"Well. And what did you wish to say to me?"

"Only that I do not like what has been happening here." Adrian paced toward the entry hall, then turned to face Mr. Danvers. "I would be glad if you could manage to return soon. I am convinced a secret passage must exist from that attic room, and I want to search more thoroughly for it. But with your niece aiding me, I must be concerned first for her safety. If you could keep her occupied—"

"Prevent me from helping, do you mean?" Daphne's voice, heavy with distaste, sounded behind him. She stalked forward. "If you do anything of the kind, Uncle, I shall be very cross. This matter deeply concerns me, and I will not be left out of it. We now have *three* specters haunting us, our pupils have begun to withdraw, and all you can think of," she added, turning on Adrian, "is a secret passage for which we have already searched and failed to find!"

Her eyes sparkled in her wrath, Adrian noted, and their gleam intrigued him. He could admire her spirit, but. . . . His jaw tightened. He would not permit her to come to any harm.

Yet try as he might, he could not rid himself of the feeling that that was exactly what lay ahead of them.

ELEGANT LOVE STILL FLOURISHES —
Wrap yourself in a Zebra Regency Romance.

A MATCHMAKER'S MATCH   (3783, $3.50/$4.50)
by Nina Porter

To save herself from a loveless marriage, Lady Psyche Veringham pretends to be a bluestocking. Resigned to spinsterhood at twenty-three, Psyche sets her keen mind to snaring a husband for her young charge, Amanda. She sets her cap for long-time bachelor, Justin St. James. This man of the world has had his fill of frothy-headed debutantes and turns the tables on Psyche. Can a bluestocking and a man about town find true love?

FIRES IN THE SNOW   (3809, $3.99/$4.99)
by Janis Laden

Because of an unhappy occurrence, Diana Ruskin knew that a secure marriage was not in her future. She was content to assist her physician father and follow in his footsteps . . . until now. After meeting Adam, Duke of Marchmaine, Diana's precise world is shattered. She would simply have to avoid the temptation of his gentle touch and stunning physique — and by doing so break her own heart!

FIRST SEASON   (3810, $3.50/$4.50)
by Anne Baldwin

When country heiress Laetitia Biddle arrives in London for the Season, she harbors dreams of triumph and applause. Instead, she becomes the laughingstock of drawing rooms and ballrooms, alike. This headstrong miss blames the rakish Lord Wakeford for her miserable debut, and she vows to rise above her many faux pas. Vowing to become an Original, Letty proves that she's more than a match for this eligible, seasoned Lord.

AN UNCOMMON INTRIGUE   (3701, $3.99/$4.99)
by Georgina Devon

Miss Mary Elizabeth Sinclair was rather startled when the British Home Office employed her as a spy. Posing as "Tasha," an exotic fortune-teller, she expected to encounter unforeseen dangers. However, nothing could have prepared her for Lord Eric Stewart, her dashing and infuriating partner. Giving her heart to this haughty rogue would be the most reckless hazard of all.

A MADDENING MINX   (3702, $3.50/$4.50)
by Mary Kingsley

After a curricle accident, Miss Sarah Chadwick is literally thrust into the arms of Philip Thornton. While other women shy away from Thornton's eyepatch and aloof exterior, Sarah finds herself drawn to discover why this man is physically and emotionally scarred.

Available wherever paperbacks are sold, or order direct from the Publisher. Send cover price plus 50¢ per copy for mailing and handling to Penguin USA, P.O. Box 999, c/o Dept. 17109, Bergenfield, NJ 07621. Residents of New York and Tennessee must include sales tax. DO NOT SEND CASH.

A Lady's Champion

Janice Bennett

ZEBRA BOOKS
KENSINGTON PUBLISHING CORP.

For Matt.
Just because.

ZEBRA BOOKS are published by

Kensington Publishing Corp.
475 Park Avenue South
New York, NY 10016

First Printing: April, 1994

Printed in the United States of America

Chapter One

Miss Daphne Selwood paced the floor of the study at Champfors Vicarage, mustering her next argument. She had to move with care, for three chairs crowded together before the blazing hearth, with a faded green sofa not far behind. A variety of pier and occasional tables stood about the cozy chamber, holding a selection of candelabra, periodicals and leather-bound books. More of the volumes spilled across the muted green carpet, and Miss Selwood stubbed the toe of her satin slipper on one of these. She muttered a word unbecoming to the niece of a vicar, but her uncle, regarding her through steady gray eyes from over the pages of the *London Times*, appeared not to have heard.

Her sister Jane, who occupied the wingback chair closest to the blaze, frowned in concentration as if trying to memorize this new offering to her schoolgirl vocabulary. Her own reading material—a delightfully diverting tale from the pen of Mrs. Radcliffe—lay open upon her lap, abandoned for the moment. All the girl's concentration remained focused upon her elder sister, whose erratic progress she regarded with the intent gaze of her green eyes.

Miss Selwood pivoted as she reached the door and directed a measuring glance at her uncle. To her annoyance, she could read nothing in the impassive countenance of the Reverend Mr. Thaddeus Danvers. Yet she knew better than to take his seeming serenity for either disinterest or weakness of will. She often had been glad of his quiet strength—but at other times, like now, she found it a frustrating stumbling block.

She returned to the hearth with measured steps, and twitched from the mantel a forgotten leaf of holly which they had missed when removing the last of the Christmas decorations that morning. After casting it into the blazing fire, she turned on her uncle.

"I cannot—and will not!—desert them." She arranged her expression into one of pleading. "If even Jane—their own cousin!—does not return after the Christmas holidays, it would seem to confirm these ridiculous stories. How long do you think the other pupils would remain? And if any more of the young ladies leave, my cousins will not be able to pay their rent for the Dower House, and they will have to close the seminary!"

"I fear you may be correct." Mr. Danvers shook his head in honest dismay. "I wish I might come up with a solution, my dear Daphne, but in truth, I cannot see a way."

"The ghost isn't actually hurting anyone," she pointed out, coaxing once more. "Only frightening some of the sillier girls a little."

"A ghost!" Her uncle's tone held nothing but scorn. "Do you actually believe that after more than two hundred years—with no rumors of dire deeds in the house—that a ghost has simply decided to move in and haunt the place? The notion is absurd! There is some person behind this."

"That is exactly my point," Daphne agreed. "I—my cousins and I—can settle this matter."

"My friend Miss Snowdon thinks it is someone playing the horridest joke on our cousins." Jane spoke for the first time, casting her earnest gaze on her sister. "And so," she added staunchly, "do I."

"Of course it is." Only Daphne wished Jane would

6

not believe everything Miss Snowdon—or anyone else, for that matter—said. She turned back to her uncle. "I *am* going to catch whomever it is who is doing this—this *idiotic* thing to those three old darlings. And do not frown so, Uncle Thaddeus. My cousins are the sweetest creatures, you know they are, and they rely on me. This whole business is just a prank, but so thoughtless, it's— it's cruel!"

"What if it is more than that? What if someone wishes to drive the seminary from the Dower House? I greatly fear the culprit may shortly turn violent to speed matters along."

"But that is absurd!"

"Is it?" her uncle demanded. "It seems to me this business has been carried too far for a mere joke."

Daphne considered his words, but could not be convinced. "We *cannot* desert my poor cousins," she declared, then tried a different approach. "Besides, I am in their employ. As long as the Seminary remains open, they stand in need of an art mistress."

"There is no need for you to be in anyone's employ. Chloe would be delighted to bring you out—"

"And see me married to some frivolous town beau. Uncle, I love your daughter dearly, but can I not make either of you understand I have no desire to make my curtsy to society? And it is *not* because Chloe—or rather her husband—would be paying the bills. I simply prefer feeling useful. I am happy at the Seminary."

Mr. Danvers shook his head. "You are too young, too inexperienced to make such a decision without first going to London. You—"

"We have this argument every time I visit you," Daphne pointed out. "Why can you not believe I know my own mind? I want only to return to the Seminary."

"And all that unpleasantness there." Mr. Danvers frowned. "I cannot like it. I would prefer to go with you."

"There is no need!" Daphne exclaimed, then continued in a more controlled voice. "Please, Uncle. It is quite unnecessary. I *can* handle this. You persist in thinking me a green girl, one who should leave all but the most frippery matters to older and wiser heads, but it is not true. I am *not* in need of a nurserymaid. Can you not accept that?"

"I promised your mama I would have a care for you." His expression remained troubled.

"I am almost one-and-twenty," she reminded him. "I am perfectly capable of—"

"Of many things, my dear. I make no doubt of it. But in truth, you must admit you have never been faced with a potentially dangerous situation. Your lack of worldly experience might betray you."

She averted her face, her teeth clenching. She *had* worldly experience. She *did* know her own mind. She had even spent eighteen months in London, thanks to her Uncle Percival Selwood—though on the fringes of society. She had capabilities of which her Uncle Thaddeus would never guess—and she could never tell him, or anyone else for that matter, for that would spell her ruination.

"How," she said with care, "can I gain any experience—enough to satisfy you that I can choose my own life—if you do not let me try?"

"Perhaps I can arrange to take a few days away," he murmured as if he hadn't heard her.

Swallowing her irritation, she crossed to his chair, dropped a light kiss on the top of his graying head, and bent her efforts to dissuading him. "You are needed here, in the parish, dear Uncle. You know that." She sank to her knees at his side, the soft blue merino skirts draping about her slippers. "Besides," she added dryly, "if you are so eager we should have masculine protection, are you not forgetting Cousin George lives next door to the Seminary?"

"Mr. George Selwood," Mr. Danvers said with considerable feeling, "would indeed be the very person to protect Selwood Seminary. Yet he sounds to me to be of no use to you whatsoever. A dandy, you say, who turns quite pale at the mention of your ghost."

Jane straightened in her chair. "I know the very thing. Why do we not send for Uncle Percival?"

"No!" The word escaped Daphne as a gasp.

Jane turned her earnest face toward Mr. Danvers. "Daphne always said he was a—" she screwed her face in an effort of memory, "a dab hand in a tight corner."

"No!" Daphne repeated, louder. "Absolutely not! Jane, you know we cannot."

"Uncle—" Mr. Danvers blinked. "Is he still alive? I thought your mama told me he had passed away."

"She—she would have used some such term." Daphne pulled herself together. "She said he was dead to us." Her mother never had forgiven Uncle Percival; Daphne, though, sadly missed the old rogue—but not enough to risk his reappearance in her life.

Jane's brow puckered. "He was always such famous fun. You said so, Daphne," she added, as if that settled the matter. "Are you objecting because Uncle Thaddeus might not like being related, even by marriage, to the owner of a gaming establishment? That's what Mama always said."

If that were indeed all there had been to it. But the past—at least that portion of it—had better stay buried and forgotten. Daphne forced a smile to her lips, which she was far from feeling, and strove for her usual light tone. "Quite the reverse, Jane. Uncle Percival always said he was quite put out when his brother married the sister of a clergyman. He claimed it to be the utmost mortification to him."

Mr. Danvers gave the matter serious thought. "Do you think he would come if you asked?"

"No!" Daphne exclaimed, alarmed. She had expected her respectable maternal uncle to be appalled at the thought of her highly disreputable paternal relative. But disobliging old dear that he was, Uncle Thaddeus would welcome anyone who might serve as protector for her in this difficulty. And that she did not want.

She swallowed and tried again. "He will not rise from the ashes," she informed him, blighting his budding hope. "He has quite washed his hands of us. The last Mama heard, he had moved from Munich to Rome—and that was a full two years before she died. There has not been so much as a single line from him since."

Mr. Danvers patted her shoulder with a compassionate hand. "I should be quite grateful if *someone* rose from the ashes to keep an eye on these goings on at your school. I cannot like it, not knowing the purpose behind these so-called hauntings."

"I am quite capable of keeping an eye on myself," she pointed out. "And we are agreed, my three cousins and I, that the fewer people involved in solving our mystery, the better will be our chances to prevent any scandal from attaching to the school."

"My dear child, I would be failing in my duty as your guardian should I permit you to return unprotected. No, do not frown at me so. I do not doubt your spirit, but your physical strength. Should this be the work of ruffians, and you get in their way, I greatly fear you might come to serious harm."

Daphne opened her mouth to refute that view, but an innate honesty kept her silent.

"And there is Jane to be considered, as well," Mr. Danvers continued, adding the clincher.

"Me?" Jane stared at him, green eyes wide beneath the delicate arch of her brows. "But Daphne says it is quite safe. The ghost only wanders the grounds, after all. My friend Miss Trevellian thinks it is only one of the other girls, making a May game of everyone."

Daphne stared at her sister, and for the first time, qualms gripped her. At fifteen, Jane was a young, coltish girl, unsure of herself and far too willing to believe—and act upon—whatever someone told her. If one of her friends suggested they could stop the ghost by simply

10

walking right up and saying "boo" to it, Jane would take it for gospel and try it at the first opportunity. The results might well be disastrous—for Jane.

Daphne braced herself. She could control Jane. She could also deal with this self-styled ghost if she could but convince her Uncle Thaddeus to give her the chance. She wanted no outsiders—even family—about the Seminary, giving the girls cause for more gossip and alarming their parents. The Selwood Seminary could not afford to lose any more pupils.

"We must go back." Daphne rose to her knees, her hands gripping the arm of Mr. Danvers's chair as she tried another approach. "Please, dear Uncle. My cousins need me, and I owe it to them. Jane is receiving the most excellent education, and you know I could never afford any of the other Bath academies for her."

"Chloe—" Mr. Danvers began.

Daphne waved that aside. "Cousin Chloe is the sweetest creature alive, but we will not impose upon her. Not only would it be quite shocking of us, but just think how Lord Richard would feel if all his wife's poor relations hung upon his shirttails."

"He wouldn't mind in the least," Mr. Danvers said, but his tone wavered.

"You are quite right, and that is exactly the problem. Lord Richard would be only too pleased to help anyone. But *I* would not like it. And neither, I am convinced, would you."

A reluctant smile touched Mr. Danvers's lips. "Indeed, I quite understand, my dear. But it seems I must be the one to consider your safety, as you will not. Unless we can hit upon some gentleman relative to act as your protector, I cannot permit you to return."

Daphne glowered into the fire, her spirits plummeting. A "gentleman relative" blundering about the Seminary, alarming the girls, was exactly what she didn't want. She could only be grateful she was not possessed of such an individual. Which meant . . .

11

She cast a sideways glance at her uncle's troubled expression, and hope resurfaced. The very goodness of his heart stood to her advantage; he could not long refuse her pleas to go to the aid of someone in distress. Once he realized no suitable gentleman could be found to play the required role, he would relent and permit her to return. They would solve their mystery without further scandal, and she would prove to him she was now a capable and sensible young woman no longer in need of a guardian's permission before making the simplest decisions.

Now, she had only to wait, and hope no long-forgotten masculine relative put in an unwelcome appearance.

The Reverend Mr. Adrian Carstairs strode through the early darkness of the icy January night, following the familiar snow-covered path from the small stable where he had left his horse and tilbury. Before him rose the ancient stone facade of the vicarage, its homey aspect as welcoming as always. To his further pleasure, he noted lights burning in several windows, glimpsed through curtains not completely closed.

After a moment's reminiscent contemplation, a slow smile spread across his face. Transferring the valise he carried to his left hand, he scooped a handful of the fresh snow that obscured the flagged stones of the path, formed it into a ball, and strode to the door. He applied the knocker with vigor, then poised himself for delivery.

A minute passed, then another, before the heavy oaken door swung inward, revealing a slender young lady dressed in a round gown of blue merino with a cream-colored woolen shawl wrapped about her shoulders. A slight frown of irritation—at being disturbed?—lingered on features meant for laughter. A riot of dusky ringlets surrounded the rather pretty face as her chin tilted upward in inquiry. Her large green eyes widened

12

as she took in his aggressive stance, and an irrepressible dimple peeped in her right cheek, smoothing away the lines of strain about her mouth.

"Miss Selwood." Mr. Carstairs's deep chuckle escaped him. He lowered his hand, tossing the ball up and down, catching it with only a minor cascade of frozen crystals across the porch. "Forgive me. I had expected Mr. Danvers."

That brought the frown back to the young lady's brow. "Mr. Carstairs. What on earth are you doing out on such a night? We had thought you at the Castle, along with the others. But Uncle will be pleased to see you, make no doubt of that. Do come inside and warm yourself." She stepped aside to allow him to enter. "Have Chloe and Lord Richard returned also?"

"Do you really think my sister Helena would let them?" Adrian heaved his snowball into an icy bank and stepped within. "It is no easy thing for Chloe and Richard to journey most of the length of England into Yorkshire with three young children. Nell says they don't visit nearly often enough. And the Castle is big enough for an army of infants. I left your young cousins playing with—" his lips twitched at the still novel thought, "—my nephew and niece."

Miss Selwood closed the front door, and the comfortable warmth of the entry hall enveloped Adrian. He allowed her to lead the way to the study, though there was no need. For the past eight years, Champfors Vicarage had been as much his home as had been Halliford Castle, country seat of his brother-in-law the duke of Halliford, or even his own spartan rooms at Oxford. Yet this would always be his retreat, his sanctuary in times of need. Like now.

He stripped off his dampened gloves, fighting back the pang of loneliness that assailed him, and stepped through the doorway. At sight of the cozy apartment, he experienced a sensation of the familiar, of coming home.

The fire blazed merrily in the hearth, welcoming in its own right.

On one side of it, Miss Jane Selwood curled into a wingback chair, her long dark hair falling over her shoulder in a thick plait. As Adrian advanced another step into the room, she raised her gaze that had been fixed on the pages of a book, and regarded him with bright speculation.

Opposite her, Mr. Danvers, his figure still lithe despite his four-and-fifty years, looked up from the newspaper he perused. A smile sprang to life in the depths of his gray eyes, and he rose, setting the sheets aside. "Adrian!" He strode forward, clasping his visitor's hand. "My dear boy. Come warm yourself. Have you driven far?"

"All of forty miles." He set his valise on the hearth, and the snow-encrusted leather steamed. He dropped his greatcoat on top of it.

"Forty—you must be nigh on frozen." Mr. Danvers poured a brandy and handed Adrian the glass. "How did you leave everyone at the Castle?"

Adrian stared into the fire, memories of the recent Christmas festivities at the ducal estate vivid in his mind. "Chloe said to give you her love. They don't plan to return until next week." And Mr. Danvers, he knew, must miss his daughter and her children, and would be glad when they returned to Champfors Manor with her husband Lord Richard, younger brother of the duke of Halliford. Mr. Danvers took great joy in his role of grandfather.

Restless, Adrian strode to the window and gazed out through the frosted pane. A wind had sprung up, and pale flakes swirled against the darkened sky. All three of his sisters married, now safe and secure. A weight of responsibility had been lifted from his shoulders with the wedding of his youngest sister Lizzie to Frederick Ashfield, now Viscount St. Vincent—yet with it had come emptiness rather than relief. For the first time in his life, he felt alone. Unneeded.

He turned back into the room and found the Reverend Mr. Danvers regarding him with an intent gleam in his eyes. "Will you be able to stay long? Or are you due back at Oxford?"

"I'm on leave, writing a dissertation. On Herodotus. Though I fear I have no more than another month to complete it." He had lost a great deal of time, busying himself with the muddled—and murderous—affairs of the new Viscount St. Vincent. He directed a quizzical glance at his host. "Why do you frown?"

"My uncle will be glad of your company." The elder Miss Selwood tossed her head. "It will seem so very quiet here once Jane and I have returned to the Seminary." Her teeth caught her bottom lip, and her bright green eyes sparkled, as if she issued a challenge.

Mr. Danvers threw her a contemplative glance as he resumed his seat. "Are you hoping I may be distracted from my purpose, my dear?"

Miss Selwood glared at him, and flounced to the fireplace where she stared moodily into the flames.

"Really, now, my dear." Amusement sounded heavy in Mr. Danvers's voice. "Has it not occurred to you that you and Mr. Carstairs might be construed to be related?"

Adrian chuckled, then noticed the intent expression in his host's pale gray eyes. "One might rather say we are connected," Adrian corrected.

"But one *might* call you a male relative, might one not?"

Miss Selwood spun about, her expression almost comical in its dismay. "But he has a dissertation to write, and he is running out of time. You heard him, Uncle Thaddeus. He couldn't possibly take on anything more. And indeed, there is no need—"

Mr. Danvers quelled her outburst with a glance. "There is every need."

15

Intrigued, Adrian strolled to the hearth and leaned his elbow on the mantel. "Open your budget, sir. What dire deed would you have me perform—that your niece would rather I did not?"

Miss Jane, who had been watching him critically, squealed in delight. "It is the very thing, Daphne! Oh, how clever you are, Uncle Thaddeus. And even though he is so very young and handsome, it will be quite all right because he is a clergyman!"

"Jane!" Miss Selwood protested.

"That does make everything all right, does it not?" Adrian agreed, keeping his expression serious only with an effort. "There is something so very respectable about this." He touched his clerical collar.

Miss Selwood turned her glare on him.

"It makes it very convenient, to be sure." Mr. Danvers's eyes gleamed. "If you will, you may become the new resident chaplain."

"Oh, it will be a splendid lark, Uncle." Jane clasped delighted hands together. "Why, with luck, no one will even guess what he will be there for!"

"Including me," Adrian agreed with complete cordiality.

"And there is no need why you should." Miss Selwood bit her lip. "I am sorry, I realize that must sound dreadfully rude, but indeed, this is *our* problem, not yours, and there is no reason why you should be involved. It would only be a great deal of bother for you. I keep telling my uncle we can manage perfectly well on our own. We *want* to."

"And I have told her they cannot." Mr. Danvers's smile flashed. "We haven't explained any of this tangle to you, have we, Adrian? It must seem to you as if we are talking gibberish, or have taken leave of our senses."

"Not in the least. I am far too accustomed to my sister Lizzie."

"It's really quite simple," Mr. Danvers began.

Miss Jane gave an enjoyable shiver. "Ghosts," she

said succinctly. "We have one haunting the school and terrifying everyone. We live in the greatest fear my poor cousins will have to close their Seminary."

"Ghosts?" Adrian swirled his brandy, but his piercing gaze moved from Miss Jane to Miss Daphne. "I collect this is the school run by your cousins?"

"My father's cousins, to be exact." Miss Daphne Selwood folded her arms before her. "So you see, it is a family matter, one which need not concern anyone else—if only," she added, directing a reproachful stare at Mr. Danvers, "my uncle will not take on so and play my overbearing guardian."

"Someone must take this seriously," Mr. Danvers responded, "since your cousins do not appear to have considered the possible implications. I repeat, there may be danger ahead, and not a man on the premises capable of lending any assistance."

"We don't need a man," Miss Selwood muttered.

Adrian straightened, his innate sense of chivalry stirring. Probably, he realized ruefully, a result of having been the virtual head of his household since his seventeenth year—and even before. Now here he was, five-and-twenty, and a confirmed manager—or meddler, as Lizzie laughingly maintained. Since his sisters no longer needed him, did he seek other defenseless females to protect?

His lips twitched in self-mockery at the thought. A lady's champion, that's what he was, one who would fight every battle or dragon that threatened. At least the prospect of *having* a battle again relieved his immediate sense of emptiness.

"Tell me all," he invited, and experienced a pleasant sensation of anticipation.

Mr. Danvers eyed him in thoughtful silence. "What do you know of the Seminary?" he asked at last.

"Only that it is operated by Miss Selwood's three cousins—"

"My father's cousins," Daphne repeated. "It has nothing to do with Uncle Thaddeus."

Adrian inclined his head in acknowledgment. "—in the Dower House on the Selwood estate. About two miles outside of Bath, is it not? I thought it did quite well."

"It did, until just the last three months."

"Someone has taken to haunting the place." Miss Jane hugged herself. "It has been quite blood curdling, I assure you. We have had several ghostly sightings."

"And that is *all* of the trouble, I assure you." Miss Selwood frowned at her sister. "The simple matter is that our ghost frightened away several of the pupils last term, and I greatly fear more will not come back after the holidays. And then there will not be enough income to support the Seminary. That is all. Someone is playing a beastly joke. There is no danger, and certainly no reason why Jane and I should not return."

"You are so certain it is no more than a joke?" Adrian watched her expression closely.

She pleated a fold in her blue skirts. "I do *not* believe in ghosts," she declared. "I am quite convinced someone is doing this out of jealousy or spite, and has not realized his actions might ruin my poor cousins. They are the darlingest old dears, no one could really wish them harm. That is why I feel Uncle Thaddeus is taking much too serious a view of all this."

"Still, one must consider other possibilities." Adrian directed his thoughtful gaze on the brandy. "Can you not think of anything that someone might gain by the closing of the school? Does the current owner of the estate—"

"My cousin George," inserted Miss Selwood.

"Does he want the Dower House himself, perhaps?"

Miss Selwood shook her head. "His income derives almost solely from the rent from the seminary. Its closing could not possibly benefit anyone."

Mr. Danvers brought the decanter to Adrian's side

18

and refilled his glass. "What do you think my boy? Will you assist them?"

Adrian, vividly aware of Miss Selwood's furious glare, experienced a flicker of curiosity. Now, why should that young lady be so against his helping? It was not as if they were strangers, though to be sure they were not closely acquainted. He trod the treacherous ground with caution, keeping his expression impassive. "What, precisely, is it you wish me to do?"

"Nothing," Miss Selwood muttered, so softly Adrian barely heard her.

"Accompany my headstrong nieces back to Selwood Seminary and remain there until this disturbance is settled and the school is once more safe."

"And what are we to tell people about having a gentleman to stay at a Seminary for young ladies?" Miss Selwood demanded. "His presence will cause the very scandal we are trying to avoid."

"That is what makes Mr. Carstairs the perfect choice. His cloth is explanation enough. Yours would not be the first Seminary to employ the services of a full-time chaplain."

Miss Selwood did not appear convinced. "And just how do you think my cousins will feel about this addition to their establishment? Do you not think you should ask them, first?"

"They will be charmed, I feel certain. And make no mistake, miss." Mr. Danvers's voice took on an edge of steel. "You will return to your school *only* in the company of Mr. Carstairs, and remain there *only* for as long as he stays under its roof. Is that clear?"

"Uncle!" Becoming color flooded Miss Selwood's cheeks, and her large green eyes glittered.

He ignored her, turning instead to Adrian. "Well, my boy? Will you go?"

A devil of enjoyment danced within Adrian. "Never," he assured his erstwhile mentor, "have I been asked to

19

play knight errant for so unwilling a damsel. You will permit her to return under no other terms?"

"None."

Adrian cast a half-apologetic, half-amused glance at Miss Selwood. "Then it appears I have no other choice. "Lady," he swept her a deep bow that mocked them both, "I am completely at your service."

"Oh, go to—to the devil," Miss Selwood exclaimed, and stormed out of the room.

Chapter Two

The chill morning wind whipped about the passengers in the tilbury, throwing the fringed end of Adrian's woolen scarf into his eyes. He caught the ribbons in one hand and cleared his vision with the other, then steadied the gait of his horse, Achilles, as the animal stumbled in the snow. When they proceeded unimpeded once more, Adrian turned his contemplative gaze on his companion.

"Neither of us had any choice in the matter." He kept his voice indifferent.

Daphne Selwood hunched her shoulder beneath the voluminous folds of her traveling cloak. "He would have relented if you hadn't shown up. Why could you not have waited until next week to return, like Chloe and Richard? Or better yet, why could you not have remained at the Castle?"

"Have you ever heard of making the best of a bad situation?" Adrian inquired, amused by her continued hostility. Her fine eyes—remarkably fine, he noted—flashed as she glared at him.

"Why did you choose to ride with me?" he continued when she made no verbal response to his last sally. "You would have been far more comfortable in the landau."

She clenched her teeth. "I wanted the opportunity to deliver a few home truths to you—in private."

"Pray proceed."

She threw him a fulminating glance. "Your presence at the Seminary is quite unnecessary."

"So you informed me last night," he agreed with complete cordiality.

"Your presence can only raise undesirable comment."

Adrian fought to keep his countenance. "I shall try to conduct myself with circumspection."

"We are quite able to manage our own affairs by ourselves."

"I believe you mentioned that, also. Is there not some new matter you wish to bring to my attention?"

"Yes! You are the most irritating, disagreeable, unwelcome, odious—" She broke off, apparently searching for words suitably vile enough with which to describe him.

"Clodpole?" he offered in a spirit of pure helpfulness. "Jackanapes? Coxcomb? How about nickninny?"

"No, vexatious!" Her lower lip trembled, as if in reluctant amusement, but she merely shivered, drawing her cloak more closely about herself.

Adrian reached down, tucking the corners of the rug more snugly about her booted feet. "I believe you mentioned that this morning."

A choke of laughter escaped her. "You are quite insufferable!"

"So my sisters have informed me. Now, I refuse to believe this is all. No one would subject themselves to such a chilling, not just for the pleasure of heaping abuse upon my head. Will you not tell me what it is you really wished to say?"

She studied her muff, into which she had once more tucked her gloved hands. "Will you just deliver me to the Seminary, then—then drive on? Go back to Oxford?" She raised her face to look up at him with the last words.

Adrian spared her a long, thoughtful glance, seeing the lines of strain etched about her eyes and mouth. "Is my presence really such a burden to you?"

She drew in a breath and exhaled it in a deep sigh,

creating a misty cloud before her face that dissipated as the tilbury continued its forward progress. "Are all men so very dense? It is not your presence, but your—your meddling I cannot support. Why must people always refuse to let me make the simplest decisions for *myself*? I am perfectly capable of handling my own affairs."

Prudently, Adrian kept his tongue.

She threw him a defensive glance. "Are you not going to tell me that a mere female must naturally stand in need of masculine guidance?"

"Why should I?"

"Uncle Thaddeus thinks so."

Adrian's lip twitched. "He is accustomed to less strong-minded females."

"Willful, I suppose you mean." She sniffed, though it might have been with the cold.

"It won't serve, you know." He ignored her last comment and returned to the greater issue. "Your uncle granted his permission for your continued stay under your cousins' roof contingent to my own."

She said nothing for several minutes. Adrian concentrated on his horse as they traversed the snow-covered lane. Branches hung low overhead, heavy with their white burden. The crisp air filled his lungs, bright and fresh and pungent with the odors of pine and spruce.

"Very well," she said at last. "It seems there is no choice but that you should stay. But there is no need for you to do anything!"

Adrian raised his eyebrows. "Not even play the role of chaplain?"

She clenched her teeth. "That you will have to do to prevent scandal. But you will do nothing more. I shall consider it the greatest impertinence should you try."

"What, may I not even attempt to gain a glimpse of your ghost?"

"You may not!" She turned away from him, hunching her shoulder in a manner that made it abundantly clear she wished no further converse.

23

A stony silence enveloped them, lasting through the next several miles. Finally, ahead of them, the ancient landau borrowed from the Champfors Manor carriage house slowed, then swung to the right through an open ironwork gate, the black bars standing stark against the snowy landscape. Adrian, still holding Achilles to a slow trot, took the curve with a deft loop of his rein. A large brass plaque adorned the wrought iron rails, proclaiming that he had entered the grounds of the "Selwood Seminary for Young Ladies."

The drive, lined with yew hedges and covered in snow, proved short. Less than fifty yards ahead stood a large, rambling house of the late Tudor period, the half-timbered walls covered in ivy, the windows set with tiny diamond panes. Smoke rose in billowing puffs from three of the chimneys, promising a much-welcomed warmth after the freezing drive.

As the landau pulled up before the door, an elderly manservant in a heavy greatcoat hurried out and began unstrapping the baggage. Miss Jane bounced down, waved gaily to the occupants of the tilbury drawing in behind, then said something to the old man which caused him to smile. Without waiting, she ran up the steps and inside.

Adrian drew the bay to a stop, secured the ribbons and jumped down. Snow and gravel crunched beneath his top boots as he strode around to extend a helping hand to Miss Selwood. She ignored it, keeping her hands tucked into her muff. As she jumped lightly to the ground, she afforded Adrian an intriguing glimpse of dainty ankle over the top of her half-boot.

"The stable is around the back," she informed him. "Would you like me to send someone to show you?"

He regarded her with a touch of enjoyment. "I believe I can just about manage to find it without getting lost."

An answering—and very reluctant—smile tugged at her lips, to be repressed the next moment. Inclining her head in an exaggerated imitation of one dismissing a servant, she headed toward the door, her long cloak sweeping a trail behind her in the new-fallen snow.

Thoughtful, Adrian swung himself once more into the carriage, turned the vehicle with precision, and proceeded around the first sharp turn toward the back of the house. There, a neat, cobbled yard met his gaze, surrounded by stone stalls and a carriage house over which a set of rooms was situated. Smoke drifted lazily into the overcast sky from the ancient chimney at the far end. Only the lightest dusting of snow covered the ground; obviously, someone tended the few animals with assiduous care.

An elderly groom hurried out, dragging on a bulky greatcoat as he came. He acknowledged Adrian with a curt nod, and fell to work at once on the harness straps. Adrian lent a hand to the unhitching of Achilles, and within minutes he led the steaming animal into a spare loose box. While the groom maneuvered the tilbury into the space next to an old berline, Adrian set to work on his bay's gleaming coat with a wisp of straw.

The groom brought a fresh bucket of water. After a few more minutes, Adrian slipped out, assured of Achilles's well-being. He picked up his valise, bestowed a final pat on the animal's hindquarters, and headed for the house. The last glimpse he had of them, the bay lipped at a forkful of hay, while the groom determinedly removed the lingering traces of sweat.

The gravel path led him around to the front, where he caught sight of the landau, the ducal crest emblazoned on its door panel. The ancient vehicle negotiated the bend in the drive and began its return journey to the Champfors stable. Did Miss Selwood include the necessity of borrowing this equipage, once the property of Lord Richard's father, among her list of grievances? Adrian had a shrewd notion she would rather hire a post chaise than be dependent upon another, but hazarded a guess that neither her purse nor her uncle would allow it.

As he passed a front window, he glanced inside to see Miss Selwood pacing the length of what must be a drawing room. Looking up, she caught sight of him, and her expression clouded. She strode from the chamber. Adrian continued along the path to the front door and found her awaiting him in the hall.

"My cousins are quite anxious to make your acquaintance." She spoke the words with disdain, making it clear how little she agreed with their sentiments. She led the way across the hall and threw open the door opposite the drawing room. "The Reverend Mr. Carstairs," she announced with only the slightest touch of sarcasm.

Adrian stepped over the threshold into a small and rather haphazard apartment furnished with two desks, a number of bookcases, and several chairs. The office, it seemed. Cream and gold draperies hung at the single window, and a stout brown carpet covered the floor. The aromas of beeswax, lemon oil and a fireplace badly in need of a sweeping pervaded the air.

He took another step, then hesitated as he found himself facing three ladies, somewhat advanced in years, all regarding him with assessing gazes. Keeping his amusement from showing on his countenance, he swept them an elegant—but circumspect—bow.

"Oh, but he is quite young," murmured the eldest of the Selwood sisters. She regarded him through brown, welcoming eyes set in a rounded face etched with the lines of her sixty-odd years of living. A thick plait of gray hair wound about her head in a crown. Her plump hands fluttered in dismay at the breast of her high-waisted gown, tugging at the pale pink ribands that relieved the severity of the somber black bombazine.

The middle sister shook her head without dislodging so much as a single strand of her smoothed-back grizzled hair which she had fastened in a chignon at the base of her neck. Her expression settled into grim lines which sat oddly with her motherly appearance. "Far too handsome."

"Oh, yes," sighed her elder, regarding Adrian with a misty smile.

Adrian fought back a laugh. "So Miss Jane Selwood informed me. But she seemed to believe the circumstances of my having taken Holy Orders will render me of no interest to your charges."

"I would not depend upon that." The youngest of the three—a strikingly handsome woman with medium brown hair streaked with gray—regarded him with a decided twinkle in her hazel eyes. "I greatly fear the little wretches will ogle you in the most deplorable manner. Do you think you will mind?"

"Elspeth!" the eldest protested. "Oh, dear, you really must not—" She broke off, her expression one of confusion.

"Allow me to introduce you." Daphne Selwood stepped into the breach. "Miss Sophronia Selwood, who is in charge of the school."

The eldest flushed and beamed at him. "So very pleased. You must forgive us. We were not expecting you, of course, though to be sure. . . . That is, I make no doubt you shall do quite the most excellent job, of course, though what, precisely, that is to be . . . ?" She broke off her floundering and finished by taking his hand and giving it a gentle, if uncertain, pat. "Such an excellent young gentleman, I make no doubt."

Daphne's lips twitched, though all she said was, "Miss Beatrice Selwood."

The middle sister inclined her head. No hint of softening showed about her stern mouth, but humor lingered in the eyes so like those of her two sisters. She took his offered hand in a firm clasp. "How do you do?"

"And Miss Elspeth," Daphne continued.

Adrian turned to the last of the sisters once more, and met her measuring gaze. Breeding lay in her fine-boned features, and intelligence and character in her expression. Even now, long past her youth, she retained an easy grace in her movements as she crossed to a chair.

Miss Sophronia Selwood bestowed her sweet smile upon Adrian and gestured for him to seat himself in one of the two visitors' chairs the office boasted. The ladies ranged themselves on the other three behind the desks. Daphne drew a low stool toward the few inches of open space by the window, and watched without taking part.

"Daphne explained her uncle's concern." Miss Beatrice took over from her elder sister. "Grateful to you for aiding her return to us. Don't know what we'd do without her. Met the Reverend Mr. Danvers, several times. Have a great respect for his wisdom. If he feels your presence is necessary, then we concur."

Adrian cast a surreptitious glance at Daphne and encountered her stony countenance. He could sympathize, but that was all; he, too, agreed with Mr. Danvers's assessment of the situation. He turned back to Miss Beatrice. "I am quite at your disposal for as much as a month, should you have need of me."

"He must work on a dissertation," Daphne broke in.

"It will not take all of my time," Adrian assured them. "What would you have me do?"

"Dear boy," murmured the eldest Miss Selwood. "So very agreeable to have a gentleman about the place."

Adrian avoided looking at Daphne. He could well imagine her indignation at such a sentiment.

"Will you look into this matter?" Miss Beatrice asked in her forthright manner, making the matter official. "Find out, if you can, who is behind this nonsense?"

"If that is your wish," Adrian said, adding a silent apology to Daphne. And since this would indeed be his official task under this roof, he might as well set about it at once. "Has this 'ghost' of yours been sighted during the holidays?" he asked.

The three sisters exchanged glances.

"We have not seen it while the girls have been away,"

Miss Elspeth answered. "But then," she added with a note of apology, "my sisters and I retire early to our rooms at the back of the house. Our ghost has been seen only in the front garden."

Adrian nodded, thoughtful. It still seemed to suggest the involvement of one of the pupils. "Can you tell me a little about the Seminary?"

"Such a very old house." The eldest Miss Selwood leaned forward in her earnestness. "Truly, I cannot imagine why a ghost has never settled here before. It is such a perfect place."

Miss Elspeth cast her sister a humorous glance. "I believe he means about our circumstances. Indeed," she went on, turning back to Adrian, "I can think of no reason why anyone should haunt us. It is not as if our ghost tries to gain entry to steal from us. I might suspect that for the motive if we had a storeroom packed with gold plate. But our grandfather, you must know, was the most shocking gamester. He lost the family fortune and shot himself in disgrace. Everything of value was sold to pay his debts—except the estate, which was entailed."

"So dreadful," murmured the eldest Miss Selwood. "Beatrice, dear, do you remember?"

Miss Beatrice gave a short nod. "Several valuable paintings stolen during the evaluation process."

Tears started to Miss Sophronia Selwood's eyes, and she shook her head as if still, after almost fifty years, she could not believe such vile conduct.

"So your father inherited the estate?" Adrian asked, bringing the discussion back to the history of the school.

Again, Miss Elspeth took up the narrative. "Our father chose to live at the Dower House, which was less costly to maintain. On his death, the entire contents of this house, from the highest attic to the bottom-most cellar, were left to the three of us. Our cousin, Mr. George Selwood, inherited the house itself, along with the rest of the estate. He signed an agreement permitting us to use

29

the Dower House for a school as long as we are able to pay a rent."

"A very substantial rent," Miss Beatrice stuck in, with feeling.

"We have operated our select Seminary for more than thirty years," Miss Elspeth went on. "But now, I greatly fear this detestable haunting may reduce the income of the school so we will not be able to make the payments."

"It isn't right." Miss Selwood dabbed at her eyes with a lacy handkerchief. "So very distressing, and the poor, dear girls being so alarmed—"

"Can't have them frightened off," Miss Beatrice announced. "Have to find out what is going on—and as soon as possible."

"I see." Adrian spoke the words to himself. Ill luck seemed to have dogged the Selwood family footsteps. These ladies had made a valiant effort, supporting themselves against all odds for thirty-some years. And now catastrophe hung once more over their heads, threatening to destroy all they had accomplished and deprive them of their livelihood.

But not if he could help it.

Miss Beatrice fixed her steely gaze on him. "You believe you can get to the bottom of this, Mr. Carstairs?"

Adrian's resolve firmed. "I will certainly try."

Daphne, by the window, glared at him.

"Such a *kind* gentleman." Miss Sophronia Selwood sighed as she gazed at him.

Miss Elspeth rose. "Daphne, will you escort him to the guest chamber? It's the only one available, but I am certain you will be tolerably comfortable, Mr. Carstairs."

"Morning chapel!" Miss Beatrice suddenly pronounced. "Won't mind taking it for the girls, will you? Not a long one, of course."

"Oh, dear." The eldest Miss Selwood looked dismayed. "I hope you will not—that is, such an imposition, and you helping us already—"

Miss Elspeth smiled. "I fear my sister is quite right. The girls' parents would find your presence here somewhat unorthodox if you do not fulfill the roll of chaplain."

Adrian inclined his head. "It will be my pleasure."

"A rare treat, I make no doubt." Daphne stood. "Will you come this way, Mr. Carstairs?" She offered him a brittle smile.

Adrian followed her from the chamber. As soon as she closed the door behind them, he said, "I am sorry, Miss Selwood."

"There is no need to patronize me," she snapped. "You are not sorry in the least. I saw your face. You are looking forward to this."

"Well, yes," he admitted. "Are not you?"

"I *was.*" She turned on her heel and marched across the hall to the stairs. "They are placing you in a chamber quite away from everything."

"That sounds perfect."

Her fingers whitened on the banister rails. "My cousin Elspeth is quite right, I'm afraid. You will have all the older girls trailing after you everywhere you go."

"Oh, surely not the more ambitious ones." His ready smile flashed. "A clergyman is hardly a great catch."

Daphne cast him a dubious look, but made no comment.

Adrian studied the rigid set of her back, the pride and independence that expressed themselves in her every movement. "Have you considered what you will do if all our efforts should fail?" he asked abruptly. "If the school is forced to close?"

Her mouth tightened. "I will seek another position, of course. One where Jane may be admitted as a student in lieu of my salary. And don't be like Uncle Thaddeus." She swung about to glare at him. "I will *not* ask aid of Chloe."

Adrian's brow snapped down. "Do you dislike her?" He couldn't conceive of anyone disliking the vicar's gentle daughter.

The reluctant dimple peeped in Daphne's cheek. "I know it is very selfish of me. Uncle Thaddeus has told me so often enough, especially when it is Jane's schooling at stake. But I cannot—*will* not—bring myself to accept charity of anyone. And before you remind me that Jane and I live with Uncle Thaddeus when we are not here at the school, let me assure you that is a very different matter."

"I—"

Daphne cut him off. "My mother was his sister, and she kept house for him after Chloe's marriage, until she died last year. And I do the same, whenever we are not at the seminary."

"I am well aware." Adrian paused at the landing, his frowning gaze resting on her. "But perhaps *you* are not aware that I have undergone a similar problem."

She regarded him with suspicion. "Have you? Do you mean because your sister married someone so wealthy?"

Adrian's lips twitched in a reminiscent smile. "Halliford, certainly, has wanted to be generous, but I meant before Helena married him. I assure you, Nell and I were every bit as averse to receiving charity as ever you might be."

Daphne started up the next flight with slowed steps. "Then if you understand how I feel, why do you insist on interfering?"

"Because I had to learn there are times you must think of something more important than your own pride, such as the well-being or peace of mind of someone else. Do you really believe Mr. Danvers could attend to the troubles of his parish while all his worries are centered on your safety?"

She paused, blinking at him, and a becoming flush just tinged her cheeks.

"Try to think of me as a petty annoyance," Adrian

suggested with an almost straight face, "to be tolerated for his sake."

Daphne rolled her eyes heavenward and resumed her climb. "Are you never serious?" she demanded.

His latent grin broadened. "As seldom as possible."

She continued her climb without deigning to respond, but some of the rigidity ebbed from her slight figure. So much determination, he reflected, and a liveliness of mind to go with it. He had a shrewd notion she would not easily forgive him for being her uncle's chosen champion.

The attic chamber, where she shortly left him, proved to be tiny, but scrubbed clean. A bed, a desk, a wardrobe, a washstand—what more did he need? He drew back the lace curtain at the paned window and gazed out over the snow-strewn landscape. Stillness and quiet greeted him—for the moment; the young ladies would begin returning for their classes at any time. He should enjoy the peace while he could.

He unpacked the few belongings he had brought with him from the Castle, and with due reverence placed his notes on Herodotus into one of the drawers of the desk. After a moment's contemplation, he repositioned a candelabrum to ensure himself the best light. If his time were to be taken up with chapel and ghost-hunting, he would have to work in sessions for his dissertation whenever he could.

And thinking of ghost-hunting, he might as well begin his investigations at once. Miss Daphne Selwood, at least, would be glad to see the last of him. On that inspiring thought, he cast a final glance about the chamber, still neat but now bearing the signs of his habitation, and departed.

He returned to the small office on the ground floor. He knocked, entered on the answering call, and drew up short in the doorway. The eldest Miss Selwood, now bereft of her sisters, still had company. Beside her, in the chair recently occupied by Miss Beatrice, sat a lanky gentleman of middle years, his sandy brown hair fashionably cropped and curled, the face beneath it commonplace. The height of his intricately tied neckcloth, the width of his lapels on his wasp-waisted coat, and the blinding extravagance of his waistcoat all bespoke rampant dandyism. The several fobs and seals draped across his expanding girth and the high gloss of his top boots completed the picture.

This gentleman raised his quizzing glass and regarded Adrian with a languid air. "A clergyman, my dear Sophronia? What new affectation is this?"

The elderly Miss Selwood hastily shoved aside the clutter on her desk and directed a vague smile at him, putting Adrian forcibly in mind of a bewildered hen. He advanced into the room. "Forgive me for disturbing you."

"But you are not, Mr. Carstairs. Not in the least, I assure you. So very good of you to help us. Allow me to present my cousin, Mr. George Selwood. He owns the Manor—and this house, of course." She blinked at Adrian.

Mr. George Selwood regarded him with an air of fascinated delight. "A clergyman for ghost catcher! My dear Sophronia, you are to be congratulated! What a truly inspired notion. I am in awe of it, simply in awe. Will you be able to exorcise it, do you think, Mr. Carstairs?"

"Oh, if only he could!" Sophronia Selwood gasped.

Adrian directed a considering gaze at George Selwood. "You sound as if you think that will be our only hope."

Mr. Selwood twisted his quizzing glass between his fingers. "I fear so, I greatly fear so. The deuce of a business, this has been. A ghost!" He shuddered. "Can't tell you how upset everyone is. Just the other day, Romney actually suggested we call in Bow Street. As if one could take a specter into custody!"

"Romney?" Adrian searched his memory, but could not identify the name.

"Mr. Harold Romney. Most people around here call him the Squire," Mr. Selwood explained.

"But not you, dear." Miss Sophronia Selwood beamed on her cousin, then turned to Adrian. "Such a delightful neighbor, dear Mr. Romney. Why, he and Cousin George have been friends for simply forever. I remember them running about the house here when they were but the merest infants, getting into everything."

"And you scolding us," George Selwood reminded his elder relative.

"And Romney—the Squire—thinks this current matter should be handled by Bow Street?" Adrian pursued.

"I only wish I could agree with him." George Selwood shook his head as well as the absurd points of his collar allowed. "Bow Street! There's nothing tangible to tell them—well, how could there be in the case of a ghost? But that's Romney, always wanting to go to the extremes at once without considering reason." His eyes narrowed, and he stared at Adrian, holding his gaze. "Perhaps you'll be able to do something where others cannot. You know, lay the poor soul to rest."

"I certainly intend to do something," Adrian said. "But what, precisely, must wait to be seen." He turned once more to Miss Selwood. "Have I your permission to prowl about the place? I should like to take a good look around before your students return."

"Anywhere you wish, and at any time—" She broke off, her face puckering in concern. "Though to be sure, it might be awkward should you need to search the girls' rooms, once they've returned. That is—"

"I shall endeavor to avoid that." With a bow, Adrian removed himself.

He paused in the hall to find his bearings, then set forth. He could understand Daphne's not minding her cousin George's involvement—as well as Mr. Danvers's lack of faith in that gentleman's abilities. Mr. George Selwood appeared to prefer taking as little part as possible in this unpleasant business.

Adrian spent the rest of the afternoon familiarizing himself with the layout of the rooms. The Dower House proved to be a fair-sized home dating from the Tudor era, with only minor adaptations having been made to accommodate its use as a school. The ground floor housed the office, classrooms, dining room, library, and a salon. The first floor held bedrooms, five of which had been devoted to the students, each with four beds. The Selwood sisters also kept a small suite of rooms for their private apartments on this floor.

The next held the attics. Along one side, overlooking the front of the house, stood the rooms of Daphne, those of two other school mistresses, his own guest chamber, and a storage room. This proved to be packed with an assortment of abandoned furniture and trunks, shrouded in holland covers and dust. Directly across the narrow corridor, overlooking the back, stood a similar lumber room. Along the rest of that side lay the servants' quarters—inhabited by the cook, the elderly retainer, and the two maids.

He next went outside to explore the grounds. These were not extensive, consisting primarily of a small terrace off the library and a snow-covered shrubbery in the front, and the stable in the rear. Beyond the grounds lay a spinney, probably quite splendid in spring and summer, but at the moment appearing merely cold and desolate. About a hundred yards up the drive he could see the Manor House, its imposing facade having been restructured during the early years of the second King George, at a guess.

He gazed about, deep in thought. The crisp air smelled of wet pine and smoke from the chimneys, and the shrill cries of birds sounded from the trees. The late afternoon light cast deep shadows among their barren limbs, lending the scene a sinister air. His sister Augusta, who was given to romantic daydreams, would undoubtedly declare the place to be haunted.

But if the ghost were real, why had it not been seen before? And if the manifestations proved to have a human cause, then why? Frowning, he returned to the house.

He barely had time to remove the dust and snow of his explorations before a knock sounded on his door, and Daphne's voice informed him that it was time for everyone to gather in the drawing room before dinner. He checked his mirror to assure himself his appearance was not so disordered as to offer insult to his hostesses, and emerged into the empty hall. Daphne had not waited.

Several of the students, it seemed, had returned to the fold. As he strode across the threshold, he found himself the focus of three pairs of eyes: one pair blue and languishing, in the face of a remarkably pretty chit with a fashionable crop of hair the color of wheat; one pair hazel and speculative in a pert face surrounded by chestnut ringlets; and one solemn pair of pansy brown set in the face of a mere child with long brown hair tied with a riband at the nape of her neck.

"I told you he was handsome," came Miss Jane's voice in an unfortunately loud whisper from a corner.

"Jane!" Daphne hushed her sister.

"But he's only a clergyman, after all," sighed the blonde in a tone not meant to carry as well as it did.

Adrian kept a commendably straight face as he entered this lioness's den. The steady gaze of the brown-haired child continued to follow his every move, no trace of a smile on her watchful features. He retired to the farthest corner and schooled his countenance into what he hoped to be an appropriately ecclesiastical expression.

Dinner proved to be a simple affair, with the girls chattering with unrestrained animation. Daphne, after directing one unforgiving stare at him, ignored his presence. Miss Elspeth, seated at his right, maintained an oft-interrupted conversation with him, as the majority of her attention remained focused on keeping her young pupils in line. As soon as the meal drew to a close, Adrian excused himself on the pretext of needing to devote himself to his writings, and retired to his room.

He did not find it easy to concentrate. Squeals of girlish laughter, followed inevitably by requests that the perpetrators strive to remember they were young ladies and not street urchins, drifted up from two floors below, punctuating his thoughts. Herodotus, while a never-ending delight, proved tricky at the best of times. Giving up at last to the exhaustion of the last few days' travel, he prepared for bed and crawled between sheets.

For a long while he lay awake, willing the knots out of tired muscles, allowing his mind to skim over what very little he knew of these supposed hauntings. No fresh ideas arrived in bursts of startling revelation, so he abandoned the pastime at last. Instead, he stared out the window, sensing more than seeing the gentle swirl of snowflakes as they drifted past, blanketing the world in silence.

Except for that squeak.

It jarred Adrian to full consciousness. By the dim light of the oil lamp beside his bed, he could just make out the face of the clock. It lacked but ten minutes until two.

He leaned back against the pillows, frowning. A *squeak?* At two o'clock in the morning? A very large mouse, perhaps? Or . . .

The grating noise repeated, muffled and drawn out, as if someone moved with stealth. The ghost? Here, inside the house?

Holding his breath, Adrian slid from his bed, pulled on his dressing gown, but disdained slippers that might scrape the floor. He didn't want to betray himself. Anticipation rushed through him, mingling with a sense of rising enjoyment.

He eased open his door and set forth in pursuit.

Chapter Three

Complete blackness blanketed the hall as Adrian emerged. In one hand he grasped his chamberstick, in the other his pocket luminary; it would be much easier to strike his light now, but he wasn't about to show a flame where his ghost might see it. He crept forward, surprised at the depth of the enjoyment that flooded him, at feeling so very much alive. An aura of danger beckoned, and something deep within him awakened, rising with alacrity as if to a clarion call.

Two steps into the corridor he paused, straining his hearing, unsure from which direction the noise had come. As he stood motionless, with even his breathing stilled, a door down the narrow hallway creaked in protest as it inched inward. Triumphant, Adrian eased himself into the deeper shadows by the wall as the wavering light from a candle cast its luminous bath toward him.

A delicate figure in clouds of pale cloth floated within the glowing circle, holding the flame on high in a trembling hand. Long dark curls peeped out from beneath a nightcap. No ghost or evil malefactor, this, but Miss Daphne Selwood, enchantingly *deshabille*. Adrian stepped forward, and an involuntary gasp escaped her lips as she drew back. He advanced into the revealing glow, and she sank against the door jamb.

"You terrified me!" she protested in a soft whisper.

"I almost attacked you." He matched her tone, more

39

a breath than a real sound. He lit his candle from hers and thrust his luminary into his pocket. "You heard something, too?"

She nodded, her wide-eyed gaze resting on him. "I wanted—I was *determined*—to find out what it was. It was so eerie. And now you've interrupted me." Her hand strayed to the throat of her high-necked dressing gown as if she suddenly realized the impropriety of her attire. "You might as well go back to your room. There is no need for us both—"

A protesting creak from the far end of the corridor interrupted her. Daphne's fingers clamped onto his arm. His own covered them, reassuring; they were cold and trembling beneath his touch.

He studied her wide-eyed face. "Why do you not wait here while I investigate?"

She gave herself a shake, as if throwing off the attack of nerves that held her rigid, and seemed to realize she clung to his arm. She released him as if the contact stung. Still, her uneasy gaze strayed down the hall. After a moment, she straightened her shoulders. "*I* will investigate." With that, she started forward.

She made no objection when Adrian followed. When they reached the first door beyond and opposite Adrian's, she paused, holding back. Adrian moved past her and placed his ear against the keyhole. A storage room, he remembered from his explorations of the afternoon.

Daphne pressed against his side, her fingers once more clenching a handful of his sleeve, her cheek brushing against his shoulder. Awareness of her surged through him, and enticing but highly unreverendish images flickered through his mind. With circumspection not unmingled with regret, he thrust them aside. Those he'd explore later, at leisure.

Now, he had a ghost to pursue.

Not a sound issued from within. In the combined light of their candles the door handle gleamed, and he turned it, allowing the ancient oak panel to swing inward with only the slightest groan. He held his taper aloft, and together they advanced into the shrouded chamber.

Shadows danced backward, retreating toward the ceiling and corners as he threaded his way farther into the room, jammed with the debris of the ages. Frowning, he allowed his searching gaze to roam the apartment, alert for any movement, any elusive shape, any betraying sound. Nothing—at least nothing untoward. The flickering light created innumerable ghostly shapes, but they all proved innocent.

Behind them, in the hall or the rooms beyond, something heavy scraped against the floor boards. With the sound of Daphne's gasp in his ears, Adrian ran out the door. He hesitated only a moment, thrust open the door opposite, then stopped, transfixed, staring at the glowing form that met his gaze.

Light seemed to fill it. It wavered, its contours changing even as he watched. Slowly it rose into the air with a soul-rending moan, then a gust of chill wind set it flapping.

Adrian's candle blew out, plunging the attic chamber into darkness. Fingers grasped his arm, accompanied by a soft moan as something pressed against his side. Daphne. His arm encircled her, folding her against himself, but his gaze remained on the pale, hazy outline hovering nearly three feet off the floor.

Another creak sounded in the darkness, then stillness engulfed them. It took a moment for Adrian to realize the wavering figure had vanished. With his one arm still about Daphne, he managed to free his luminary from the capacious pocket of his dressing gown and light it behind her back. A subdued glow once more illuminated the chamber.

This time, no ghostly apparition hovered anywhere in sight.

Gently—and not without a measure of regret—he disengaged Daphne's hold on him. "I want to look."

She shivered. "Was—was it real?"

"Very real, I should imagine. Human, that is."

41

She looked up at him, her shadowed eyes huge, her face enchantingly pale in the flickering light. "Have you ever seen a *real* ghost?"

Adrian's lips twitched. "Two of them," he admitted. "There is a gray monk at Halliford Castle, and poor old Archbishop Laud up at St. John's College at Oxford."

"Archbishop . . ." Her voice trailed off, but her wide-eyed gaze rested on his face.

"He was Archbishop of Canterbury, until he was beheaded. Mid-sixteen hundreds, if I remember aright. He likes to bowl in the library."

"Bowl—you mean with a ball?"

"Well, no. With his head. He rolls it across the floor, you see."

A touch of amusement glinted in her lovely green eyes. "You take this quite calmly. I should imagine I would run screaming if I ever encountered any such thing."

Adrian shook his head, smiling. "The old monk is quite harmless. I doubt he's ever done more than shake his cowled head at anyone. I think he's lonely, and hangs about for the company. And as for the Archbishop, I think he stays about to plague the new students more than the dons. Feeling better?"

She stared at him in indignation. "You were trying to divert me!" After a moment's reflection, she added, grudging but fair: "It seems to have worked. And I think you are quite right about our visitor. He might have terri— *unsettled* me, just a little, but he didn't *feel* like I'd imagine a real ghost to feel." In spite of herself, she shivered.

"Hold this." He handed her his candle, lit the other, and strode into the long attic chamber.

She followed. "Where did he disappear?"

Adrian shook his head. "I'm not certain. I must admit," he added, a touch rueful, "he certainly accomplished his purpose. I was so startled at the picture he made, I completely failed to notice anything pertinent—like where he stood, or how he managed that cold blast."

Daphne hugged her robe about her. "It is freezing in here, even without him."

He glanced at her inadequate wrap, aware of the gentle curves beneath the clinging fabric. Very unreverendish, he reminded himself, and grinned. "You had best return to your room. But don't worry, you won't miss anything. I'll wait to explore this until tomorrow, when there's adequate light to see any secreted devices to open trap doors."

Daphne hesitated, frowning. "You will wait for me until after lunch, won't you? You won't come in here while I'm tied up with the girls? I won't be left out."

He could find no objection to that. In fact, the prospect pleased him, and not just because two pairs of eyes and hands would make the work go faster. She would come to no harm, not in the daylight and under his watchful eye, and being included would assuage her pride. Already, he noted, pleased, she did not seem to object to his presence as much as she had earlier in the day. All in all, not a bad night's work.

Yet after he'd escorted her to her door and seen her safely within, uneasiness crept over him. He sought his own bed, thoughtful, his doubts growing. Someone went to a great deal of trouble to ensure any chance observers would believe this to be a real ghost, and that gave him pause. This matter might well prove to be a very dangerous business.

And he definitely did not want Miss Daphne Selwood to come to any harm.

Daphne studied the sketch defiantly thrust at her by Miss Marianne Snowdon, and stifled an inward groan. Somewhere, if she searched hard enough, she might—just might—find a resemblance to the vase and candelabrum she'd artistically arranged for the girls to draw, but she doubted it. "Very nice," she managed.

The girl frowned at her, wrinkling her freckled little

43

nose. "No it isn't, Miss Daphne. This is *terrible.*" Her pleading gaze rested on Daphne, a touch of calculation in the dark depths of her eyes. "There is really no point in trying to make me proficient at sketching, for you must see I have not the least aptitude."

"You mean desire. You seem more than capable enough when it comes to things you like. No, you are not to argue. Your mama specifically requested me to teach you the basics, and teach you I shall. When you show me you have applied yourself, then you may go. But not until."

With an air of indignant injury, Miss Snowdon returned to her chair.

Daphne cast a frustrated look out the window, across the winter-shrouded garden. This morning, for a change, the sun shone, the rays glistening off the patches of snow. A perfect day for ghost hunting. And here she was, stuck with her reluctant pupils who still longed to return to the delights of their Christmas holidays.

From behind her, an all-too-familiar voice rose with its lilting laugh, and Miss Louisa Trevellian declared: "He is quite the most handsome man I have ever seen."

Daphne's hands clenched. The girls were talking about Mr. Carstairs already, although that wretched little flirt could have seen him only briefly. Still, the words surprised her, for she would have thought Louisa would prefer Classical perfection of feature rather than the rugged charm of their temporary chaplain. She would have called his features arresting or compelling. Of course, the way the candlelight played off the thick waves of his light brown hair—she broke off that thought, appalled by how her mind dwelt on the man.

"I shall be quite the envy of the *ton* when I have wed him," Louisa went on, smugness in her voice. "Imagine, I shall be a viscountess at only seventeen, and a countess when he inherits his papa's earldom."

Not Mr. Carstairs. Daphne's cheeks warmed, and she kept her back to the room. Louisa Trevellian had become engaged over the holidays—captured for herself quite a matrimonial prize, it would seem. What ever had made Daphne think she spoke of Mr. Carstairs?

Because he haunted her own thoughts, Daphne realized.

Not that it was *he* who occupied her mind, of course, but the reason for his being at the seminary. To be her watchdog, her nurserymaid. She *didn't* look forward to seeing Mr. Carstairs this afternoon; only the lure of the search they would undertake beckoned her. She even considered it a shame Mr. Carstairs would be taking part in it. It would be much more fun to rummage through the old lumber room on her own.

She considered that last thought and owned that perhaps she stretched the truth a trifle. After all, the search would proceed more quickly with two instead of one.

She glanced at the clock on the mantel, willing the hands to speed their circular journey. The hours seemed to linger like unwelcome morning visitors. If only more of the girls had returned, then at least they would have kept her busy. Tomorrow would be better, she reminded herself, with more girls back—but that didn't help *now*.

With resolution, she picked up a sketching pad and went to work. Yet after only a few quick strokes with her pencil, her thoughts drifted upward to the attic chambers. Mr. Carstairs had surprised her last night. He hadn't hesitated a moment; he'd certainly shown no trace of fear or even nerves. In fact, he seemed to enjoy himself despite the fact she'd been reduced to a quivering heap.

She didn't know him very well, she realized with a touch of surprise. His visits to her Uncle Thaddeus rarely coincided with her own; and when they'd met, she'd seen him as bookish, wholly enthralled with whatever Greek text her uncle recently had unearthed. Yet it seemed Mr. Carstairs possessed another side, and one of great humor and courage, unexpected in an Oxford don.

When the lunch hour chimed at last, Daphne dismissed the girls. Louisa made her stately way from the room with all the dignity required of a young lady betrothed to a viscount. Jane, her expression one of awed envy, followed her friend, begging for more information about the young lord. The other girls clustered about them, chattering in a manner that made Daphne heartily glad to be rid of them for a little while.

At the doorway, she paused, frowning. Too many of the girls had surrounded her cousins at breakfast; she hadn't yet had a chance to tell the Selwood sisters about the ghostly encounter of the night before. Almost, she didn't want to. They had hoped—how often they had expressed it!—that with the school almost empty over the Christmas holidays, their ghost might grow bored and leave. To learn it still haunted the place would distress the old darlings.

She found Miss Elspeth ushering the girls into the dining room, a distracted expression on her face. Daphne waited.

Elspeth looked up, caught sight of Daphne, and drew her aside. "Mr. Carstairs has told us of your dreadful experience last night. And actually within the house, this time! That makes it so much worse. Sophronia is quite distraught."

"I preferred its remaining in the gardens, too," Daphne admitted. "Where is Mr. Carstairs?"

"He has taken a plate to his room—to avoid the girls, I fear—and says that as soon as you are free, to knock on his door." Elspeth hesitated. "Do you know, I quite got the impression he looked forward to this."

Daphne waved an airy hand. "There is no accounting for a gentleman's tastes, is there? I do not believe he turned so much as a hair when that beastly apparition moaned at us. I nearly fainted!"

Miss Elspeth's easy smile started in her hazel eyes, then spread to her generous mouth. "Do you know, I think I might come up and have a look myself. In the daylight, of course. I want very much to know how this disappearing trick is managed."

Then Daphne would not have to spend the afternoon alone with Mr. Carstairs. To her annoyance, that realization did not please her as much as it should. She thrust the thought from her and turned her attention to a luncheon which she ate quickly. That finished, she excused herself and made her way up the stairs.

Mr. Carstairs answered as soon as she knocked. For a long moment she regarded him, taking in the tumbling waves of his thick brown hair, the serious expression of his gray eyes—a seriousness that could melt in a moment, she'd discovered, leaving them laughing and carefree. Why, though, did he have to come here, playing nurserymaid to her, robbing her of her chance to prove herself able to make sensible decisions? Under other circumstances, she might have liked him.

She shook off her regrets. "Am I interrupting your studious endeavors?"

He glanced across at his desk, where papers lay scattered over the surface, and merely grimaced. "Why do you not change into an older gown—one that will not be ruined by the dust? Then join me next door."

She should have thought of her gown herself. It irritated her to be less than efficient, to appear dull-witted in his eyes. She changed quickly, then made her way along the corridor.

The lumber room stood open, and out of it drifted her cousin Elspeth's melodic voice. Good, she told herself, and was dismayed this sentiment struck no true chord within her. It would be much easier to search with three—and she would feel Mr. Carstairs's intrusion the less for it.

She entered to find them standing side by side, Mr. Carstairs towering over Cousin Elspeth, whom Daphne had always considered to be quite a tall woman. She advanced into the room, determinedly averting her gaze

47

from the breadth of the gentleman's shoulders, exquisitely set off in a coat of excellent cut.

They had thrown back the curtains, letting in what little light they could; a dreary overcast had replaced the welcome sunshine of the morning. Now all looked dark and threatening. Snow before nightfall, she guessed.

She drew her shawl about herself, shivering in the chill chamber. "Have you found something?"

Mr. Carstairs glanced over his shoulder. "Only that our ghost left no trace last night. The room is surprisingly clean. There is no dust on the floors or furniture."

Daphne ran a hand over the nearest chest and examined her pristine fingertips. "How odd."

"Mr. Carstairs believes our ghost does not want to leave any tangible evidence of its passing, such as footprints or smudges." Cousin Elspeth frowned. "Yet I wonder what could be the purpose?"

"And why did it appear in here, at all?" Daphne asked. "The chances of our seeing it were very slim."

"Then perhaps it didn't intend to be seen, but came for some other purpose. Shall we see if we can discover what might have brought it?" Mr. Carstairs wended his way amid the clutter on the floor of the crowded chamber, then set to work opening cupboard doors and drawers at random.

Wardrobes, trunks, chests—anything out of date or damaged—had been stored here over the generations. With a sense of fascinated wonder, Daphne joined the other two. Yet for what sort of thing did they look? Or perhaps more to the point, for what might the ghost have been looking?

After two hours of peeking into everything that opened, Elspeth reluctantly called a halt to their explorations. "We must return to the girls soon, Daphne," she said.

Daphne turned with regret from an ancient cabinet stuffed with gowns from the early part of the previous century. "But we have not found anything!" Nothing, at least, that might indicate a reason for last night's unorthodox visitation—whether human or other-worldly.

Miss Elspeth rose from the teetering chair on which she had perched. "I would much rather stay here, too, but Sophronia and Beatrice will be counting on us. And we cannot go down in all our dirt."

Daphne examined her skirts. "Our ghost isn't as excellent a housekeeper as you would have me think, Mr. Carstairs. We are all of us covered in dust."

Mr. Carstairs nodded absently, his gaze fastened on the window.

"Do you see something?" She moved with care amid the clutter to join him.

"I just wondered—" He broke off, his gaze transferring back to the center of the chamber. "We only *assumed* our ghost vanished from over there." He waved in that general direction. "Could we not have seen a fabricated apparition set there to confuse—and frighten—prying eyes? Whoever it was might then have made his escape out the window in perfect safety, while we gaped at his creation."

"Of course!" Daphne stared at him, vexed with herself for having missed something so obvious. "Oh, how foolish we were—but I must own, it was rather an awe-inspiring sight. It cannot be wondered at that we were diverted. And the window would explain that gust of chill wind. *Not* an other-worldly presence, at all." And that relieved her, more than she had expected.

Mr. Carstairs, though, continued to frown. "It is only a possibility," he reminded her. He reached across a small chest and pushed the sash wide. An eerie protest rasped in their ears, even as a blast of cold wind swirled about them.

Daphne leaned against the edge of a chest of drawers. "I don't remember that sound."

Mr. Carstairs closed the window once more, securing it with care. "No," he said after a moment. "Neither do I. I heard a creak, but not like this." With no apparent thought for his buckskin breeches, he sank onto the top of an old sea chest. "Miss Elspeth, can you remember any mention of a secret passage in this house?"

That lady's brow puckered. "My papa never mentioned one," she said, "but it is possible he might not have known."

"What is behind all this?" Daphne exclaimed. "Does someone want to ruin the school?" She looked from one to the other of her two companions. "Cousin George certainly has everything to be gained by keeping it open. Has he not?" She turned to Cousin Elspeth for corroboration.

"I believe he only would be harmed by our having to close Selwood Seminary," she agreed. She drew a long, trembling sigh. "You must know, Mr. Carstairs, that the rent we pay him for the Dower House supports him. To lose the school would be to lose his own income."

"Might the house be more valuable used for something else?" Mr. Carstairs asked.

Daphne stared at Cousin Elspeth, and encountered a blank look in return.

"Not that I can think of," Elspeth declared at last. "It is entailed, so he could not sell it, and I do not believe he would receive any more for it from a private party. No, whatever is happening, Cousin George cannot be responsible."

Mr. Carstairs rubbed his chin. "It's very possible this is naught but a schoolgirl prank. I remember some of the more outrageous larks kicked up by my classmates at Oxford—"

"Not by you?" Daphne interrupted with feigned innocence.

His slow smile lit his eyes. "Occasionally," he admitted.

"It seems quite elaborate," Miss Elspeth demurred.

"The girls can be very inventive," Daphne pointed out dryly. "And did you not say the hauntings stopped while everyone was away for the holidays?"

"Stopped as far as we could tell." Miss Elspeth

frowned. "For all I know, a ghost might have popped in and out of this room every night, and I would have been none the wiser. I had thought the manifestations took place outside. At least, that is what the girls have always reported." She rose and took several agitated steps. "Of course, no one comes up here that often, and night-time noises are so very frequently no more than an old house settling. We might never have suspected this room, had not you and Mr. Carstairs come to investigate last night."

"It might have been a prank staged for my benefit," Mr. Carstairs suggested. "Several of the girls were once more in residence last night, and they must know the only available chamber for me to occupy is next door to this one."

"Pranks," Daphne murmured. "But who—oh, the little wretch! I wonder—" Daphne stared at Cousin Elspeth. "What do you think of Miss Snowdon as the instigator?"

"Marianne?" Miss Elspeth stared back, her expression one of no little consternation. "I would sooner suspect Louisa!"

"*Not* since she has become engaged," Daphne protested. "It would be too far beneath her dignity, now."

"True." Elspeth smiled. "But before?"

"We saw the ghost last night," Daphne reminded her. Elspeth twisted an escaped tendril near her cheek. "Surely Marianne would do no such thing. I admit she has a lively mind, and—and a certain disregard for the proprieties, but surely she would do nothing harmful to the school!"

"Would she realize it as such?" Mr. Carstairs asked when that lady broke off.

Daphne's mouth tightened. "I'll find out," she declared, and rose. She could see Miss Marianne Snowdon taking revenge for those drawing lessons she despised. Revenge . . .

Another face flickered through her mind, another girl who had not liked the seminary and sworn eternal enmity when she'd been dismissed from the ranks of the students. Yet Miss Susannah Ingels had left months before the hauntings had begun, and her only connection with the academy now lay in the fact that her ancestral home lay less than two miles from the Selwood estate. She remained a possibility, but how could she—or anyone else, for that matter?—have gained entry into the school last night?

"Daphne." Mr. Carstairs followed her into the hall. "Is there a room into which you might move on the floor below?"

At once, she bristled. "Why? Do you feel too crowded up here?"

"I would rather you were safe with your cousins if our ghost returns."

Her watchdog. She glared at him. "I am hardly alone up here. What with you and the servants—"

"The servants never heard a thing last night. I would rather—"

"*You* would rather?" Her indignation swelled. "May I remind you that my uncle required that I submit to your *presence*, but he said not one word about your *orders?*"

Infuriating amusement flickered in his gray eyes. "Did I issue any orders?"

"Can you deny you were about to?" she shot back.

His lips twitched. "Not orders, precisely. Call it a suggestion. Or perhaps sound advice."

"You may call it whatever you will. *I* call it interference. This is *our* problem—my cousins and mine—and I will not submit to sitting tamely out of the way and doing nothing when I am perfectly capable of investigating matters and making decisions on my own. Is that understood?"

Without waiting for his reply, she turned on her heel and stalked down the hall, her face burning. How dare he regard her with laughter dancing in his eyes. And how dare he try to take charge. She spun around to find he still watched her. "You will do nothing further in that room without me! And that *is* an order!"

She stormed down the steps, only to pause at the next floor as she heard Cousin Beatrice hail her. Daphne looked down to see the stolid figure beckoning her with an imperious hand. Curious, Daphne hurried down the last steps.

"There you are." Beatrice cast a disapproving glance over her shoulder into the drawing room, then grasped Daphne's arm and marched with her purposeful stride into the library. "That Davenport female," she said by way of explanation.

"Do you mean she's here? She has actually left the lofty heights of her own Seminary and lowered herself for a visit to us? Whatever for?" Daphne stared down the hall, dismayed.

"Come to gloat, I shouldn't wonder. Can't find Elspeth, and Sophronia's no use. You'd better bear me company. Keep me from saying things I might regret. Though don't see why I should."

Reluctant, Daphne straightened her gown, removed the smudges of dust as best she could, and accompanied her cousin into the unwelcome presence.

Miss Isobel Davenport sat on the wingback chair before the fireplace, back straight, hands folded, her sharp features now wreathed in contented smiles. An elaborate hat, decorated with artificial roses, perched upon steely gray hair that she wore coiled into a chignon at the nape of her neck. She looked up at their entrance and inclined her head, rather as if she had been a royal personage acknowledging the arrival of supplicants instead of herself being the visitor.

Beatrice, not to be outdone, sailed into the chamber and regarded the proprietess of the rival Davenport Seminary with an air of haughty tolerance. "Well, Isobel. What brings you out here? Need assistance with your lesson planning?"

Faint color tinged the high cheekbones on the narrow

53

face. A moment of silence passed, then Miss Davenport said, "I have come to pay a call of condolence. One hears that the Selwood Seminary may close its doors at last." Only the slightest touch of satisfaction colored the last two words.

Beatrice's mouth showed white as she forced it into a smile. "Uninformed gossip. Never pay any heed to such vulgarities myself. Suppose you're used to it, of course."

The bony figure—not frail, by any means—stiffened, and the dark eyes gleamed with malice. "You can't tell me you are *not* losing pupils. In the last couple of days I've had four new girls, their families positively begging me to rescue them from your . . . care."

Four? Daphne searched the pinched face for signs of exaggeration. Only satisfaction met her gaze, and her heart sank. She only knew of two who had withdrawn because of the hauntings. Were there indeed more, some who had not yet informed the Selwood ladies of their decision?

"It will seem so very strange when—*if*," Miss Davenport corrected herself with painstaking care, "Selwood Seminary is no more. But you need have no fear. We will accept the more elegant of your pupils into our establishment. Only the more elegant," she repeated. "After all, we must maintain our standards. My dear cousin the viscount would be appalled should they be slackened. As for the other girls—" She wrinkled her pointed nose. "Well, I'm sure there are many schools of *your* sort—not so fastidious, I mean—who will take them on."

"Won't be the need." Beatrice transfixed her with a steely glare. "Our Seminary is not shutting its doors. Those four won't be missed in the slightest. Plenty of young ladies whose families want them educated in an atmosphere of *refinement*."

"I hardly think one can consider ghosts to be refined." Miss Davenport permitted herself a thin-lipped smile as she rose. "Well, you have my deepest sympathy, my dear Beatrice. So very wise of you to keep up a

54

brave face. No, there is no need to show me out. I know you must be quite at your wit's end." Somehow, she made it sound as if that were a very short journey.

Daphne followed the woman from the room, saw her to the door, and barely prevented herself from slamming it in her wake. She turned back into the hall to find Beatrice, hands clenched, shoulders trembling, advancing on her.

"The nerve of that woman. Her 'dear-cousin-the-viscount,' indeed!" Beatrice sniffed. "Third cousins, they are, and by marriage only. I doubt he has the least interest in her trumped-up little school."

"She said *four* girls." Daphne led the way to the office. "Is that true?"

"Not to my knowledge." Beatrice's ire wavered, then abated. "Though fewer girls have returned as yet than we expected. Only two have formally withdrawn, but that does not mean there won't be more."

Daphne settled on one of the chairs and fixed her thoughtful regard on her cousin. "How long has this rivalry existed between you?"

Beatrice snorted. "Since our own days at a Seminary. Everything we did—riding, dancing, even household management—she made into a contest between us. Every time I excelled, Isobel did something to ruin my success."

"And if Miss Davenport excelled?" Somehow, Daphne couldn't imagine the malice to have been one-sided.

Beatrice snorted. "Her? Excel? Don't be ridiculous. Except at gloating, of course. Just like her, to come and crow over us. Though it would be more like her to—" She broke off, eyes widening.

"To—?" Daphne prompted, though suddenly she thought she knew what had occurred to her cousin.

"Exactly what she did with everything else I did better. Sabotage it, of course."

Chapter Four

Daphne checked the clock before leaving Cousin Beatrice; it lacked only an hour before time to dress for dinner. She knew a craven impulse to retreat to her chamber to regroup before facing the girls again, but knew she could not. She still had her sister Jane to see concerning the possible peccadilloes of one Miss Marianne Snowdon.

If that girl were up to anything, Jane would know. From the moment Miss Snowdon had arrived at the seminary, she and Jane had become particular friends, constantly in one another's company, far too frequently with their heads together in whispered conversation. From the shocking things Jane upon occasion repeated in artless innocence, it appeared the lively Miss Snowdon looked upon Jane as a confidante, one to whom the most outrageous thoughts could be revealed in safety.

Daphne found Jane in the music room, seated at the pianoforte, but not playing the aged instrument. Marianne perched on a chair at her side, her crop of blonde ringlets tilted close to Jane's darker head. Both were giggling, which filled Daphne with foreboding.

As the door opened, the pair pulled guiltily apart as if they had been caught doing something they should not. Marianne froze a moment, then leaned over and whispered to Jane. She rose with exaggerated decorum, smoothed out her skirts, and made a stately exit which was marred at the last moment by her muffled giggles.

Jane composed her expression into one of such innocence that uneasiness again assailed Daphne.

"What are you two planning?" she demanded as she closed the door behind her.

"Why, whatever do you mean?" Jane raised wide, questioning eyes and batted her long lashes.

"Do cut line." Daphne took Marianne's abandoned chair. "Jane, you are not planning mischief, are you?"

"As if we would!" The girl's indignation lacked conviction, and tell-tale color tinged her cheeks a becoming rose.

"Jane . . ." Daphne allowed the name to trail off on a threatening note.

"Well, it's not so *very* bad," Jane countered.

Daphne covered her face for a moment, composing herself so as not instantly to berate her young sister. "You would not—you *could* not—engage in any activity that might harm the school. Jane, you *know* how our cousins dote on the seminary. They would be heartbroken—"

"I'd never do anything to hurt them!" Jane glared at her. "How dare you think any such thing."

"You would *not* engage in a little harmless haunting to scare someone?" Daphne watched her, her eyes narrowed. "One of the younger girls, perhaps, whom you did not quite like? I noticed last night you did not seem pleased with Miss Alden."

Jane gave her a disdainful look. "How childish. Of course I would not." Her eyes widened. "Last night. Do you mean the ghost has been seen since then? How exciting! By whom?"

"By me, and by Mr. Carstairs. And in the house, not in the garden."

Jane's mouth rounded to an astonished "O."

"Jane." Daphne possessed herself of her sister's hands. "Marianne has such a lively mind. Do you not think it

57

possible *she* might be behind these hauntings? As a lark, or a—a trick on the other girls?"

Jane pulled free, her eyes flashing. "Of course not! What a terrible thing to suggest. Why, she is quite devoted to our cousins. She's said so!"

"But if it did not occur to her the harm she did——"

"No!" Jane sprang to her feet. "You do not like Marianne because she hates to sketch, but indeed, there is no harm in her. It is quite detestable of you to suggest such a thing."

"You are very right, and I do apologize." It did Daphne no harm to placate. Jane appeared sincere, and Daphne wanted other information from her sister, as well. "Instead, tell me about this engagement of Louisa Trevellian's. Where did she meet her viscount?"

Jane's delicate brow puckered. "Her father had invited him to stay at their home for the holidays. She *says* she is very pleased about the arrangement."

"But she isn't?" Daphne caught her sister's slight stress on the word.

Jane resumed her seat at the pianoforte. "Marianne says Louisa makes too much of a show of pleasure, and it doesn't ring quite true." She looked up, troubled. "I do not know which one of them to believe."

"I thought this morning," Daphne said slowly, "that when Louisa looked out the window, and forgot the other people in the room, she looked unhappy."

Jane blinked. "She did. Then it is Marianne who is telling the truth. I am so glad. Marianne thinks Louisa is not as enamored of her viscount as she would have everyone believe."

Daphne stood, paced to the fire, then looked back. "You know her better than do I. Tell me the truth. Is Louisa on the catch for a title?"

Jane hesitated, her mouth twisted into a frown. "Marianne does not think so, but——" She broke off and looked up at Daphne. "Miss Breame does. They cannot both be right."

58

"What do *you* think?" Daphne asked.

Jane wrinkled her nose. "I think Marianne is right," she said after a moment. "She told me first."

As if that settled the matter. Daphne let it pass. "I wonder what sort of man this viscount of hers is, if he is truly all that is amiable."

"And an excellent dancer and leader of fashion. She has made much of his abilities." Jane brightened. "I know the very thing! Let us ask Mr. Carstairs, for he is sure to be acquainted with her viscount."

Daphne stiffened at this mention of her watchdog. "Indeed, why should he be?"

"Why, he moves only in the first circles when he visits London—at least, that is what Miss Breame and Emma Pembroke say. After all, he is *Halliford's* brother-in-law. Of course he knows everyone of importance."

Daphne's irritation kindled. "I would not deign to trouble him with the matter. It is of no real moment, after all."

Jane tilted her head on one side and regarded her sister with a puzzled frown. "Why do you dislike Mr. Carstairs so? All the girls say he is quite amazingly good fun, especially considering he is a clergyman. There is such laughter in his eyes, have you not noticed?"

"All I have noticed is that he is as managing as any other gentleman where 'mere helpless females' are involved. I wish he could be brought to understand that we are able to take care of ourselves."

Jane opened her mouth, then prudently closed it once more, her expression both puzzled and thoughtful. After a moment, she said, "Do you think he would remain here had Uncle Thaddeus not insisted upon our having a gentleman in attendance?"

"He is enjoying himself no end," Daphne declared with suppressed savagery.

"Well, we could be rid of him easily enough, if you wished it."

Daphne stared at her sister. "Whatever do you mean?

Mr. Carstairs is so odiously honorable, you know he would not go back on his word, nor desert what he considers to be his duty. He would never leave unless he were assured someone else could protect us more effectively."

"What of someone with a better right to protect us?" Jane's eyes twinkled. "We *could* send for Uncle Percival. I don't know why you made such a fuss about it before."

"Uncle—" Daphne felt the color drain from her cheeks. "Oh, no," she managed.

"But if you are so eager to dismiss Mr. Carstairs, though to be sure I cannot understand why—"

"*Uncle Percival?* Jane, have you no memory of him?"

Her sister considered. "Not really."

She could be grateful for that, at least. What Jane didn't know, the girl couldn't blurt out. "Mr. Carstairs would never approve of him," she said, grasping for an excuse. "Rather than leave us in his care, I fear Mr. Carstairs would be more determined than ever to remain. And then we would have *two* gentlemen with whom we must contend," she added, bitterly.

She left the room, depressed, and made her way to the library. Thoughts of Uncle Percival played about her mind, but as if hiding behind a gauze curtain, afraid to come out into the open. Even if she were to need his aid—even if she dared admit him into her safe, respectable world—she doubted he'd come. The last time she'd seen him—was it just under four years ago?—his sole family feeling had been irritation that none of his relatives had been able to loan him money. A delightful old rogue, but not a ha'porth of proper feeling in him. She could not imagine the so very chivalrous Mr. Carstairs approving of him in the least.

She picked up the poker and stirred the embers on the grate back to a flame, then added more wood. Sinking onto a chair, she gazed into the fireplace. What, exactly, had she learned—if anything—from her talk with Jane?

The door opened behind her, and she sank lower in her chair, hoping whomever it was would go away. Instead, she heard even, solid footsteps crossing the ancient carpet and coming to a halt beside the next chair. She raised her gaze to meet Mr. Carstairs's.

"You look as if you have learned something that distresses you." His deep voice offered compassion, invited confidences.

She rejected it. "Not in the least. I have learned nothing. That is all that ails me."

"Miss Snowdon is not engaged in any illicit activities?"

Daphne's breath escaped on a long sigh. "I wish I knew. She is bound to be up to some mischief, but Jane became quite angry when I suggested as much. I can only hope Jane will drop a hint to Marianne that I am suspicious."

"Perhaps there is no need." He strolled to the mantel, then paced to the window before turning back to face her. "The more I think about it, the less likely it seems that any of the girls here would be able to create a phantom the likes of which we saw last night."

Her temper, strained already, flared. "You would appear to have a very low opinion of their abilities—of the abilities of all females. I suppose you think we are fit for only the most frivolous of lives."

He raised his eyebrows, but made no comment.

"Oh!" she gasped. "You are quite odious! You think females are incapable of anything that matters."

"Is creating ghostly apparitions something that 'matters?' " he mused, as if to himself.

"If there is a reason for it, then yes, it is!"

Mr. Carstairs rubbed his chin, on which a late afternoon's shadowy growth had become visible. "And what would that reason be?"

She glared at him. "How am I supposed to know that?"

He took the seat opposite her. "It is what I—we— hope to discover, is it not? Do you think it possible one of the young ladies does have sufficient reason?"

She regarded him with suspicion. "I see no reason

why they should be any less mischievous—or enterprising—than young gentlemen."

Disconcerting lights danced in the depths of his gray eyes. "Indeed, more so, if my sisters are anything to judge by. But that specter we saw required considerable ingenuity. And it disappeared without a trace. If it had been naught but the girls bent on a lark, do you not think we would have found something? Thread and hooks, perhaps? Even a length of gauze? If the purpose were no more than mischief, why go to lengths to leave no trace?"

"No trace," she murmured. "As if what we saw possessed no substance, only an image . . ." The idea struck her as blindingly obvious, so much so that she could only wonder why it had not occurred to her before. She stared at Mr. Carstairs and found him watching her, his lips twisted into an odd smile. She swelled with triumph. "A magic lantern!"

"I thought of that." He shook his head with maddening omniscience. "There would have to have been something on which to project the image. Again, there should have been gauze."

Injured, she bit back her retort. Must he always be so insufferably superior? With effort, she schooled her features into an expression of deceptive sweetness. "Since you gentlemen are so all-capable and all-knowing, I am surprised you have not yet discovered the answers."

He remained silent, watching her with a gentle appreciation she found disconcerting. She looked away as warm color seeped into her cheeks. His scrutiny unnerved her.

"What do *you* think about all this?" His tone held interest, a touch of concern.

She kept her gaze on the fire, fighting a suddenly compelling urge to reach out to him. He had no right to make her long to rely on his judgment. She didn't need to rely on anyone's! And so he should be told.

"I think," she said with care, "you should content

yourself with playing the role of nurserymaid assigned to you by my uncle, and allow my cousins and me to pursue inquiries on our own. We have no need of a scandal to round off our problems."

"How am I likely to cause a scandal?" His tone held polite inquiry, coupled with a touch of enjoyment.

She gritted her teeth, infuriated by his amusement. "Do you have to be so—so condescending in your attitude? How I do wish you had never come to the vicarage that night!"

He leaned forward, his expression for once serious. "If you honestly desire me to leave, you have only to say so."

She clenched her teeth. "You know perfectly well I cannot ask you to go—though heaven knows, I should like nothing more!"

It hurt, more than she'd realized, to acknowledge once more how her uncle had bound her to this gentleman. It was so—so *insulting* that she would have to return to the vicarage if he left. To her consternation, her eyes stung, smarting with angry tears she refused to shed. She rose, keeping her bearing stiff, refusing to show any weakness in his presence. "If you will excuse me? I have a number of things I must do."

He stood, but spoke not a single word. He opened the door for her, and she swept out, chin high, keeping a rigid control on herself. She made it halfway up the second flight of stairs before her temper deserted her.

She shivered, suddenly chilled, both within as well as without. The early night of January closed about her, she told herself. The house was old, drafty. And she'd slept very little last night. Tonight, if she heard any odd creakings, she would be hard put not simply to bury her head under her pillow.

The normal after-dinner sounds of the girls laughing and talking in the drawing room carried upstairs to

Adrian as he donned his greatcoat. Innocent laughter. Or was some of it not so innocent? Miss Marianne Snowdon might well weave webs more intricate than mere larks; nor was she the only schoolgirl within these walls who might possess reason or need—or determination—sufficient to go to such lengths.

On the whole, though, it still sounded like a practical joke to him. Or did he merely cling to that explanation as preferable to the alternative? For if it were not a lark gotten out of hand, then someone seemed determined to do Selwood Seminary great harm.

And he was just as determined to see that this person failed.

He made his way down the stairs and into the back reaches of the house, moving quietly, even though it seemed impossible anyone could hear him over the cacophony emanating from the drawing room. One of the girls—it could hardly be anyone adept—pounded on the ancient pianoforte while several other voices rose in song, almost—but not quite—on key. The racket put him forcibly in mind of his sister Lizzie and her ongoing attempts to persuade their eldest sister Helena to allow her to abandon her practice on the detested instrument.

He nodded to Moffett, the elderly man of all jobs, as he passed him in the corridor. The man grunted an agreeable acknowledgment and continued in his chore of laying out fresh chambersticks. Adrian reached the back hall and let himself out into the freezing night air.

For a long minute he stood still, gazing up into the overcast sky. A glow from the hidden moon bathed the snow-blanketed landscape, highlighting the leafless trees, sparkling off ice crystals as the branches stretched toward the low clouds. A bright night, in spite of the flurry of flakes that had fallen a few hours earlier. Not an evening he would choose to be abroad, if he hoped to conceal his movements. He'd just walk about to make certain no one lurked in the spinney with a ladder.

He stopped first at the small stable, exchanging a few

words with Hobson, the lad who, bundled up from head to toe, made his final inspection before turning in. Adrian's own bay seemed snug enough, though glad of the carrots his master unearthed from the depths of his pocket. After patting Achilles on the neck, Adrian set forth around the corner of the house.

The stillness seeped through him, peaceful, as if he were alone in this frozen white world. Not a single owl hooted its questioning call, not a single dead branch cracked beneath the paw of a foraging animal. He shoved his gloved hands deeper into his pockets and trudged on toward the line of shrubs. A fire would be welcome upon his return, and a glass of brandy to warm his chilled veins. A pleasant prospect to contemplate.

He did contemplate it as he continued his round. A very large brandy, he promised himself, and a very warm fire.

He paused in the drive, turning back to study the Seminary's facade. No stealthy figures crept through the underbrush, bent on reaching the lower windows. No one scrambled across the rooftops. The only discernible life inhabited the drawing room windows, where a multitude of candles burned, throwing shadowy shapes against the drawn curtains. At least the pianoforte player had desisted.

He scanned the other windows, and his gaze stopped at one on the second floor up, where the girls had their chambers. A pale figure stood silhouetted by the candelabrum behind her, gazing across the bleak landscape. Adrian moved to one side, staring hard at her, and recognized the perfect features of Miss Louisa Trevellian. Even without her normal animation, she was lovely. Now, melancholy marked her expression, and her shoulders sagged as if with a great weight too much for her to bear.

Something of considerable importance troubled the girl, he decided. Yet when in the company of others, she chattered incessantly about the magnificence of her viscount, as if only a future of untrammeled joy awaited her. Apparently, it did not.

That offered new possibilities. Perhaps the whispered rumor he'd overheard about Miss Trevellian's not caring for her viscount had been correct. If the girl found herself forced into a match not of her liking, did she rebel in the only way she could? And might that rebellion take the form of flitting about the school grounds at night, frightening the other pupils?

He turned about, allowing his gaze to sweep the countryside, the path, the garden, the hawthorn shrubs lining the drive leading to the Manor House some hundred yards beyond. Movement caught his attention, and as he watched, a dark shape detached itself from the leafy covering of the hedge and, stooping low, angled across the drive toward the sheltering wood.

Adrian cast a rapid glance about his darkened surroundings. His best chance of cover lay in that same hawthorn hedge, but that would put him on the opposite side of the drive from that lurking figure. He'd have to risk it through the spinney and rely on his luck to keep him from crashing through shrubs and alerting his quarry to the pursuit. At least the reflected glow from the cloud cover illuminated his way.

He grinned. Something tangible at last, a human form with which he could come to grips. Energy filled him, a satisfaction that perhaps he could confront the prankster and stop all this haunting nonsense. Driven by that hope, he ran lightly over the snow-strewn path, ducking to avoid low-hanging branches.

Here, amid the undergrowth and trunks, with the boughs thick above his head, he could see very little. He slowed, now creeping along, but could make out no movement ahead. Doggedly, he continued until he reached the upper end of the spinney, and with a sense of disgust realized he had lost the figure.

His quarry might have headed off in any number of directions, his actions screened by the same undergrowth that sheltered Adrian. He offered himself the sop that this prankster must know the woods better than he, having "haunted" them for several months, now. This was only his own first foray. He'd have to familiarize himself with the lay of the land, he decided.

He started toward the drive, only to pull up short. There, just ahead, a dark shape separated from a shadow cast by a gnarled oak and sauntered toward the great Manor House. Sauntered! Adrian regarded it for a moment, then followed, this time making no attempt to disguise the sound of his passage.

At the first crack of a broken branch, the figure whirled around to face in his direction. Adrian continued, and at the rustle of a bush, the figure backed one step away, then another. His hands came up before him, as if to ward off an attack. Hardly the attitude Adrian would expect from a man bent on evil.

Adrian emerged from the masking brush and called: "Good evening."

The man hesitated. By the soft light, Adrian saw him stretch his head forward, as if peering. Adrian approached, and the odd breadth of the man's shoulders resolved itself into a greatcoat with upwards of a dozen capes hanging down his arms. A broad nose, set between high cheekbones, dominated the wide face. He appeared in his late forties, Adrian decided. The man kept his hands up, and Adrian, no stranger to mills, recognized a classic boxer's stance.

"Who the devil are you?" the man demanded in a raspy, but carrying, voice.

Adrian repressed a smile. "The new chaplain at the Selwood Seminary. The name is Carstairs."

"The new—" The man broke off, his eyes widening. "Good God. So it's true. Thought he must be joking."

"Indeed?" Adrian waited for further comment. "You thought who must be joking?"

"Selwood, of course. Told me his cousins had brought
67

in someone to lay their ghost." His lip curled. "Sounded nonsensical to me."

Adrian rocked back on his heels, his gaze narrowing. "You don't believe in ghosts, I take it?"

The man frowned. "Well, as to that, can't say that I don't, exactly."

"You just don't believe in this one?"

The man pursed his lips. "The devil's in it that I'd like to. Rum business, this. You see, I've encountered it myself. Twice, now. Don't know what to make of it."

"Twice?" That surprised Adrian.

"Ummm. While walking back from visiting Selwood of an evening." The man gestured toward the hedge and beyond. "Live at Romney Court, you know, just the other side of this park. I'm Romney."

Romney. Squire Romney. The one, Adrian remembered from his meeting with George Selwood, who recommended calling in Bow Street. "I understand," Adrian said with deliberation, "this haunting threatens the very existence of the Seminary." He kept a close watch for his companion's reaction.

Romney's mouth tightened. "Don't see why they don't do the obvious about it and call in the sheriff or the Runners. But Selwood persists in thinking it a real ghost. Can't say I blame him, at times." Romney grimaced. "Have you seen it? Demmed floating thing, all glowing, hovering over the drive, then lifting off into the trees? Enough to make a believer out of anyone."

"But not you?"

Again, Romney frowned. "Not in the daylight. At night, though—" He broke off, shaking his head.

"At night," Adrian said, "it is far easier to fool people."

A short bark of laughter escaped the man. "Like just now, thought I saw someone moving in the woods over there. Was that you?"

"I only came to investigate *you.*"

The man nodded. "Things like that make me wonder

against logic. I saw it, you didn't. If it were some poacher or other demmed fellow, we should both have gotten a glimpse of him."

"But your advice is still to call in Bow Street?"

"Hedging bets, you know, hedging bets. After all, they've got you here to handle the spiritual miscreants. Best to guard against the other kind, as well—just to be safe. At least a ghost ain't like to murder you in your sleep."

"If it is a ghost," Adrian said, "have you any idea why it never bothered anyone before this? I understand the Seminary has been operating for more than thirty years, and the house has been inhabited continuously for several hundred."

Romney rubbed his chin. "Possible some of the young ladies disturbed it, what with all their squeals and rumpus. Well." He glanced at the sky. "Not getting any warmer, is it? Best be off for my piquet with Selwood. Glad to see you having a look about. Must make the ladies feel a good deal safer." With a curt nod, Mr. Romney strode toward the Manor's front door.

Adrian watched the retreating figure with a slight frown puzzling his brow. He couldn't say what he made of Romney, he decided at last. A Corinthian, from the multitude of capes and the solidity of his stance. Yet he had seemed cautious, almost afraid, as Adrian had approached him.

Nor could Adrian tell what the man believed about the hauntings. Perhaps he was just careful by nature, "hedging his bets" as he claimed. He'd seemed scornful of the presence of a man of the cloth, preferring the assistance of temporal authority. Or would he accept any and whatever protection he could find? Bravery did not appear to be his strong suit.

Still thoughtful, Adrian turned his steps back toward the Dower House and the warm fire waiting within. He had gone no more than a few feet, though, when he heard his name shouted from behind. He looked back and saw two figures on the porch, standing in the glow of the lights within the Manor.

"Carstairs!" Mr. George Selwood waved as he descended the shallow steps and started toward him. "Come in, man, come in! You simply must have a drink to warm you."

Adrian retraced his steps halfway. Even from here, he caught the heady scent that clung to the dandy—or perhaps to the puce velvet coat he wore. Its buttons gleamed in the moonlight as Selwood minced his way across the snow. "Thank you," Adrian called, "but I must be returning to the Seminary."

"The Seminary. Of course." Selwood cast an uneasy glance along the drive and shivered. "I can't tell you how glad I am that you're there to keep an eye on them. It's a devilish thing, all those females with only that fellow Moffett on the premises. He means well enough, I know, but I can't see where he'd be the least bit of use in this matter."

The Squire strolled up behind his friend. "Persist in thinking this an affair for the church, do you?"

Selwood spun to face Romney. "Who else should have dealings with a ghost? Innocent, helpless females?" He shuddered. "Much better a man of Mr. Carstairs's calling to get to the bottom of this. You will, won't you? Lay this poor, restless spirit for them?"

"If there is need," Adrian said, phrasing his answer with care.

Selwood nodded, though lines of strain marked his face, and a touch of desperation shadowed his words when he spoke. "It has to be stopped."

"That, certainly, is my intention."

"It can't be allowed to ruin the school." Selwood continued as if he hadn't heard Adrian speak. "My poor cousins, everything they've worked so hard to achieve."

Romney's lip curled. "Not to mention your own income."

Selwood waved that aside. "They must not lose their

Seminary. You'll see to that, won't you?" His voice rose with a note of anxiety. "Keep them safe?"

Adrian rubbed his chin. "I doubt they have much to fear—at least for their physical safety—from a mere specter."

Selwood moistened his lips. "One can never tell. Promise me you'll keep my cousins from doing anything rash."

"Nonsense!" Romney slapped his friend on the shoulder. "You'll be frightening Mr. Carstairs next with your fidgets."

Adrian offered them his blandest smile. "Have no fear. I don't frighten easily."

"Good man," pronounced Romney.

Selwood glanced at Adrian. "But there is no need to run any unnecessary risks, is there? They—my cousins, you know—would be devastated if anything happened to you. They'd feel they were responsible."

"Be easy," Adrian assured him. "I'll not come to harm at the hands of any ghost." He placed the slightest emphasis on the last word.

Romney regarded him with a touch of amusement, Selwood with relief. Adrian said his goodnights and headed back toward the Dower House, moving with deliberate slowness to allow himself time to consider this exchange before being inundated by the noise and clamor of the girls.

Romney appeared to take a practical view of the matter, blaming human contrivance, showing concern and wanting action. Much what he'd expect from a country squire. Selwood, on the other hand, showed the fastidious taste of a dandy, shrinking from the whole affair. He seemed to prefer transferring blame for the whole deplorable business to the spirit world, though he cowered at that prospect.

If, of course, he could believe either of them. Adrian had not yet made up his mind about that.

Chapter Five

Muffled strains of unmelodious singing and the strident chords of the pianoforte broke the stillness of the night as Adrian strode up the path toward the front of the Dower House. He hesitated, then headed around to the entrance at the rear. He would rather not encounter any young ladies.

Moffett looked up from the boots he polished as Adrian let himself in. "All secure, sir?"

"I hope so." Adrian bade him goodnight and headed toward the stairs.

Daphne's soft voice, calling him, drew him up short. He turned to see her approach, her simple gray evening gown fashioned high in the neck and fastened at her throat with green riband that matched her eyes. Only a single flounce decorated the hem; the garment, he noted, came from the hands of an obviously inferior modiste. Long years of his eldest sister's assisting a fashionable seamstress—during the years of their hand-to-mouth existence before the advent of the duke of Halliford into their lives—had taught him a great deal about feminine furbelows. Only the elegance of her carriage saved her from appearing dowdy.

A soft flush, barely discernible in the flicking lights from the wall sconces, touched her cheeks. A moment passed before she said, with a note of censure, "Did you see anyone? You were gone for a very long while."

He regarded her with amusement. "Now, do you resent my escaping that infernal racket in the drawing room or my pursuing *your* investigations without you?"

The flush deepened, yet she kept her chin high, her gaze unwavering. After a moment, though, her lips twitched and she shook her head. "You are quite insufferable."

"I have lost count of the times you have so informed me."

Her eyes sparkled, and the smile won out. "I make no doubt of it. And yes, I certainly resent both. Could you not have waited until I was free?"

"My need to escape must stand my excuse." He drew off his gloves and idly slapped them against his palm. "I met Mr. Romney."

Her eyes widened. "The Squire? Why, whatever brought him out on such a night? Piquet with Cousin George, I suppose."

"And a bit of looking about, as well. I found him in the wood by the Manor House."

She stared at him. "Is he trying to lay our ghost, as well? How very kind of him."

"He seems convinced our culprit is all too corporeal."

Daphne nodded. "I cannot understand why Cousin George insists it is a genuine specter. It is not as if possessing a haunted establishment confers any *congé* upon him."

"Perhaps he prefers an insubstantial menace to a concrete one."

She shook her head. "I know he has become a dandy—a veritable tulip, I believe—but truly, he is not cowardly. Oh, you meant for the sake of the school. It's true, a ghost is likely to do less physical damage than a person, but in the long run, do you not think them equally harmful?"

"For the sake of the school's finances," Adrian told her with complete sincerity, "yes."

She drew in a quavering breath. "Yes," she repeated.

73

"And it will not just be us, but poor Cousin George, as well, who will be ruined. What a dreadful situation this is! We must stop it soon, before it is too late." She gazed up at him, her expression guarded. "Do we keep watch in the lumber room tonight?"

Adrian fought a sudden urge to stroke back a dusky tendril that swept her cheek. "I doubt we can hope for a repeat performance so soon. I intend to watch from my own chamber."

She tilted her head to one side. "When do you sleep?"

He grinned. "After breakfast," he admitted. "Will you care to assist me with another search tomorrow?"

"You mean would I care for you to assist me? But the bother is that I must chaperone two of the girls to Bath, to visit their grandmother. She is taking the waters, you see, and sent a message to have them brought to her." She fixed him with a stern gaze. "You will not do anything without me."

He inclined his head. "Nothing of any importance, I promise."

The noon hour approached before Daphne and her two charges, the Misses Pembroke, set off on the short carriage ride to Bath. Daphne sank back on the facing seat, wishing herself in the lumber room instead. Time spent in any pursuit other than laying their ghost and solving the school's problems seemed wasted. With an effort, she assumed a relaxed manner and turned her attention to the girls.

Miss Juliana, a solemn thirteen, gazed out the window while Miss Emma Pembroke, with all the dignity of her sixteen summers, sat with hands demurely folded in her lap. This pair might be easy to handle, but on the whole, Daphne decided, she would prefer livelier company. Unless, of course, it happened to be that of Miss Marianne Snowdon. Count your blessings, she told herself sternly, and pointed out a particularly fine prospect to the two girls. They responded with polite but unenthusiastic interest, then returned to their own thoughts. With a silent sigh, Daphne abandoned the attempt.

In a very short time—fortunately, for Daphne's frayed nerves—they entered Bath and pulled onto Westgate Street. Pedestrians, huddled into a variety of greatcoats, capes, and other wraps, strode briskly along pavement swept clear of snow or dawdled in front of the shop windows. Light carriages whisked their passengers to innumerable destinations, while sedan chairs carried others disinclined to go afoot. Miss Juliana leaned forward, showing the first spark of animation.

"Oh," the girl exclaimed. "Look at that gown!"

Daphne turned to inspect the elegant creation hanging in the display window of a modiste's, and experienced a pang of wistfulness. Of a light and filmy pale green muslin, wholly unsuited to the January snow that surrounded them, it boasted a single deep flounce and trim of a darker green. Over all draped an open robe of the same fabric, worked in delicate embroidery about the opening and hem. Beside this hung a spencer of a rich dark green, together with a frilled sun shade that spoke of spring and *al fresco* parties in flower-filled gardens.

For a moment Daphne tried to picture herself in this enchanting toilette, but failed. It had nothing to do with the simple round gowns of gray and brown merino or muslin she usually wore. The lot of a schoolmistress, she reminded herself.

Yet she wouldn't have it any other way. She wanted to accomplish things. She wanted to be thinking, using her abilities, knowing herself useful. Life with dear, impossible Uncle Percival had spoiled her for the frivolous life in the fashionable world.

But one pretty gown or an occasional party would not be unwelcome.

The carriage jolted to a stop, jarring Daphne out of

her reverie, and she saw they had arrived at the Pump Room. Resuming her brisk manner, she bundled her charges' pelisses about them, and ushered the two girls onto the pavement. After arranging for the driver to return for them in just over an hour's time, she shooed the awed girls into the building.

A surprising number of fashionables filled the large room, either strolling about or sitting at the numerous tables provided. Daphne took an uncertain step forward, wondering how, among so many, she would find the dowager Lady Leamington. She cast an uncertain glance at her charges, who gazed about wide-eyed.

Miss Emma Pembroke brightened. "She is over there, Miss Selwood." Yet she made no move to go to her maternal grandmother.

Nor did Miss Juliana. They waited, watching Daphne, and did not step forward until Daphne, with a sigh, led the way. They were dear girls, of course, so very easy to instruct. But so deadly dull. Glad to discharge her duty to them—at least temporarily—she approached a table where a demure little woman sat, clad in a simple walking gown of blue merino.

Miss Emma touched her arm, then lowered her hand at once. "Oh, no, Miss Selwood. The next table."

The next . . . Daphne blinked at the vision that met her startled gaze. The dowager Lady Leamington sat in a chair facing them, her massive figure swathed in yards of purple satin. A turban wrapped about her head, from which emerged three ostrich plumes and a few sparse gray hairs. Pale blue eyes regarded her from a plump and ruddy countenance, but not by a single flicker of an expression did she indicate she recognized the two girls who stopped a few feet away.

"Lady Leamington?" Daphne hazarded. "I'm Daphne Selwood. I've brought your granddaughters."

"Hah!" The woman peered at the two girls with a flicker of interest. "You've grown to be every bit as fubsy-faced as your mama. Knew you would."

A thin-featured female in a drab round gown sprang to her feet. "Oh, dear Lady Leamington. And you dear girls. Do sit down." She reached for an ermine muff of enormous size. "Shall I—"

"Leave it where it is," Lady Leamington commanded. "And stop your fussing about, Margaret. You know I can't bear your flighty nonsense. Be still."

Margaret sank onto her chair with the manner of one accustomed to such snubs. A paid companion or indigent relative, Daphne guessed. She herself would find such a life insupportable. She preferred being in charge, as she was over her students—and as she frequently had been in Uncle Percival's establishment.

"Sit, sit." Lady Leamington waved at the chairs. "Give me an account of yourselves. And you," she turned back to Daphne. "Won't be needing you. Come back in an hour." Without giving Daphne time to so much as take her leave, she turned back to the girls and eyed them with an expression of acute distaste.

Daphne strolled away, not sure whether to be amused or affronted by so abrupt a dismissal. Those poor children would suffer a dreadful morning, but she could do nothing to help. Perhaps she could find some treat for them before returning to the school to make up for it. She no longer wondered at their docile natures.

She found a chair on the far side of the room, and prepared to amuse herself by speculating about the occupants of the Pump Room. An elderly gentleman in military-cut clothing, missing his left arm, caught her easy sympathy, and she began to weave a highly romantic and fantastic story about his heroic figure. She should have brought her sketch pad; she would have depicted him astride a gallant charger, leading his men into battle, banners fluttering in the breeze behind him, his sword held aloft—

"Miss Selwood, I believe." The high-pitched voice made it a statement, not a question.

Daphne looked up in dismay into the bright, malicious eyes of her accoster and managed a false smile. "Good morning, Miss Davenport."

"Has that dreadful ghost distressed you?" Without being asked, Miss Isobel Davenport pulled out a chair and seated herself next to Daphne, making a great show of settling her skirts. "Have you come to take the waters as a restorative?"

Daphne eased a bit away. "Are they indeed used for such a purpose?" She kept her tone cool, skeptical, and wondered how to escape without giving unwarranted offense.

Miss Davenport reached across with a hand enclothed in lavender kid leather and patted Daphne's arm. "You do not come into Bath very often, do you, my dear? It must be dreadfully uncomfortable to be situated so far outside of the city."

"We are not above two miles," Daphne protested.

"Two miles." Miss Davenport waved that aside. "It might as well be ten or twenty. You can hardly visit Milsom Street or even exchange a book at Duffield's on a whim. It is so very agreeable, you must know, to live right here. I vow, I must pop into the Pump Room at least once a day, and my instructresses are forever slipping out for a delightful half hour among the shops."

Daphne wrinkled her nose. "So much noise and bustle. I find the country far more agreeable."

Miss Davenport frowned. "As to that, I find Sydney Gardens very refreshing."

For a moment, Daphne considered returning to Lady Leamington as an excuse to escape. It didn't seem likely the dowager would receive her with any degree of civility, though. Still, that might be better than remaining here. Her gaze strayed to where the Misses Pembroke sat stiff and quiet under their grandmother's ferocious glare.

Miss Davenport peered forward. "Are you in attendance on Lady Leamington's granddaughters?" she asked with unfortunate perception. "Well, they do appear to be unexceptionable. Quite a credit to any establishment."

"They attend Selwood Seminary," Daphne said through gritted teeth, "as did their mother before them. I doubt they intend to change schools."

Miss Davenport laughed, sounding very satisfied. "They might not have much choice, my dear. Such a dreadful business, your pupils being frightened away. I fear you will find yourself seeking new employment soon." She cast Daphne a glance from half-lidded eyes. "I daresay a very comfortable position might be found for you among my staff—if, shall we say, we were to take on several more girls whose families would be willing to pay for all the extras? No, no need to say anything now."

She rose, a small, smug smile playing about her thin lips. "Though to be sure, we must make our decisions soon. I greatly fear we could not go to the expense of a new art mistress unless we were to be assured of five or six new young ladies—all of the most impeccable lineage, of course. And now I must be going. Dear Miss Selwood, always a pleasure to see you."

Daphne opened her mouth, found herself too furious to find words, and shut it again. With a conspiratorial smile for her, Miss Davenport departed, threading her way among the tables toward the door. Inwardly, Daphne raged. She should have said something—anything!—sufficiently cutting.

Did that woman actually believe Daphne would desert her cousins—and take away their highest-paying pupils into the bargain? That Miss Davenport had meant her offer in that vein, and not as an option if the Selwood Seminary were forced to close, Daphne had no doubts. Miss Davenport hoped Daphne might help bring about that closing.

Sitting quietly indoors no longer appealed to her. She stood, restless, and looked about the room. Joining the fashionable promenade held no lure for her, either. Yet there was no reason she must stay here; Lady Leamington chaperoned the girls, and she'd made it clear she did not need Daphne. She would walk outside, where the chill wind might tame her burning temper.

Daphne started for the door, keeping her angry stride in check by determined effort. Too many people crowded the room to make rapid progress possible. She sidestepped knots of loitering gossipers and made slow but definite progress toward the door.

As she neared it, it swung wide, and in a gust of wind three newcomers sailed in, laughing as they attained shelter. The two young gentlemen in the party, fashionably dressed to the point of excess, bore all the air of playing off the Exquisites. The one in the lead, a tall, dark, brooding man, swirled off his cloak, then stopped as his gaze fell on Daphne, only a few feet away. A slow, speculative smile dawned.

Behind him, the other gentleman, as fair as his friend was dark, bent over the bonneted head of the girl who clung to his arm. The young lady cast a roguish glance at him through languishing lashes. Daphne's heart sank. Of all people she least wanted to see at this—or any—moment, she would rate her former pupil, Miss Susannah Ingels, and her brother very near the top. As for that rake hellion who now murmured in Miss Ingels's ear, she had hoped never to set eyes on him a second time. Once had been unpleasant enough. Daphne forced herself to stand her ground; it was too late to escape.

Young Mr. Ingels drew off his gloves, never taking his gaze from Daphne's heated countenance. "Miss Selwood, how very pleasant. Susannah, look whom we have met."

Miss Susannah Ingels raised limpid blue eyes, saw Daphne, and malice gleamed in their depths. "Miss Selwood." She almost purred. "Why, it has been quite an age. How *do* you go on in that dreary seminary of yours?"

80

Daphne bit back the impulse to tell her they went on far better since the Selwood ladies had requested Miss Ingels's parents to remove her from the establishment. That had been an awkward business, for the Ingels estate stood less than two miles from Selwood Park, bordering Squire Romney's lands. Instead, she gritted her teeth and smiled. "We do very well, thank you. Our young ladies excel, as always."

Miss Ingels raised a delicate brow. "Do they, indeed? Do you now instruct your pupils in the finer points of ghost watching?"

The blond gentleman—Wembly, Daphne remembered, Charles Wembly—snickered.

Mr. Reginald Ingels threw his sister a smirking glance. "Really, my dear, it is hardly kind in you to tease Miss Selwood, when her cousins' Seminary is so soon to be closed."

Miss Ingels's eyes gleamed in vengeful delight. "Oh, indeed," she declared in a gush of overdone sincerity. "It is so very dreadful. Positively, my heart bleeds for you. Your cousins must be devastated." Satisfaction sounded in each of the last words.

Daphne squared her shoulders. "Not in the least. We have every hope of ridding ourselves of the problem in the very near future. It is really quite absurd, so much fuss being made over the matter. It will be forgotten in less than a fortnight, I make no doubt."

"Indeed?" Reginald Ingels swung his quizzing glass by its riband, then raised it to his eye. Through it, he inspected Daphne in lingering detail.

Miss Ingels gave an affected sigh. "How very brave of you, Miss Selwood, to be taking it this way. Though of course, you must put up pretences before the world, I suppose. But there is no need with us, you know, not with people who—love—your cousins as we do." Her smile glittered with falsity. "Do tell them I think of them—often." The last word held an unmistakable hardness, making her pronouncement a threat. She waited a moment, as if making sure Daphne had caught her meaning, then nodded dismissal and swept away, dragging Mr. Wembly with her.

Reginald Ingels still watched her through his lens. "You have grown even more delightful than since the last time I laid eyes on you."

"You mistake, sir. It wasn't your eyes but your hands you laid on me. And you had your ears soundly boxed for your efforts." At least his arm about her waist had been preferable to Mr. Wembly's attempt to kiss her.

Mr. Ingels chuckled. "Ah, so you do remember that little gathering. So dull, with so many schoolroom chits and their so-staid parents milling about the school. And then you walked in." He reached out, touching her cheek before she could pull away. "You may always come to me if you find yourself without a position. I feel quite certain I could offer you far more agreeable employment." With that, he left Daphne to follow his sister and Mr. Wembly.

Her cheeks burned, then the next moment a chill crept through her. Had there been more than spite in Miss Susannah Ingels's words? The girl had seemed so smug. And Susannah had always been one for action, taking swift and sometimes violent vengeance on any student who thwarted or angered her. Did she do the same to the Seminary now, out of revenge for being thrown out?

Slowly, Daphne turned to regard the threesome where they stood at some distance with heads close together. Now they watched an elderly woman in a startling gown of puce satin and a head of plumes. Daphne was willing to wager one of these would be plucked before long, and dared not contemplate the other indignities to which this unholy trio might subject the unfortunate lady.

There was little that Susannah Ingels would not dare to do—especially with her brother and Mr. Wembly to lend their assistance. She could easily see them staging

82

an elaborate haunting of the school, and being delighted by results that probably far exceeded their original intentions.

Daphne closed her eyes. Miss Ingels, for revenge. Miss Isobel Davenport, to destroy her long-time rivals. Were there others who might wish the Seminary harm? She could not forget Miss Marianne Snowdon, who might have carried a joke too far. With a sinking sensation, Daphne realized their best hope of getting to the bottom of this morass lay in catching the ghost actually engaged upon his—or her—disreputable antics.

Chapter Six

Adrian slipped out of the dining room after dinner as soon as he could politely excuse himself. An evening spent with Herodotus appealed to him far more than one spent in the company of giggling schoolroom misses. The sooner he caught this ghost so he could take his leave, his obligation completed, the better he'd like it. Yet he'd miss Miss Daphne Selwood's antagonism. He'd come to quite enjoy it.

As if the mere thought conjured her, he heard her light step in the hall behind him, and looked back to see her trim figure striding toward him. He waited, allowing her to catch up. A frown still marred her brow, he noted; it had been there since she returned from her excursion to Bath that morning. He would be glad if she chose to confide in him, but knew he could not force from her the disclosure of her troubles.

She stopped in front of him and visibly squared her shoulders. Determination gleamed in her eyes, arresting his attention. She possessed remarkably fine eyes—and a remarkably determined spirit.

"Will you watch in the lumber room tonight?" she asked without preamble.

"I thought I would take up a hiding place at about eleven o'clock." His gaze lingered on her expressive countenance, watching the play of emotions that flickered across it, clear to be seen. Anger, resolution, chagrin—this last because she must defer to him in this business, he guessed. He didn't like causing her distress.

She nodded. "I intend to watch with you."

That prospect appealed to Adrian, but for all the wrong reasons. Steeling himself, he searched for a way to phrase his answer that would not injure her pride. "You would find it most uncomfortable, I fear." He tried to keep his tone indifferent.

The light in her soft green eyes flared. "I would not mind in the least," she snapped. "I am not so poor a creature as to fret over something like that. I intend to see our ghost captured, at whatever cost."

No, she was no poor creature at all. He thrust that thought aside. "You might well find yourself waiting all night for nothing," he pointed out.

Her jaw tightened. "You are merely supposed to act as my nursemaid, not take my place completely."

The door to the drawing room opened, and a tall feminine figure in a dark gown hesitated on the threshold. "Daphne?" Miss Elspeth's voice reached them.

Daphne glared at Adrian. "Here," she called without moving her gaze.

"There you are, my love." Miss Elspeth stopped short, eyeing the pair with tolerant amusement. "Now, whatever are you two at outs about?"

"He is quite insufferable," Daphne declared with vehemence. "I merely wish to do my share of hunting our ghost, and he is being top-lofty and self-important and taking charge where he is not wanted."

"Daphne—" Miss Elspeth protested, startled.

Daphne drew a long breath, and when she spoke again, she had steadied her voice. "I realize my uncle and Cousin Beatrice have asked him to investigate, but it is the outside of enough that he insists on doing everything himself."

"Does he?" Miss Elspeth eyed him with mild surprise. "To be sure, none of us wished this to become a burden on him."

85

"I am here," Adrian said evenly, "to *assist* you. If you," he added, turning to Daphne, "wish to sit up all night under cramped and freezing conditions, you may do so with my goodwill. Unfortunately, your uncle would never forgive me if I did not bear you company—"

"You mean play my watchdog," she inserted.

"—on the off-chance," he continue with determination, "—that our ghost chose to lay violent hands on you." And there were moments, such as now, when he wouldn't blame it.

Daphne blinked at him, for the moment speechless.

"Very proper sentiments." Miss Elspeth nodded approval. "But I believe I see Mr. Carstairs's dilemma, my dear."

"Do you?" She sounded suspicious.

"But of course." Miss Elspeth's eyes twinkled. "It wouldn't be at all the thing for you to spend the night thus in his company. Only imagine the ruin to his reputation if word ever got out."

Adrian fought back his smile. "Just so, ma'am."

Daphne glared from one to the other of them. "Of all the absurd, ridiculous, mutton-headed ideas!"

Miss Elspeth sighed. "Would you permit Louisa Trevellian to spend the night alone in his company?"

"I—" Daphne broke off. "But this is nonsense." Yet the vehemence had faded from her tone.

"Of course it is," Adrian agreed. "But I cannot think Mr. Danvers would approve. I will tell you what, though," he added, "and this is no palliative. I will have to remain still and in hiding, which means I will not be able to see out the window. If our ghost chooses to haunt the gardens this night instead, I will miss his performance. You have a clear view over the spinney from your room, do you not?"

"We could keep separate vigils." She spoke the words slowly, as if considering the merits of this plan.

"And you are more likely than I to see something, as well as having the advantages of warmth and comfort."

She sniffed. "I hope the dust makes you sneeze!" Yet she sounded somewhat mollified. In a soft swirl of skirts, she spun about and made her stately way back into the drawing room, from which the discordant strains of a butchered ballad drifted.

Miss Elspeth watched this retreat, then turned back to Adrian. "Do you indeed intend to sit up all night?"

"It may not come to that. There's always the chance our ghost might honor me with a visit before I've had time to regret it."

Her soft laugh broke from her. "I will wish you good hunting, then. But do you not think we should ask Moffett to bear you company? I cannot help but think it might become awkward for you if our ghost *does* come, and he proves to be quite solid."

"What a poor adventurer you must think me." He regarded her with an assumed air of injured hauteur. "I assure you, I am quite able to defend myself."

She hesitated a moment before saying, "Very well, then."

She followed Daphne back into the drawing room, leaving Adrian in little doubt that she would at least mention his nocturnal plans to the elderly Moffett. Resigned to this likelihood, he mounted the stairs. He could spare an hour or two for his dissertation and still be in his hiding place before such time as he could reasonably expect any apparitions—unearthly or otherwise—to appear.

It seemed he had barely sat down at his desk and resumed the analysis of his translation when a light rap sounded on his door. He glanced at the mantel clock and was surprised to see that a little more than two hours had passed. Setting aside his quill, he called for his visitor to enter.

Moffett opened the door, garbed in a heavy driving coat made for one of shorter height and stouter girth. A sour expression lay heavily on his lean countenance. In his right hand he clutched an ancient fowling piece. "Ready, sir?" he asked.

It took considerable tact for Adrian to convince Moffett that more than one occupant in the room might warn off their expected visitor. This news considerably cheered the man, the only check to his growing enthusiasm a sudden fear that Adrian might assume Moffett would be the more suitable man to hide in the cramped recesses of the attic chamber. Of this thought Adrian quickly disabused his mind, and the elderly servitor, considerably relieved, took his departure.

Adrian just had gathered his own coat when a knock once more sounded on the door. It opened without ceremony and Moffett again entered. He thrust the fowling piece into Adrian's hand, nodded twice to himself as if pleased with this decision, and took himself off. Adrian stared at the gun in distaste and laid it on his bed. The last thing he needed to do would be to shoot some silly chit of a schoolgirl.

At the next knock, he rolled his eyes heavenward. He opened the door, and to his surprise found the rigid Miss Beatrice Selwood in the hall, her steely eyes regarding him with their customary sternness. In her hands she held a tray containing a decanter, a brandy glass, and a plate piled high with a selection of biscuits, cakes, rolls, and wedges of cheese.

"May be a long night," she informed him as she thrust this into his hands.

Adrian thanked her, she snorted, and he found himself alone once more. He set the tray on top of a pile of papers, absently selected an almond macaroon, and grinned. After a moment's consideration, he settled in his chair, stretched out his slippered feet, selected a piece of poppyseed cake, and waited.

He didn't have long. Less than four minutes later, someone once more rapped on his door. He hoisted himself to his feet, and this time admitted Miss

Sophronia Selwood. A quilt hung over her plump arms, which she held folded before her.

Her bright eyes beamed on him from above her rounded cheeks. "There, now, so very kind of you, to offer to sit in that dismal, cramped room." She proffered the quilt. "Will this be of any help?"

He accepted it gracefully, laying it on his bed.

Miss Sophronia clasped her hands beneath her ample bosom. "I do hope you will not be too uncomfortable. So cold, I make no doubt."

"I shall do very well," he assured her. "But I had best take up my position, or our ghost will start wondering why there is so much activity on this floor tonight."

Her mouth rounded in an "O" of comprehension. "I shall give orders that *no one* is to come up here, not for any reason, though of course the servants will have to seek their beds. And Daphne, of course." She hesitated. "That is, unless you think you should like company?"

It took him several more minutes to convince her that prudence dictated he should keep his nocturnal vigil alone. Apparently satisfied at last, Miss Sophronia bade him goodnight, hoped he would sleep well, recalled his purpose and corrected her last sentiment, then beamed at him in a hopeful manner. He thanked her and watched her bustle down the corridor, her pale pink, knitted shawl trailing behind her.

A moment after she passed Daphne's room, that young lady opened her door, peeked out, and raised supercilious eyebrows at him. "I thought you so eager, you would have been in place hours ago."

"You aren't watching your window," he pointed out, then grinned as she slammed her door. That was not well done of him, he knew, yet he couldn't resist. Nor could he blame her for her sense of outrage. Had anyone tried to exclude *him* from this scheme, he would have considered it shabby treatment indeed, and resented it just as strongly.

The time lacked but ten minutes before midnight

when Adrian at last worked his way through the cluttered attic room and took up his position in the farthest corner. He sat on the floor, half the quilt beneath him for padding, the other half wrapped about him to alleviate the icy chill of a chamber that never knew the drying warmth of a fire. He extinguished his candle, and almost at once the odor of mildew assaulted his nose.

He poured a measure of brandy and leaned back against the wall. This location placed him at exactly the opposite side from where he'd been when he saw that ghostly apparition before. If it appeared again—or rather, if it *dis*appeared again—perhaps he would gain a better idea of where, precisely, this stunt occurred. Unless this ghost were real, there had to be some means of egress from the room, other than the door.

He possessed his soul in patience—and his stomach of another macaroon—and waited. His gaze traveled about the room. He could make out shapes, but little else. The door made itself obvious by the crack at the top, though only the faintest light shone through. Someone had left an oil lamp burning low in a wall sconce in the hall beyond.

Grayness filled the window, he noted; it must be snowing again. That would explain the complete silence that enveloped him, broken only by the distant groan of a settling timber. Time crept by; he caught himself yawning, and shook his head to keep awake.

A floorboard creaked. Adrian tensed, suddenly alert, and realized he must have been near to drifting off. He had no idea how much time had passed. He strained his ears, and the sound repeated, coming from the hallway. He drew his stockinged feet beneath him, pulling himself into a crouch.

Now he could detect the susurrant sound of a slippered foot brushing rapidly across the loomed runner that stretched the length of the corridor. A brighter light glimmered through the crack, and the door handle squeaked as someone touched it.

Adrian remained coiled, ready to spring, as a sudden rush of cold anger assailed him. This was no ghost, but a very real person, and one who did very real harm to three kindly ladies. The precept of forgiveness, so basic to his calling, faded from his mind as his hands clenched into punishing bunches of fives.

The door eased open on hinges that barely protested. For a moment Adrian crouched, centering his balance for his attack, then the figure filled the doorway, holding aloft a candle.

"Mr. Carstairs?" Daphne's hushed voice quavered. The shadows that leapt about her face gave her a frightened appearance.

The next moment, Adrian realized her hand trembled. He reached for his own candle.

"Mr. Carstairs, are you—?" She broke off.

"Here." Adrian stood, then picked his way on stockinged feet toward her. Her single taper, after the complete darkness, provided more than enough light to keep him from tripping.

Daphne huddled into her dressing gown, drawing her shawl closer about her shoulders. "He's outside," she breathed. "Our ghost."

Adrian's jaw tightened. "You saw him?"

"I thought I heard a noise, down in the garden, so I went to the hall window, and saw this—this *thing*—" She broke off, shivering. "I—I know I should have gone down and tackled it—"

"Certainly not. Here." He blew out the candle. "We don't want anyone outside to see unusual light movement, especially in this room." He made his way to the window, picking his way with care over the jumble of discarded items. "Where is he?"

"You must think it very hen-hearted of me not to go out at once," she continued, sounding diffident.

"And leave me freezing and cramped in here? I am exceedingly grateful to you. Now, where did you—?"

A shape—it was too amorphous to be called a figure—flitted from one tree to another, then approached the house. It swept in a small circle, then drifted back to the covering. Fingers clutched Adrian's arm, and he placed his hand over Daphne's chilled one.

"It—it isn't a real ghost?" She sounded more fascinated than afraid.

"Just someone capering about in a bed sheet, I should imagine." His anger hardened. "I'm going to put a stop to it." He strode from the room. Behind him, he could hear her following.

He stopped at his own room long enough to rekindle their candles and thrust his feet into slippers, the first foot gear he could find. The ridiculous fowling piece he left lying across his bed. It might go a long way toward frightening some silly student bent on a lark, but at its age, the dangers far outweighed any benefit it might bring. All he would need would be to have a faulty spring cause a misfire.

At the ground floor, Daphne took the lead. "We can go out through the bookroom," she whispered. She led the way, then eased free the bolt securing the French door which let them out onto the terrace.

Adrian touched her shoulder. "Has the house been locked for the night? Securely?"

"I went around with Moffett and Cousin Elspeth myself."

A blast of icy air and a flurry of flakes greeted them as they slipped out into the frozen night. Adrian hesitated, not liking to leave this entry vulnerable in their wake for anyone else to enter, but he had little choice. He could always send Daphne back to watch it if he had to go too far.

Dark clouds still covered the moon, but the snow had all but ceased; only an occasional flake floated past their faces. Daphne stood very near his side.

"You'll freeze," he told her. "Go back and put on something warmer."

"You will *not* deprive me of this hunt," she informed him, huddling closer.

Adrian set her aside and dragged off his greatcoat. "At least I come prepared for the weather." He draped it about her shoulders.

She thrust her arms through the sleeves. "Do you?" She cast a significant look at his slippered feet.

He'd been trying to ignore the frozen dampness that enveloped his toes. The thinness of the fine wool of his coat now added to his discomfort, doing little to ward off the cold. "Let's find our friend and get this over with before we both develop an inflammation of the lungs," he said.

They set forth toward the spinney, moving with caution, checking every possible hiding place. Daphne moved away from him, whispering they were more likely to come upon their culprit if they approached from different sides. Adrian agreed with this concept in theory, but found himself too concerned for the impulsive girl's safety, and kept her well within easy reach. Only the occasional snap of a twig under their own feet broke the silence of the night.

"Not so much as a rabbit did I see," Daphne announced in disgust as she rejoined Adrian at last. She looked back the way they had come. "And we searched with the greatest care."

"Whoever it is must have left before we came down." Adrian took her elbow and guided her toward the Dower House.

Daphne hugged herself, shivering, her warm breath hanging in a cloud before her face. "We did see it, didn't we?"

"We did." He spoke through teeth gritted against the cold. His cramped hiding place in that attic chamber began to hold a certain charm for him, and he found himself thinking of it with fond reminiscence.

Daphne frowned. "Do you think we can follow his footprints as soon as it is light? Surely there has been enough new snow so we should be able to make them out."

Adrian looked up into the glowering sky. "There will be more within the hour, I fear, and there will be no traces left. Come, it is too cold to enjoy ghost chasing when it proves this futile."

With that, Daphne agreed. She showed no reluctance whatsoever as he led her back toward the house.

"Do you think we can defrost——" He broke off both word and stride.

Ahead, a shadowy shape emerged from the line of trees nearest the school and flitted across the grass toward the bookroom door.

Chapter Seven

Daphne stared at the unearthly apparition, transfixed. It had actually come back; it was *here*. She became aware of Mr. Carstairs's pushing against her arm. Too shaken to object, she allowed him to ease her against the line of shrubs. With a whispered "Stay here," he slipped away in silent pursuit.

She held her breath, not wanting to make any sound that might alert the specter to their presence. They were so close; they might have their chance to unmask this malefactor, stop his ruination of the Seminary . . . and she just stood here, doing nothing, letting Mr. Carstairs do all the work!

Disgusted with herself—with the cowardice that had gripped her—she gave her head a vigorous shake to clear the lingering muddle. Here she had a chance to accomplish something, prove she wasn't helpless, and what did she do? She, like everyone else, had promptly called for Mr. Carstairs! There had been no need for her to run to him at his attic post. She could have come down here alone and waylaid this capering sheet-wearer.

Yet here she was, letting Mr. Carstairs pursue the figure—and without even her assistance.

Sincerely disillusioned with her own claims of capability, she set resolutely forth.

This proved more difficult than she expected. Even

though she repeated, over and over, that help lay close at hand, still a chill crept down her spine and settled in the pit of her stomach. How could Mr. Carstairs set off so blithely—no, with positive delight!—on this chase?

Something large rustled in the shrubs all too close, and Daphne froze. Turning slowly, she saw a second ghostly figure looming through the trees. Her heart filled her throat, beating so loud it blotted out all other sound. A *second* ghost? No, it couldn't be. . . . She swung about and spotted the first, which stood immobile on the tiny terrace by the library, staring right toward her. . . .

No, toward the other apparition.

As she watched, the first ghost seemed to fly toward the corner of the house. Mr. Carstairs set off in pursuit. Which, Daphne told herself with an uncomfortable shiver, left the second specter to her.

She looked back, only to find the apparition had vanished. For a moment she stared, too startled to react, then determination set in. She wasn't letting it get away that easily. If Mr. Carstairs could do it, then so could she.

Silence would be wasted, she decided. Throwing caution to the winds, she pushed through the first available hole in the shrubbery, and the sharp twigs snagged at her shawl and tore Mr. Carstairs's greatcoat from her shoulders. She detached herself and grasped the too-ample garment across her breast. Next time she went ghost hunting, she'd wear better-fitting clothes.

Ahead of her, branches snapped as her ghost made its escape. Then abruptly all sounds ceased. Silence surrounded her, punctuated only by the breeze rustling through the evergreens. Daphne halted, listening intently, trying to control the rapid, nervous pounding of her pulse in her ears. She inched forward, shoving aside a snow-capped limb.

Before her she saw not one specter, but two.

She blinked, watching the eerie figures as they hovered perhaps twenty feet apart in the clearing. Then the one farthest from her raised its arms, and a low, soul-wrenching moan pierced the night air, filling Daphne with a sick dread. The figure nearest her took heel and fled. An overpowering urge to follow suit swept through Daphne, but she held her ground. It hadn't noticed her, had made no threatening gesture toward her. But why . . . ?

The clearing stood empty. She stared in disbelief at the spot where a moment before that misty white figure had stood—or floated. It had simply vanished.

A twig snapped off in her hand where her fingers had convulsed about it. No, it couldn't be a real specter. She must have been so startled she took her eyes off it for the one critical moment in which it slipped away. This was Mr. Carstairs's ghost. It must have circled about and encountered hers—

But why had the first tried to chase off the second? Or had it been a show for her benefit? Surely they must be working together. Unless a *real* specter had taken exception to someone's untenable pranks . . .

Speculations jostled about in her mind, colliding with one another, making the waters of thought too muddy to make sense. With slow steps she returned to the drive, and saw Mr. Carstairs approaching with his determined stride. Relief swept through her, startling in its intensity, and she hurried forward.

He slowed as she neared, allowing her to join him. "It got away," he said.

"I know. I—" She broke off.

He took a long look at her face, and his brow creased in a frown. "Come inside," he said.

With one hand under her elbow, he guided her back toward the bookroom. To her further discomfiture, she welcomed his support. He ushered her inside, pushed her gently onto the sofa before the hearth, then tossed kindling on the embers. These he fanned into a blaze, then added two logs.

He turned back to her. "What distressed you?"

She swallowed and held out her hands toward the growing fire. "There were two ghosts. I saw them together."

"You—" Mr. Carstairs's brow snapped down. "What do you mean? Where were you?"

"Across the drive from you. The second ghost appeared behind me, and I followed it. Then the two of them ran into each other, and yours scared off mine."

"Mine," Mr. Carstairs said with slow emphasis, "escaped in the woods behind the stable." He held her gaze.

Daphne's eyes widened as she took this in. "Then it couldn't have been—Do you mean there were *three* specters?"

Mr. Carstairs's lip twitched. "Three specters." He spoke the words softly, drawing them out. "And to think I found *one* a challenge. Three," he repeated, his tone musing. He sank into an arm chair and thrust his dripping slippered feet toward the fire. "At least one of them knows the grounds better than do I. This complicates matters a trifle."

"Complicates," Daphne breathed. *"Complicates?* Mr. Carstairs, do you realize—" She broke off, not quite sure what it was he *should* realize.

"Certainly." An easy smile of pure enjoyment lit his eyes, slowly spreading to his generous mouth. "There are at least three people involved, who may or may not be working together."

"But—they *must* be together. Mustn't they?" She added the last with a touch of dismay.

He drew a slow breath, but the enjoyment never wavered from his expression. "It doesn't make sense either way, does it?" His smile invited her to share his comment as a joke.

"Three people." With difficulty, she forced her disordered mind to function. "Three—" She leaned forward, excited. "Three! Miss Ingels and her brother, and Mr.

Wembly! Oh, it would be just like them. I do believe we have the answer!"

"And who might be Miss Ingels, her brother, and—er—Mr. Wembly, was it?"

"I beg your pardon." Quickly, she told him of Miss Ingels's infamous career at the Seminary and her summary dismissal as a pupil, then added a few choice—but carefully expurgated—accounts of the two gentlemen in question.

When she finished, he nodded agreement. "They do sound a likely choice. And this Miss Ingels is now a boarding student at Miss Davenport's establishment?"

"I would not put it beyond Miss Davenport to encourage her in this dreadful affair."

"I think," he said slowly, "I will have to make the acquaintance of these gentlemen."

"You may do so with my good will." Daphne wiggled her toes, and discovered she could feel them once more. She wished she couldn't, as tingling pain shot through them.

Her gaze strayed to Mr. Carstairs's frowning countenance, and she quickly glanced away. She found it a little too pleasant—almost companionable—sitting here with him by the firelight, talking over a problem that had by insidious degrees become "theirs" instead of "hers." The realization troubled her, as did the fact she found their present occupation far too enjoyable.

She went on very well without Mr. Carstairs. If they were correct in their assumptions, this whole matter might be settled in another day or two, and then Mr. Carstairs would return to the almost monastic cloister of Oxford, and she would see him again but rarely, as she had in the past. That was best. An Oxford don had no place for a female in his life—any more than she, in her useful, rewarding position here, had a place for a gentleman.

But what if they were wrong, and these ghosts had nothing to do with Miss Ingels? Then Mr. Carstairs would remain longer to trouble her peace of mind. If she did not watch herself at every step, she might far too easily come to rely on him, forgetting her own capabilities, leaving her lost when he at last said goodbye.

Abruptly, she rose. "What do we do now?"

Mr. Carstairs stretched. "I believe I will return to my attic."

"But surely no one would dare come back tonight!"

"Perhaps not," he conceded. "But I cannot help but feel we should maintain a watch."

Her confidence sank. "You aren't satisfied that the Ingelses and Mr. Wembly are responsible, are you?"

He rubbed his chin on which a shadowy beard showed. "Why all three in one night? They had no guarantee we would be there to see them. It seems a great deal of effort for no guaranteed results."

"Then—" She gripped the back of the chair. "You're not implying . . ."

"That we have more than one set of haunters." He considered a moment, then nodded slowly. "It's a possibility we cannot overlook."

With this she reluctantly agreed.

Mr. Carstairs made no further comment; he merely gazed into the fire in quiet contemplation. Daphne hugged herself against a chill that had little to do with the snow outside. In fact, her fingers no longer felt frozen—but her toes still could be vastly improved. She sank onto the sofa once more, holding them out toward the comforting blaze.

After a minute, she glanced up at Mr. Carstairs. He remained silent, as if at the moment oblivious of her presence. The light from the hearth flickered and danced, casting shadows across the planes and angles of the face she saw in three-quarter view. An interesting face, not so much because of his features, which were well-formed, but because of his expression, which indicated both kindness and firmness of will. And something more.

100

She studied him covertly, trying to analyze this illusive quality that hovered just beyond her comprehension. His firm jaw indicated strength, the high forehead intelligence, the patrician nose his noble heritage. Yet it was more than that.

Authority, she realized suddenly, naming the aura that hung about him. Authority and conviction of purpose. Here was a gentleman who had endured much, like the tempering of steel for a fine blade. He turned, catching her watching him, and warmth flooded her cheeks.

"Go to bed." He spoke with a gentle firmness.

She rose, giving way to his request because she found it difficult to disobey such a reasonable, practical tone. That startled her and she glared at him. "You've done more than your share this night."

His smiling eyes seemed to understand her resentment. "Without our working together, we would not have known of the other two specters. Get what rest you can, one of us must have a fresh mind for devising new stratagems in the morning."

He made it so easy. Not sure whether to forgive him or not, she found her chamberstick, lit it, and left him to stir the wood with the poker, breaking up what remained of the logs.

She was tired, that was her problem. She had found too little time to sleep of late. Tonight, she would thrust her worries from her mind and not lie awake trying to seek out solutions for the seemingly insolvable.

She mounted the steps to the first landing. Above, movement caught her attention, a pale figure standing at a window. Daphne gasped, drawing back, then caught herself on the railing before she lost her balance. The ghost . . .

The figure shifted and gave vent to an audible sigh. Not a specter, but one of the girls. Swallowing her discomfiture, Daphne climbed the last few steps.

As Daphne's slippers scuffed the carpet, the young

lady spun about in a swirl of pale blue muslin dressing gown and gaped at her. From beneath her nightcap emerged a long plait of fair hair, and even in the meager light Daphne could make out the perfect features of Louisa Trevellian. As she drew closer, she also detected the lovely dark eyes reddened and swollen from weeping.

"Whatever are you doing out of your bed?" Daphne held her candle aloft. She looked the girl over, noting her dry slippers. Whatever else Louisa had been about, it had not been playing ghost in the garden. Daphne didn't know whether to be relieved or sorry. Louisa as a ghost she could have dealt with.

The young lady blinked back the tears that brimmed in her eyes, and color tainted her cheeks. "I—I couldn't sleep."

"That seems to be a common problem here tonight." Her voice softened in sympathy. "What is troubling you?"

An odd expression that might have been fear flickered across Miss Trevellian's face, to be followed at once by guilt. She turned away. "Nothing. It—it is nothing. I will go to my room, now."

Daphne accompanied her, her mind too numb to determine just what had been going on. Perhaps it would make more sense in the morning. It could hardly make less. She followed Louisa into the chamber the girl shared with three other students. Two, at the moment. One had not yet returned from her Christmas holiday. Daphne thrust that thought from her mind. Another problem to be faced—tomorrow.

She pulled back the covers, assisted Louisa out of her dressing gown, then covered the girl once she had climbed into bed. Louisa gave a convulsive sniff, dabbed at her eyes with her handkerchief, and turned over, facing away from Daphne and the two sleeping figures in the room. Daphne hesitated, then whispered "Goodnight," and let herself out.

What had made the girl cry? Regrets for her forth-coming marriage, perhaps? And why had she gone into the hall—unless, of course, she had done so to prevent the other girls from hearing her unhappiness.

Or was there another reason? Daphne made her way to her own chamber, puzzling out a new possibility. What if Louisa knew the "ghost?" Had she started to meet it, only to see Daphne and Mr. Carstairs pursue him through the spinney? But why the tears? Had she wanted to see the ghost—or been afraid of it for some reason? If only any part of this would make sense!

Adrian jerked awake, shaking his head to clear it of the cobwebs that cluttered his mind. They cluttered his coat, as well, he noted the next moment as the sticky fil-aments stuck to his chilled fingers. He peered through the darkness in the attic chamber. No, not complete darkness. A dim light penetrated the gloom, announcing the arrival of morning. He had fallen asleep at his post.

It probably was just as well, he decided, giving way to a cavernous yawn. Two nights without sleep would im-pair his ability to think clearly. He rose from his crouched position behind the chest to the accompani-ment of his muscles' protest. He had remained cramped back there for too long.

Nothing good had come from it, either. No ghostly apparitions had hovered over him, no chains had clanked or clattered, no unearthly screams had torn the stillness of the night. Nor had any human presence dis-turbed his watch, either. Even in the fitful sleep he had attained, he would have heard the creaking of floor-boards beneath the shifting weight of a person. He'd heard Daphne clearly enough earlier that night, and she was a slight little thing.

He eased the stiffness in his shoulders and neck, then dusted the clinging dirt from his breeches. A great deal of good he accomplished in here. The Selwood ladies would have done better to have brought in a Bow Street Runner, hiring him for a private job, rather than a man of the cloth. Yet here he was. And all he could say for certain was that no one had entered this chamber except for himself. Had he and Daphne frightened their specter away from this room that first night they saw it? He made his way to his own chamber to shave and make himself presentable for the day.

When he at last emerged once more into the hall, he saw Daphne approaching him with her graceful yet determined stride. She paused a few feet from him, her gaze studying him. Dark smudges outlined her large eyes, unspoken testimony of her own sleeplessness.

"Nothing?" she asked, her voice resigned.

"Not yet."

She sighed. "Perhaps we frightened them off last night."

"Or they frightened each other."

She cast a swift glance at him. "We have to find out soon." They descended the first flight before she spoke again. "Cousin Sophronia looked on the verge of tears last night."

"We'll lay these ghosts of yours," he assured her.

She hesitated, then turned to peer into his face as if she hoped to find the answers written there. "Can we do it in time to save the school?"

"Yes." He held her gaze, and had the satisfaction of seeing a softening in the strained lines about her mouth.

Her lips twitched in a self-deprecating grimace. "I suppose you think me the most dreadful defeatist."

"Not in the least. You merely need a dose of confidence. And a good night's sleep."

"That we could both use."

The unexpected warmth of her parting smile lingered in his mind throughout morning prayers and accompanied him to his chamber when he retired to work on his dissertation. It progressed well, in spite of his distractions of late—though not as quickly as he needed it to.

104

Still, and in spite of his worries, he found himself slipping back into the frequently fanciful world of Herodotus. A portion of his mind, though, remained on his current problem, and when he at last reached a stopping place, he laid aside his pen and papers and rubbed his strained eyes.

How *had* that ghost vanished from the lumber room the other night? Try as he might, he could think of no other explanation than a priest's hole—or possibly a secret stair. Their cursory search so far had produced no results—but then they'd been concentrating on the "why" rather than the "how."

He fought back a yawn. He should probably try to catch a few hours sleep to keep him more alert this night, but at the moment the question of "how" burned in his mind.

He would sound the walls, he decided. If any hiding hole or secret passage existed, he might locate it with relative ease. Ready as ever to forge ahead, he went next door and considered the walls. Or rather, what he could see of them. Massive pieces of ancient furniture lined them, crowding together like guards prohibiting access. Well, if the specter had been able to reach a hidden passage, then he should be able to, as well.

It took less than an hour, stepping with care amid the jumble of furniture, to convince him that finding any secret doors would be no easy task, after all. He'd tested every available space, each massive cabinet, and found nothing. He retreated to the vantage of the door and frowned into the chamber.

The ghost had seemed to vanish from the middle of the room, not any of the sides. Yet how could that be possible? He eyed the clutter and shook his head. That had to have been an illusion; he could think of no other explanation.

Maybe he just went about the problem backwards. If a hidden passage *did* exist, then it obviously must lead

105

somewhere. If he failed in discovering it at this end, perhaps he might succeed at the other.

But where might it lead? Sideways? The only possibility was his own chamber—or into the outside wall. Upward? There might be space between the ceiling and the roof. He'd have to investigate that. Downward still seemed the most likely and obvious, which meant that somewhere that hypothetical passage had to have an exit. Unless, of course, it was only a priest's hole.

He leaned against the jamb, musing. One exit had to exist here, in this chamber—on this top floor. Did that mean the other let out on the ground floor? He reviewed the rooms on that level and settled on the library as the most likely choice.

Thoughtful, he rubbed his chin. Carved woodwork could easily conceal an opening mechanism. And who would search for one, if they didn't suspect its existence? Those shelves, crammed from ceiling to floor with books, gave an illusion of solidity, of immovability. That would make a perfect entryway.

If that failed . . . he considered a moment. If he failed in the library, he would try the basements, next. Yet those rooms below ground level led nowhere, allowed no exit from the house. On the whole, the library, with its French doors leading onto the terrace, made the most sense.

He made his way down the stairs to the ground floor and was surprised to hear light laughter coming from the dining room. A glance at his pocket watch assured him he had worked well into the luncheon hour. He had no desire to join the young ladies; instead, he headed down to the kitchens, where he found a ham still resting on the cutting board and a knife lying near by. A little foraging provided him with bread, cheese, and several pieces of fruit to go with it. Bundling his booty into a large napkin, he set off to the library to commence his explorations.

A brief examination of the dark oak shelves proved a

106

leveler to his hopes. The cabinetmaker had designed the cases to be perfectly plain, devoid of carvings or even knotholes. Not so much as a single crevice or knob could he find that might conceal any mechanism.

He munched an apple, his thoughtful gaze resting on the leather-bound volumes before him. He had heard of opening devices hidden not on the exposed woodwork but behind a specific book, a precaution to deter anyone from searching or even suspecting. He regarded the multitude of reading matter which filled every available niche on the walls, and his heart sank.

He would have to take them out, he supposed, every single one of them.

Resigned to the task but by no means eager, he set the apple core aside and started to the left of the door at about waist height. An armload at a time, he transferred the books to the floor. As he cleared each shelf, he checked the wood with care, then replaced the volumes and set to work on the next area.

Some two hours later, the door opened and someone hesitated on the threshold. He sank back on his heels where he knelt before the lowest shelf near the terrace and brushed the dust from his hands before turning. His shoulders and neck protested their stiffness.

"Dusting?" Daphne advanced into the room, a quizzical note in her voice.

"I might as well be." He came stiffly to his feet. "I don't seem to be accomplishing anything else."

She cocked her head to one side, considering. "Did you lose something?"

His lips twitched. "A secret passage."

The corners of her bright green eyes crinkled with amusement. "A very small one, it would seem."

He directed a pained look at her, then dropped to one knee and restored an armload of heavy books to their place.

She perched on the arm of a chair. "You might try the dining room. Fewer things to move."

"I'll bear that in mind." He scooped out another arm-load, set the volumes aside, and checked the recess for any triggering device. Failure again.

"And I had thought your stores of patience and good humor to be boundless." Smugness sounded in her voice. "Are you truly as exasperated as you look?"

He sat back and regarded her, frowning, and wiped a tickling speck of dust from his temple with the back of his dirtied hands.

The satisfaction in her expression faded into sympathy. "Do you have much more to do?"

"Only these three walls." He fought a losing battle against his chuckle at the horror in her expression. "No, only this last shelf. I am almost done."

She glared at him. "For that you deserve to be left alone." Yet she made no move to leave. Instead, when he drew out the next stack of books, she grabbed another.

With her help, they finished in fifteen more minutes. Daphne stepped back as Adrian replaced the last volume once more in its position, dusted her hands, and cast a rueful glance over her blue muslin skirts. "Nothing," she said in disgust, and fixed her accusing gaze on him. "What a dreadful waste of time."

He shook his head. "I never promised anything," he reminded her.

She sniffed. "I expected at the least a winding stair with a fortune in jewels strewn about."

"And here was I thinking you'd be satisfied with nothing less than skeletal remains."

Her lips twitched. "I suppose that would be appropriate. Where do we search next?"

"I had thought the cellars. No, do not look so dismayed. There is no need for you to accompany me."

"Of course there is. What there is no need for is your doing everything, as if the rest of us are not fit for anything constructive. In case you did not realize it, I am perfectly capable of performing simple tasks if they are adequately explained."

He smiled at her heavy sarcasm. "It will be cold and dank."

"Don't forget the mildew." She looked down at her gown and wrinkled her nose. "That will be even worse than this dust. Will you wait while I change into an older gown?" She started toward the door, only to be brought up short as it opened.

Moffett entered, a frown on his lined features. He nodded in morose satisfaction at the sight of her, and jerked his head indicating the hallway behind him. "Mr. Ingels to see you, Miss Daphne."

"Mr.—Oh, bother!" she muttered.

Adrian raised his eyebrows. "Do you want me to remain?"

"There's no need." She squared her shoulders. "I can deal with him."

Ingels. That would be the brother of Miss Susannah Ingels, who had been dismissed from the school. Admitting to considerable curiosity, Adrian strolled into the hall and cast a seemingly casual glance at the young gentleman who preened before the mirror there. A coxcomb, Adrian decided, eyeing with disfavor the lanky figure in its elegant town dress. A jackanapes perhaps too young to have learned discretion or taste.

Mr. Ingels turned, and Adrian's gaze narrowed on the thin face. Not handsome, he decided, not even particularly good looking. But any number of females might swoon over that brooding expression. He certainly appeared at pains to assure himself the arrangement of his neckcloth remained impeccable.

He accorded the young cub a curt nod and strolled toward the office. He would allow him ten minutes with Daphne, then find an excuse to interrupt. And he would stay within earshot.

* * *

Daphne drew in a steadying breath as first Mr. Carstairs, then Moffett, left the library. She had told Mr. Carstairs the truth; she *could* deal with Mr. Reginald Ingels. She just didn't enjoy doing so.

But she could be glad Mr. Carstairs gave her the chance.

The young gentleman entered a moment later, swaggering into the room as if assured of a joyous welcome instead of the chilly one he would receive. He swept her an elaborate bow which lacked grace and carried her stiff fingers to his lips for a prolonged kiss. She pulled her hand away.

He lowered himself onto the sofa without waiting to be invited. Lounging back, he extended his gleaming top boots toward the embers in the hearth and awarded her a smile meant to dazzle. It failed singularly in its purpose.

"My dear Miss Selwood. Miss Daphne." His lazily smiling gaze traveled over her in appreciation. "It is such a relief to find you still safe and your school still open."

"A situation," she said, "that will continue for a very long time, I assure you." She remained standing, making it clear this would be a short interview.

He laughed, and idly swung his quizzing glass by its riband. "How delighted I am to see you endeavoring to keep your spirits up. Such determined optimism, and in the face of such bleak prospects. Really, my dear, I marvel at you."

She barely prevented herself from telling him she was not, under any circumstances, his "dear." Instead, she said, "If you believe our position to be so dreadful, I may relieve your mind and tell you that you have been misinformed."

His eyes narrowed, and the quizzing glass stilled. "Have I? Then you are still visited by only one specter?"

"How——" she began, startled, but bit back the question. Did he have specific knowledge of the three ghosts

110

who had cavorted about the spinney last night? Had he, perhaps, been one of them?

A slow, unpleasant smile spread across his face. "Ah, so it is true, then." The glass resumed its rhythmic dance. "Now, I wonder what it might be worth to you to stop these hauntings. So very distressing, they must be. And with such disastrous results for your beloved Seminary."

Daphne stiffened, and a chill seeped into the pit of her stomach. "What do you mean?"

He rose and strolled with languid steps to stand before her. He was very tall, she realized with a touch of unease—though not as tall as Mr. Carstairs. Yet she had never found Mr. Carstairs's size anything other than comforting.

He brushed her cheek with one finger. "If I could do something about your ghosts, stop them from playing off their tricks, you'd be grateful, wouldn't you?"

She forced herself not to cringe. "Do you mean you *could* stop them?"

His soft laugh sounded unpleasant. "It would hardly be wise to promise anything, now would it? But one never knows what can be accomplished when there is sufficient reason." His arm slipped about her and he drew her a step toward him.

She went without protest, forcing herself to remain relaxed, raising her face to his. A gleam lit his watery blue eyes, and as he shifted his hold on her, she swung up her fist and delivered a ringing box to his left ear.

He jumped back, covering the afflicted area with his hand, his expression one of stark fury. At that moment, Daphne didn't care. She glared at him, seething in anger.

"How dare you threaten me? And how dare you put your filthy hands on me?"

He drew in a shaky breath, his features livid. He waved a finger under her nose for a moment before he seemed able to command his voice. "You'll regret this, my girl, you mark my words. Your academy is finished, and so are you." He gave a short, angry laugh. "Your reputation—"

"Her reputation," came Mr. Carstairs's steady voice from the doorway, "will remain as impeccable as ever."

Heat flooded Daphne's cheeks as her startled gaze flew to the new arrival. How long had he been standing there? Yet in her relief at his presence, her embarrassment seemed insignificant.

He strode forward, his features rigid, his presence filling the room like an avenging angel. As his assailant bore down on him, Mr. Ingels shrank back a step, cowering in the face of so much power and determination. Daphne regarded Mr. Carstairs with new and startled awareness.

He stopped before Mr. Ingels, his fists clenching at his sides as if he longed to behave in a very unclergyman-like manner. Daphne could almost wish he would. Almost. She noted the white lines outlining his knuckles, and respected his control.

When he spoke, though, his voice sounded surprisingly mild. "I fear your little jest is ill-timed, Ingels. Miss Selwood is in no mood for your funning humor."

The pale eyes blazed. "I—" he began, but the brief flare of defiance died aborning, and Mr. Ingels fell silent.

"Exactly." Mr. Carstairs smiled, but no pleasantness lurked there. "It would not be healthy for you to return here, under any guise. Do I make myself clear?"

Mr. Ingels's gaze traveled the length of Mr. Carstairs's sturdy figure and lingered a moment on the fists that remained clenched. He licked his lips and nodded.

"Excellent." Mr. Carstairs flexed his fingers, then took Ingels by the arm. "I will see you to the door." With no apparent effort, he propelled the young exquisite out into the hall.

Daphne remained where she stood, wrung by the

112

emotions that had swept over her. Fear, fury, and then . . . awe? Gratitude? Or admiration?

She found a chair just as her knees buckled, dropping her into it. She knew she was capable. She knew, despite Uncle Thaddeus's concerns, she had chosen the right life for herself. Dedication and hard work suited her. So did managing on her own.

But when Mr. Carstairs calmly took over, protecting her, sheltering her from frightening or disagreeable occurrences, she *enjoyed* it.

Traitorous, traitorous heart . . .

He returned to the room and leaned against the door jamb. "He's gone," was all he said.

Daphne stared back, and experienced an almost overwhelming desire to burst into tears.

Chapter Eight

The exuberance of the students, who demanded Daphne's company for a sketching expedition to catch the late afternoon shadows, prevented the immediate exploration of the cellars. She did not break away from them again until after she had seen them into their beds late that evening, by which time the hour was too advanced to begin that massive undertaking. Now, she needed to take up her ghost-watching position for the night.

Assured that Mr. Carstairs intended to keep his attic room vigil again, Daphne sought her own station at the window of her bedchamber. For a long while she gazed out, but no specters of any description disturbed the quiet of the grounds—leaving her all too much solitude to look back over the disturbing happenings of the day. Yet in spite of the emotions that whirled through her, her eyelids grew heavy and her thoughts became muddled.

She awoke abruptly to a brisk knock on her door. Daisy, one of the two housemaids, announced it was time and past she was up and doing. Daphne stretched, found herself still curled in her chair, and came none too steadily to her feet.

Her cousins would probably be in their office already, planning their day. Daphne's late rising meant the girls would be running amuck downstairs with no one to stifle their high spirits. Still heavy-eyed, she splashed water over her face, then scrambled into the somber gray gown she felt suitable for an art mistress and brushed her long hair. Arranging it with any style would take too long, so she fastened the unruly mass at the nape of her neck with a bright blue riband, then hurried along the hall toward the attic chamber where Mr. Carstairs kept his lone watch.

Before she reached it, he emerged from his own chamber, impeccably attired in the habiliments of his calling. At first glance, he appeared rested; then her surprise faded to compassion as she noted the lines and shadows of exhaustion about his piercing gray eyes. "Did you—?" she began, then broke off. There was no need to ask; the futility of his night's endeavors lay clear to be seen in his strained face. "Why do you not try to get some sleep now?"

He shook his head. "I have duties this morning. Come." He ushered her ahead of him toward the stairs.

She glanced back, worried. He strode erect with his usual springing step that bespoke repressed energy. How did he manage it? He could have done no more than dozed for brief spells for two nights, now. She hoped he would take a few hours of rest in the afternoon, but from what she had learned of him, she doubted it. He would probably either work on his dissertation or explore the woods more thoroughly so he would not lose track of any ghosts again.

Guilt flooded through her, for causing him so much trouble, for taking him from his own work. And in exchange for all his efforts, she had given him only resentment in return. She sought words of acknowledgment which refused to come, though the need to say something grew and grew until she thought she would burst with it. At last, she grasped at something wholly inadequate. "We will be late for morning prayers," she announced.

Adrian's devilish grin flashed. "They will hardly start without me."

At least he had not lost his humor. He had retained

115

it throughout this business far better than had she. Probably because he wasn't personally involved in the outcome, she assured herself—and realized that was not quite true. From what she had come to know of him, he entered wholeheartedly into everything he did, accepting the cares and responsibilities as his own.

When they reached the crowded drawing room which they used for morning chapel, Mr. Carstairs strode ahead, making his way to Cousin Sophronia where, in that compelling, deep voice, he proffered his apologies for keeping everyone waiting. Daphne eased in behind him and closed the door. Her three cousins sat in various places about the room, where they could best keep watch over their charges.

Cousin Elspeth appeared neat and unruffled as ever in a simple round gown of dove gray merino, her hair wound about her head in a crown. She directed a searching glance at Daphne, to which Daphne responded with a negative shake of her head. Elspeth sighed, then turned her attention to Marianne Snowdon and hushed her where she sat giggling with a friend.

Daphne turned a quelling frown on Jane, but found her sister for once a model of propriety. The girl's gaze rested on Mr. Carstairs, and a dreamy expression settled on her face. Startled, Daphne cast a rapid glance about the room, and noticed that most of the young ladies watched their new chaplain with an intent enthusiasm that had nothing to do with religious fervor.

Oh, dear. Her lips twitched in rueful acknowledgment. She understood their girlish heart-flutterings a little too well. What had happened to her? Covertly, she subjected Mr. Carstairs to a thorough study, her reflections both troubled and wondering. When had she stopped seeing him with the eyes of prejudice? For several years, he'd been naught to her but a scholarly acquaintance of her uncle, with whom she had little contact and in whom she had little interest. Then he became her watchdog, and she had resented him.

116

But after that? What did she feel now?

He was very handsome, in a rugged, commanding way. His features were regular and good—and strong. Compelling. Confidence and authority radiated from him. He had no need to depend upon brooding Byronic theatrics or extravagant fashion to make an impression on others. In fact, she felt certain he made no attempt to make any impression on anyone at all. He had no need.

As she watched, he left Cousin Sophronia's side and strode to the front to take up his position. Each movement held an athletic grace that drew the admiring attention of every girl in the room. As he opened his prayer book and started to speak, his congregation stilled to take in his every word.

Why had she never realized how very attractive he was? So—so masculine. And infinitely capable, as she'd been finding out. She simply never had let herself really look at him before. And it would be best, she realized, for her peace of mind, if she did not do so again.

Yet now that she had allowed herself to see him with unbiased, open eyes, she found it difficult to forget.

She closed those eyes and allowed the deep, sonorous tones of his voice to wash over her. And this was only morning prayers. How many would flock to hear him preach a sermon on a balmy spring eve?

But he wouldn't preach sermons. He would lecture to a select handful of young gentlemen, upon whom his dynamic voice would be wasted. He had chosen the life of an Oxford don, isolated away from the world into an academic cloister. No troubled parishioners would be able to seek his calming wisdom for guidance.

The brief service drew to a close all too soon, and Daphne found her attention fully absorbed by the lively girls. With a sigh, she summoned Juliana Pembroke, then barely managed to prevent Marianne Snowdon from trailing after Mr. Carstairs as he left the room. And to think Uncle Thaddeus requested that gentleman to accompany her here to make her life easier and safer!

She brought up the end of the procession that made its erratic way to the dining room for breakfast, shooing the stragglers ahead of her. She could use a cup of strong coffee, very hot and very sweet. She started toward the sideboard, only to draw up short at the unwelcome sight that greeted her.

Four girls gathered about Mr. Carstairs, casting the most revolting sheep's eyes at him. Amazingly, he appeared oblivious—or at least completely unmoved by such youthful adoration. Marianne Snowdon touched his arm, fluttering her lashes at him; he merely smiled, extricated himself with finesse, and left the girl sighing at his back.

Poor Mr. Carstairs. He must find these silly chits a sad bore, yet he never betrayed it by either word or gesture. Nor, she noted with pleasure, did he betray any sign of liking the attention.

At the earliest opportunity, she departed the dining room with her first class. The next two hours she spent attempting to explain perspective to a group of young ladies who consistently drew all objects as if they existed on a flat plane. She clung to her temper by the merest thread; her heart wasn't in it today. She would far rather be devoting her energies to the Seminary's problems.

Her second class she found even more insupportable than her first. Her time, she felt, would be better employed searching the grounds, the lumber room, even the cellars with their cold and mildew. Before the hands of the clock neared noon, she began to have wistful thoughts of strangling a few of her pupils. But then if she did, the Seminary might have real ghosts haunting it.

That thought helped restore her humor, and she—and her charges—survived until the great clock in the hall struck one. As the girls darted out the door to seek their luncheon, Daphne made no attempt to rebuke them for their lack of decorum. She would far prefer to rush right along with them.

Cousin Sophronia, her expression distraught, emerged

from the midst of the chaos at the doorway. For a moment she stood bewildered, glancing from side to side as the girls streamed past, then shook her head as if to clear it. "A word with you, Daphne, dear, if you don't mind. In the office?"

"But the girls—"

"Beatrice already knows. Dear Beatrice. So very forceful. She will preside over luncheon. She has decided to leave all this unpleasantness to you and Elspeth, you must know, though why—but that is neither here nor there. She merely says she will tend to the girls, though what she thinks I am doing—"

"Beatrice will manage very well," Daphne said. Sophronia's manner concerned her, and she abandoned the drawing supplies on their tables and followed her aging relative from the room.

Cousin Elspeth awaited them in the tiny chamber, her expression perplexed. "My dear sister—" she began, but Sophronia cut her off.

"So dreadful. So very dreadful. In the morning post, you must know." The eldest Selwood lady sniffed.

Daphne exchanged a perplexed look with Elspeth. "What must we know?" Daphne prodded gently.

"This!" Sophronia declared in tragic accents, and held out a much-folded sheet of writing paper.

Elspeth took it, adjusted her reading glass, and scanned the page. Her smooth brow furrowed in dismay.

"What is it?" Daphne looked from one to the other, her apprehension growing. "Is it bad news? Has something else occurred?"

Elspeth sighed as she laid the paper on the large desk she shared with Sophronia. "Miss Lydgate will not be returning to us. Her parents feel that our Seminary is no longer suitable for her."

"The ghosts," Daphne exclaimed, furious. "I—I could wring their necks!"

"If they were not already dead," murmured Elspeth.

"You shall not divert me so." Daphne cast her favor-

119

ite cousin a rebuking glance. "Not for a moment do I believe the specters to be real. It is some jokester, making sport of Selwood Seminary for his own amusement, and ruining us into the bargain!"

Sophronia wrung her hands. "Miss Lydgate's parents wish us to return her fees for the remainder of the term."

"They what? You shall do nothing of the sort!" Daphne took an agitated turn about the room. "It is not *our* fault the silly little wretch has listened to the nonsensical stories the other girls are creating."

Sophronia's face rumpled, as if she were about to dissolve into tears. "They have enrolled her in Miss Davenport's Seminary."

"In—" Daphne broke off, too outraged to speak. After a moment, she recovered enough to say between gritted teeth, "Have they, indeed? How very— fortunate—for Miss Davenport."

"Oh, Elspeth," Sophronia wailed, "if that is not the most crushing blow of all. To think That Woman will take on our own dear Miss Lydgate."

"And our fees," murmured Elspeth.

"And three of the other girls are not yet back from their holidays," Sophronia went on in the voice of doom probably favored by Cassandra.

Elspeth looked up, alarmed. "You fear they will not, as well? But we cannot possibly afford to return so many fees. It will ruin us. And even if we do not return these fees," she added hastily as Daphne opened her mouth, "what will we do for the *following* term? We cannot operate a seminary with no pupils."

Daphne turned away, her heart aching. Perhaps their ghost just didn't understand the harm caused by his pranks. Maybe next time instead of chasing him, she should call to him, tell him the disastrous results of his ridiculous playacting. Perhaps he would stop. Perhaps. But it wasn't likely.

Too agitated to remain in so confined an area, she

surged out into the corridor, then paced its length. She didn't want her luncheon, she wanted to go outside and scream until their specter promised he would behave in the future. She turned and made her way to the library door, knowing her feelings could only be relieved by a long hike through the woods.

The Seminary simply could not be forced to close! What would Sophronia, Beatrice, and Elspeth do? For that matter, what would *she* do? The school was her livelihood as well. If she lost this position, she would never turn to Miss Davenport! But what choice did that leave her? She would have to rely on her Cousin Chloe, now Lady Richard, to pay Jane's fees at another school. Chloe would do it gladly, but Daphne could not bear the idea of charity. Not for anything would she impose on someone.

And she would have failed, at helping her cousins when they needed her most, at providing for both Jane and herself. Uncle Percival had lectured her always to keep an ace tucked somewhere about her person in case of emergency. Where was one now when she needed it? Had she forgotten all the principles of surviving that lay behind everything he had taught her?

Perhaps she *was* suited for nothing but the frivolous, pointless life in London so enjoyed by most young ladies.

Half-blinded by angry tears, she unlatched the French doors that led outside. As she started through, a deep voice, calm but compelling, hailed her. She turned, and beheld Mr. Carstairs standing just inside the door to the hall.

He came forward to join her, and his steady gaze searched her face. "What is amiss?"

She dashed a hand across her eyes. "It is the unfairness of it, that some cruel prankster—pranksters!—" she corrected herself, "—can ruin the lives of three wonderful old dears like my cousins, and there isn't a single thing I can do to prevent it!" To her dismay, tears prickled in her eyes, but she refused to give in to them.

He raised a questioning eyebrow. "When did we declare defeat?"

She fought back a sniff.

"Beaten to snuff?" he suggested. "You're not just going to fight a crib, are you, then cry off?"

She straightened and regarded him with suspicion. "And what, pray, does that mean?"

"To only pretend to fight, then back down. It's considered very unsporting, I might add."

"And quite shocking of you. Boxing cant, is it not?" She shook her head, a reluctant smile tugging at her lips. "Most reprehensible. And you a man of the cloth!"

His eyes lit as his slow grin spread. "But you don't look nearly so blue-deviled any more. Now, what's toward?"

She sank onto a long couch and told him the day's tale of woe. He perched on the arm of a wingback chair opposite her, his gaze resting on her face in a manner that brought a touch of warmth to her cold cheeks. She shouldn't be confiding in him; he didn't need to know their financial difficulties. Yet she could no more prevent herself than she could fly to the moon.

When she finished, he transferred his gaze to the small fire burning in the hearth. "So it is Miss Davenport who profits—at least this time. And she already has taken in another girl who used to attend here?"

Daphne nodded. "She has always hated Cousin Beatrice. I know it is shocking to suspect her, but I cannot put it from my mind. Do you think it possible?"

He studied his gleaming topboot, his brow creased. "It is difficult to know to what lengths a person might be driven, given sufficient motivation. If Miss Davenport believes herself to have suffered some great harm at the hands of your cousin, and has allowed that thought to fester within her for thirty or more years, she might indeed plot the Seminary's ruination. Or perhaps she covets some special pupil, and merely seeks to discredit your cousins so she will have no rival for the prize."

122

Daphne nodded, her thoughts straying between the good sense and steady judgment of his words, and the deep, calming tone of his voice. He made her *feel* better. Challenged rather than defeated. Even if this weren't the answer, they would soon find the solution to this deplorable bumblebroth. There was something about the Reverend Mr. Adrian Carstairs that filled her with confidence and hope. No, she would not give up.

And in the very near future, she would arrange for Mr. Carstairs to make the acquaintance of Miss Isobel Davenport.

Adrian remained in the library after Daphne returned to her chores about the school. He hated to see her so troubled, worrying about her cousins, worrying about the Seminary, worrying about her own future. She had every right to resent his interference; but he still intended to help her in any way he could.

And that meant getting to the bottom of this haunting business.

He shoved at the log with the poker, then threw on another, his thoughts drifting back to that first night in the attic chamber and the ghost who had disappeared as they watched. He closed his eyes, trying to remember the way the figure had glowed, the gust of cold air, the eerie creak that had accompanied the vanishing act. Human. It had to have been. But *how* had it been done?

He jabbed at the log before him, sending it into the midst of the flames. Back to secret passages, he supposed.

He'd already spent a profitless few hours combing this room. Nor did any of the others on the ground floor seem more likely. He supposed, the way his luck had run of late, he would be reduced to measuring every inch of this place to discover if any unaccounted for space existed between the walls. It would be a long and laborious process, and one he would rather avoid.

But it would allow him to spend time in Daphne's company while he did it.

Of course, he could think of far more enjoyable ways to do that.

Still, if all else failed, he would certainly measure. Yet there might be an easy way to avoid the process. Records of the house's construction might exist somewhere. If he could unearth those, he might be able to determine the most likely locations for hiding places and secret stairs, even if they weren't marked. Feeling considerably elated—and wondering why that obvious solution hadn't occurred to any of them before—he went at once to the office.

There he found Miss Elspeth dwarfed behind the great mahogany desk, poring over an account book. She raised a face lined with strain and managed a wan smile. "Did Daphne tell you?" she asked.

"It seems I must speed up my investigation." He explained why he had come.

For a long moment, Miss Elspeth stared off into space, then nodded. "I don't remember seeing any, but we can always look."

They began a methodical search, delving into the contents of every cabinet and drawer. But while they discovered a set of misplaced records, they found nothing of relevance concerning the construction of the Dower House. Measuring, he realized with a sinking heart, it might well have to be.

As he started to take his leave, a knock sounded on the door, and it opened to reveal Moffett. "Gentleman to see you," the man announced in his casual manner, and stood back to permit the entrance of a slender man garbed in black.

"Mr. Danvers." Adrian stepped forward, pleased to see his old friend the vicar standing in the hall. He at once drew the man into the room.

Miss Elspeth half rose, and becoming color touched her cheeks. She greeted him with formal courtesy, yet a

124

hint of warmth lingered in her soft voice as she invited him to be seated.

"How goes your ghost hunt?" Mr. Danvers looked from one to the other of them, and his expression sobered. "I see. Tell me all." He took the seat opposite the desk and directed his comforting smile toward Miss Elspeth.

She lowered her gaze. Adrian noted this in fascination, then strolled to the hearth and leaned his elbow on the mantel, from which position he could better watch them both. Mr. Danvers, he noted, appeared oblivious to the signs of confusion present in the lady.

Adrian took pity on her. "The whole business is dashed peculiar," he said, freeing Miss Elspeth from the need of answering.

Mr. Danvers regarded him from beneath bunched brows. "As odd a situation as Daphne hinted?"

"More so, I should say. And though I have no reason to suspect it, I cannot rid myself of the notion this may prove dangerous."

"Oh, no," breathed Miss Elspeth.

Mr. Danvers drew in a deep breath, and his gaze strayed once more to the lady. "Mr. Carstairs's suspicions tend to prove accurate."

Adrian drummed his fingers on the wooden ledge. "And the devil is in it that I cannot convince Daphne to stay safely in the background."

"Of course she will not. Nor will any of us." Miss Elspeth's eyes gleamed with her determination. "Why, what a shocking thing it would be if we made no effort on our own behalf. We cannot leave the matter solely to you. It would not be right."

"But it might be wisest," Mr. Danvers said. "I will talk to Daphne and Jane before I leave." His frowning gaze rested on her a moment, then transferred to Adrian. "Have you discovered anything yet at all?"

Briefly, Adrian told him about the eerie experience in

125

the attic chamber and the three separate ghosts who had haunted the woods at the same time.

Mr. Danvers listened, his frown deepening. At the conclusion of the tale, he paced the length of the small apartment, then turned back to face Adrian. "We should send for a constable."

"I tried," Miss Elspeth said. "But they told me they cannot take a ghost into custody. They seemed to find considerable humor in our situation," she added with feeling.

"One cannot blame them, I suppose," Mr. Danvers said, though with obvious regret. "You have no proof your nocturnal visitors are human. Nor is there any law that I know against dressing up in a sheet and capering about. If there were something of value contained in this house, I make no doubt they would send us a guard at once."

Adrian straightened. "Then we shall have to find out something. And let us hope it is nothing more than someone playing an elaborate practical joke on the school."

Mr. Danvers glanced at the clock on the mantel. "I shall have to return to my parish. I am sorry I could only spare so short a time—but I found myself too anxious to wait until I could stay away for a longer while. Before I go, though, I must pay my respects to your sisters, Miss Elspeth. Are they free?"

Miss Elspeth looked down at her desk and idly shuffled several papers that lay beside the account book. "They are with classes at this time. They will be so sorry to have missed you."

"Next time, perhaps. I shall return as soon as I possibly can to learn how you go on."

Adrian crossed to the door. "I will help you find your nieces." He inserted a gentle edge to his voice.

Mr. Danvers blinked at him. "Oh. Ah, of course." He exited into the hall, then looked back as Adrian closed the door behind them. "I must admire Miss Elspeth's devotion to the school. She is quite determined to save it, is she not?"

"They all are, and who can blame them? It is their life."

Mr. Danvers brooded on this for a moment. "And Daphne's also, do you think?"

Adrian frowned, recognizing the unspoken meaning behind his friend's question. "I believe she knows her own mind."

"And she wouldn't thank me for consulting you about her, would she?" Mr. Danvers shook his head. "Well. And what did you wish to say to me?"

"Only that I do not like what has been happening here." Adrian paced toward the entry hall, then turned to face Mr. Danvers. "I would be glad if you could manage to return soon. I am convinced a secret passage must exist from that attic room, and I want to search more thoroughly for it. But with your niece aiding me, I must be concerned first for her safety. If you could keep her occupied—"

"Prevent me from helping, do you mean?" Daphne's voice, heavy with distaste, sounded behind him. She stalked forward. "If you do anything of the kind, Uncle, I shall be very cross. This matter deeply concerns me, and I will not be left out of it. We now have *three* specters haunting us, our pupils have begun to withdraw, and all you can think of," she added, turning on Adrian, "is a secret passage for which we have already searched and failed to find!"

Her eyes sparkled in her wrath, Adrian noted, and their gleam intrigued him. He could admire her spirit, but—his jaw tightened. He would not permit her to come to any harm.

Yet try as he might, he could not rid himself of the feeling that that was exactly what lay ahead of them.

Chapter Nine

Daphne glared at her uncle and Mr. Carstairs in frustration. "Why can you not understand how I feel?" she demanded. Somewhat to her surprise, she found herself facing Mr. Carstairs.

"It seems I might ask the same question of you," he said. "What would you have me say to your uncle if I permitted you to be harmed when he has placed you in my care?"

"He shouldn't have!" She drew a deep breath, fighting for control. For a moment, it hovered on the brink, teetering toward explosion, then with an extreme effort she brought it under rigid restraint and turned to her uncle. "Dear sir," she said with infinite care, "will you not finally agree that here—where I work, where I belong—I am no one's responsibility but my own? I have sufficient sense to behave in an intelligent manner. I have no need for a nurserymaid to watch my every step."

"My dear Daphne—" Mr. Danvers shook his head. "It was never my intention to imply—"

"Well, you did, and only see where it has gotten us." To her dismay, tears of anger stung her eyes, and she blinked them back before continuing. "How can I tolerate such—such an insult? His presence is a constant reminder—" She broke off, wishing those last words unsaid.

"I seem to excel at my role as a thorn in her side," Mr. Carstairs said. His warm smile lingered in his eyes, but otherwise his expression remained as solemn as she might wish. He raised an inquiring eyebrow toward her uncle.

Mr. Danvers looked from one to the other of them, an arrested gleam in his expression. A slow smile played about the corners of his mouth. "So be it, my dear. You are completely free of Adrian's intervention. He may leave this afternoon if you wish it."

She blinked, taken aback by such complete and unexpected acquiescence. She'd expected a struggle, renewed hostilities . . . a continued reason to regard Mr. Carstairs in the light of a tolerated enemy. She felt deflated, as if the wind had suddenly shifted course and left her sails hanging limp and useless.

She opened her mouth, closed it, then straightened her shoulders. "All right, then," she said, and knew that as a victory speech it lacked a certain panache. After a moment, she added, "Will you also grant that I know what is best for myself?"

Her uncle's eyes gleamed. "I believe I should be able to answer that by the time this matter is settled. And now I must take my leave, my dear. Give my love to Jane. Adrian, if you do not arrive on my doorstep in the next day or two, I shall most assuredly ride back to see how you all go on here." With that he inclined his head and took himself off. Mr. Carstairs accompanied him out the door, apparently bent on escorting him to the stables.

Daphne remained where she stood, still stunned by her partial victory. She could ask Mr. Carstairs to leave—she had full permission. She could free herself from her watchdog. She'd longed for nothing else since he'd been thrust upon her.

Yet somehow he'd become more than that hateful role. Perversely, she wanted him to stay. She'd come to rely on his presence—which was no easy thing for her to admit. At least she didn't have to admit it to him.

Her Uncle Percival, she remembered, had warned her never to rely on anyone but herself. But perhaps that had been because Uncle Percival had himself been totally unreliable. She could never accuse Mr. Carstairs of that.

Several girls approached, and Daphne slipped into the library where she could be alone a little longer. She held no *real* grudge against Mr. Carstairs, she realized. He made no attempt to influence her, to urge her into the typical life of a young lady of quality. He did not extol the delights of a London Season and all the things her Uncle Thaddeus told her she *ought* to want—and which she didn't.

And he'd better not try!

She roused herself. Right now, she wasted time. She looked about the room, frowning, more determined than ever to solve their mystery. Mr. Carstairs had already searched in here for his secret passage. If she tried the dining room now, or any of the other rooms on this level or the one above, she would encounter the girls, which she had no wish to do. That left either the attics—a singularly fruitless task, so far—or the basements.

The basements. They would be dank and freezing with the January ice seeping into their gray stone. Not even a fire to alleviate the chill. She could think of far more pleasant ways to spend a late afternoon. Unless, of course, she had Mr. Carstairs's company . . .

The door opened behind her, and she braced herself, knowing without turning who must stand there. She hadn't been aware of the steady tread of his booted feet, yet she had not a doubt. Slowly she turned, and encountered that devilish gleam of enjoyment sparkling in his eyes.

He strolled to the hearth and tossed on another log. "Shall I pack at once?"

Daphne stiffened. The devil take the man, did he hope to make her grovel? With care, she shrugged an indifferent shoulder. "As you please. I know you have far more important concerns than our ghosts." *He* could jolly well be the one to grovel if he wished to remain—which she felt certain he did.

"True, there are any number of matters that require my attention." Maddeningly, he leaned back against the mantel, his expression unreadable. "Do you wish me to leave?"

She thrust out her chin. "It is of no consequence to me what you do, Mr. Carstairs." She saw the resolution settle in his face as he straightened. He *would* go.

Panicking, yet loathe to lose face, she struggled, casting her mind about for something—anything—to make him change his mind on his own. And then she had it. She trailed her fingers along the back of the sofa and said, in her most off-hand manner, "Of course, my cousins might feel you have deserted them, but I suppose that cannot be helped." *That* should make him squirm.

His rich chuckle broke the silence. "On no account would I wish to earn their bad opinion. Have I your permission to remain, then?"

She sniffed. "The decision is entirely up to you."

"Very well. For the sake of your cousins, then." He seated himself in the chair nearest the hearth. "What may I have your permission to do next?"

For a full ten seconds she stared at him, struggling, then burst out laughing. "You are quite abominable! Shall we call *pax*, then? For the moment, at least?"

"Fair enough." He leaned back, stretching out his booted feet toward the fire, and rubbed a thoughtful finger along the squared line of his jaw. "So far, we have failed to discover the motive behind the hauntings?" He made it a question.

She settled on the sofa and clasped her hands in her lap. "Unfortunately."

He nodded. "Then I fear my best suggestion is one which you do not like. Keep searching for a hidden passage to learn how, which might eventually lead us to why and who."

She studied her entwined fingers. "I fear I came to that conclusion earlier."

"You don't look pleased about it."

His deep voice held a lingering smile which warmed her. She tried to shake off the sensation, but failed. "Do you look forward to searching the basements in such raw weather?" she countered.

He surged to his feet. "It will only get darker and colder, the longer we put it off."

She inclined her head. "Will you obtain lanterns for us while I change my gown?"

His intriguing grin flashed. "I promise I will not begin without you."

She ran up the stairs to her room, and, out of breath from the several flights, threw open her wardrobe and pulled out what she now dubbed her "ghost-hunting gown," an aged green merino mended in more than one spot. She scrambled out of her dress and donned this one as quickly as she could, then paused before her mirror. It still became her, perhaps more so than ever now that frequent washings had muted the shade and softened the folds of the fabric. Though why she should care was beyond her. She certainly didn't concern herself with what Mr. Carstairs might think of her appearance.

She descended to the ground floor, then made her way to the back steps leading down to the kitchens and the basements beyond. Like the attics, where inhabited rooms shared the floor with almost-forgotten storage areas, the kitchens occupied the same level as a long subterranean chamber. Windows set high in the walls permitted light to filter in from barely above ground level.

The kitchen, with its blazing fire and intriguing

smells, tempted her. Instead, she resolutely turned her back on it and entered the other door into the dim, dank basement. As she stepped within, the sharp odor of mildew surrounded her.

She shuddered. She always felt uncomfortable down here, as if the whole house hovered over her, ready to collapse. At least the cellar was large and not a confined space.

Mr. Carstairs stood just inside the cavernous stone chamber, a lantern held high in one hand, a frown creasing his brow. On one of the long, narrow tables that ran down the center of the vast area stood a multi-branched candelabrum, as yet unlit. Daphne took a step toward it, and something squeaked and scampered away. Rats.

Mr. Carstairs glanced over his shoulder at her. "It appears we are not alone. Would you rather wait for me in the doorway? That way you could call suggestions to me."

For a moment, Daphne actually caught herself considering his suggestion. She didn't like rats. She could just imagine them, large and dirty with sharp teeth and scaly tails, running across her slippers . . .

She swallowed. "I am not so easily put off."

She looked about through the dimness. Against one wall, beneath the darkening windows, a variety of trunks and portmanteaux stood neatly stacked. On the opposite side of the chamber, seven huge oak casks took up most of the space. Against the far wall stood four more, and next to them a long wooden rack held several grime-encrusted bottles of wine. An arrangement of shelves, mostly empty except for a few dusty jars, extended to the corner.

She advanced another two paces, and this time encountered a cobweb. She batted it away in distaste.

"Unless our ghosts are partial to the bottle," Mr. Carstairs said, "I can see little that would draw them here."

Daphne found herself in complete agreement with him, and her enthusiasm for the project dropped to new depths. "Perhaps they come to keep the rats company."

Mr. Carstairs cast her a quizzical glance. "It was my idea, wasn't it? Shall we get on with it?" He strode toward the nearest wall, held the light close, and subjected the masonry to a thorough scrutiny.

Daphne watched for a moment, then joined him. "Sounding the stones? How delightful. Tell me, how does a hollow one sound?" She made an experimental rap and winced, then examined her knuckles. "I see we are in for a treat of no mean order."

He pushed a portmanteau toward the center of the room and knelt in the empty space, his gaze fixed on the stonework. "I'm searching for a section that might swing outward. Mortar that doesn't quite meet."

She collected the candelabrum, lit the wicks from the pocket luminary he handed her, then walked to the opposite end of the basement near the shelves and began a methodical check, working her way back to meet him. "What delightful ways you do think of to pass the time," she called over her shoulder.

He made no response, and they continued their work in silence broken only by the occasional scraping sound as he tested a suspect portion of the wall with his pocket knife. When they at last met near the middle, both admitted utter defeat. More companionably, they turned to the back wall with its wine, shelves, and casks.

Daphne eyed the huge oaken containers with dismay. "We won't have to move them, will we?"

"Not unless our ghosts do."

She brightened. "That wouldn't be practical, would it? Unless they move easily. I must say, that does seem more likely than any section of stonework, doesn't it?"

"If any of it moves." He tested the wooden wine rack, which did not so much as budge under his efforts.

She watched, frowning. "That person we saw in the attic didn't simply vanish. He had to go somewhere."

Mr. Carstairs gave the wood another, testing shove. "The passage—*if* one exists—may simply lead through a wall and out of a fireplace," he reminded her.

"Or even outside," she suggested.

He shook his head. "I've examined the exterior—at least, the ground floor." He turned his attention to the massive casks, then set his lantern on the floor so he could use both hands to pull and push.

The chill of the cellars crept through Daphne, and her fingers numbed. She held her candelabrum to give Mr. Carstairs the best light, and he thanked her absently. His attention remained on the cask. Together they moved on to the next one, and so around the gigantic room.

They reached the door again at last, having found nothing. Daphne rubbed her fingers, sore from their constant tapping and prying. She shivered, and wished she'd brought a shawl. Or a fireplace.

Mr. Carstairs strode back along the length of the chamber and returned with his lantern, frustration evident in every line of his tall frame. His hands and face, in the wavering light, showed streaks of dirt and cobwebs. Daphne leaned against the table, watching him, too spent to move at the moment. She must look as begrimed as he.

"More wasted time?" she asked.

His grin flashed, sudden and unexpected. "No effort is wasted, you know. Even negative results are still results. We have eliminated all the obvious possibilities down here, and may now, with a clear conscience, turn our attention to the rooms above."

"The warmer rooms above." She shivered. Slowly, she paced farther into the basement, then turned back to him. " 'From the topmost attic to the bottom-most cellar.' " The words sounded to her like a quotation, but she couldn't remember where she'd heard them. "That does make sense, doesn't it, from an aesthetic point of view? But it isn't practical. A passage linking the kitchens with the dining room would be more to the purpose—" She broke off, staring at him, awed by the possibilities she had just broached.

"The kitchens are down here, not in the attics," he pointed out. "And there is a servants' stair, so there would be no need to provide a hidden way for them to get about."

She sighed and leaned back against the trestle table behind her, half-sitting on it. "I feel so very dull-witted."

His smile warmed. "I have yet to find you so."

"We have yet to find *anything*." The cold and dampness closed about her, and she shivered again. "Is it not time to change for dinner?"

He drew out his pocket watch. "Still an hour or more. I think I'll take a turn about the grounds to see if anyone has been rigging up sheets with strings."

Outside, she told herself, it would be even colder and wetter than down here. But at least they'd be free of the oppressiveness, of the eternal musty odor. And the rats. "I'll come too," she announced.

For a moment she thought he'd protest, but he merely advised her to don appropriate footwear and a heavy pelisse. To this plan she found no objection, so together they mounted the back stairs to avoid any of the girls, whom they might startle with their disheveled appearance.

Five minutes after arriving at her room, Daphne set forth once more, her feet now protected by sturdy walking boots and her rumpled, dirty gown covered by her pelisse. As an added precaution, she wrapped a shawl about her head.

Mr. Carstairs waited for her in the corridor, a tall, broad-shouldered figure in his greatcoat, shadowed and mysterious in the near darkness. Awareness of the power of the man washed over her, and for a moment she hesitated. But she had nothing to fear, not from him at least. Or did she?

He had certainly begun to trouble her peace of mind.

His devilish humor, his courage and determination, his complete capability. Lord, the man was wasted in his cloistered retreat.

Warmth flooded her cheeks, but she kept gazing at him, aware of the deep currents that eddied beneath his still surface waters. He disguised his passions and concerns with a seemingly calm exterior, yet what tempests roiled within? She could sense his enjoyment of their puzzle—and much more, now that she knew him better. Determination burned deep inside, a driving force that could accomplish who knew what? He was a gentleman to be reckoned with, she realized—and very much a man.

She looked down, confused, and hurried past him to the stairs. What a shocking direction for her thoughts to take! Did she seek to cast him in a heroic role? As her chosen champion? He was certainly made in that vein. Not the dark and brooding Byronic type, but a knight in shining armor. Sir Galahad.

At the moment, though she knew it should, the comparison did not seem in the least absurd.

They let themselves out by the door at the back of the house, checked that all remained quiet at the stables, then started through the wood toward the drive. Stars glimmered in an early evening sky almost clear of clouds, and the pungent odor of pine permeated the crisp air. Daphne drew a deep breath, savoring the freshness.

Mr. Carstairs paused by the hedge nearest the library windows, studied it a moment, then peered up into the sky. "The moon will rise late tonight."

"Does that mean our ghosts will be out early?" Daphne took a step closer to him—for the warmth he generated.

"There's sufficient light from the stars to illuminate anything that moves. This should be a good night for haunting. In fact—"

He broke off, his stance rigid, listening. The next moment, Daphne heard the distant snap of a twig, as if some incautious foot had trod upon it. Mr. Carstairs grasped her shoulder and drew her back into the sheltering shadows of the hawthorn hedge, placing himself in front of her. She pushed around him to see.

His left arm relaxed its protective hold. "Sorry." Ruefulness sounded in his whispered word.

"You should be." But she didn't feel offended, only nervous, and very grateful for his solid presence.

Another twig snapped, then another, followed by the crunch of footsteps on gravel. Mr. Carstairs eased himself along the line of shrubs to their edge, and Daphne pressed close to him, trying to see over his shoulder.

In the pale glow of starlight, a bulky figure strode toward the Dower House, muffled from head to toe. No ghostly phantom this, to flit amongst the trees, but a very solid visitor. Mr. Carstairs stepped forward, and the man swung about to face them, drawing back a pace as if in alarm.

Daphne peered at the pale face that could barely be glimpsed from within its shrouding scarf and greatcoat. "Cousin George?" she hazarded.

"Daphne? Is that you?" The words came out heavy with relief. "My dear, you gave me quite a start." Then, his tone rife with suspicion, "Who is that with you?"

"Carstairs." That gentleman strolled forward. "Rather a cold night to be paying calls."

Mr. George Selwood wrapped his arms about himself. "That it is. I would have come earlier, but I've been gone for a couple of days. Up to London, you know. My tailor. Quite an important visit. Daphne, my dear, you will be enchanted with my new waistcoat. Dark green velvet, embroidered with silver threads. And—"

"You surely didn't come out this evening just to tell me about it," she interrupted.

He blinked at her. "No, of course not. I came to discover what has been going on here. But Daphne, I found the most exquisite snuff box—"

"Since you are so concerned, you will be glad to know the school has yet to close," Daphne informed him.

He brightened. "No new occurrences, then?" He peered at her, as if trying to read the answer in her face. "The ghost, you know."

"Our time has not been dull," Mr. Carstairs said in a masterly avoidance of a direct answer.

George blanched. "So it has been active," he breathed. "Dreadful, so very dreadful. My dear——" He turned to Daphne, but could only shake his head as if too overcome to speak. "Have you found no clues?" he managed at last.

Daphne glanced at Adrian. "There is more than one ghost, we have learned that much."

"More——" George broke off and shuddered. "More," he repeated, and shook his head. "How will this all end?"

"I wish we knew," came Mr. Carstairs's dry comment.

"Ghosts." George made it a pronouncement of doom. "If you've found no physical traces after all this time, they can only be real specters." He gripped Daphne's arm. "Perhaps it would be best if you all left—just for a little while, just long enough to let those poor troubled spirits settle once more into quietude."

"But the school——"

"Surely you can postpone your classes for a month?" His gaze held earnest entreaty.

Daphne shook her head. "We would lose our fees. And you," she added, pointedly, "would lose your rent."

He blinked, then swallowed whatever words had sprung to his tongue. "The rent," he repeated, crestfallen.

Daphne cast an anxious glance at Mr. Carstairs, then turned back to her cousin. "Will you not come inside? I am certain a glass of wine could be found for you."

"No, no, thank you." He straightened. "It is very kind of you, to be sure, but I'm quite all right. I mustn't disturb anyone. I know how busy our cousins must be at this time, what with the dinner hour approaching. It is not in the least necessary, really it isn't." Still murmuring assurances to himself, he headed back toward the Manor.

Daphne opened her mouth, then closed it again, and looked at Mr. Carstairs. "One might almost say he is upset," she said.

His lips twitched. "But why? Is it that we have *not* discovered anything—or that he fears we *might* discover something?"

Daphne shook her head. "You saw how he reacted to my comment about his rent. He needs it. The tenanted farms don't cover the half of his expenses."

"And so," Mr. Carstairs said, "it remains a mystery."

Chapter Ten

As soon as the young ladies and their schoolmistresses departed the dining room that evening, Adrian went to work on its walls. So far he'd checked thoroughly only the library on the ground floor; but the seemingly obvious room might have been avoided by the builders of any secret passage for just that reason—it would be too obvious. He would now, as time and opportunity permitted, repeat the process in every chamber until he found what he sought. Somewhere, there had to be an entrance into a passageway. Somewhere . . . and somehow. Whatever device triggered it must be cunningly concealed.

Shoving aside the nagging worry he should be spending an hour or two with Herodotus, he started on the paneling. This he examined inch by inch, running his fingers lightly over the surfaces to detect any unevenness. The process revealed nothing except an occasional knothole, which refused steadfastly to divulge any secrets. Tapping the walls produced only the most solid of sounds.

When the flames in the fireplace died to embers, he took the poker and prodded the interior stones. The coating of soot made the search difficult, and though he persevered, he could find no trace of any hidden mechanism—no metal rings, no decorative devices. Even the grating proved innocent. He rose, thoughtful, and wiped his begrimed hands on a napkin.

He had now ruled out both the library and the dining room. That still left any number of other rooms, but he refused to let the prospect daunt him. Like a horse with the bit firmly between its teeth, he was away and racing. Hot on the scent, as his hunting-mad friends would have it—though "faint but pursuing" was actually more like it. Well, he wouldn't turn tail.

The remainder of the evening he spent in the office, schoolrooms, and finally the drawing room, repeating the same process he had followed in the dining room. As he finished the last, he was forced to admit he had achieved nothing for his efforts except the growing conviction he made no progress whatsoever. As the hands of the clock now stood at seven minutes before two a.m., he gave in to exhaustion and called an end to his labors for the night. Tomorrow, he decided as he mounted the stairs to his room, he would return to the attic chamber and check every wall panel once more.

If the ghosts walked during the night, Adrian slept through them. He rose in the morning feeling considerably rested and far more his usual, determined self. Or stubborn and pig-headed self, as his sister Lizzie would fondly phrase it. Every part of him felt ready to tackle his self-appointed chore. Every part, that was, except his conscience. First, he had morning prayers to conduct, and his neglected dissertation weighed heavily on his mind.

As he stood at the front of the drawing room—a well-searched drawing room, he reminded himself—he allowed his gaze to travel over the girls. He had begun to know them a little, which ones were particular friends and were forever in each others' company, which ones could be counted upon to disrupt lessons. And which ones could be trusted not to hold the line.

With studious care, he ignored the languishing glance directed at him by Miss Fanny Breame, a ravishing beauty on the verge of her come-out. She counted the days—to anyone who could be brought to listen to her—and described the gentlemen she would have casting their hearts at her feet. Adrian could only be grateful that the marriage of his last sister meant it would be unnecessary for him to attend any of the numerous and boring social functions if he visited London during the coming Season.

Miss Marianne Snowdon, he noted, sat in a corner by herself, her gaze fixed intently upon him. Jane had taken the seat next to Daphne. Adrian began his reading, but his attention wandered between these two, normally so inseparable. Something had come between them. Perhaps Jane's learning that Marianne played one of the ghosts? Or did he become too fanciful? He would have to ask Daphne if Jane had confided in her.

When the girls at last filed from the room, Adrian caught Daphne's attention with a slight movement of his head. She lingered while the others disappeared next door to the breakfast parlor, then moved to join him.

"I don't know what has caused this rift between them." She hadn't needed to wait for his question, but hurried into speech. "Jane only says that she is quite disappointed in Marianne. Do you think it possible . . . ?" The question trailed off, but hope sounded in her voice.

"She *might* be one of our ghosts," Adrian said slowly, "but then who are the other two? I cannot imagine Jane—"

"No, of course not! Jane wouldn't. And Marianne has no other close friendships here." Daphne's pensive gaze rested on his face.

A high-pitched squeal of laughter sounded from the next room, and Daphne emitted a vexed exclamation. "I had best hurry. There is no telling what they will be about. Do you join us?"

"I shall take something in the kitchens." He held the door for her.

"How very wise," she said over her shoulder as she passed him.

Still smiling, Adrian went in search of a meal he could carry to the quiet of his room.

For once, Herodotus failed to hold his attention. Still, he kept doggedly at his work, forcing himself toward the minimum amount he required of himself each day to complete the dissertation on time. Occasionally he found himself pacing the tiny chamber, but not so much while his mind searched for the right word as to stare down into the snow-covered garden below and speculate about ladders.

Shortly before one o'clock he slammed his book closed in frustration and went down to the kitchens for rolls and cheese, then headed for the attic chamber to begin one more thorough search.

He entered the apartment, brooding, and his gaze wandered over the assortment of chests, wardrobes, trunks, tables, and chairs that crowded the area. Getting to the floorboards wouldn't be easy. He might as well start on the walls—again. He might have missed something before. After all, he'd now gained considerable experience in the art of sounding panels. Beginning where he stood in the doorway, he began once more to rap on the ancient oak.

He had covered half of the first side when he heard footsteps in the corridor, a muffled knocking on a door, then Daphne's soft voice saying, "I made quite certain he would be in his chamber."

Mr. Danvers's deep voice answered, but Adrian didn't catch the words. Pleased by this visit, he maneuvered his way back through the clutter to the door and opened it. The group in the hall turned, and he saw that Miss Elspeth accompanied Daphne and her uncle.

"There you are." Mr. Danvers hurried forward to take his hand. "I have come to help."

Daphne and Miss Elspeth at once volunteered their services as well, and Adrian ushered them inside and explained his purpose and how far he had gotten. Dutifully, each of his assistants selected a wall and went to work. For a very long while, silence reigned in the chamber, except for the constant tapping of knuckles on wood.

At last, with a frustrated exclamation, Miss Elspeth leaned against the back of a shrouded chair. "It is quite hopeless!" she exclaimed. "We cannot even reach the wall most of the time, and the furniture is far too heavy to move out of our way."

Daphne brushed off a trunk with her handkerchief, sneezed at the cloud of dust she raised, and perched on the top.

"Think of it as a challenge," Adrian suggested. "There are still," he added with a touch of apology, "the floorboards."

Mr. Danvers shook his head. "You said the figure disappeared from the center of the room? I simply cannot see how that could be possible. From next to a wall, yes. But *not* from the center of the room."

Miss Elspeth nodded slow agreement. "It had to have been an illusion. How could someone vanish otherwise, except by dropping directly into the room below? And that is occupied by—" She broke off, considering.

"By four of the younger girls, not one of whom is likely to be involved in this business," Daphne finished. "If Marianne or Louisa occupied that room, I'd feel certain we were on the right track."

Adrian studied the center of the room, frowning. "I can see no other solution," he said at last. "There might be a crawl space."

"A—" Mr. Danvers blinked. "But why?"

"This house was built at the time of Henry the Eighth, was it not?" Adrian glanced at Miss Elspeth for confirmation. "A priest's hole—or perhaps even a more cunning escape route—might well have been part of its plan."

Daphne leaned forward, intent, her eyes bright. "And the plans might have been destroyed to keep it secret."

"But our ghosts—or one of them, at least—know about it." Miss Elspeth looked from Adrian to Mr. Danvers, and faint color tinged her cheeks. "How? When we, who live here, do not?"

Adrian stretched his cramped muscles. "Is it possible your father knew of it but did not tell you?"

"My father—" Miss Elspeth's eyes flashed. "It would have been just like him. He would not have considered it ladylike for us to go clambering about in hidden passages. But if George had wanted—" She broke off, her eyes widening. "George? He and his friends were forever about the place, for Papa positively doted on him. Daphne, my love, that must be the answer!"

"If George were responsible," Daphne said slowly, "it would explain why he is so anxious to convince us the ghosts are real."

"Yet the hauntings continued while he was in London," Adrian pointed out.

Daphne's chin thrust out. "*If* he went."

"That should be easy enough to check." Adrian rubbed a thoughtful hand along his chin. "I'll ask around the stables. But for now—" He hesitated, frowning, then nodded to himself. "I had best clear everything from this room to examine the floorboards."

"Everything?" Daphne regarded him in dismay, then swallowed. "I suppose you are right, that would be easier than trying to shift things back and forth, for we would be certain to miss the right area in the confusion."

"We have nowhere to move it *to!*" Miss Elspeth protested. "The other storage room is as crowded as is this one. Or do you mean to carry all that heavy furniture down to the cellar?"

"I should have thought of this before," Adrian said, not answering Miss Elspeth. "The floor is the only place in here I have not thoroughly examined." He looked up from the clutter to find the others all watching him, and he smiled. "Why do you not all return to whatever it is you need to do? I'll begin shifting things in the other room to make more space."

Miss Elspeth rose, her expression grim. "We'll all help. And Moffett—no, he's far too old. Oh, dear. Perhaps the groom?"

"He'd be sure to talk." With a sigh, Daphne rose. "I fear it is up to us."

Adrian led the way, and the sight that met their tired gazes in the other lumber room did not raise their spirits. If anything, this chamber contained more abandoned relics than did the first, and the coating of dust lay thicker and undisturbed. Miss Elspeth advanced into the room and sneezed.

The work proved every bit as back-breaking as Adrian had anticipated. No one, it seemed, throughout the history of the Dower House, had ever thrown out so much as a single item. They discovered whole rooms of furniture, hardly damaged at all, stacked against the farthest wall. Gigantic trunks, crammed with ancient clothing, bundles of letters tied with ribands, mildewed books and torn linens, defied all efforts to lift them. Adrian shoved these as far back as possible, and stacked the lighter articles on top.

Their efforts lasted until the encroaching darkness forced Daphne to go in search of a lantern. Mr. Danvers and Miss Elspeth settled on chairs to await her return. Yet Adrian continued, pushing the heavy furniture into more convenient positions, straining muscles, determined to complete the task as quickly as possible. His search waited on this.

And what if it all proved in vain? What if, once he'd cleared the other chamber and ripped up the floorboards if he had to, he found no trace of any crawlspace or passage? To *fail* to find it—the thought didn't seem reasonable. What possibilities would that leave? A *real* ghost? No, a believable explanation required finding a hidden passage.

Daphne returned, and the others resumed their labors. At last, Mr. Danvers stacked the last broken lamp, and Adrian shoved an escritoire with a damaged leg against a fragmented bed frame. Miss Elspeth examined her begrimed hands in dismay.

Adrian leaned back against a wardrobe, flexed his stiff arms, and grinned at his exhausted helpers. "Shall we begin moving things in, now?"

Daphne regarded him with a kindling eye. "I do hope that is your idea of a joke."

"If it is," said Miss Elspeth, "I fail to see the humor in it."

Mr. Danvers shook his head. "This has become far more involved than I ever envisioned. I wish you would just call in the authorities."

"What could we tell them?" Miss Elspeth's frayed temper flared. "We have not the slightest shred of evidence that anything is going on here, except the growing number of pupils who have been frightened away, and the resulting dwindling of our income."

Mr. Danvers pursed his lips. "If this were nothing but a mere prank—"

"—the means to perpetrate it would have been easy to discover," Daphne finished. "We are well aware of that."

"Which implies there may be some danger involved." Mr. Danvers met Adrian's frowning gaze. "It really would be best if the ladies did not remain."

Miss Elspeth glared at him. "Are you suggesting we should move out?"

"Simply that it might be wisest if you do not come up to this floor."

"That is absolute nonsense!" She rose to her feet and shook out her skirts, setting motes of dust flying in the lantern light. "This has been going on for a little over two months now, and not one of us has come to any

148

harm. And so far, I might add, we have managed quite well on our own—without outside interference." With that, she stalked from the chamber.

Adrian watched the door slam behind her. "Where have I heard those sentiments before?" he mused.

Daphne glared at him. "How can you be so—so—" She shook her head, at a loss for words. "You're *enjoying* this," she accused.

"Would you rather I let it wear down my temper?"

She drew in a shaking breath. "No. The rest of us have become quite ill-natured enough with exhaustion." She used the top of an aged trunk to help herself rise. "Not to mention with hunger. Uncle Thaddeus, you will stay to dine, will you not?"

"Your cousin—" he began.

"My cousin will be quite distraught if you leave. I assure you, she rarely loses her temper, and will now be suffering agonies of remorse. It would be most unkind of you to leave without permitting her to make amends."

"If you are quite certain . . ." He allowed his niece to lead him downstairs to the library for a revivifying cordial.

Miss Elspeth, when she descended the stairs at last, wore a silk gown of a very flattering shade of violet. Her long hair she wore in her usual crown, but braided with matching silk ribands. The effect, Adrian noted with appreciation, was stunning. Mr. Danvers seemed to notice, as well. He went forward, taking her hand and bowing over it with a courtly grace that sat well on him.

As he straightened, Miss Elspeth's gaze faltered for the first time. "You must forgive me," she said, her soft voice barely carrying to where Adrian stood nearby. "I spoke in haste—"

"And in exhaustion. But you were quite right. I have no right to interfere."

"Nor I to be so rude, when you meant well." Somehow, her hand had become tucked within the curve of Mr. Danvers's elbow. He led her toward a chair and

149

himself poured her a glass of sherry—a luxury only offered on rare and special occasions at the school.

Mr. Danvers took his leave directly after the meal, pleading the length of his drive and an approaching storm as his excuse. Adrian saw him to the stable, then prowled the grounds, inspecting for artificial contrivances to aid the haunting. Tonight, though, no ghostly figures flitted in and out of the shrubbery. Of course, he was probably hours too early for that. With a sigh, he returned indoors. He'd have to make his tour of inspection closer to the midnight hour. In the interim, Herodotus awaited.

The sounds of someone walking down the hall interrupted his translation some time later. He stiffened, then heard Daphne's door open, then shut behind her. She must be turning in for the night. He checked his clock, surprised to see it was almost eleven-thirty. Time to resume his duties as night watchman. He stacked his papers neatly, dragged on his boots and greatcoat, and went out.

A three-quarter moon peeped out at him, only to vanish again behind a fast-moving cloud. He watched for a minute, but it did not reappear. Snow again at any moment, he supposed. He slipped behind the line of trees, keeping out of sight of the house, and circled the building.

Nothing unusual met his searching gaze, no ghostly apparitions hovered before him. Somewhere overhead, an owl hooted its nocturnal call to be answered, some distance away, by another. Peace enveloped the landscape—for the moment, at least.

He returned indoors by the rear entrance, then hesitated, one foot on the bottom step. Energy surged through him where he knew he should be exhausted from the day's labors. Restlessness, that was it. In the back of his mind, he remained convinced the answers lay just beyond his grasp, as if he had missed something important yet obvious.

But what could he do now? Move the furniture from that lumber room? He'd wake the whole household if he tried.

Well, if he couldn't accomplish anything by going up, he'd go down. He retraced his steps to the back premises, picked up the lantern that hung near the door, and descended the steps to the basement.

He entered the cavernous chamber, and the chill, damp air wrapped about him. His light cast wavering shadows, and from everywhere came the scurrying rustle of rats scampering for cover. Ignoring them, he strode forward, lantern held high. It would help, of course, if he knew for what he looked.

He paced to the far end, then stood for a long minute in silence, staring at the row of wine and ale casks. If he were building a secret stair, he would put it into one of these. Yet he had found no mechanism, nothing that indicated they ever had held anything but alcoholic—not other-worldly—spirits.

The rumbling noise must have been going on for several minutes before he became aware of it. It grew on his consciousness, an indistinct, elusive sound, nothing he could name. He roused from his contemplation and looked around, but could detect nothing different. No new lights glowed—but then his own provided enough illumination for anyone else who might have entered the basement to see without needing an additional one.

Had someone joined him? He strode toward the door, and realized the sound faded. Behind him? Curious, he backed up a pace, and it rose in volume—though only enough to be just barely audible. He turned, his fascinated gaze resting on the stone wall at the rear, half covered in huge oaken casks, half in wine racks and shelves. Without making a sound, he set the lantern on the floor, then set his ear against the first cask.

Nothing. He moved on to the next, then the third

151

and the fourth. Silence from each. Yet the sound continued, a low mumbling noise, vague and unidentifiable.

If it didn't come from the casks, what did that leave? Against all logic, he turned to the wine rack. Nothing could be concealed there. Yet . . .

He unloaded the several bottles that filled the nearest section, moving them out of his way. This done, he leaned between the shelves, positioning his ear as close to the dank stone wall as he could.

The mumble resolved itself into the rumbling tones of two voices.

Chapter Eleven

Voices. Adrian studied the wall, his thoughts racing. *Voices?* That didn't seem possible. He moved away from the slimy stones and studied them in thoughtful silence. The mumbling sound continued, fainter and irregular now, but still present.

Voices. As far as he knew, nothing lay behind that wall except solid earth. And unless the worms and moles had gotten noisier of late, he had better look for another source.

He moved back a pace, scanning the heavy timbers of the ceiling a good six feet above his head. Could it be coming from the next floor up? A couple of students who had sneaked downstairs after everyone should be abed? Yet even if several of them clustered about a fireplace, surely sound traveled upward, not down.

Of course, this might be some strange effect of the old house, projecting noises that actually came from behind him, in the kitchens. Yet that room, as well as the pantries beyond, had been empty when he came down. Nor had he heard anything like this on his previous expedition to the cellar when the kitchens *had* been occupied.

He took another pace back, his gaze moving to the narrow line of windows which marked the ground level more than four feet above his head. Someone outside? He tested the shelves, found them solidly built, and hauled himself up until he faced one of the panes squarely.

For a moment, he heard nothing. Then a brief spate of mumbled sound followed. Only he would swear it came from below him, not through the glass. Below, through a stone barrier backed only by solid ground. Unless the ground wasn't so very solid after all.

He lowered himself to the stone floor and pressed his ear once more to the dank wall. Nothing, now, only the sort of silence that had been likened to that of a grave. Had someone been sealed up behind this wall, and his spirit now roamed the Seminary?

As that thought flickered through his mind, he grinned. It was worthy of his sister Augusta, who had always let her romantic, nonsensical notions carry her away. No, this would have a simple explanation. All he had to do was find it.

His first instinct, to waken the Selwood ladies and ask about the possibility of another room beyond the cellar, he checked with difficulty. He would hardly get coherent answers out of anyone at this hour. He would do better to catch some sleep himself and tackle the problem fresh in the morning. At least then he might think more clearly and make some sense out of it all.

Before retiring to his own chamber, he checked the lumber room one last time. Everything appeared undisturbed, just the way they had left it after their search earlier. All quiet. He could sleep with a clear conscience.

Yet he lay awake for a very long time.

When he at last dragged his eyes open once more, sunshine filled his tiny chamber. He groaned, stretched his stiff muscles, then sat up, alert. What time was it, anyway? He fumbled for his watch, saw the hands standing just short of ten o'clock, and sprang out of bed. Why hadn't someone called him?

He splashed cold water on his face, then scrambled into clothes, taking time only to ensure he did not present a harum-scarum appearance. It must have been going on four before he sought his room last night, and he had been stinting himself on sleep for too long. But ten? He'd never been abed so late in the morning in his life.

He took the stairs two at a time, and found everyone gathered in the drawing room. Apparently, all had proceeded apace without him. Sunday, he realized in relief. They must have gone to church, leaving him to sleep.

Miss Elspeth sat with some of the young ladies, hands clenched in her lap, while Miss Sophronia assisted the redoubtable Miss Fanny Breame through a ragged rendition of a ballad on the pianoforte. Several of the other pupils gathered about Miss Beatrice, who appeared to be offering criticism on a stack of papers she held. Daphne sat near a multi-branched candelabrum, hemming a handkerchief with neat stitches.

She looked up at his entrance, and started to set aside her sewing. He shook his head, and turned to the youngest of her three cousins. "Miss Elspeth?"

She turned to him with eagerness, as if anything would be better than listening to the painful chords that issued from the elderly instrument. She held up a hand to prevent him from speaking, then led the way from the room and closed the door behind them with decided emphasis. "That child is hopeless," she said by way of explanation. "Now, what may I do for you? And I can only hope it will take some little time. Enough, at least, so I need not go back in there until Miss Breame has finished."

"Only tell me if there at any time could have been another room attached to the cellars."

"Another—" She broke off and her eyes narrowed. "Have you found something? A hollow sound, perhaps?"

"A sound, yes, but not hollow." He told her of the voices.

"If only we could find the building plans." Miss Elspeth stared into space for a long moment, then shook her head. "They might be at the Manor, I suppose."

Adrian paced the length of the hall, then turned to face her. "I would rather not ask for them," he said at last.

Miss Elspeth's hazel eyes clouded. "No, I suppose you cannot. But it is quite dreadful suspecting my own cousin."

"There is no proof he is involved," he reminded her. "I merely would rather not take any chances."

"But Cousin George—" The furrows deepened in her brow. "No, the school provides his income. He *cannot* wish us harm."

The door to the drawing room opened, and Miss Beatrice came out, carrying her handful of student papers. She stopped on the threshold and regarded them with frowning intensity. "This is where you disappeared to, Elspeth. What is the matter?"

Three of the girls emerged into the hall, and Adrian prudently led the way to the office where they could talk without disruption. They seated themselves about the desks, and in as few words as possible, he explained.

Miss Beatrice frowned as she fingered the pages she still held. "I wonder—" she began, then broke off.

"Have you thought of something?" Her sister regarded her with anticipation.

"Just a ridiculous old tale my uncle used to tell. To scare us, I make no doubt. All nonsense, of course—at least Papa always said so."

"What is?" Adrian asked.

"The underground passage. My uncle claimed it went all the way from the Manor over to here, but we never could find any trace of it. You'd be too young to remember, Elspeth, but Sophronia and I spent months hunting for it. Sophronia cried when we realized it was all a hum."

"There is quite often a grain of truth in every story." Adrian leaned back in his chair, considering. "There might once have been such a passage."

Miss Beatrice snorted. "If there was, must have been

sealed off long ago, certainly before we ever searched for it. Unsafe, I should think."

Adrian nodded, his certainty filling him with satisfaction. "It's possible it has been walled shut at this end, but it's Lombard Street to a China orange it's been opened on the other."

"If only we might try it from *that* side." Miss Elspeth sat forward, her expression bright with her enthusiasm. "Would this explain our ghosts? Someone trying to find—or force—the exit on this side?"

"It might," Adrian said, but kept his further reflections to himself. Such an explanation seemed less than satisfactory. A simple passageway couldn't be important enough to warrant the elaborate hauntings to which they'd been subjected. It would be an oddity, nothing more.

Girls' voices, raised in argument in the corridor, recalled the ladies to their duties. They hurried out, leaving Adrian seated before the great mahogany desk, puzzling out possibilities. When the door opened a few minutes later, he heard it, but made no response. Silence stretched on, but the arrival had broken his concentration. He looked up, and found Daphne studying him, her delicate brow furrowed.

"Has something occurred?" She took a step into the room. "You look so—so solemn."

He repeated his tale, adding the revelations made by the Selwood sisters, and her eyes widened. "An underground passage," she breathed. "A tunnel! What a horrid thought."

He raised his eyebrows. "Why?"

A very becoming flush touched her cheeks. "Just the idea of being so enclosed, I suppose. I know it's silly." She perched on the edge of the chair at his side. "How do you think it might be involved? No ghostly apparitions have ever been spotted near the cellars. Only in the gardens—and by us, once, in the attic."

"Just because we haven't seen them doesn't mean they haven't been here," he pointed out.

157

Her eyes widened. "What if the secret way from the attics lets out not anywhere in *this* house, but in the underground passage beyond?"

He rubbed his chin. "That might explain parts of it."

"But not enough?" Her expression fell.

"It would mean the underground passage would have to have been planned at the time the Dower House was built. That could, of course, very well be the case. But I would be willing to wager there is also an entry in the basement. And if we find the hidden door to one passage, we may well have found the one to the other."

Daphne nodded, her gaze fixed on his face. "It *must* be used by our ghost for making its escape."

"But if it only leads to the Manor?"

"Then—" Daphne stared at him, and her eagerness faded. "Oh. You are quite right. What possible reason could Cousin George have for playing such tricks?"

Adrian opened his mouth, then closed it again. Having met the gentleman, he did not share Daphne's conviction of his innocence. Yet it hardly behooved him to cast aspersions on one of her relatives based on nothing more than personal opinion. He had no proof—and for Daphne's sake, he hoped he was mistaken.

"There is undoubtedly a secret passage between the attics and the cellars," Daphne went on. "If only we could find it!" She rose and paced back and forth between the door and the hearth, as if unable to remain still.

Adrian's gaze followed her delicate form, then came to rest on her clouded face with the full lips and large, sparkling eyes. Once more, he found himself caught up in the innate sweetness of her expression. She roused all his protective instincts—and she was about as helpless as a fox. Keen and intelligent, that was Miss Daphne Selwood. Perfectly capable and poised, and not in the least in need of a championing knight errant, especially not one given over to the life of a scholar.

Marriage, as his sister Lizzie often informed him in that lofty tone of hers, was not for everybody. Of course, she'd meant herself, not him. All three of his sisters had indulged in a spot of matchmaking where he was concerned—and all three, even the determined Lizzie, had given it up as hopeless. Even had he not embraced the single life of an Oxford don, no young lady in her right mind would choose to cloister herself away with a man who found London society a dead bore. How could any female admire mere scholarly achievements when other gentlemen flaunted their abilities with their neck-or-nothing riding on the hunting field or set society astir with their cutting wit or the intricacies of their neckcloths?

Abruptly he rose, excused himself on account of Herodotus, and made for his own chamber, calling himself every kind of fool. With considerable force, he reminded himself that the life he had chosen suited him to perfection. The last thing he needed—or wanted!—would be to leave Oxford—or for that matter to have some fluttery female about who would misplace his notes and disturb his concentration.

Unfortunately, he found Daphne, while not in the least fluttery, already distracted him in a very enticing manner and played havoc with his long-laid plans for his orderly—and solitary—future. He sat for a long while staring at the page printed in Greek before him, and tried to force all thoughts from his mind except Herodotus and his rapidly approaching deadline. He almost succeeded.

But not quite.

A knock sounded on his door less than an hour later. He opened it to find Miss Beatrice, her stance purposeful, her eyes gleaming.

She cleared her throat and fixed her penetrating regard on him. "Mr. Carstairs, several of our young ladies have expressed an overwhelming desire to learn a little Latin or Greek."

"Have they?" He hoped his lack of enthusiasm didn't sound in his voice.

The woman gave a bark of laughter. "I doubt scholarship is on their minds. Just want to escape their regular studies. And spend time with a gentleman."

Adrian grinned. "I feel certain a dancing master would be preferable to a mere clergyman."

"They're being philosophical," Miss Beatrice said.

"You mean they are willing to settle for what they can get."

Miss Beatrice nodded. "One lesson should prove more than enough to discourage them. Won't mind, will you? Know it's an imposition, but they're becoming importunate."

"And you would be glad of a break?"

"We all would," Miss Beatrice pronounced with considerable feeling.

If he were to take time away from his dissertation, he should really spend it at work in the attic chamber. But the plea patent in Miss Beatrice's normally brusque voice could not be ignored. Thus a short while later, Adrian found himself ensconced in one of the schoolrooms, surrounded by a flock of eager, giggling girls, recounting to them some of the more decorous of the Classical myths. The presence of Daphne might have made the situation bearable, but she did not put in an appearance. She was probably only too glad to be free of her charges, as well.

He escaped with considerable relief after a little more than an hour and returned to his own chamber to spend a few hours crossing Egypt with Herodotus. For once, though, this entertaining—if somewhat difficult—occupation failed to hold his enthusiasm. His thoughts kept straying to the basement and the voices heard beyond that wall in an area where nothing should exist except earth.

An underground passageway. Was one feasible, he wondered? How long would it have to be? There was one way to find out.

He donned his boots and greatcoat, and slipped down

the stairs to the library where he silently let himself out into the afternoon chill. He could hardly have chosen a more pleasant time for a tramp through the woods. The sun shone, brilliant and inviting in the clear sky. Only the icy nip in the air and the lung-chilling smell of dampness warned of more snow to come.

He shoved his hands deep into his pockets and paced far enough from the Dower House to obtain a clear view of the surrounding area. At the edge of the building, where the cellar windows rose three feet above the ground, someone long ago had planted a hawthorn hedge, which, judging from its height and breadth, thrived. Snow covered the ground everywhere in swirling heaps, trapped between fallen branches by the heavy winds.

Adrian frowned. If he were to play ghost, he would have picked a balmy spring eve, not the depths of a frozen winter's night. Which meant there must be a reason for three unknown individuals to engage in so uncomfortable a pursuit. *But what?*

That line of thought had already proved fruitless. He might as well concentrate on this possibility of a tunnel.

He scanned the garden and the shrub-edged wood that lay between the Dower House and the Manor, then on impulse paced the distance as well as he could with so many limbed obstacles in the way. After sixty or so yards, he paused. Only about half again that distance now separated him from the huge columned facade of the Manor House. He had thought it farther—a trick of the trees, he decided.

It would be difficult, but not impossible, to dig the underground passage—especially if it were shored up with timber, possibly even archways, to prevent it from collapsing.

If, indeed, it existed. Yet the more he thought about it, about the voices, the more likely he found it to be.

He looked down at the snow-littered path. He probably stood on top of the tunnel at this very moment The thought pleased the speculative turn of his mind.

He turned his attention back to the Manor. As with the Dower House, a line of windows showed at ground level, permitting daylight to shine into the basements. That implied similar construction. Good.

After a minute more, he headed deeper into the wood. Curious, and possibly hostile, eyes might well watch him. He stood a better chance of discovering what occurred if his ghosts didn't know he had learned one of their secrets.

If, indeed, he had.

A deep voice hailed him, seconded by another, and he looked up to see George Selwood and Squire Romney riding toward him. Selwood's chestnut, a great brute of a creature, plodded along, head lowered, as if the crisp air meant nothing to it beyond an impending attack of rheumatics. Romney's black, a tall, lanky animal, raw boned with a Roman nose and broad chest, swung its head from side to side, snatching at the bit. A showy beast, but short in the pastern and seemingly touched in the wind. The two men left the graveled drive and allowed their horses to pick their way through the drifts of snow and fallen branches, pulling up at last at his side.

"Good afternoon," Romney said. "Forgive me for not remaining, won't you? Just seeing Selwood back. Hunters to condition, you know. Melton, that's the place for me." With a wave of his gloved hand, he barely touched his heel to his mount's side, and the black lurched forward.

Selwood watched their retreat, then shook his head. "He's such a thruster, you know. He's bound to break his neck in the field one of these days. I keep telling him so, but he just won't listen. I never could understand why he's so hunting mad. So much mud." He wrinkled his nose in distaste.

Adrian's gaze lingered on the black's jolting stride. "Romney looks like he knows what he's doing."

A short laugh escaped Selwood. "Lord, the man *always* knows what he's doing. He's up to every rig and row in Town, as they say. But——" His face clouded, then he forged on. "The thing is, he don't always hold the line. He's a gamester, you know. He bets on the most outrageous things."

"Many gentlemen do."

Selwood hunched a shoulder. "The devil's in it, I'm as much to blame as he is, this time. I shouldn't have done it, there's no need to tell me that, but we were in our cups, you see. It started as just a discussion, then became a friendly disagreement. The next thing you knew, we'd made the wager, and—well, there it is."

"What is?" Adrian smoothed a hand over the chestnut's neck, then gently fended off the great equine head in its search for a rubbing post.

"About the Seminary." Selwood looked miserable. "Romney didn't think they could remain open. I laid a monkey they could. Well, they're my cousins. I had to support them. You see how it is."

"Certainly." Adrian kept back his smile. "Though I cannot but think they might not like being the subject of a wager."

"No. But—well, it's more than that. I don't like to say it, but it's been weighing on my mind. I thought it best to tell someone." Selwood met Adrian's gaze. "He never loses, you see. *Never.* He's got quite a reputation for it. I can't see him wanting to start now, especially when he's being dunned at his door."

Adrian caught the chestnut's bridle and once more averted a threatened rub. "Strapped for the ready, is he?"

"Oh, he'll come about, never fear. He always does. Especially with his uncanny way with wagers." George shook his head. "Don't you ever bet against him, that's my advice. It's a good way to come home by Weeping Cross." With that he turned his mount and made his de-

163

jected way toward the Manor and the spacious stable behind.

So Squire Romney never lost a bet. Adrian turned his steps toward the lane beyond the spinney; he needed a brisk walk to clear his head. Would the Squire go to such extremes as haunting the Seminary just to win a ridiculous wager?

Adrian bent to pick up a broken branch, then slapped it against his leg as he quickened his pace. What, he wondered, might the terms of that wager be? He could only be sorry they didn't record it in the betting book at White's. A monkey wasn't a staggering sum of money— yet in spite of the Squire's currently being under the hatches, the money might not be the issue. Selwood said Romney never lost a wager. The man possessed a determined streak—but would he go so far as to ruin the school—and the Selwood ladies—just to maintain his unblemished track record?

He continued his walk, but came no closer to finding any answers.

When he at last slipped once more into the library, Daphne rose from a chair before the hearth, alert and eager as she laid her mending aside. "What have you been about?"

Wisps of dark hair escaped her chignon, brushing her cheek, and he suppressed an urge to smooth them away. "Just some measuring. The houses are not situated so far apart as to make the existence of an underground passage out of the question."

Her face brightened. "Then we are getting somewhere at last!"

He said nothing. The glint that danced in the depths of her eyes fascinated him, and he hated to dispel it.

Her expression sobered. "Oh, pray do not say we have gained *nothing*."

"Something, perhaps," he temporized. "I must now determine to what use—if any—this passage is being put—if it even exists."

"Oh." She considered a moment. "Have you made plans?"

"If you will keep watch on our attic, I believe I shall do best to go to the Manor and see if anyone goes down into the cellars this night."

Tiny creases formed once more in her brow. "If only we could actually get inside, we might be able to find the opening on that end. Do you not think——"

"I do not!" he said quickly. "You will remain here." Now, he guessed, would not be the time to tell her that an unauthorized exploration of the Manor's basement was exactly what he had in mind. She would insist upon coming with him; and while he couldn't imagine her cousin George actually doing her any harm, he couldn't like any of this. No, he would rather she stayed behind, in safety.

Aloud, he added, "You may spend your time devising a way to introduce me into the house without letting your cousin know what we suspect. Will you do that? And meanwhile, one of us must watch the attic for our ghostly visitor. It would be a shocking thing if he came to call and no one was there to receive him. Of course, if you would rather huddle beneath your cousin's windows in this weather . . ." He let his sentence trail off.

She cast him a suspicious look, but accepted the post in the attic.

He would have to find a hiding place near the Manor at an early hour, he decided. If someone came, he wanted to be there to see the arrival. If someone were already there, he wanted a chance to observe that person before he took himself down into the basements—providing, of course, that was what he would do. The prospect of sitting in the snow for four hours or more didn't appeal in the least to him, but he saw no hope for it.

The clock in the library showed the time to be not quite nine as he set off that evening. He stepped out into the freezing night, shrugging into his greatcoat and fastening the buttons. He could use a little more certainty in this endeavor, he decided as he trudged through the dark. It would help if he had definite evidence, some reason to *know* he would actually see something, that someone might actually descend to the cellars and disappear into a tunnel, that he did not propose to spend a freezing and uncomfortable night for nothing. But then he could have called in the authorities.

He had seen no ghostly activity at all for the past couple of days, not since that night when three specters had haunted the garden. That meant they were long overdue for another "visitation." Three days had been the longest interval so far between sightings—except for when the Seminary had been all but vacant for the Christmas holidays.

He hunched his shoulders deeper into his greatcoat. At least he'd assured that Daphne would be somewhat warmer and more comfortable. He wouldn't have minded her company on what promised to be a very long and boring vigil, but it was better for her this way. But then he had the worry that the ghost would pop up at her in the attic instead of out here somewhere.

He neared the Manor and slipped deeper into the shadows provided by the shrubs and trees. Darkness clouded the ground floor windows, except for three or the far end of the house. No light at all shone through the cellar casements.

By the dim glow of the waning moon, he made his way around to the back of the house. At once, he saw the lights gleaming from the basement windows on this side. Curious, he crept closer, watching his step to avoid any tell-tale snapping of twigs that might attract attention. At last, he peered inside to see a woman of ample proportions standing behind a maid while the girl dried a cooking pot. He'd found the kitchens.

A fire burned high in the hearth, promising a warmth Adrian was far from feeling. A huge kettle of water simmered over it, sending steam wafting into the air. On the long table nearby stood a fresh loaf of bread; he could almost smell it.

It would be a safe bet, he told himself, that it was far more comfortable within than without. A glass of hot rum would go very well, right about now. He dragged himself from the tempting scene and continued along the back of the house. It wouldn't be safe to seek an entrance while the servants were still up and about.

No other lights greeted him, except for one two stories up. He continued with caution around the corner, making his way to the front once more, toward the first window showing the flickering glow of candles. Gripping the lower edge of the casement, he raised himself up as high as he could. Had he been even an inch shorter, he realized, he would not have been able to see inside. It proved to be a wasted effort, though; the room, a salon, stood empty.

At his next attempt he had more luck. Mr. George Selwood, garbed in yellow-striped, ankle-length pantaloons, Turkish slippers, and a pale blue brocade dressing gown, sat in a wingback chair before a blazing fire, idly turning the pages of a periodical. Beside him on an occasional table stood a decanter and a glass. He bore every appearance of a gentleman prepared to spend a quiet, comfortable evening.

Adrian wished he might do the same. He dropped silently to the ground, rubbed some feeling back into his frozen hands, and crept once more into the shadows. Resigned to a long, cold, and probably pointless wait, he settled on a bench deep enough within a shrubbery to provide cover, not only from prying eyes but from the wind, as well.

The cold kept him from any danger of falling asleep at his post. He shifted his position so that he could see along the drive. If any ghost chose to caper about the garden, either here or at the Dower House, he should be able to see it.

And if it instead appeared in the attic, where Daphne

167

waited. . . . He rejected that thought, refusing to allow that fear to eat at his mind. So far, the ghosts had done no one any actual physical harm. Daphne would be safe. Probably, the ghost would avoid the attic now that they had discovered its presence there.

Movement inside the bookroom caught Adrian's attention. A portly man had entered—a butler, by his appearance. Selwood waved him away, probably giving him permission to lock up for the night. If anything peculiar were to happen, it seemed likeliest it would occur after the servants had gone to bed. Unless . . .

He straightened. Could the servants be using the underground passageway for something? *They* would have no reason to worry about the closing of Selwood Seminary. And George Selwood might know nothing about it.

He slipped from his position, following as best he could the progress of the butler. He heard the rattle of the windows as the man checked them, and the bolt being thrown at the great front door. So far, nothing suspicious.

At last, the house settled into a stillness broken only by the leaping flames in the library hearth. Adrian found a position where he could see into that window. Selwood remained in his chair, though now the paper lay in a heap on the Aubusson carpet and he held the wine glass in his hand. The man stifled a yawn and cast a frowning look at the mantel clock, then hunched deeper into his chair. Waiting for something, perhaps?

Adrian's interest stirred once more. He'd probably been wrong about the servants. He could see no reason for Selwood to sit up so late, obviously sleepy, unless he expected a visitor. Gritting his teeth against the icy wind, Adrian remained alert for other subtle signs that something might yet occur.

The minutes crawled by, but Selwood's continued glances at the clock kept Adrian's spirits rising. After all this fruitless waiting and searching, the prospect of action—even of just learning something definite—enthused him. The clouds gathered overhead, and snow began to drift about him. He couldn't see a clock himself, but the layering of white on his arms told its own tale. Selwood rose, but Adrian's hopes faded when the man only threw another log on the fire.

Adrian stamped his feet, trying to work some feeling into them, and thought of Daphne. He hoped she'd given up by now and sought the warmth of her bed. Yet she was not a quitter.

He had been thinking for some time he should have brought a flask of a restorative—brandy had appealed at first, but at the moment a hot rum toddy had taken precedence—when he became aware of the crunching of gravel. He turned to see two horsemen crossing the drive. Drawing farther back behind a tree, he watched them ride up to the house and one swing to the ground. The other, who slumped negligently in his saddle, held both mounts while the first climbed the steps and rapped on the front door.

In growing satisfaction, Adrian noted their rough garments and general air of slovenliness. These were far from genteel visitors for a gentleman's country estate. Not at all the sort of acquaintances to be cultivated by a dandy like Selwood. And that could only be of interest to Adrian.

In the library, Selwood sprang to his feet and raced from the room. Adrian, his slow grin of enjoyment growing, repositioned himself for a better view of the front door. Barely a minute later, it swung wide and the disreputable visitor pushed his way inside. Selwood backed away, his expression obscured by distance and shadow. His manner, though, made his sentiments clear.

Now, why should George Selwood be frightened of these men? Was this not the visitor he expected? Adrian moved closer, sure now he had discovered something of importance.

But what, exactly?

Chapter Twelve

Adrian followed the line of shrubbery, circling as close as he could to the front doorstep while still remaining out of sight. The Manor had not been designed with observation in mind, he noted; an open expanse of lawn, now white and humped with snowy drifts, separated him from the drive and the house. If he advanced any farther, the men could not help but see him. Frustrated, he could do nothing but watch.

The man holding the horses rubbed his arms and called an occasional desultory request to " 'Urry along, there" to his comrade. The other man stood just inside the doorway as if he were quite at home. Not their first visit, Adrian decided. But what brought them?

George Selwood backed another step away as the wiry man before him wagged a finger in his face. Adrian peered through the darkness, wishing he could make out Selwood's expression—*any* of their expressions—or hear more than the sharp tones of the voices. Not a single clear word reached him. Still, he knew the two men argued; that much was obvious.

Selwood drew something from his pocket—a bag? a purse?—and held it out to the rough figure who towered over him. The man gave a sharp crack of laughter and shoved Selwood's hand away. More low-voiced argument followed, and Adrian cast a measuring glance at the mounted ruffian. He could probably knock him out with little trouble—he'd always had an excellent aim with a rock—but it would cause a commotion. He could see no way to do it without alerting Selwood and his companion they had an observer.

Seething at this feeling of helplessness, Adrian turned his mind to speculation on the identity of these two midnight visitors. Their host seemed to be afraid of them. So who were these men of obviously low order—and what hold did they have over Mr. George Selwood? He could see these two haunting the school for some fell purpose, frightening people away. *But why?*

Adrian cast a thoughtful glance back toward the Dower House and froze. There, in the middle of the drive, stood a ghostly figure. It hesitated a moment, then seemed to float along the line of hedges, then capered for a moment in the center of the garden.

Adrian's glance flew to the two ruffians, then back to the specter. A moment ago he would have sworn these men were responsible. Or was this third their accomplice? The men—Selwood included—appeared oblivious to what went on less than a hundred yards away. Surely, if the ghost were one of their group, those two visitors would watch it, at least cast surreptitious glances in its direction even if they wished to keep its presence secret from Selwood.

The specter faded into the trees, and Adrian made his decision. He could do no good here, listening from too far away to hear anything; but he stood a very good chance of catching that ghost. He set off in silent pursuit, cold and stiff from his long vigil, but glad to have something to do that might help end this whole ridiculous game.

Except Selwood hadn't looked as if he thought this a ridiculous game. His manner had portrayed real fear. All the more reason to get to the bottom of this.

Keeping part of his attention on his footing and the rest on the ghost, he crept along the line of trees. As he slipped from shadow to shadow, his grim enjoyment continued to rise, buoying him. Tonight he would catch the fellow, and demand a full explanation.

The ghost emerged from behind a sheltering hedge and ran toward the French door that led into the library, then swerved away, following the line of windows. Occasionally it leapt into the air as if to aid itself in seeing inside. Then it crossed the drive, this time vanishing into the trees.

Adrian hesitated, then selected for himself an ancient oak where he could blend into the darkness and remain hidden. His steady gaze searched the night for signs of movement, some clue as to where his ghost had gone. He scanned the trees, the undergrowth, the bushes . . . *there*. The flutter of white caught his attention, and a slow, determined smile tugged at the corners of his mouth. He had it.

With every measure of stealth he could muster, he eased from his hiding place, then ducked low and moved as swiftly and directly as prudence allowed, always keeping the glimmer of sheeting—or whatever it was—in sight. Somewhat to his surprise, it remained in one place, making no attempt to continue its ghostly prowls. Had a piece of fabric been torn off by the grasping twigs of a bare limb? If so, his ghost might be escaping in an entirely different direction.

He looked over his shoulder, and caught a glimpse of the shrouded figure breaking through the line of trees and heading once more for the Dower House. He'd let himself be fooled. Disgusted, Adrian shifted, reorienting on his new target—when the glimmer of white he'd been stalking vanished, only to reappear again several feet away. It *was* a person.

With a muttered word somewhat questionable for one of his calling, Adrian pulled back into the concealing darkness of the shrubs to regroup. He could not reach that capering specter without being seen by the other— and possibly by both. He would, though, have that first one, and before many more minutes passed.

The ghostly shape moved again, and Adrian eased himself through the underbrush, circling around to come on it from behind. Closer he crept; he could see the pale, trailing fabric where it touched the snow-covered ground, the wrap about the head that disguised all features. Elation filled him as he inched ever nearer, his hands clenching into fists, then relaxing, flexing, preparing to grab. Only a little farther . . .

He stepped with care, taking no chances, keeping complete silence. . . . Springing, he tackled the person about the upper legs, knocking them both to the ground.

A terrified sound emitted from his victim, half scream and half gasp. The body seemed surprisingly slight beneath him. He pinned it to the snow, and the full curves of a feminine figure pressed against him. Anger filled him as he realized it must be one of the students. Well, he hoped he'd given the chit the fright of her silly life.

He raised himself on one hand, and with the other dragged the muffling shawl from her face. Daphne's eyes, wide with terror, stared back at him. For a long moment he gazed at her, as awareness filled him of her body forced tightly against his.

And a very soft and yielding body he found it. His fingers just touched her hair, the dark curls like strands of silk. Her warm breath misted between them, mingling with his. Her face could be no more than inches from his, her expression now more startled than afraid. An urge surged through him to kiss her, so powerful it could not be denied.

He denied it anyway—but not without a serious struggle. He scrambled to his knees, then assisted her to a sitting position. "Are you all right? Did I hurt you?"

She brushed white flakes from her shoulders. "Just cold. I'll have you know I might have caught our ghost, if you hadn't interfered." She looked up at him, her expression accusing. "Did I really look like one, too?"

"Of course not. I tackled you for practice." His brows

173

snapped down as he took a closer look at her. "What the dickens are you doing out here in nothing more than a dressing gown? You must be frozen!"

"Well, I hadn't intended to roll about in the snow." She turned a considering eye on him. "That was a very effective attack," she offered, possibly as a sop to his self-esteem.

He grinned. "Yes. A pity I didn't pick my target with more care." He rose, brushed himself off, then extended a hand to assist her to her feet. He retained his hold on her chilled fingers, rubbing them between his own gloved ones. All in all, he had found it a decidedly pleasurable interlude.

Too pleasurable. The memory of her softness pressed against him sent a yearning through every part of him, stronger than any he had ever before experienced. While part of his mind registered that this was an experience he would very much like to repeat—with or without the snow—another part of him recognized that not just any female would have stirred such a reaction in him. Daphne's liveliness of mind, her determination not to become an object of charity, her sincere desire to help her cousins—yes, it was Daphne herself who intrigued him.

And she, now that they had called a truce, treated him like an elder brother. One of whom she was growing tolerant, true, but with whom she seemed to prefer to be at odds. He could hardly blame her for thinking no more of him. Amidst his illustrious connections, he knew himself to be no catch. Annoyed with himself, he dragged off his greatcoat and draped it about her shoulders.

She huddled into it. "It's long gone, isn't it?" She sounded resigned. "We must have given it a bit of a fright, at least. How did you get on at the Manor?"

The memory of those two men jolted back to Adrian. He told her about them, and had to restrain her from going at once to take a look for herself. At last she accepted the futility of attempting to overhear, and the wisdom of waiting in hiding along the drive to try to get a clear look at them as they left. To pass the time, he also told her about Selwood's revelations concerning the bet.

Daphne listened, her expression one of growing indignation. "How dare they! Oh, I know of their ridiculous wagers. They are forever making a bet about one thing or another, all of them quite silly, but it is quite odious of them to make sport of our problems."

"So your cousin has come to realize."

"He should show more sense," she declared. "George has nary a feather to fly with—he squanders it all with his tailor—and the Squire isn't all that plump in the pocket, either."

"But I gather, for Squire Romney at least, that the amount of the wager is of less importance than the simple fact of winning."

She frowned. "Do you mean—oh, no, surely he would not be the sort of man who would ruin my cousins just to assure his winning a bet. Besides, the haunting must have already started before ever the bet was made."

"He might have aided it since," Adrian pointed out.

"It's such a cruel thing to—" She broke off, alert, and looked over her shoulder.

The crunch of gravel reached Adrian, too. Without pausing to check, he grasped Daphne's arm and propelled her deeper into the thicket. Then gesturing to her for silence, he positioned himself where he could see the drive.

The two men rode toward them. Beyond, Adrian could see the door to the Manor had been shut, apparently with Selwood within. The lantern still flickered by the steps.

He returned his gaze to the nocturnal visitors. Their hats concealed their faces from what little moonlight filtered through the heavy cloud covering. This hardly seemed a night for a horseback ride—and certainly not for cavorting about in sheets—without a very compelling reason. As they passed, their heads turned briefly in the direction of the Dower House, then they continued on their way toward the lane.

"Do you suppose they know about tonight's ghost?" Daphne's question sounded on the merest breath.

Adrian straightened. "I wish I knew. Did you recognize them?"

"They might be from around Bath, I suppose. Common laborers, don't you think? But what connection have they with Cousin George? He's always so—so fastidious." Her voice turned cold. "And as for his ill-judged bets . . ." She left their hiding place and started not toward the Dower House but up the drive.

"What do you think you're doing?" Adrian asked as he caught up with her—though he feared he knew.

"He's got a thing or two to explain. No, I won't accuse him of anything, but wouldn't you like to see his reaction when I ask about that dreadful wager?"

Adrian's grin got the better of him. "I wonder if he will be at pains to remind us that it gives Romney a reason to wish the Seminary to close?"

"But if he tries to throw suspicion elsewhere—oh, no, Mr. Carstairs. That would mean he wishes it away from *himself*. And before you point out the possibility of the underground passage between his house and the school, please remember someone might be gaining entry into the Manor without his knowledge."

"Or those voices—and the tunnel—might have nothing to do with the haunting. The possibilities," he added, enjoying himself hugely, "are endless."

She cast him a frustrated look and marched ahead. "If we do not hurry, he will have retired to his chamber, and then we will either have to raise the entire household or abandon our purpose."

"There is still a light shining in his bookroom. There, he has extinguished the candles. We will have to hurry."

176

He lengthened his stride, and Daphne broke into a run to keep pace with him. They mounted the steps, and Adrian applied the knocker.

For perhaps two minutes, silence stretched. Then the sounds of movement in the hall beyond reached them, followed by the creak of the bolt being drawn back, and the door opened the merest crack. George Selwood peered around the edge, holding high a chamberstick with a wavering flame.

"What do you mean by—" He broke off, his eyes widening as his gaze rested on them. "Daphne? And Mr. Carstairs? What ever are you doing about at this hour?"

"Freezing," Daphne said and waited, her expression expectant.

Selwood blinked. "To be sure. Do come in." He stood aside to let them enter, and his gaze traveled over their disheveled appearances. "This is a little—just a little—early for morning visits, do you not think?"

Daphne, arms akimbo, faced her cousin. "I want to know about this wager of yours with Squire Romney."

Selwood cast an uneasy glance at Adrian, and even by the meager light Adrian could see a dull flush creep into the man's face. Apprehensive—or merely embarrassed?

Selwood ran a finger inside his wilting collar and cleared his throat. "You told her about that, I see. But really, my dear Coz, there's nothing in it, you know. It's all my mistake, making too much of it." He led the way into the library, and for the next couple of minutes busied himself with the lighting of a candelabrum, the stirring of embers in the hearth, and the pouring of three brandies—two quite large and one very small which he gave to Daphne.

He gestured for them to take seats, and settled himself on the sofa. After swallowing a large mouthful, he cleared his throat once more. "It turns out it was all a hum." He glanced at Daphne. "It was a detestable thing

177

to do, I admit it, to make a wager about the Seminary. But we didn't mean any harm by it, I assure you. You must know how these things come about. And now I've been worried over nothing, and distressed you as well."

"Cut line, George." Daphne fixed her compelling gaze on him. "You're not making any sense."

"No. Well." He fingered the quizzing glass that hung about his neck by a puce riband. "I *thought* we'd made a wager. It turns out I was wrong, you see. I rode over to see Romney this afternoon—after I talked to you." He nodded toward Adrian. "It bothered me, you know. I meant to call it all off, only it turned out I didn't have to. Care for more?" He rose and started for the decanter.

"George . . ." Daphne's voice trailed off on a threatening tone.

He refilled both Adrian's glass and his own. "Romney claims to have no memory at all of any wager, you see. He quite agrees the whole thing would be unsuitable, so we called it off—if it was ever officially on. Well, I'm not such a rum touch as all that. Nor is Romney," Selwood assured them.

Still, in Adrian's opinion, the man looked pale and shaken. He glanced at Daphne; she didn't appear satisfied, either. He turned back to Selwood. "Who were your visitors tonight? Odd sort, they looked."

He blanched. "Visitors?" He sounded hoarse. "Oh, them." He gave a short laugh. "Just laborers. I hired them to repair a fence for me. I also meant them to have a look at the Dower House, but I decided they're too uncouth. Not at all the sort of fellows to inflict upon my cousins."

"Odd time for them to come, wasn't it?" he suggested.

Selwood examined his immaculate manicure. "They're unreliable. Quite hopelessly unreliable. I expected them in the early evening, and they had no good excuse whatsoever for being so late. It was a lucky thing

I was still awake. I wouldn't have put it beyond them to raise the household with some dreadful clamor if we'd already turned in."

"And was that," Daphne asked a few minutes later as they started once more down the drive, "a pointed comment directed at us for paying so late a visit?"

Adrian smiled. "Do you think your cousin so unhandsome?"

"I suppose," she went on, "he might well have been afraid if they'd come demanding money he owed them."

"Very true." Or if they were blackmailing him for having them haunt the Dower House. He kept that reflection to himself, not wanting to distress her further.

"What a night!" Daphne huddled deeper into Adrian's greatcoat. "George and those men—and we might have caught one of the ghosts if—"

"If I hadn't caught you, instead," Adrian finished when she broke off.

She said nothing. He looked down at her, and found she studied the snow-covered ground as if it fascinated her. Was she remembering sensations similar to those that had raced through him as he'd held her close? He certainly was. Or was she merely embarrassed by his reminder?

He touched her shoulder. "Did—?" Something moved among the trees ahead, and Adrian broke off.

Daphne glanced at him. "What?" She kept her voice to a whisper.

"I don't know. But it's possible . . ." He took her arm and propelled her toward the darkness of the towering hedge. "Best we stay out of sight."

Several minutes passed, during which time Adrian tried to ignore the fact they would be much warmer if they shared his greatcoat. He wouldn't mind holding her close—just to keep her from freezing, of course—but she gave no indication of welcoming such an arrangement. He gritted his teeth to keep them from chattering and thrust his hands into his pockets.

Then Daphne leaned against him, her slight frame shivering, and that settled the matter. He wrapped an arm about her beneath the heavy folds of the coat, gaining some of the warmth himself, and drew her against his chest. His chin just rested among her disordered curls. She smelled of violets and sunshine, he noted. Somehow his other arm encircled her also, and he pulled her closer, awareness of her softness, of her every curve, flooding through him.

She buried her face against his lapel and his hand stroked the silkiness of her dusky curls. With another order of female, he knew full well where this might end; the ways of the flesh held no mysteries for him. He had not taken to a monastic lifestyle until his recent ordination. But other females had roused only a passing desire in him, easily sated—never regretted, but never making a lasting impression, either. Daphne stirred him to depths never before plumbed.

If he kissed her, as every part of him wanted, would she be outraged? Just because she sought protection and warmth from him did not mean she invited his advances. Yet the urge to put it to the test grew stronger every moment she remained in his arms. Her breath warmed his neck, and she raised her face. . . .

A ghostly figure flitted across the drive, less than twenty yards from them. Daphne stiffened against him, her hand clutching his arm. The specter glided from side to side, then back toward the sheltering trees. Reluctantly, Adrian set Daphne aside.

"Stay here," he breathed.

"Wait." She pointed back toward the school. A dark shadow climbed out of a lower window and hurried across the snowy lawn to disappear into the bushes where their phantom had vanished a moment before.

"Can you reach those shrubs by the window without being seen?" he asked. "Then go. If anyone tries to get

180

back in through there, don't try to intercept the person. Just see who it is."

"But—"

"I'm going to try to catch our ghost and its companion. If they think they're being chased, one of them, at least, might try to escape into the school. And whoever it is might be feeling a bit panicky. Be careful." His fingers gripped hers a moment, then he slipped away.

He crossed the drive at a point that seemed darkest, and could only hope his quarry did not look in this direction at the moment. It seemed unlikely either of those two were aware he and Daphne were wandering in the grounds; the ghost had taken no pains to conceal itself. Rather, it seemed to have been bent on attracting attention in the house, probably to bring its companion out to it.

Adrian reached cover on the other side and looked back to where he had left Daphne. He could see nothing—or was that movement farther down, nearing the school? He turned his attention to where he stepped, and made his stealthy way deeper into the underbrush.

Ahead, the murmured tones of a masculine voice reached him. He slowed, seeking the shelter of a massive oak, and spotted the two figures, less than ten yards away. He had them this time.

Then a second ghostly shape separated from the shrubs, approaching from an oblique angle, slightly to the left of from where Adrian himself had come. Adrian hesitated, looking from the new arrival to the other two, knowing that to pursue one would allow the other to escape. And they might well warn each other.

A twig snapped under the foot of the newcomer. The couple by the trees jumped, spinning about, and Adrian strode forward, knowing the time for caution had passed. The newcomer charged the other two figures, and Adrian lunged to intercept.

The next moment he lay sprawled in the snow, his jaw aching, unsure which of the ghosts—if not both—

had turned the tables on him. He pulled himself up on his elbow and winced as sharp pain shot through his left wrist and up his arm. He must have landed on the heel of his hand. He struggled to a sitting position, and was not at all surprised to discover no one remained in sight.

Even telling himself the odds had been three against one did little to salvage his self-esteem. His pride, he decided, had suffered more than had he. He dragged himself to his feet, setting his teeth against the angry throbbing of his wrist. With his good hand, he brushed off the worst of the debris clinging to his breeches and coat, and set off for the Dower House, calling himself every uncomplimentary name that came to mind. He might as well go to bed. He did little enough good out here.

Daphne must be hiding not far away. From near the window she wouldn't have been able to see the ignominious end to his chase. He didn't look forward to telling her about it. She'd realize soon enough, though, that he'd blundered; he saw no way of hiding the damage he'd done to his wrist. Some champion he turned out to be.

He neared the shrubs. The window remained open, and beneath it—

Beneath it lay a crumpled figure, the muslin whiteness of her dressing gown showing from beneath Adrian's greatcoat.

Chapter Thirteen

Daphne. Dear, beloved Daphne. . . . He dropped on his knee at her side, his fingers searching for the pulse at her neck. It beat slow but steady beneath his touch, and relief washed over him. Gently he gathered her into his good arm, wrapping the other about her with care, cradling her close as a low moan escaped her. She struggled erect, and he eased his hold on her at once.

Her eyes flickered open, then focused on him. With a groan she sank back to rest against him. "What—?" she began.

He touched her lips with his fingers, smiling in his relief. "We were both taken out the same way," he told her. "And when I get my hands on him—"

She pulled herself shakily into a sitting position. "It knocked *you* out as well?" she asked, disbelief rife in her voice.

His right hand strayed to his jaw. "Not quite, but he might as well have." He found it much easier to make his confession than he'd expected. Fellow sufferers, and all that.

A soft rustle behind him caught his attention. He kept talking to Daphne, telling her who knew what, while all his concentration centered on that stealthy noise. Footsteps of someone creeping along at some distance, perhaps?

Daphne peered up at him through the darkness with

the oddest expression on her face. He must be speaking nonsense, he reflected, but no help for that at the moment. The low sound of his voice would be all that was heard by anyone else listening out there, not the exact words. He had to keep speaking or he'd alert whoever it was that he'd heard him—or her.

To where would this person be making? Certainly not the window. He and Daphne effectively blocked any entrance or egress by that route. That probably left the library door; one of their ghosts, at least, seemed to be trying to get back into the Seminary. It was a safe assumption, he decided, this would be the same person who scrambled out the window not so very long ago. Which meant, very likely, it was one of the girls.

Heartened by that reflection, he whispered to Daphne to keep talking. She nodded and began, mouthing something about how ridiculous it felt to be sitting about in the snow under windows, waiting for someone who was probably miles away by now. Adrian, grinning, slipped away.

There was no chance of reaching the door first, which he found regrettable. Still, he moved as quietly as he could, sneaking up on the figure—definitely a feminine form warmly garbed for the inclement weather. The girl reached the terrace, glanced from side to side, and reached for the handle.

"What an interesting time to take a walk, to be sure," Adrian said in a normal speaking voice. It sounded *ab*normally loud in the stillness of the night.

A soft shriek escaped the girl, and she spun about. Her trembling hand hovered before her mouth, and her eyes widened in alarm. Adrian stared, without too much surprise, into the aghast face of Louisa Trevellian.

"I—what—Mr. Carstairs!" She tried an artificial laugh, but apparently it fell flat in her ears as well, for she abandoned it almost at once. "Whatever are you doing out here?" she demanded.

184

"Ghost watching," he said, quite cheerfully. "And I've tallied a fine selection this evening."

"Have you?" She regarded him with considerable trepidation.

"Indeed I have." Adrian kept his steady gaze leveled on her. "It's been quite a night for specters. There was one of the girls from the school—I watched her climb out the window. Then there was the one who called her out, and then the third one."

She shivered. "That one—it was dreadful, wasn't it?"

"I admit," Adrian said, "I hadn't expected three of you in one night. Who, by the by, was your companion?"

"My—what? I—I didn't meet anyone."

Adrian fixed his gentle smile on her and said nothing, merely waiting. Steadfastly, he ignored the heat and throbbing in his wrist. Injuries always hurt like merry blazes at first.

Her gaze dropped to her clasped hands. "I—I suppose you saw us? It's not so very dreadful—at least, not what it might seem. After all, we are betrothed," she added with defiance.

Adrian raised his eyebrows. "Had I the honor to encounter your viscount?"

Her face worked, obviously trying to hold back emotion. "No," she finally gasped. "Not my—my viscount."

Still Adrian waited, making no comment.

She raised her clasped hands before her breast. "Oh, please, don't tell on me, sir," she wailed. "It is the most dreadful fix. Not for worlds would I have this come to the ears of any of the mistresses."

"It's a little late for that." Daphne stepped somewhat unsteadily from the concealing shrubs to join them.

Louisa gasped at sight of this new arrival, and burst into tears. Adrian prudently stepped back, leaving the girl to Daphne's not-so-tender ministrations. Daphne produced a handkerchief, handed it to Louisa, then waited, arms folded, anger glinting in her eyes. After a

185

couple of minutes, Louisa sniffed and straightened somewhat.

"Who is he?" Daphne demanded. "I do not mean to pry," she added through gritted teeth, "but as he seems bent upon haunting the school into ruination, I would like to know a little more of his motive."

"But he doesn't!" Louisa protested. "That is, we have played ghost, but—" she broke off, confused.

Adrian, looking at Daphne's wan but furious face, decided this had gone far enough. "Inside," he pronounced, and opened the door, ushering both ladies within.

Very little of the fire remained, but a few embers still glowed in the hearth, enough for his purposes. While Daphne guided Louisa to a chair, he threw on several sticks and a log and fanned them until they caught. Sure of his blaze, he straightened and turned back to the other two.

Louisa appeared a little more composed, though still distressed. Daphne, pale and weaving a trifle on her feet, he simply wanted to send straight to her bed, but knew he hadn't a chance. She'd see this through, no matter how she felt. He experienced a rush of warmth, mingled with exasperation.

"Who is he?" Daphne repeated.

"M—Monty," Louisa sniffed. "It is not what you think, he is my oldest friend. We grew up practically living in one another's houses."

Daphne threw Adrian an exasperated glance over the girl's head. "Then why," she demanded, "does he not come openly to the school in a normal manner?"

"Oh, you do not understand," Louisa wailed. "He cannot! Mama would not allow it."

Adrian began to have a glimmer of understanding. "Monty is not from an important family?" he asked.

Louisa threw him a grateful look. "That is it exactly. How ever did you know?"

186

He let that pass. "And your mama has worldly ambitions for you?"

She sniffed and nodded. "We—she has forbidden me to see him," she said, her voice quavering. "It is the most unkind thing, as if any harm could ever come of seeing my dearest friend."

"And so," Daphne began, the edge in her voice taking on steel, "he decided to play ghost and haunt the place so that he could meet you. Of all the foolish, deplorable, childish tricks! Did it not occur to you that you might destroy the Seminary?"

"No!" Louisa cried, aghast. "We would never do anything so shabby. Oh, you think *we* have been responsible. But we haven't. Truly we haven't. We've only met this way three times, now. The haunting merely gave us the idea of how to meet. Since the ghosts were frightening the students away, none of them would come out, or even look out the windows at night, which gave me the most splendid opportunity to slip out and—and talk to him. But we would never do anything to harm the Seminary, truly we wouldn't."

"Has he ever come inside?" Adrian asked.

Louisa twisted about in her chair to face him. "Of course not. That would be shockingly improper." She said this with complete sincerity, apparently unaware of the questionable propriety of the rest of her actions. "It has been so very dreadful. I never know, you see, when he can get away. I have to watch for him."

The door into the hallway opened, and all three jumped. Guilty consciences, Adrian reflected. Just as if they had been responsible for the hauntings themselves.

Miss Elspeth stepped over the threshold, a candle in one hand, her other clutching the opening of her dressing gown. She stopped, taking in the trio with patent surprise—and a touch of relief. "Daphne, my love? What is all this? I thought I heard noises down here."

Louisa looked from one to the other of them, her expression pleading.

"We were out ghost hunting," Daphne said after a moment's hesitation, "and awakened Louisa."

Fortunately, Louisa's back was to Miss Elspeth, who therefore missed the girl's look of abject gratitude.

"She should go back to bed now," Daphne added, and gave Louisa a quelling glance.

Miss Elspeth came forward, directing a shrewd look first at Daphne, then at Adrian, and gathered Louisa up. "I will wish you all a goodnight," she said with pointed emphasis, and led the girl from the room.

Daphne sank onto the sofa and let out a deep sigh.

Adrian smiled. "That was kind of you, but do you think it wise?"

Daphne shook her drooping head. "I am beyond thinking. What did you make of her story?"

Adrian paced to the hearth and poked a recalcitrant log into the comfortable blaze. His wrist hurt abominably, but he refused to acknowledge it. "I think," he said slowly, "that I believed her."

"Then Louisa and her Monty are not responsible for this fix we are in." A note of regret, mingled with relief, sounded in Daphne's voice.

Adrian shook his head. "It's possible her Monty landed me a facer when I came at him suddenly, but I can't see either of them cold-bloodedly knocking you out. And if either of them did, you may be sure Miss Trevellian would have taken that opportunity to scramble back into the school—which she didn't. No, this attack on you makes the matter more serious than mere schoolgirl indiscretions. But for now," he went on, "I believe it is time we both went to bed."

She hesitated.

"And you cannot tell me you do not have the headache," he added with mock sternness.

She managed a wan smile in return. "No, that I cannot," she agreed. "Very well, then. It has been rather a long night, has it not?"

He nodded. "And before much longer," he agreed, "it
188

will be time to get up and begin a new day with the girls."

She cast him a reproachful look. "I admitted I had the headache. Did you have to add to it?"

He smiled, relieved. She sounded far more like her usual self, now. Perhaps he need not worry too much. But the sight of her lying there, crumpled, so very vulnerable—he'd been frantic for her. He supposed he should be grateful to the ghost for only knocking her unconscious. Perhaps that implied the business was not as desperate or dangerous as he feared. She might very well have been dead.

That thought left a wrenching ache within him.

He helped her to her feet and slid his left hand into his pocket. He'd have to tend it soon. He tried to give his fingers an experimental wiggle, but they refused to cooperate.

She frowned at him. "Have you hurt yourself?"

It pleased him she'd noticed, but it also embarrassed him. "It's nothing," he said, more curtly than he'd intended.

"Let me see." She eyed his arm, then transferred her gaze to his set face. "What is it, your hand? And you can stop looking so stubborn. If you don't show it to me, I'll drag it out of your pocket and look for myself. I will," she added, threatening, as he made no move to comply.

Reluctant, yet curious himself as to what he would find, he raised his wrist, drawing back his sleeve.

"What—?" She broke off, her expression horrified as she gazed at the discolored swelling. "Is it broken?"

He ran a finger over the inflamed joint. "Only sprained, I should think." He smiled in reassurance at her, but it took a bit of an effort.

"Snow," she announced, and grabbing his good hand, she led the way outside. She knelt at the edge of the terrace, scooped up a double handful of the frozen flakes, then looked back at him, uncertain. "We need a towel."

189

"A bowl will do. I'll take it to my room." He returned within, located a vessel undoubtedly meant to hold flowers, and carried it out to her.

Daphne, who had dropped her first handful of snow, collected more. "We'll have to bandage it."

Adrian managed a grin. "Why don't I just go around to the stable and ask Hobson for a little of whatever liniment he keeps on hand for the horses? No, don't look like that. I don't need anything. I'll put the snow on it, then wrap it with a spare neckcloth. And while I am doing that, *you* will go to your bed."

"It looks terrible." She still eyed his wrist in concern. "Are you quite sure—"

"Quite. Now, come. It was not I who was knocked unconscious this night. I have only my own clumsiness to blame."

"And the ghost who hit you," she stuck in, but otherwise went docilely enough when he urged her back inside.

He escorted her up the stairs and to her door. A low fire burned within, glowing, lighting her way. "Throw another log on," he ordered.

She turned about. "I suppose you will stay up to see if anything more happens?" she asked, accusing.

"I doubt it will. Not tonight, at least. It's far too late. Any self-respecting ghost will have long since sought his couch. Besides, I imagine every one of them has already paid us a call."

Her lips twitched. "But if you do hear anything, you will let me know, won't you?"

"I promise."

"And you will take care of your wrist?"

"I need the use of it too much to ignore it." With that, he went on to his own chamber where he dealt swiftly but efficiently with his injury.

He wouldn't mind a shot of brandy to aid in his falling asleep, he decided. The hunt for a bottle led him down to the kitchens, where he found one in the cupboard. Armed with this, he returned to his room, sought his bed, and tried not to let nightmares of Daphne lying so very still in the snow haunt what little remained of the night.

Daphne awoke abruptly, alert, her mind racing with all that had happened during the long night. George and his visitors, Louisa and her Monty, Elspeth's shrewd assessment of the scene. And Mr. Carstairs . . .

Memory of his strong arms encircling her, holding her close and protected, sent a flood of warmth through her. He'd only done it because they'd been so cold—hadn't he? She shied from examining her feelings about that. It would not be wise, she had chosen a useful, purposeful life, and she would not permit a gentleman who would be part of that life for so brief a time to shake the foundations of her contentment.

Instead, yet still unable to drag her thoughts from him, she concentrated on his injury. Had he wrapped it tightly enough? Did it pain him? He'd never admit it, of that she felt certain. She'd have to give him as much help as she could—without his realizing it, of course. She dressed quickly and hurried downstairs, eager to see him—or rather, she told herself firmly, eager to see that he had cared properly for his wrist.

He had, she discovered a short while later. In fact, he managed perfectly well at morning prayers. If she hadn't known, it never would have occurred to her he had suffered any injury last night. Only the cloth that bound his hand between thumb and forefinger betrayed him, and no one seemed to notice it. Mr. Carstairs, she realized, needed no one's help. And that included hers. Depressed—no, only tired from her eventful night, she assured herself—she made her way to her first class.

She would have done better to sleep through it, she decided an hour and a half later. Marianne Snowdon's venomous glares grated on her nerves as the girl pursued her half-hearted attempts at a watercolor rendition of Jane. Daphne had posed her sister in a languid attitude upon a day bed, an open book in her lap. That Jane had a tendency to forget herself and read, turning the pages and shifting to a more comfortable position as the whim took her, did not help in the least.

Nor did her own lack of real attention, Daphne reminded herself. Despite her best endeavors, her thoughts continued to return to Mr. Carstairs. Had he avoided speaking with her before breakfast? Or had it been chance that placed so many girls between them? She would not have embarrassed him by making a fuss before the others, drawing attention to the wrist he obviously wished ignored. Surely he must know that.

Nor could she help but blame herself for what he endured. Had it not been for her and her problems, at this moment he would be comfortably ensconced at Champfors Vicarage with her Uncle Thaddeus, probably nearing completion on his dissertation, looking forward to his return to Oxford. . . .

She dragged her thoughts back to her present duties and wandered from girl to girl, making a suggestion to one, giving a word of praise to another. As she reached Louisa Trevellian, the girl looked up with a quavering smile, then returned to her efforts at once. It was mediocre, Daphne decided, but passable.

Louisa's attitude, on the other hand, was not. The girl's manner was all meekness and subservience this morning, as if she were a gentle miss who had been severely chastised, and had determined never again to give the least offense. Daphne well knew her for no such thing. Louisa's lively behavior frequently set the whole school on end. That brief interview with her in the library would bring no such drastic change. Which could only mean she was up to something.

A sigh escaped Daphne as she moved on. She would have to keep a closer eye on the girl, and she already had quite enough on her plate at the moment.

With the arrival of lunch came her release for the day. She couldn't be glad—the withdrawal of so many pupils had caused the cancellation of her afternoon classes—yet she could look forward to the quiet as she turned her attention to her other duties about the Seminary. She tidied the art room, then sought her meal.

Mr. Carstairs, she noted, was not in sight. She could only hope he slept—though he probably attended to his beloved Herodotus. With determination, she forced her thoughts from him, yet perversely, they returned at once.

It was not in the least fitting he should occupy her mind to so great an extent—and it was not just because of his injury, she acknowledged. He was quite unlike any gentleman she ever had known. He made her laugh, he made her feel at ease, he made her more aware of him than she ever before had been of any gentleman. And when he touched her . . .

No, she would not think about the unsettling and wholly delightful sensations he created within her. He had his own life, and she had hers—provided she could convince Uncle Thaddeus to allow her to remain here. She would *not* think about the way Mr. Carstairs made her long to share her burdens and allow him to carry them on his very capable shoulders.

He had already done so much for her—and for her cousins. How could she hope to repay that debt? She had nothing to offer, nothing he did not already have. Even if she or her family possessed influence enough to win for him an even greater position at Oxford, he would not need their intercession; he had abilities and intelligence and energy enough to drive him to the top of any profession he chose.

Depressed—only because of her sleepless night—she finished her roll and sliced beef quickly and went to the office. There she settled behind the great mahogany desk and drew out the enrollment figures. Perhaps, if they raised their fees just a little . . .

Cousin Elspeth joined her twenty minutes later, and together they spread out the accounts. "We could grow more of our own food," Daphne suggested at last, staring at the staggering sum demanded by a greengrocer.

"And keep cows and pigs and sheep, as well, to provide meat?" Elspeth wrinkled her nose and indicated the amount due the butcher.

"If only the rent were not so very high—" Daphne broke off as voices sounded just outside the door.

Someone knocked, and on Elspeth's call, Uncle Thaddeus looked inside. He crossed the threshold, then halted, frowning, looking from one to the other of them. "Has something occurred?" he inquired at once. "You look so very solemn, the pair of you. I hope I have not come at a bad time."

Elspeth smiled, albeit somewhat wanly. "Of course you have not. Indeed, we must always be pleased to see you."

His gaze rested on her lightly flushed countenance, and the furrows in his brow deepened. "Tell me what has gone on since my last visit."

Daphne exchanged a glance with Elspeth. "Tell him," Daphne said, deferring to her cousin. After all, Elspeth knew less, and might not alarm him as much. She sat back in her chair, hoping she did not look as tired and distressed as she felt, while Elspeth described what she knew of the events of the last couple of days.

When Elspeth finished, Mr. Danvers shook his head, his expression troubled. "I cannot like this," he said.

"No more do we." Elspeth picked up the pen she had set aside on his arrival and twisted it between agitated fingers.

A silence fell between them that did nothing to ease Daphne's nerves. It was broken by another knock on the door, followed at once by the entrance of Mr. Carstairs. Relief flooded through Daphne, and she smiled a warm welcome.

His gaze, with reassurance in his steady gray eyes,

rested on her a moment, then moved on to the others, whom he greeted. "Moffett told me you'd come," he added to Mr. Danvers as he drew up a chair at the older man's side. His left arm hung naturally, as if the bandage were a mere affectation. Still, Uncle Thaddeus noted it, but Mr. Carstairs merely waved his question aside. "A slight sprain, just clumsiness on my part. Have they told you everything? Even about Selwood's visitors last night?"

"Selwood's visitors?" Elspeth looked up sharply.

Daphne shook her head, wary, and Mr. Carstairs took up the narrative, filling in several details of which Elspeth had not been aware. He omitted any mention of the attack on himself and, to Daphne's relief, of her being struck unconscious and of Louisa's Monty. He certainly possessed discretion, she noted, her gaze lingering on the burnished waves of his hair and the gleam in the depths of his penetrating eyes. How did he manage to be so capable, with such an air of authority, yet not be in the least overbearing?

"I cannot like the sound of those two ruffians," Uncle Thaddeus said when Mr. Carstairs finished. "While Mr. Selwood himself is not likely to wish any of you harm, these associates of his might. The authorities might well be interested in them."

"They are more likely to believe Selwood's tale of them—which, I might add, we have no real reason to disbelieve ourselves." Adrian held up a hand, silencing Daphne's protest. "What *tangible* proof have we to make the authorities take this matter seriously?"

Uncle Thaddeus frowned at Elspeth, then Adrian. "I cannot approve of the danger. I still feel the ladies should be induced to leave."

"We have had this argument before," Elspeth reminded him, amused now more than indignant. "Why ever should we leave? And where should we go?"

"There is not the least need," Daphne protested. She regarded her uncle in concern. He remained her legal guardian; he could require her to obey him. If he ordered her to go home, it would place her in an intolerable position. She hated the thought of defying him, yet how could she abandon her cousins?

Mr. Danvers looked at her for a long moment, then turned to Adrian. "How do you feel about this?"

Mr. Carstairs met Daphne's pleading look with a slight frown. "I do not believe," he said slowly, "that we have cause for such drastic action yet. And you may be very sure I shall not let things reach such a head."

"Very well, then," Mr. Danvers said, though obviously still far from being reconciled. "Continue as you think best. I must return to my parish now, but rest assured I shall come back as soon as I may."

Mr. Carstairs rose along with him. "Be at ease," he said as he escorted Mr. Danvers into the hallway. The rest of his comments faded as the door closed behind them.

He returned within a very few minutes. Pausing in the doorway, he looked at them, and his warm smile flashed. "We have been ordered to take every care," he informed them, "but he has granted his permission for you to remain."

Daphne glared at him. "Did he ask you to keep me on a leading string?"

His disarming grin flashed. "Not quite. But I do have a request to make of you."

"What?" she demanded, hackles rising.

"I believe," he said, and his eyes twinkled, "it is time you swallowed your pride and visited Miss Davenport about her offer of employment."

Daphne's jaw dropped, and she closed her mouth again with a snap. "If that is your idea of a joke, let me inform you it is ill-timed."

"I am quite serious. I desire an opportunity to meet the lady, and have not been able to think of a better pretext. Can you? Besides," he added in a dry tone, "I won't be able to do much good in the attics this day."

196

She regarded him with considerable suspicion. "What do you expect me to say if she offers me the position?"

"See to it she doesn't. Make it clear at the outset you only wish to learn a little more. You might even hint you are considering one or two other schools."

"And what will you be doing?"

"Trying to form an opinion of her. I wish to see her reactions when you tell her your cousins are at their wits' end, and are talking of closing their Seminary."

Elspeth eyed him with fascination. "Are we?" she asked, politely.

His smile widened. "But of course. If she has been attempting to bring that about, she might let her triumph show."

"She might, anyway," Daphne put in. "I cannot think of anything she would like more." She looked back to Mr. Carstairs. "And what will be *your* excuse for accompanying me?"

His expression turned solemn—almost humble. "Young clergymen without preferments are always in search of positions," he informed her in pious tones.

They didn't fool her in the least. "When do you wish to go?"

Within twenty minutes, she watched him drive up before the Dower House in his tilbury. One ribbon draped over his injured left hand, but he held a loop of it in his right. The horse, though moving with spirit, responded to his slightest touch.

She moved forward to meet him, then slowed the eagerness of her step. Behind her, she knew quite well, several of the young ladies would be gathered at the windows, watching their departure, speculating upon the reason. She set her teeth. Some of the bolder ones—Miss Snowdon, for example—would tease her about it later. Long practice had inured her to the girls' questions and weavings of fanciful romances for her, and taught her to deftly turn them aside.

Still, she declined Mr. Carstairs's proffered hand and

climbed in without assistance. She settled primly as far from him as she could manage, and sat, back stiffly erect, as he turned his horse and started down the drive. *That* should disappoint the little cats.

She glanced at her companion, and the set of his jaw warned her not to offer any assistance. She could handle a single horse easily enough, but so, it seemed, could he—even with an injured wrist. She relaxed into the seat and allowed him to set his own pace, sure there would be no mishap.

The drive passed pleasantly in rehearsing the roles they would shortly play. Daphne struggled with a creeping invasion of nerves, but Mr. Carstairs appeared perfectly at his ease. Enjoying himself, in fact, she noted with a touch of envy. Would he never be discomfited or even out of sorts? Somehow, she doubted it, and that thought warmed her.

When they reached the outskirts of the city, she gave him the direction of Davenport Seminary. He located an inn a short distance from their destination, left his equipage, and they set off for a brisk afternoon's walk. With every step, her courage faltered.

All too soon for her taste they arrived at the Seminary. She hesitated in the street, but Mr. Carstairs strode up the steps to the front door and rang the bell. A minute passed, then a gaunt-featured maid of middle years, garbed in severest black with a muslin apron and mobcap, admitted them. She directed an assessing look at them, asked their names, then ushered them into Miss Davenport's study and departed to fetch her mistress.

Daphne entered the spacious apartment, impressed in spite of herself at the understated elegance that met her critical eye. No lack of funds dictated anything inferior here; from the silver candelabra to the leather-bound volumes to the paintings on the wall and the rich carpet on the floor, all spoke of excellent taste and the money to indulge it.

She cast an uneasy glance at Mr. Carstairs. "I wish we had not come."

A wicked gleam lit his deep gray eyes. "Just remember it is *your* pupils' fees that are now paying for all these trappings."

"I do remember it," she said, knowing it pointless to hide her bitterness.

The door opened, and Daphne spun about to face it—every bit as nervous as Mr. Carstairs wished her to pretend to be. Not Miss Davenport, but a tall young lady with limpid blue eyes and dusky ringlets arranged á la Sappho. Miss Susannah Ingels.

The girl leaned against the door jamb, a lovely picture in her figured muslin—except for the malice of her expression as her contemptous gaze rested on Daphne. "Have you come to grovel for a position?" A throaty laugh escaped her. "It won't be long now before *all* the Selwood ladies are out of business. Such a terrible shame, is it not? Of course, they can always go as governesses."

Daphne opened her mouth for a cutting retort, caught Mr. Carstairs's almost imperceptible shake of the head, and remained silent but seething.

Susannah's gaze narrowed. "I understand Reginald paid you a call the other day. Really, there is no accounting for a gentleman's taste, and I'm certainly not one to begrudge him his amusements. If I were you, I would think twice about giving him a cold reception."

"But then I'm not you, thank heavens," Daphne said before she could prevent herself.

The door opened again, saving Daphne from any further response. On the threshold stood Miss Davenport, regal in a gown of dove gray silk, her long silver hair wound in a thick chignon at the nape of her neck.

She turned a steely eye on Susannah. "You will kindly tell me, Miss Ingels, what you are doing here."

To Daphne's utter amazement, the girl flushed.

Daphne glanced at Miss Davenport with a grudging respect.

Susannah straightened her shoulders. "I came to ask you a question, Miss Davenport, but it is no matter. I will return at a more convenient time." She hurried out the door, casting a nervous, calculating glance at her preceptress as she went.

Miss Davenport watched her departure, then stepped into the room and closed the door behind her. Her gaze rested first on Mr. Carstairs, then traveled to Daphne. "This is a pleasant surprise, Miss Selwood." She gestured toward chairs and seated herself behind a cherrywood desk. "How may I help you?"

Daphne glanced at Mr. Carstairs, and derived a measure of comfort from his solid presence.

Miss Davenport smiled. "My dear, you need not be afraid of me. I am not quite the ogress Beatrice and Sophronia would have me. We have been much at odds, I admit, but the fault probably has been shared equally between us."

Daphne's face heated. "I do find this awkward," she said. "You mentioned the possibility of a position here, at your establishment." She inserted what she hoped to be just the right touch of defiant hauteur and desperate uncertainty. "We have come to town today to visit two or three Seminaries."

Miss Davenport's raised eyebrows acknowledged the point. "I did not know there was such a crying need for art mistresses."

Daphne gritted her teeth. "For capable instructresses, I believe there always is."

"And what has prompted this visit? Has anything new occurred at Selwood Seminary?"

Daphne studied her clasped hands. "Another student has withdrawn." She looked up, meeting Miss Davenport's gaze directly. "My cousins have begun to discuss the possibility of losing their school."

Miss Davenport's eyes gleamed. For a minute she occupied herself with shifting objects on her desk, then she looked up. "I will not hide from you, Miss Selwood, that taking on *another* art mistress would be quite an extravagance for us. Still," she toyed with a pen, "if our own enrollment were to increase, it might be possible. Six more girls, perhaps, and one of them your sister Jane? I fear even then we would have little money to spare. But then Jane's tuition would be more than any salary you might expect, anyway, would it not?"

"But it would be covered?" Daphne held her temper in check.

Miss Davenport inclined her head. "I believe we could make such a concession. But as for you . . ." Her voice trailed off as she regarded Mr. Carstairs. "A chaplain." She awarded him a condescending smile. "Such a silly conceit in the Selwood ladies—though perhaps you could instruct the young ladies in some useful subject. Well, I must think about it." She rose, effectively bringing the interview to an end. "You may call upon me next week."

"As if she were conferring upon as an invitation to Court!" Daphne hissed as they at last stepped once more onto the street.

Mr. Carstairs's slow smile lit his eyes. "Impecunious young instructresses and chaplains should be properly grateful for not having been merely shown the door forthwith, remember."

She strode in silence at his side for the length of the street. "Did you form any opinion?" she asked at last.

"Not the one I had expected." He rubbed his chin. "On the whole, I rather think I prefer Miss Ingels and her brother for sheer nastiness. Whoever is doing this seems to be taking a positive enjoyment in ruining the school."

"They are, aren't they?" And that fact depressed Daphne even more.

Chapter Fourteen

Adrian maneuvered his tilbury through what seemed a great amount of carriage traffic along Stall Street. Beside him, Daphne sat as if lost in thought, gazing straight ahead without apparently seeing anything. As they pulled outside the town at last, a great sigh escaped her.

She leaned back against the seat. "I think I fancy Miss Marianne Snowdon to be responsible," she announced, "out of sheer hatred for drawing classes."

Adrian smiled. "Or your Louisa. She might be afraid to admit the whole haunting had been their doing from the beginning. But seriously, the Ingelses could have managed it, if Mr. Wembly served as their assistant. Miss Susannah Ingels might well be malicious enough. For that matter, even if she has nothing to do with your Seminary's troubles, I would not be at all surprised if the same sort of thing starts happening to Miss Davenport."

"Unless," Daphne inserted, "she *is* responsible, and Miss Davenport is behind it."

Adrian frowned, considering the proprietress of the school they had just left. Certainly rivalry between the two schools existed; Miss Davenport admitted it freely. But he had also found the woman to have a shrewd sense of business—to be sharp witted and clear thinking. Such a mind *might* be behind the haunting, but he had by no means made up his mind. He had, he suddenly realized, rather liked her.

Feuds, he knew well, were almost a tradition for some people, who derived satisfaction and purpose from them. Some, in truth, led to serious consequences, even to murders. This one *might* have led to the haunting and the driving of her rival out of business.

Yet he wasn't convinced that lady possessed such a ruthless nature. She would take every advantage of the Selwood's difficulties, of course, but would she have instigated them? Nor could he see how those two mysterious men who had visited Selwood fit into any plans she might have made. Of course, the same could be said for Marianne and Louisa, if either of them were involved.

"Which brings us, I suppose," Daphne said after he voiced this opinion, "to Cousin George."

Adrian urged Achilles to a faster trot. "The motive— the reason," he reminded her, "remains obscure."

"But those two men—" She broke off, shaking her head. "I cannot see what role they play in any of this."

"The voices at the end of the passage," he suggested.

"But why?"

He drew a deep breath. "For that, I fear, we will have to either enter the Manor and discover the entrance from that end, or find a possible entrance through your basement."

Daphne slumped in her seat. "Which we have already tried and failed to do." She was silent for a couple of minutes. "We are forgetting Squire Romney," she said, brightening.

"Of course." Adrian nodded. "And his bet. Perhaps he started the haunting in the first place, just so he could make that wager and then arrange to win it."

She directed a darkling glance at him. "Pray do not be absurd."

Unable to stop himself, his deep chuckle escaped him. "This entire situation is absurd." He sobered at once. "If

203

it were not for the seriousness of the consequences to yourself and your cousins, and that attack upon you, I would be inclined to dismiss the whole thing as childish pranks."

She nodded. "But the consequences *are* severe, especially for my cousins, the poor dears. This is all so dreadfully unfair to them. And if it is Miss Davenport's fault—" Her fists clenched.

"You may haunt her for revenge."

She ignored this sally, merely casting him a searching look. "Have we gained anything by this trip—beyond a lesson in humility?"

He considered that, and the possible effects of various answers on her before he at last admitted, "Something, perhaps. Enough to make me certain we must look further for our answers."

She turned her brilliant eyes on him. "And what, now?"

He studied a spot between his horse's ears. They had nothing substantial to go on, no hint at where to look next. He needed to return to the attics, he knew. He had an unfinished search awaiting him there. But as for the nightly watches . . .

"I think," he said at last, "that if you will keep an eye on the attics at night, I will patrol the grounds."

"Oh, no," Daphne protested. "I mean—there should always be two together. For safety."

Yet he had not been able to keep her safe last night when someone had been desperate enough to strike her, rendering her unconscious. He could not be everywhere at once, especially if he were up against three ghosts. Nor would he show to advantage at the moment if it came to a bout of fisticuffs. He could do with a helper or two—yet the only ones upon whom he could call were the very ones he must either suspect or seek to keep safe. No, his best choice would be to leave Daphne indoors, where she would not be as cold, and help might be forthcoming if she screamed. He would take the outside watch alone.

As they neared the turnoff from the Bath road to the Dower House, a rider approached them from the lane. Squire Romney raised a hand in greeting, then drew his showy black abreast of them as Adrian reined Achilles to a halt. "How do you go on at the Seminary?" he called. "Hope there've been no ghostly sightings of late."

"Last night." Adrian watched the man closely, but could detect nothing but dismay in his expression. What did he expect? Blatant satisfaction? If Romney had aught to do with the matter, he would not betray himself so foolishly.

Romney glowered. "Nasty business." He studied his hands for a moment where they clenched the reins, then looked up to meet Adrian's gaze. "Not sure I should mention this or not. Might concern the ladies."

"Does it?" Daphne eyed him with suspicion. "In what way?"

Romney's gaze flickered over her, then he turned back to Adrian. "Selwood," he said succinctly.

"A matter that concerns him need not necessarily concern his cousins," Adrian said evenly.

Romney's horse sidled beneath him. "Might. Not sure. Don't like the company he's been keeping of late. Hah! Disreputable men. Common. Not as if they were sportsmen, even."

Daphne wrinkled her nose. "I doubt sportsmen would be of any interest to Cousin George."

"Can't see where these two would be of interest to him at all," Romney said bluntly. "Insists on breaking engagements with me to meet with them, though."

"Most peculiar," Adrian agreed. He kept his tone even, as if the matter were only of the mildest interest to him.

Romney frowned. "Know you're concerned for the ladies. Can't help but wonder if those two are involved

205

in the school's problems. Well, won't hurt if his cousins keep a closer eye on old George. Invite him over more often. Give him a taste for better society." He gave them a curt nod, wheeled his horse about, and set off at a canter.

Daphne raised her eyebrows. "So we are not the only ones privileged to encounter Cousin George's new friends. What do you make of that?"

Adrian's gaze followed Romney's vanishing figure. "I don't know—yet." He set the bay forward once more at a trot. "You'd think your cousin would have told his friend about the work those two supposedly did for him."

Daphne hugged her pelisse about herself. "Squire Romney implied they were more than mere laborers, don't you think?"

With that Adrian agreed. The Squire had also implied those two spent a great deal of time with George Selwood—enough, at least, to bother him. It bothered Adrian, too.

It still bothered him the following afternoon, as did the need to search the attics. He had devoted most of the last twenty-four hours to Herodotus, taking time off only to pace the quiet grounds in the early hours of the morning, then to catch a very few hours sleep. He had not found it easy to focus his attention on his scholarly pursuits, yet he had not had any choice. Mystery might beckon, but his still-swollen wrist demanded prudence.

Prudence, he decided, be damned. He flexed his left hand and ignored the stabbing pain. He'd rested it long enough. He'd be careful. In fact—and this ought to please Daphne—he'd request her help. A satisfactory situation all around.

He went in search of her, finding her at last in the art room, paper on the easel before her, her watercolors at her side. A landscape spread across the sheet, more beautiful, he decided, than even the one through the window beyond. That it was the same scene was obvious, but her light touch had rendered her version more aesthetically pleasing—which surprised him, for he usually felt nature, on its own, far outshone man's feeble attempts to recreate it.

He remained where he stood so as not to disturb her, appreciating the work she produced, appreciating her concentration, her gentle touch with the brush. She had very real talent, which was something he admired. And she possessed the dedication to pursue it and refine it, to make the most of her ability.

Without glancing up, she said, "Tomorrow's lesson."

He came closer, examining what she had done in more detail. "They'll make a botch of it," he said.

She laughed. "Not all of them. A couple—Miss Breame and one of the Pembroke girls and Jane—will probably do quite well."

He sat on the edge of the table. "Do you enjoy this? Trying to discover some scrap of talent or desire in these girls?"

Her brush stilled, her head tilting to one side as if she considered. "I'm good at it," she said at last, with no trace of boasting. "There is such a satisfaction in helping to overcome problems, seeing potential reached. Even if they will never truly be proficient, they are learning to try. Some of them, at least," she added.

His gaze rested on her smooth dark hair, its full length confined in its chignon. Memories of it loose about her shoulders haunted him. The rush of warmth, of pure emotion that filled him, surprised him. That she could have become so very dear to him in so short a time amazed him. And that he should welcome such a feeling rather than shun it seemed more a mystery to him than anything else.

She dipped her brush in the water at her side, contemplated the scene beyond the window, and turned to her colors once more. "What will you do when you're done here? Return to my Uncle Thaddeus to finish your dissertation?"

"You are assuming," he said, "we will settle this matter in the near future."

A shaky sigh escaped her. "We have to." She sat back and looked at him for the first time. "And after that, do you return to Oxford? I don't suppose it will be so very quiet there after all, not with all the larks one hears the young gentlemen kick up."

"No, it is sometimes quite lively there," he admitted. Yet he still found considerable time to pursue his scholarly inclinations. It was the ideal life for him . . . or was it perhaps just a bit lonely?

He had his students, as did Daphne. But while only an occasional one of Daphne's—like Marianne Snowdon—despised art, it was the opposite with Greek and Latin and the other Classical subjects. Most young gentlemen regarded them as pure drudgery.

His students gained little from his efforts, he realized suddenly. Little, at least, that any of them acknowledged. The lessons of life that awaited, layer upon layer, in the dramas of the Classical world passed through their minds without leaving any discernible trace.

At least what Daphne taught might some day provide diversion for her young ladies. But his classics? One or two of his pupils, with intelligence and enthusiasm for the study, might benefit from his time and efforts. But the others? A true scholarly mind, he realized, was a rare and wondrous thing. Far rarer than he had ever realized.

Did he waste his time—his life—in a meaningless endeavor?

He blinked, and saw she still watched him with a touch of surprise on her face.

"I hadn't thought the question of when you return to be so thought provoking," she said.

"I hadn't, either," he said slowly. He had never before considered leaving the position for which he had longed since he had been very young. But now the possibility of another—more satisfying—life just formed in his mind.

"I might not go back," he said, still wondering at the vistas opening before him.

"Of course," she said wisely. "With your connections, you probably have your eyes set on a bishopric." Sudden color touched her cheeks and she gave a shaky laugh. "Don't look so startled. If you ever left Oxford, what else could you become? Even without your connections," she added. She looked quickly back to her painting with such absolute concentration that he might no longer have existed.

He left her, his mind still reeling. Leave Oxford? For what? To pursue a prestigious position in the Church? No, that way held no allure for him. He didn't hanker after a miter or palace; he'd taken Holy Orders only as a step toward his scholarly future.

Yet the academic cloister satisfied only his intellect. Something was missing, something necessary to him. The certainty that his efforts mattered.

Mr. Danvers, he reflected, indulged his passion for Classical studies while enjoying a very useful life.

Six young ladies, led by Marianne Snowdon and Miss Breame with Jane in their wake, swooped down upon him, demanding his attention. Miss Snowdon caught his arm and cast a languishing glance at him. He extricated himself, his thoughts still far away on the problems encountered in day-to-day village life, and of the role of a vicar in sorting it all out.

"Will you read more stories to us?" Marianne begged, fluttering her long lashes at him.

Adrian tried to step back, but found the girls now surrounded him.

"Oh, please," Fanny Breame begged.

"You do it so very well," put in Miss Emma Pembroke.

"And Daphne is busy," added Jane artlessly. She tugged at his arm, pulling him into the library.

One of the girls dragged a chair toward the hearth. Another pressed the book into his hands. Marianne,

Fanny Breame, and Emma Pembroke settled on the floor about the chair, gazing up at him, obviously expecting him to take a seat.

The attic required his attention far more than a flock of silly girls. Yet their expressions were far more eager than any of the ones that faced him at Oxford. Short of being bluntly rude, he did not see any escape. And his wrist did ache, still. Another hour of resting it might allow him to work more efficiently later. He would wait to begin his explorations until the girls went to dinner.

They kept him far over his allotted hour, not appearing to tire in the least of his tales and explanations. Instead, they bombarded him with questions, Miss Breame going so far as to beg him to show her the Greek alphabet. With this the others chorused agreement, and one of the youngest was sent to fetch paper, pens, and ink.

It occurred to Adrian, watching their rapt interest as they set up at makeshift desks, to wonder what they were about. If their purpose had been to prevent him from searching attics and basements, they could not have done it more effectively. Did one of them, perhaps, actively seek that?

His gaze traveled to Miss Marianne Snowdon. She remained oblivious of his regard, all of her concentration focused on the relatively simple *psi* she tried to copy. The tip of her tongue protruded from the corner of her mouth as she labored.

Did she try to divert him from his purpose here? It would have been easy to round up several innocent girls to aid her. It would never occur to them they did other than spend a pleasant hour or so. But Marianne—if this were deliberate, that would mean she must know what he searched for.

He corrected Miss Breame's *omega*, his mind on far more pressing issues than Greek letters. It would not be impossible for one or more girls, engaged in illicit exploring, to have stumbled across a passage. He could even see them keeping it secret for their own purposes, such as midnight raids upon the kitchen, or frightening an unpopular schoolmistress. He could not tie this in, though, with the haunting of the school. Marianne, although despising her drawing lessons, had no other reason to do the Selwood ladies harm.

He strolled among the girls, making suggestions, awarding praise, exhausting the possibilities for motives. He gained little by this, he decided at last. Instead, he turned his mind to devising a scheme to rid himself of his self-appointed charges.

In the end, he did not need it. Miss Beatrice charged into the library, looked around, arms akimbo, face stern. "You should be dressing for dinner," she informed them. "Off with you."

They scurried, with Miss Breame pausing for one last lingering glance at Adrian. Marianne lowered her lashes and peeped up at him at her most flirtatious. Her murmured "thank you" dripped with sweetness.

Jane glowered at her erstwhile friend, then directed a speculative look at Adrian. "I am sure Daphne would have liked to join us." She blushed, cast Miss Beatrice a defiant glance, and hurried after the others.

Miss Beatrice turned back to him, shaking her head. "Plaguing the life out of you, are they?" she demanded.

"Not really. Will you hold me excused from dinner, though? I think I should get on with my search of the attic."

At last, he made his way up the several flights of stairs and down the long corridor past his own chamber to the lumber room from which he suspected most of the troubles emanated. So far, he had rummaged among the furnishings but had found no ready means of egress. He had checked the window and sounded the walls and found nothing. Now he would move every last stick of furniture so he could reach the floor boards.

He crossed the hall, opened the door to the other storage room which he had already prepared, then began the back-breaking process of dragging the heavy chests across. From those he could, he removed the drawers; the rest he emptied. It took a great deal of time, but his wrist, which he had wrapped tightly for the job, did not let him down.

From below, the desultory strains of someone's playing the pianoforte drifted up to him. Didn't anyone in this establishment do credit to the aged instrument? Of course, few students remained this term; so few, in fact, he didn't know how the Selwood ladies would meet their expenses. And so far, he'd accomplished very little to help them. He returned to his work with renewed determination.

He progressed with a slowness he found frustrating, yet he continued doggedly until a heavy armoire which he could barely manhandle lodged in the doorway. Why did people create such massive furnishings? he wondered. He eyed the crude carving with distaste. He preferred a cleaner line, a smoother appearance than this depressingly dark and coarse piece. He could not blame whomever had consigned it to this room. He would have consigned it to a bonfire.

Light footsteps approached down the hall, hurrying, then slowed as they neared. He could not see over the wardrobe, which stood a full seven feet in height, but he could detect a crack around it, indicating enough space so that if he could only maneuver it over whatever impediment stood in his way, he could get it out the door.

"Mr. Carstairs?" Daphne's soft voice sounded from without. "I'm sorry I couldn't come earlier."

"You wouldn't be if you had been here," he said. "This is hardly an enjoyable way to spend the evening."

"But you should have help! Do not tell me you have dragged that alone."

"Oh, no," he assured her. "I have a passel of ghosts to help me."

212

Silence greeted his sally. After a moment, she asked, "Are you stuck?"

"For the moment," he admitted.

"This is dreadful," she exclaimed. "You should not be doing all of this. Your wrist is in no fit state. Let me call Moffett."

"Don't," he objected. "He is too old for this sort of work."

"Perhaps we could hire a man—" Daphne broke off. "Mr. Carstairs, do you think that is what George did? Hire those men to move furniture?"

"Are you proposing to go to the Manor next time they come and hire them yourself?" On the whole, he preferred to see her when he spoke to her.

He flexed his sore wrist and eyed the armoire with distaste. He would have to tilt it back toward himself, shove it several inches, then lower it again. He shrugged his shoulders to ease their stiffness, grasped the massive cabinet, and pulled. With a protesting creak, it rocked toward him. He saw Daphne's fingers grasping the sides near the bottom, and she pulled as he pushed. Slowly it inched forward, until at last he stood in the hall where he could set it once more on its legs.

Daphne regarded it with a brooding expression. "I think it looks quite elegant exactly where it stands right now. Don't move it another inch."

Adrian stood back to consider it. "Perhaps two inches," he said, and positioned it against the wall. "It's rather in the way."

"Not for our ghosts. They can go right through it," she assured him. She entered the room he had just left and looked about. "You haven't gotten very far," she said, then flushed. "I didn't mean that the way it sounded. It's—how can I help?"

He set her to work pulling out drawers from a chest while he moved a chair next door. He then took the cabinet she had emptied, and she followed with its bottom drawer. This she slid into position as soon as he placed the chest against the wall.

She leaned against the top, her eyes smiling. "What delightful ways we do find to spend our evenings. Is it not time for our nightly rounds?"

He drew his watch from his pocket, surprised to see the hands standing at just after eleven-thirty. "Get your pelisse," he said, and tried to ignore how pleased he was to have her company.

He ought, he knew, to leave her inside; yet altruism only went so far. He wanted to keep her with him—at least for the initial stroll about the grounds. He'd send her back later, to keep watch up here while he stood vigil without.

He awaited her on the landing, gazing out through the window over the snowscape. All seemed quiet, not a sign of anyone below. He wondered how long that would last.

Daphne rejoined him in a few minutes, now garbed in pelisse and half boots, and with a warm shawl wrapped about her head and neck. Eagerness radiated from her, shining in her lovely eyes. He resisted the impulse to gather her into his arms and kiss her, and instead led the way down the stairs and toward the back of the house. At the doorway leading down to the basements he hesitated, then crossed the hall to the outside door. He would check down there later—when he didn't have Daphne with him.

They stepped from the warmth into the icy chill of the night. Above them spread a canopy of stars and a waning crescent moon. Wisps of clouds, a hazy gray against the vast darkness, drifted high overhead. A clear, beautiful night, filled with glowing light. Not, Adrian decided, a good time for the ghosts to play their loathsome tricks—unless they wanted to be caught. Daphne should be safe.

Satisfied, he set forth to the stable, where all lay sleeping; not even the groom did he glimpse. Daphne strode at his side, huddling into the warmth of her wrappings, casting searching gazes into the shadowed darkness. They circled around to the front of the house, keeping to the hedges and as much out of sight of any possible watching eyes as they could manage. Still nothing. They stood for several long minutes observing the drive and the spinney beyond, where only an owl broke the stillness. Not even the nocturnal animals prowled.

"Do we go to the Manor?" Daphne stood on tiptoe to whisper in his ear.

"Wouldn't you rather go back into the house? I can go alone." His hand covered her fingers where they had come to rest on his arm.

"I intend to stay out here as long as you do, so don't think you can get rid of me."

He didn't mind as much as he should. They retreated a few paces through a gap in the shrubbery, then started under this new cover toward the great house down the drive. Here, too, only stillness greeted them. No lights glimmered in any of the windows; apparently Selwood expected no visitors this night. Adrian wished he could feel certain that meant none would come.

With Daphne just behind him, he made his careful way to the back of the Manor, where the basement windows stared back at him, cold and dark and empty. This might, he realized, be an ideal time to break in and look about. Except for Daphne's presence . . .

She wanted to help. She had every right to, he acknowledged—and with this injury, he needed someone's assistance. But could he protect her if need be? He touched the wrapping on his wrist, considering; his use of it might be difficult, but not impossible.

He'd risk it. The chance was simply too good to miss. He picked his way through a line of shrubs and tested one window after another. Daphne, her eyes wide with comprehension and excitement, hurried to his aid.

As he released the last one, he sat back on his heels,

frowning. All locked. He would have to force one of them—which he doubted he could do in silence.

Yet who would hear him? If they were caught, he might have trouble explaining why he chose to search the Manor in secret rather than telling Selwood of his intention, but what could Selwood do to him? As for Daphne, he doubted Selwood would hurt his cousin. Those two ruffians he didn't trust in the least, but there was no sign they were here.

Thinking of difficulties only wasted his time. He checked the windows again until he found one where the casement no longer fit the warped frame. "With something strong yet flexible . . ." His voice trailed off for a moment. "Like the stock of my driving whip," he finished.

Daphne, eager, examined the area. "Do you think you can reach through and drag back the bolt?"

"There's a chance of it." He flashed her a quick smile. "Come, let's go back to the stable."

She shook her head. "I'll stay here and watch. What if someone comes while you're gone?"

He regarded her with fond exasperation. "That's exactly what worries me."

"Go, or we'll be arguing all night."

Knowing her, they might. Settling her at last well out of sight, he made the trip to the stable and back as quickly as he could—bringing both whip and rope. The former felt ideal in his hand for the purpose—unless it proved too thick.

It nearly did. The top end slid through easily enough, but a bare two inches short of the latch the stock caught and had to be forced, a fraction of an inch at a time.

"You did it!" Daphne, kneeling in the dirt at his side, hugged his arm. "There, just a little—you've caught it. Pull back."

He did, a grating sound reached them, then the window popped open a half inch as the catch slid free.

Adrian withdrew his whip, and Daphne grabbed the frame and dragged it wide.

"We should have brought a lantern," she whispered. "How far down do you think we must drop?"

"Here." Adrian set her aside, then lowered his whip into the basement. It went down a goodly way before he felt the gentle thud as it hit the floor. Holding the thong at his measuring point, he drew the stock back, then frowned. "Ten feet, about. You'd best wait here."

"Don't be absurd. Go first, then you can catch me with your good arm."

His good arm. He'd have two of them if he hadn't been so clumsy. And Daphne—bless her—spoke no words of reproach to her tarnished knight errant. Instead, she lent a hand of her own. She could be a real partner for a man, he realized.

He secured the rope to a tree, then checked the length. It would reach the floor with no trouble, but he'd never be able to climb it with his wrist. Unless . . . he started to knot a loop at the bottom, but found he couldn't apply enough pressure with his left hand to tighten it sufficiently. Again, he needed Daphne.

With her assistance, he soon secured four loops into the rope, strong enough to hold his weight. Satisfied, he threw the end through the window. It would be short now, but as long as he could reach the bottom loop with a foot, he could make his escape—and help Daphne out, as well. Reassured, he sat on the window ledge, turned himself around, then gripped the frame and, with his good hand, lowered himself as far as he could reach. With his height, the drop would be no more than two to three feet. He let go and landed easily.

Darkness engulfed him, though not quite complete. Some of the glowing light filtered through the other windows. The one directly above him proved blocked; Daphne sat in the opening, then the next moment had emulated his movements and hung by her hands. He wrapped his good arm just below her waist and lowered

217

her slight weight to the ground before him. His other hand came up, holding her gently, and he sensed more than heard the quickening of her breath.

For a long moment they remained that way, her hands resting on his shoulders, his lingering about her waist. Instinct raged against common sense, and won. His arms tightened, drawing her closer, and he bent toward her until the fresh scent of her hair filled him and a stray tendril tickled his cheek.

She stepped back abruptly. "We need a lantern."

That wasn't at all what he needed. He ran his hand through his hair, angry with himself—and still wanting her in his arms, wanting to feel her lips beneath his. He was a cad to try to take such advantage of her when she was so completely in his power.

Being a cad, he reflected, could be a great deal more enjoyable than being a gentleman.

He forced his mind back to his surroundings. His eyes had grown accustomed to the darkness of the basement, and he could make out objects and walls at close range. The room in which they stood could be no more than twenty feet square, and held very little. It also, he remembered, did not face toward the Dower House. Any underground passages would leave from a different area.

They found the door by the simple means of feeling their way along the wall. A minute later they stood in a long hallway. Daphne cast an uneasy glance upward, as if she found the cellars oppressive. Adrian couldn't blame her, not in the dark and cold. He paused long enough to reoriented himself, and struck off toward the end of the Manor nearest the Dower House.

The corridor ended in a long chamber lined with oak barrels similar to those that filled the cellars at the Seminary. Numerous windows high in the walls opened onto this room, allowing a greater degree of visibility. A rack, into which Daphne bumped, rattled with disturbed bottles. Wine, Adrian guessed. If the tunnel indeed opened from in here, and was in use, it might be easy to find.

An hour later, though, Adrian admitted defeat—for the moment, at least.

Daphne rose from where she knelt beside a great oak cask. "I thought it would be obvious," she whispered. "If someone is going through here, you'd think they would leave some trace."

"True," Adrian agreed. "The least they could have done would have been to leave it open for us."

She sighed. "Or post a sign pointing toward it. 'This way to underground passage,' or some such thing. What do we do now?"

Adrian strode the length of the wall once more, grasping the edges of the casks, finding nothing that yielded or twisted. "If it weren't for those voices, I would be convinced no tunnel exists. As it is—" He broke off.

"You could have been wrong?" Her voice sounded very small.

"It might have been an odd trick of acoustics, but I don't think so. No, I heard voices, and they came from beyond the wall." He slammed a hand against the last cask. "There's a way through, and we just haven't discovered it yet. But I suppose we'll be able to search more easily from our side, where we at least can bring down all the light we need."

She glanced around the dank chamber, then up toward the ceiling, and shivered. "I suppose we had better leave before we get caught."

Moving cautiously, he guided her back to the room with the open window. The rope remained where he'd left it; so far, they had not been discovered. He grabbed the end, located the first loop, and thrust his booted foot into it. With his good hand he pulled himself up, put his other foot into the next loop, then hauled himself to the sill. In another moment he swung a leg over the edge and rolled out.

By the time he leaned back through, Daphne already had clambered into the first loop and waited, arms extended. He caught her hand and helped her to the next.

219

Then she was scrambling through the casement and away from him, turning her back to straighten her disheveled clothing. Adrian's gaze lingered on her slight form for an agreeable few moments, then he pulled up the rope and shut the window. On the fourth attempt with the whip, he succeeded in closing the latch. Only a couple of minutes with a branch sufficed to smooth over the snow they had trampled; when he finished, he didn't think they had left any noticeable trace of their unorthodox expedition.

Satisfied, he brushed the clinging ice from his breeches, turned back toward the Dower House, and stopped abruptly. With the brightness of the star-strewn night, he could clearly see even at that distance the figure standing in the drive, its sheet flapping in the breeze. It made no attempt to hide itself; in fact, it planted itself in plain sight and stared up at the windows as if waiting.

"Louisa's Monty," Daphne exclaimed. "No one else would be so brazen about it. But how dare he, after last time!"

"Possibly Louisa hasn't had a chance to tell him they've been caught," Adrian pointed out.

"Then it's high time someone informed the young jackanapes his game is over." Daphne strode forward.

Adrian caught her up after only a few steps and drew her into the sheltering cover of the hedge. "I'm not so sure it is Monty," he whispered. "This one doesn't seem to be trying to lure anyone out of the house."

As they watched, the figure approached a window and tested it, then moved on to the next. "It's trying to get in," Daphne breathed. "But—I thought our ghost entered through the underground passage."

"Maybe we were in its way." Adrian realized he stroked her arm, and let her go. "Come, I want you to wait just inside the back door. No, don't argue. I need you there. If he tries to go in that way, you can scream to let me know."

"And what will you be doing?" she asked.

"Trying to follow it, in case it finds another way in."

He escorted Daphne around to the rear of the house and saw her safely indoors, then hurried back to the front. For a moment he could detect no trace of their specter, then he caught a glimpse of unhurried movement near the far side of the building. The ghost had worked its way along the entire front, apparently without success. Adrian set off after it, moving with stealth.

Yet he wanted to overtake it before it reached the door behind which Daphne waited. He increased his pace and reached the corner, only to see no one along the side of the house. There was no reason for the ghost to linger; few windows looked out this way, at least on an easily reachable level. He followed the path and peered around the next corner.

There. His specter had moved quickly, and even now approached the rear door—almost as if it had been making for that destination. As Adrian started forward, he heard the faint click of the latch being lifted. Daphne . . .

He ran headlong, tensed for her scream.

It didn't come. Instead, the specter stood as if transfixed on the doorstep. Adrian crashed through a bush, and the figure jumped, then bolted down the steps and vanished into the shrubbery.

In another minute, Adrian reached Daphne where she now stood on the porch, clutching her shawl beneath her chin. Even by moonlight she looked pale. He caught her into his arms, holding her tightly, his cheek pressed against her hair; then he set her away from him, his hands gripping her shoulders as he searched her face. "Are you all right?"

She turned wide, shocked eyes toward him. "I—yes, of course. Just—" She shuddered. "It was just so very—distressing. No," she added as Adrian started down the steps. "He—it must be long gone, by now. Don't bother chasing him. I—I would rather you see me upstairs."

221

Adrian returned to her at once, his arm wrapping about her waist for support. She must be badly shaken, indeed, to beg him to abandon pursuit. "What did it look like?" he asked.

She shook her head. "It—I can't describe it. There was no face. I—please, I just want to forget about it."

He frowned, but knew he could not press her, not at the moment. He would have to content himself with offering her what comfort he could. He secured the door, but not until they started up the stairs did Daphne stop trembling.

Chapter Fifteen

The long hours of the night dragged past. Daphne lay awake in her bed, listening to the distant chiming of the clock in the hall two floors below. Her fingers pleated then smoothed the sheet, then repeated the process, over and over.

The dim glow of the stars and crescent moon gave way at last to a gray haze that seeped into her chamber, giving shape to the furnishings. When she could discern the outline of the chair opposite her, she threw back her comforter and, shivering in the chill air of early dawn, climbed out of bed. What she needed to do had best be done at once, before anyone else rose and discovered what she was about.

She padded to the hearth, laid a fresh fire with the kindling and peat that waited in a bucket, then struck a flame from her tinder box. The resulting blaze, though friendly, did little to dispel the iciness of the morning. She crossed to the wardrobe, drew out her warmest gown, and dressed quickly. Her stoutest boots would be best; it would be a long walk. She donned her pelisse, wrapped a warm shawl about her head and shoulders, then put her hand to her door. This part had to be done in complete silence. If Mr. Carstairs should be awake and hear her . . .

Holding her breath, she eased the door open, cast a rapid glance about the corridor, and gasped as a dark shape loomed at the far end. That armoire. Relief left her weak; but she had no time to waste. She closed the door behind her and crept toward the stairs.

If only she dared light a candle . . . and if only that second step didn't creak. . . . She leaned on the railing and skipped it to be safe.

Two agonizingly slow minutes later, she reached the ground floor. So far, all went well. She let out the breath she held, and when she inhaled again, the scent of baking bread filled her. Cook was awake and at work in the kitchens.

Daphne hesitated. She could slip out the library door onto the terrace, but Mr. Carstairs might see her from above—if he were awake. Or, she could surrender to the sudden hunger brought on by the scent of baking dough and—yes, of cinnamon. The delicious aroma served as a will-o-the-wisp, tantalizing, beckoning her, luring her onward. She followed her nose, feeling her way along the dark hall to the back stair, then descending to the kitchen.

Light filled the room, and Cook stood by the hearth, plump and welcoming, in one hand a pan of rolls which she had just drawn from the great oven. Wisps of gray hair escaped from beneath her mobcap and clung to her flour-dusted cheeks. The woman looked around as Daphne entered, and her eyebrows rose in her heat-reddened face.

She set the pan down, inserted the next into the oven, then turned to her visitor. "Well, now Miss Daphne, what brings you down at such an hour?"

"I couldn't sleep." Daphne leaned against the edge of the wooden table and eyed the cooling rolls. "May I?"

Cook waved a permissive hand and returned to her rolling pin.

Daphne selected one. "I feel so restless," she announced in what she hoped was a normal voice, "I'm off for a walk."

Cook stopped in the act of shaping another roll. "At

this hour, miss? Surely you won't be off a-tramping through the snow in the dark."

"It's growing light. And thank you." She waved the roll by way of explanation and scuttled for the door. Two minutes later she had mounted the stairs and let herself out the back way. Munching her breakfast, she set off through the wood along the shortcut to the Bath road.

Two miles on a cool spring afternoon made a pleasant walk. That same distance in an icy January dawn was quite another matter. Daphne huddled into her pelisse and wished her gloves were warmer. At least no snow fell at the moment, she reminded herself as she trudged through a deep drift to reach the relatively cleared stretch of road.

A bird trilled out its song in the trees above, and the pungent odor of wet pine filled her nostrils. Everything felt fresh and new—and frozen. She increased her pace—though she dreaded what she would find at the end of her journey.

At last—and all too soon—she reached the outskirts of Bath. She could find the major sights of the town, but other than those, she knew little. Where, for example, would a gentleman put up if he wished to stay here at little expense to himself? Definitely not the York, which was the only hotel with which she was acquainted. So what did that leave?

Any number of lesser establishments, she realized with a sinking heart. That her quarry might not be here at all, and her morning's expedition futile, she acknowledged. But she had to start somewhere, and Bath seemed the most likely place.

She walked until she reached a modest hostelry of comfortable if not extravagant aspect. She went inside the dark common room but could see no one; she would have to venture farther, it seemed. As she stood there, hesitating, uncertain, something metallic clanged in the distance, a promise of life. More sounds of activity followed, and they led her to the kitchens.

A rotund man of middle years and cheerful aspect, a towel tied about his waist, stood at a long wooden table. He looked up from the list he perused, set it down at once, wiped his hands on his begrimed makeshift apron, and came forward. Daphne asked about a possible guest, and received a polite but negative response. After thanking the man, she left to continue her tour of the least costly of Bath's many hostelries.

On her sixth attempt, the proprietor, a gaunt man of morose countenance, listened to her question, then let out a deep sigh. " 'E's 'ere, all right and tight. You'll be wanting a word with 'im, I suppose?" He made no move to leave.

"Yes, I would," Daphne prompted. Perhaps she could bribe him into lumbering up the stairs.

The man grunted. "Well, you can't. Left word 'e doesn't want to be disturbed, 'asn't 'e?"

"Has he?" Daphne countered. "You needn't give the matter another thought. Go right ahead and disturb him. You may take a message to him that I'll await him in the parlor. And if he's asleep, you will wake him up." She fixed a compelling eye on him that had sent many a young lady scurrying about her appointed tasks.

The man shuffled his feet and regarded her askance. "Won't like that, 'e won't."

"And I shan't like it if you do not do as I ask. Am I to be forced to go up to him myself?"

The landlord considered. "That don't seem proper," he said at last.

"Very true. So you will go for me, and I shall await his coming."

The man nodded. "Aye," he said in desultory tones. "That'll be the ticket, it will." With another heavy sigh, he dragged his feet out of the room.

And he hadn't told her where to find the private parlor. She found a tapman able to give her this information—along with the caveat it had been hired for the next week or more by the gentleman occupying the best front chamber. As that was the very gentleman she had come to see, this information did not in the least dismay her. She ordered coffee, mounted the steps, and located the chamber on the second try.

She had barely time to strip off her gloves and unwind her shawl before a light tap sounded on the door, and a maid entered to lay a fire. It caught quickly, and as Daphne moved to warm herself, the tapman arrived bearing a tray with a steaming pot of coffee, two cups, and a plate of rolls and biscuits. The aroma filled the cozy chamber, reminding Daphne that her early walk had made her ravenous. She settled down to her wait in relative comfort, seated in a wingback chair, her feet propped on a footstool and extended toward the blazing hearth. She sipped coffee, ate a roll, and began to feel slightly less as if the world had collapsed about her.

A little more than half an hour passed before a florid gentleman of ample girth and genial aspect, clothed in a flamboyant dressing gown of purple and green hues, hurled open the door of the room and posed in dramatic fashion on the threshold. Daphne remained where she sat and regarded him critically.

"Me darlin'!" he exclaimed, his Irish brogue, normally barely discernible, now emphasized for effect. "How I have yearned for this hour, to clasp ye once more to me bosom."

"Oh, no, don't risk mussing your ruffles." She stood, but only to put more distance between herself and the exuberant gentleman.

He pulled up short, drew himself erect to his full five-foot-four, and huffed. "I am affronted, my dear." He abandoned the brogue in favor of a more theatrical flair. "The coolness of your reception, the curtness of your tone, the aloofness of your manner. Indeed, they must all combine, to my sorrow, to tell me you are not as delighted to see your long lost Uncle Percival as I am to see you."

"Long-lost, indeed. I saw you on your last visit to England just under four years ago. Or was it your last? We certainly have not heard from you since shortly after that. And what do you mean by reappearing now, of all times, and in such a manner? Playing ghost, of all things!"

He gave an affected sigh, drew a handkerchief from his capacious pocket, and dabbed at his eyes. "My little Daphne. You, whom I nurtured and housed, and thought of as my own daughter. Who could have believed you would have turned out so unfeeling. How your poor mama must turn over in her grave."

"So you got my letter saying she had died. I wasn't sure." She folded her arms. "Now, cut line, Uncle. What game are you playing? I—we all—thought you safely ensconced on the Continent operating your latest gaming hell. In Italy, was it not?"

"It was, my dear, it was." He poured himself a coffee and helped himself from the plate of rolls and biscuits. Around a mouthful, he said, "An excellent establishment, too. In Milan. I quite miss it."

She refilled her own cup and returned to her chair. "Let me guess. I suppose you had a little run-in with the local authorities?"

"It was no such thing," he declared, the picture of indignation. "Mine was a most reputable establishment— well, for the most part. Just a run of ill luck. And now I find myself forced to turn my mind to other ways of raising the wind." He beamed at her.

Her unease grew. "You have hit upon a plan?"

"But of course. My child, can you doubt me? I remembered the family legacy."

"The family—" She eyed him with suspicion. "*What* family legacy?"

He paused with a roll halfway to his mouth and shot her a quick look. He took a bite with deliberation, then

228

aved the rest in the air with a casual hand. "Thought
ou knew. Well, nothing really to know, I suppose. So
ll me, how do you go on? Still at the Seminary, I sup-
ose? And speaking of it, shouldn't you be there right
ow? Shouldn't skip your lessons, you know. You—"

"Uncle!" She broke across his ramblings. "You will
ot misdirect me. What, exactly, do you mean about a
gacy?"

He looked uncomfortable. "Just a rumor, you know.
robably nothing in it."

"In what?" She kept her patience by the merest
read. "Do explain yourself. You would not have gone
o the expense of coming here for a mere rumor."

He finished the roll and stared into the bottom of his
up. "Some silly story about a fortune buried some-
here in the Dower House," he mumbled.

"A—" Daphne shook her head. "Oh, no, Uncle.
hat's doing it too brown. A fortune? The Selwoods?"

He straightened, indignant. "You doubt my word? I'll
ave you remember, my girl, that my father was a
ousin and close crony of the father of Sophronia,
eatrice, and Elspeth. Too brown, indeed. I know
hings," he added with a wink.

"Such as the fact that their grandfather lost every-
hing? Uncle Percival, there was no fortune left to hide."

"Your skepticism, dear child." He shook his head. "I'll
ave you know that just before the old gentleman blew
is brains out, he hid several valuable paintings—which
eren't entailed, mind—at the Dower House. Didn't
ant them sold to pay his debts along with everything
lse. His way of providing for his family's future." Uncle
ercival beamed on her in triumph.

Paintings. . . . She remembered Cousin Beatrice say-
ng something about valuable paintings going missing at
he time of the evaluation. Had they indeed been hid-
en instead of stolen? Valuable paintings . . .

She turned on her uncle, her outrage welling. "You've

been haunting the Dower House, haven't you? T[o] frighten everyone away so you could hunt for them."

"No." He shook his head in sorrow. "I cannot tak[e] credit for such an inspired scheme. I merely copied i[t] when I learned others were trying it. And I must say,[''] he added, sounding aggrieved, "there are so many ghosts creeping about that place, it's a wonder we don'[t] bump into each other more often."

Daphne rested her forehead in her hands. So Uncle Percival was one of the ghosts—well, she'd known tha[t] since she ran into him at the back door last night, shock ing her more than any of the other specters had suc ceeded in doing. But he wasn't responsible for the original plot against the school. Her Uncle Percival Louisa's Monty—did *everyone* flit around the seminary a[t] night garbed in old sheets? So many ghosts . . .

With so many, the potential of scandal for the schoo[l] increased dramatically, looming over her like a threaten ing thundercloud.

She drew a steadying breath. "What do you know o[f] these paintings?"

Uncle Percival's gaze shifted from her. "Well, now, a[s] to that, I have need of them, me darlin'."

"That's nonsense." Daphne straightened. "The paint ings, as contents of the Dower House, belong to my cousins Sophronia, Beatrice, and Elspeth, and they need them to save the school!"

Percival pursued his lips. "This lack of family feeling I detect in you is to be deplored, my girl. I, your blood uncle, have a very pressing need of those paintings, too!"

"You are ignoring the fact that my cousins—*your* cousins, I might add—are also very close blood relatives. And they have a *legitimate* claim."

"Claim!" Percival waved that aside as irrelevant. "They have lived in that house all of their lives, and have they bothered to unearth their treasure? No! They have no interest in it!"

"They don't know about it, you mean."

"There!" Percival beamed at her. "If it belongs to them, they should know about it, should they not? That *proves* my claim. No." He held up his hand. "You do not need to apologize." He swept expansive arms wide. "I forgive you."

Daphne forbore to argue. What she was to do about her exasperating uncle escaped her at the moment. If he remained in the neighborhood much longer, she doubted she could count on his discretion; he possessed none. He would start with simple games of cards or dice, but his Greeking ways would soon land him—and the Seminary—in fresh scandal. Perhaps Mr. Carstairs . . .

The horror of that thought left her weak. Mr. Carstairs must never learn of her delightful but disreputable relative. The things Uncle Percival could—and undoubtedly would—reveal. . . . The thought left her ill. There was no controlling her uncle's wayward tongue. Let him have but a bottle of canary, and he would recount his shocking history—and her own. It would be all over Bath in a trice that she had spent eighteen months gracing the gaming tables in that ill-fated hell in Covent Garden.

She shuddered at the thought. She'd been only fifteen, and her mother had been preoccupied with her eldest daughter's infant son, her second daughter's imminent confinement, and her third's approaching wedding. Mrs. Selwood had been only too happy to let her fourth daughter "keep house" for an uncle, never dreaming of the sort of establishment over which he presided. But then Percival had a run of luck and moved to more genteel quarters in Jermyn Street, and Daphne's mother had at last been alerted to the true nature of her brother-in-law's house. She had sent for Daphne forthwith, forbidden any further communication between them, and strove to achieve a far more respectable background for her daughter.

Well, Daphne reflected, she had become respectable An art mistress. But if the truth came out, she would be ruined. She could not remain in her position to blemish the reputation of the Seminary, no respectable family would take her for governess, she would be denied the possibility of ever doing anything worthwhile with her life. For that matter, no gentleman would ever consider any but the shadiest of alliances with her.

As for Mr. Carstairs . . .

Warmth crept into her cheeks, then rushed throughout her body. An alliance with Mr. Carstairs. So far, during the course of their growing friendship, she had refused, by sheer determination, to permit her thoughts from going too far in this direction.

But they were there now, and far too enticing. He had long disrupted the tranquillity of her mind. His humor and sheer enjoyment of a challenge appealed to her more than she'd wanted to admit. When he put a comforting arm about her, her pulse quickened and she wanted only to remain at his side, to explore the wild, unfamiliar sensations that raced through her.

She loved him, and that realization shattered her.

She took a revivifying sip of coffee, but it didn't help, not in the face of this—this disaster. Mr. Carstairs didn't want a wife. He had chosen the life of an Oxford don, a bachelor's existence.

But now he said he *might* not go back. What if he sought a parish, to work with those who needed him . . . ?

She clutched her cup. She had rejected the thought of marriage before; the frivolous, pointless existence of the *ton* held no appeal for her. If she ever married, she wanted it to be a partnership with a gentleman who strove to achieve some purpose, as did she. And she wanted to bring to that partnership every bit as much as she would receive from it.

Marriage to a man of the cloth—to this particular man of the cloth—would be the only one to suit her.

But what could she bring to him for her share? Only ruination.

That realization sent pain knifing through her. If the truth ever became known—and disreputable secrets had a way of becoming common knowledge—she would be a millstone about his neck, destroying his chances for advancement. She could never do that to Mr. Carstairs—to Adrian.

His name, spoken in her mind, sent a thrill through her, which she fought back.

She had to keep him at a distance from now on. She couldn't bear it if he learned the truth, the tale of her past that Uncle Percival could—and undoubtedly would without thinking—someday reveal. The threat hung over her like a Sword of Damocles, and the hair stretched very thin indeed.

Not that Adrian would be disgusted at the thought of her dealing cards at the tables amidst the hangers-on of society, the lowlifes shunned by the gentlemen who frequented the more acceptable hells. Yet he should be. Instead, he undoubtedly would be amused, and his chivalrous instincts would rise to the occasion and he nobly would sweep her into the security and respectability of marriage, sacrificing without a thought his own interests.

That would sever his ties with Oxford, denying him the chance to make that choice for himself.

She couldn't allow that. She wanted to be with him—more than anything—but she would not be so selfish as to take her happiness at the expense of his future. He must be free to make his own choices, choose his own life, just as she had wanted to choose hers.

And whatever path he followed, she could not be part of it, for her past would forever be a stumbling block to him.

From now on she must discourage the intimacy she cherished, and at all costs keep him out of reach of Uncle Percival's betraying tongue. At least she need not struggle for long. Soon—all too soon—Adrian would leave Selwood Seminary, and she would see him again only at rare intervals. That would solve the problem—but how could she bear to watch him go, knowing she had no right to do otherwise? She rose, fighting back tears.

Uncle Percival looked up from where he'd been contemplating the fire in peaceful silence. "Going, m'dear? You won't spend another half hour with your old uncle?"

She shook her head, battling for control. "I must get back," she managed. "Now, I want you to promise me something."

He eyed her, his expression rife with suspicion. "What?"

"I want you to behave with the utmost decorum and not, under any conditions, to indulge in any card-sharping practices. And whatever else you do, stay away from the Seminary."

Percival humphed. "Really, me darlin'—"

"Promise! You know how scandal follows you."

He hung his head and gave vent to a gusty sigh. "There's just no accounting for it."

"I don't want it touching the Seminary. Is that understood?"

He sprawled back in the chair, shaking his graying head. "To think it has come to this, my own beloved niece implying—"

"I'm implying nothing," she broke in. "I'm *telling* you. Behave yourself, I beg of you."

She succeeded in extracting a half-hearted consent from him, and took her leave. Her heart heavy, she began the long walk back to the Dower House. Thoughts of Adrian—of all she could never have—jumbled in her mind until she forced them out. Instead, with considerable effort, she concentrated on the Seminary's shaky future.

Uncle Percival spoke of the paintings as if certain of

their existence. Did others share this knowledge? Cousin George, perhaps?

Really, she reflected, her life was quite simple. All she had to do was locate that secret passage within the ancient house, find the paintings, and make sure they were placed far beyond the reach of anyone but the proper owners. Then she had to see Uncle Percival safely off to the Continent once more, where he could create as many scandals as he chose where they would not touch his beleaguered family. And of course she had to avoid any further enjoyment of Adrian's—Mr. Carstairs's—company. Truly, what could be easier than all that?

She trudged on, her eyes stinging with unshed tears.

Adrian set down his pen and frowned at the words he had formed on the paper before him. He had made progress this morning, but enough? It didn't make up for the time he had spent of late in vain pursuit of ghosts. Or did his dissertation really matter that much to him any more?

Not, he realized, as a means of advancing in his position at Oxford. Yet as a personal goal, it meant a great deal—but not as much as helping the Selwood ladies and outwitting the miscreants responsible for their troubles.

He regarded his volume of Herodotus for a long minute, then closed the book. He would not resume it, he determined, until he had solved this mystery and seen the Seminary safe. He could work as long and hard as he wished once no threat any longer hung over the ladies' heads.

The decision heartened him, filling him with a sense of purpose he had not known since—he paused. Since the last time he had dedicated himself to someone's aid. A rueful smile tugged at his lips. He did not think of himself as a knight errant. More, a meddler. Well, he would meddle now to his heart's content.

He let himself out into the hall just as Daphne emerged from her chamber, gowned in the soft blue merino she had worn that night he arrived at the vicarage and tumbled headlong into this imbroglio. Memories flooded back of her antagonism, of her fighting spirit, of the light flashing in those lovely green eyes. He had admired her then; now he knew her so much better.

He started forward, but she turned from him, closing her door and hurrying down the hall.

"There you are." It surprised him how much he'd missed her. "I wondered where you had gotten to this morning."

She hesitated, but did not face him. "I went for a long walk," she said, "but now I have duties I must get back to."

"Have you? I thought perhaps you might help me move furniture."

She had taken another step away, but now stopped. "I have other things to do," she repeated, her voice toneless, and continued on her way.

He watched her retreating back with a frown. Her shoulders seemed slumped, almost defeated, which was not at all like her. Perhaps exhaustion, he thought. They had spent so many sleepless nights keeping watch and chasing uselessly through the snow after ghosts who vanished practically beneath their hands. It would be enough to discourage anyone, he told himself. Yet he had not expected that from someone of Daphne's fighting spirit.

He had barely reached the attics and started to work when Miss Sophronia appeared. She stood in the doorway and exclaimed, "Why, how far you have come! But such a dreadful amount of work. Dear boy, and you all alone. Allow me to assist you."

He set her to removing the drawers of the chest he had next to haul, but no sooner had she dragged out the top one than she exclaimed over the contents, drawing out a packet of yellowed letters that she cried had been written by herself and her two sisters to their mother, while they attended school. Nothing would do for her but to open and peruse them. As she did this perched upon a rickety chair balanced against the chest, Adrian had little choice but to turn his attention to a different cabinet in a more awkward position.

"But how silly of me, to be sure," she said when she realized what she did, and apologized profusely. "But what could one expect? So many years, so very many memories." She sighed and laid the letters aside with obvious regret. She replaced them in the drawer that now rested on the floor, only to exclaim again in delight as she unearthed a ream of papers she declared to be Miss Elspeth's earliest attempts at schoolwork.

Resigned, Adrian turned his attention once more to the cabinet and allowed Sophronia her dreaming into memories. He found it difficult working around her, and she no longer made even a pretence of assisting him, so totally absorbed was she in the ancient treasures she discovered. Ruefully, Adrian wondered what would have happened if she had uncovered old accounts, or something else of a very boring nature. But being of a philosophical turn of mind, he accepted the situation. Short of bodily ousting her from the room with her booty, which he briefly and humorously contemplated, there was nothing else he could do. And should he banish her from the chamber with her treasures, she would be quite hurt and protest how silly she was for at least the next twenty minutes.

They continued thus until she had finished the contents of that drawer, and happily removed the next. Here she found a selection of gloves, lace mittens, and shawls, all of which she wanted to try on. So delighted was she in these latest discoveries that she hurried off in search of one or other of her sisters with whom to share the joys.

Adrian wasted no time, but instantly pulled out the remaining drawers, shoved them aside, and maneuvered the chest across the hall into the waiting room. Here he set it where it would not be in his way, but where the sisters could continue their explorations to their hearts' content.

He had barely replaced the last of the drawers and returned for the next trunk when Daphne appeared in the doorway. She regarded him with a solemn gaze, the usual light extinguished in her lovely eyes. She went at once to help him, grasping one ancient brass handle and trying to pull it. He pushed, taking the greatest share of the weight, and in silence they dragged it to its new resting place.

She straightened up, easing what must be a stiff back. "How grateful I will be," she said, "when this is all over."

Something in her voice alerted Adrian that she did not speak simply of the hauntings and the peril in which the Seminary stood. He watched her closely, noting the almost breeziness of her manner as she smoothed the dark tendrils of hair back from her forehead.

"If all goes well," she went on, "you will be able to leave soon, and I know how glad you will be."

He made no response.

Her gaze flickered to his face, then dropped. "I know I shall be only too pleased to return to a normal routine. Can you imagine, I might be able to paint once more with only the girls to interrupt me?"

Meaning she looked forward to his own departure? He could place no other interpretation upon her words—or her manner.

She dusted her hands. "It will be quite delightful when it is quiet here once more. I do most sincerely appreciate the freedom to paint as I wish."

"I had thought you free to do so, now," Adrian said.

She gave a laugh that sounded odd, not quite sincere. "With so many strangers running about the place? I want a familiar routine, no intruders." She straightened

238

abruptly from where she had leaned against a table. "I have chores below," she said shortly, and left.

Adrian could not help but take her meaning. He was the only intruder, aside from the ghosts. She had just informed him she wished him to leave and allow her life to return to normal. But what had brought this on? he wondered. They had seemed well on the way to an excellent understanding the last few days. Certainly as late as last night.

Last night. He remembered leaving her just within the house, guarding the back door, and the ghostly figure that had confronted her there. Had it frightened her that badly that she had retreated within herself? The thought puzzled him. His only recourse, he knew irritatingly well, would be to lay these ghosts once and for all, free her from whatever fears loomed great at her shoulder, and allow her to actually choose what life she wanted next.

That that life might not include him, he realized, was a very real possibility.

That he wanted it to, he now knew for certain.

By the time he quit to ease his aching wrist and to seek nourishment from the kitchens to avoid the girls, he had cleared most of the wall with the windows overlooking the drive, and as far as ten feet into the room. Had he yet reached the point where his specter had vanished that first night? He couldn't be sure. But he had certainly seen no trace of any secret passages through either the wall or floor. He found this depressing.

After eating a thoughtful, solitary meal in the kitchens, he crossed the hall and paced the length of the cellar, pausing to listen at that far wall. Nothing. Not even voices drifting down from above. The young ladies by now must have moved on to the drawing room.

There. He heard the first strains of the pianoforte, not quite in tune and played with more verve than finesse. Obviously not a music lover at the keyboard. He hesitated, straining his ears, but couldn't convince himself that was anything like the voices he had heard the other night.

He walked along the walls, pausing by the great oak casks, running his hands along them. Did one of those intricate carvings hide an opening mechanism he had so far missed? He could spend the next few weeks here, examining them, to discover the right spot. And in the end, he knew full well, he might find it securely fastened from the tunnel end. He even might have encountered the mechanism already, only to have it remain locked and immovable—and unnoticeable.

On that cheerful thought, he returned to the hall leading to the kitchens, then mounted the stairs. Too many young ladies infested this floor, he decided, so he made his way up one more flight. Here, he had already explored the rooms, the sleeping quarters for most of the school. He doubted he would find anything more there.

Restlessness drove him back to the attics, where he stared at the room in which he had done so much work. Another day of hard labor might well finish it—if his wrist allowed. But what might it produce? A great deal of dust and cobwebs, he knew already. But would it also reveal the passageway he sought? Only tomorrow would tell.

He set down his lantern and drew out his watch. Barely ten o'clock. Far too early for ghostly activity. He considered the remaining furniture in the room, but common sense won out over his rejection of his injury. If he didn't let the joint rest now, he would accomplish little heavy work on the morrow.

Frustration at this weakness sent him out of doors, pacing the grounds as far as the Manor House, then across a small field until he realized he had ventured deep into Romney's property. He turned back, following a well-worn path—testimony to the length of the friendship between the two men—until he once more reached

240

the gardens delineating the border of the Selwood estate. The exercise did little to ease either the pain in his wrist or the turmoil in his mind.

He returned indoors, started up the stairs toward the attics, then reversed his steps, knowing the sight of the unfinished work up there would only grate on him further. Instead, he made his way once more to the cellar where he could glare as much as he wished at the oaken casks and wine racks beyond.

He had been there for perhaps half an hour, running his fingers along the carvings, when the soft rumble reached him once more. He tensed and crept to the wall. Still nothing distinct, but definitely voices. He couldn't even tell if they were the same ones—though most likely they would be.

This, he felt certain, contained the key—but he didn't yet know to what, or how it all worked, or even why.

The voices retreated, leaving him once more in silence. Frustrated, he struck the edge of the cask with the fist of his good arm, then stalked out of the cellar and made his way up the stairs. Stillness shrouded the Seminary; no one even tortured the old pianoforte. Everyone must have retired to their beds.

He climbed to his chamber where he strode to the window and glared out into the night sky. What was he missing? What hadn't he yet connected that would explain all that went on here? None of the explanations yet forwarded made sufficient sense. Nothing even began to. . . .

Below, by the faint light of the cloud-veiled moon, a pale shape slipped among the trees, approaching the house. One of his ghosts. And not, he noted, much past midnight. Anger surged through him. He grasped his greatcoat, eased his injured wrist into the sleeve, and set off.

This time, he would not be denied.

Chapter Sixteen

Adrian crept down the hall toward the stairs as silently as he could. He was getting very tired, he reflected, of this chasing after specters in the dark of night and having nothing to show for it—aside from a sprained wrist. Tonight, he determined, he would catch someone.

He eased down the steps, skipping the one that creaked, and turned at the landing to begin the next flight. A scraping sound reached him from the floor below, and he drew back at once, keeping well within the shadowed recesses. Someone else, it seemed, also crept through the darkness.

He had a minute or two to wait. Then a cloaked figure emerged into his view, carrying a band box clasped tightly before her. The girl cast a furtive glance down the hall, then up the stairs, and he recognized Louisa Trevellian. Another meeting with her Monty? He would be quite glad to have a few words with that gentleman, and they were likely to be quite sharp and to the point.

Louisa started down the stairs, and Adrian, keeping just far enough behind her to stay out of sight, followed with extreme caution. On the ground floor she looked about, then made her way to the library with its exit onto the terrace and garden beyond. Adrian gave her a head start, then moved to the door.

She had not closed it completely, probably fearing the

sound of the latch. He touched it, and it eased open under only the slightest pressure. Not a breath of sound did it make.

She had reached the French doors. Just outside, he could see a dim figure, more a hazy gray shape silhouetted in the moonlight against the darker shrubs. She set down her bandbox, fumbled with the latch, then threw the door wide. The figure stepped inward, and Adrian gained a quick impression of dark eyes set in a narrow face, unruly sandy hair, and a ruddy complexion, before Louisa, with a slight cry, flung herself against the young man's chest. His arms came up, hesitated, then patted her uncertainly on the back.

Adrian strolled forward, curiosity replacing his anger, even edging out his sense of triumph over at last catching one of the ghosts. "A very affecting sight, to be sure," he said, his voice purely conversational.

With a cry of alarm, Louisa sprang away from what could only be her Monty. The young man let her go and stared in open-mouthed alarm at Adrian. Louisa cast a frustrated glance at her tall, gangly gallant and returned to his side, gripping his hand. Her sudden pallor vanished beneath a deep and becoming flush. The young gentleman glanced at her in frantic appeal.

Adrian looked him over, assessing that anguished gaze, the honest features, the callow expression, and dismissed any lingering suspicions about his motives in haunting the seminary. Adrian had chosen his opening approach correctly. He folded his arms, eyebrows raised in a combination inquiry and invitation.

"Mr.—Mr. Carstairs." Louisa gave her companion's arm a slight, encouraging shake.

"Carstairs?" The youth blinked at him. "This the man you told me about?" he asked Louisa.

Louisa straightened, taking on all the air of a tragic heroine. "I suppose you want to know what we are doing? We are eloping."

"Are you?" Adrian asked politely.

"We are," Louisa assured him.

Or did she reaffirm that fact to her reluctant swain? Never could Adrian remember encountering a more uneasy looking bridegroom. He fought back a smile. "It seems a rather drastic step. I can imagine few things more uncomfortable than a headlong race up the Great North Road in the depths of January."

Monty nodded. "Just what I've been telling her."

Louisa glared at him, then turned back to Adrian. "You can't stop us."

"I have no intention of it." Adrian glanced at the youth, caught the flicker of disappointment in the boy's expression, and steadfastly looked away before he burst out laughing.

This endeavor to maintain his countenance must have produced a sterner result than he'd intended, for Louisa regarded him with renewed alarm. "Oh, please, Mr. Carstairs." She inserted a considerable amount of desperation into her whispered plea. "You must stand our friend. Someone must. We have no one to turn to for help, and my plight is quite desperate."

Adrian's brows rose a fraction higher, but he refrained from pointing out just how many friends at the Seminary Louisa could command should she need them.

"I am in the most terrible fix," the girl went on. "You can have no idea how dreadful it has all been, what I have suffered."

"No, I haven't," Adrian agreed, leaving implicit the invitation to inform him.

A quavering sigh escaped Louisa.

"Don't see how he can help," Monty said with a shake of his head. "Only wish he could."

"But I want him to understand why I must do something so—so repugnant to a gently bred female." Louisa turned to Adrian. "I have received a letter from my mama, you see." Tears hovered on her lashes, then one slipped down her cheek, followed quickly by another.

Monty nodded. "She did. Saw it."

"But I haven't," Adrian pointed out. "What did it say to—er—cause so rash an action?"

"Mama is planning to bring me out in May with—with an engagement ball." Her voice broke on a shaking sob. "My wedding is already planned for the first week of June, and I cannot go through with it. I cannot!" She ended on a soft wail.

Monty patted her somewhat clumsily on the shoulder. "Promised I wouldn't let anyone force her into anything. And I won't," he added manfully.

At whatever dreadful cost to himself? Adrian regarded the young man with amused compassion. "Have you any objections to your betrothed?" he asked Louisa, "beyond the fact, of course," he added diplomatically, "that your affections have been given elsewhere?"

Louisa blinked rapidly, dislodging several more tears. "He is quite the most horrid man," she said, her voice still unsteady. "Mama only encouraged his suit because he is a viscount and the heir to an earldom. She wants so much for me to marry a title."

"As far as I know," Adrian pointed out, "being a viscount and heir to an earldom is not really a reason to despise a man as a marriage partner."

Her chin quivered. "Oh, if that were all. But he has the coldest eyes and clammy hands, and when he speaks to me—he has no conversation at all. And I cannot bear the thought of his—" she shuddered, and forced herself to go on, "of his touching me."

"Heard some bad reports of him." Monty nodded vigorously, setting the unruly shock of sandy hair dancing on his forehead. "Not the sort of thing to discuss in the presence of females." Censure hung heavy in his tone.

Louisa sniffed. "He—he means he is a loose fish."

Monty blinked startled eyes at her, apparently taken aback by her outspokenness.

"Well, he is," Louisa asserted. "You said so yourself."

245

"*I* called him a rake and libertine," he corrected.

"And what, pray," Louisa demanded, "is the difference?"

Monty launched into an argument about proprieties and the vocabulary of a gently bred young lady, which Adrian ignored. Instead, being well-acquainted with the upper strata of society, he ran in review every eligible heir to an earldom he could call to mind. "Bromley," he said in distaste after a moment.

Louisa broke off her stinging retort to Monty and stared at Adrian. "Do you know him?" she asked, obviously shocked.

Monty frowned. "Wouldn't have thought him a suitable friend for a clergyman."

"He's not," Adrian said shortly. "So your mother has betrothed you to Bromley." He regarded Louisa with more compassion, feeling she had some cause, beyond her love of dramatics, for those tears. "The only thing I can say in his favor," he said at last, "is that he's titled. He has not even the vestige of a fortune."

Louisa sniffed. "Mama is providing that. I am quite an heiress," she added, naively.

"Have you explained your feelings to your mother?" he asked gently.

Louisa stared at him as if appalled at the mere prospect. "Not even Papa dares stand up to her," she exclaimed. "It's quite impossible."

"Dragon of a female," Monty added, glum.

Adrian nodded in understanding. If the woman were even a tenth as cold-blooded and determined as his own Aunt Maria, she would be a formidable opponent. Louisa—for once—had all his sympathy. He crossed to the hearth where the embers had died to darkened coals. "Why do you not write—"

Monty looked horrified. "Would take an army to stand up to Mrs. Trevellian."

"—and tell your mother," Adrian continued, ignoring the interruption, "that on the authority of the Duke of

246

Halliford, Viscount Bromley is not considered socially acceptable. It would do her little good to wed you to him if she hopes to climb the social ladder on his coattails. She would be shunned as surely as is he."

Louisa's mouth dropped open. "You are certain of it?"

"Very." Adrian's lips twitched. "You may be sure he is not welcome at Almack's—nor in any respectable household."

Monty's face brightened. "Think that will put paid to her wedding plans?"

Louisa frowned. "But mama is so mad for a title, it might not matter."

"But it *might*." Monty's alarm descended upon him once more.

Adrian took pity on him. "What good is a title if it is sneered at?" he asked Louisa. "And if it will slam doors on her rather than pry them open?"

Monty actually grinned. "No need for *us* to rush into anything, now."

"But Monty, I—I'm ready—" She broke off, her expression suddenly calculating.

"I daresay it will take your mother months to find another eligible *parti*," Adrian suggested. "And in the meantime, why should you not finish your term here at school, then enjoy the Season in London?"

"That's the ticket!" Monty threw Adrian a look brimful of gratitude. "No telling what may happen."

Louisa sniffed, still considering. A slow gleam lit her eyes. "I—I hate to disappoint you like this, Monty."

"Not at all. I mean—" he recovered quickly, "no point damaging your reputation if we don't have to."

"No." A smile played about the corners of her mouth, which faded the next moment. She regarded Adrian with no little trepidation. "What do you intend to do, sir?"

"Nothing," he assured them. "I'm no marplot. My

sole role here is to suggest an alternate—and perhaps less drastic—solution to your difficulties."

Louisa took that in, then with a soft cry she flung her arms about his neck. "Thank you," she breathed. "I—" She looked at Monty, then back to her bandbox. "I had best remove all traces of what I intended." She collected her things and, without so much as a glance over her shoulder at her intended bridegroom, she fled the room.

Adrian watched her departure, wondering half-whimsically how many of the other girls she would awaken in this determined purpose of hers. Shaking his head, he turned back to Monty, and found that young gentleman watching him with an expression of such relief that Adrian was hard put to it not to laugh. "I would recommend," he said, "that you return to your home for the time being and pressure Louisa's parents into investigating Bromley further."

Monty opened his mouth, closed it, then grasped Adrian's hand, wringing it thoroughly. "I will," he said. "Don't want to risk anything going amiss." He let himself back out into the freezing night.

A gust of cold wrapped about Adrian. Monty waved once more from the terrace, then hurried across the paving stones and disappeared into the darkness. Adrian turned back into the room, then stopped. Daphne stood in the doorway to the hall, watching.

She entered, closing the door behind her. "That was well done of you," she said, though she sounded grudging about this admission. "But then it was very easy for you, was it not? What would you have done had you been in ignorance of her betrothed's character?"

"I would have suggested the same, that they learn why their viscount has ventured so far from London to exchange his title for a fortune. I have no right to interfere, only advise."

"Which you appear to have done with convincing effect." She stared into the fire, not looking at him.

248

"Just common sense." *Why* wouldn't she meet his gaze?

She picked up the poker and held it before her, but made no move to stir the embers. "I must thank you for averting another scandal from the Seminary."

"I have my reward," he said. "I have finally laid one of our ghosts. You can have no idea how satisfying I find that."

She looked up, opened her mouth, then turned away from him, an infinite sadness touching her eyes. "I believe I do know." Her voice sounded muffled. "Let us hope, in the future, this Monty will visit by more acceptable means."

"I doubt Louisa will encourage him, once she knows herself safe from Bromley. And as for him, he would much rather be her friend than her husband."

"The little wretch," Daphne said without passion. "She used him abominably, did she not?" She turned away, walking quickly toward the door.

Adrian opened it for her, and ushered her into the hall. At the landing to the sleeping floor he paused, but heard no sounds coming from any of the girls' rooms. Assured—and somewhat surprised—that Louisa had made her return in safety, he continued up the stairs. Daphne kept a few steps ahead of him, not looking back, but not hurrying away, either.

He saw her safely to her chamber, then went on to his own, troubled. One part of the night's work, at least, he had found satisfying. He had managed to assist Louisa, and without being pompous or dictatorial or any of the other traits he so loathed in advisors. He had enjoyed preventing their ill-judged start, replacing their panic with a level-headed approach.

He must indeed be a meddler at heart. He could well imagine the derisive snort his sister Lizzie would give at this stage of his reflections. Smiling, knowing Lizzie safe and happy, he settled in a chair where he could gaze out the window in case he had a chance to catch any more ghosts that night.

Now, if only he could aid Daphne in resolving whatever troubled her. Here, though, he knew better than to interfere; he cared too deeply about the outcome. If he could not convince her to share a life with him, his own future appeared very empty indeed.

He awoke stiff and cold in his chair to a room filled with dim light. Voices sounded from below, the girls preparing for their day. He had slept through most of the night, he realized in surprise. He checked his wrist, found the swelling mostly gone, but wrapped it once more against the coming exertions of the day. After donning fresh clothes, he set off to conduct morning prayers.

This obligation completed, he excused himself as usual from breakfast with the young ladies and instead went down to the kitchens. Cook presented him with a heaping platter, and he settled down to a hearty meal. He was just finishing this and enjoying a cup of coffee before heading to the attics when Moffett appeared in the doorway.

The elderly man eyed him with the glum reproof of one who had sought him high and low. "Gentleman to see you, sir."

Adrian raised his brows. "Mr. Danvers?"

Moffett gave his grizzled head a jerking shake. "Squire."

Squire Romney? Curious, Adrian drained his cup, set it down, and made his way upstairs to where his visitor awaited him in the library.

Romney, looking rumpled in spite of his excellent tailoring, stood by the hearth, gazing down at the fire that burned merrily in the grate. He looked up as Adrian entered, and a broad smile spread across his ruddy face. "Carstairs," he said, sounding pleased. "Thought perhaps you could do me the honor of having a game of chess with me this evening."

Chess? The idea appealed to Adrian. But with Squire Romney? He studied the man, but could detect nothing but guileless hope in the man's countenance. "I fear," Adrian said slowly, hiding his suspicions, "I must decline, though it goes much against the grain. My dissertation must stand my excuse—I have devoted too much time of late to the chasing of ghosts."

Romney drew a snuff box from his pocket, flicked it open with his thumb, and held it out to Adrian, who took a pinch. "Come no closer to finding the answers?"

"Not for lack of trying."

Romney shook his head. "Well, stop by any time. Could use a good game of chess—or even piquet, for that matter. Selwood's a good fellow, but lacks finesse. Ever that way, even when we were boys." He shook his head, brooding. "Anyway, would be pleasant to match wits with a worthy opponent."

"You may be sure I'll come when I can." Adrian conducted his visitor to the door and saw him off, and watched the purposeful stride as the man crossed to where he had tethered his horse. Frowning, Adrian returned to the hall, to find Daphne peeking out of her art room.

She slipped into the corridor to join him, closing the door softly but firmly behind her. "What did the Squire want?" She listened as Adrian told her, and her eyes widened. "And you refused?" she exclaimed. "You just turned down the chance to enter his house and learn who knows what about him!"

He forced his attention from the sparkle in the depths of her vivid green eyes. "What do you think I might find? Evidence of a bet that has been called off—if it ever existed at all? No," he stopped her indignant protest. "Playing chess with him, I doubt I could learn more than the workings of his mind."

"Wouldn't that help?" she demanded.

Adrian resisted the impulse to stroke back a tendril of hair that touched her cheek. "If the man *is* guilty of any-

251

thing, why should he invite me over for any reason other than getting me out of the way—or trying to gain information from me?"

Daphne hunched a shoulder and did not meet his gaze. "This way, we learn nothing."

"True, but I'll be here in case any villainous sorts try to gain entry to the Seminary tonight."

Daphne raised her unhappy gaze to his face, started to speak, then turned away.

"Daphne—" He caught her hand, drawing her back. She pulled free. "I—I must return to my class."

He drew a deep breath. Rather than precipitate a scene in front of who knew how many silly schoolgirls, he would wait. Tonight, though, he would find some way to induce her to tell him what troubled her. If he couldn't help, perhaps he could comfort and console. Somehow, he would see to it that unhappiness faded from her eyes. On that thought, he made his way to the attics.

Daphne leaned against the closed door, listening to his footsteps receding along the hall, then his steady tread on the steps. She'd evaded him once more. But how much longer could she bear it? If only he would leave, so she wouldn't have to see him every day, his strength and humor wrecking havoc on her peace of mind, making her long to melt into the haven of his capable arms.

He could never have more than a passing interest in her, she told herself savagely. Even if it weren't for those eighteen months spent with Uncle Percival. That episode made her ineligible to be the wife of a clergyman— but Adrian was more than that. He must know what was due to his name. Hadn't Uncle Thaddeus once said one of Adrian's uncles was an earl, another a baronet?

And his sisters—the eldest married a duke, the second a diplomat, the youngest a viscount. They undoubtedly planned their only brother's marriage to some wealthy beauty of influential family, one whose name would not disgrace the titles of Halliford and St. Vincent. How could they do anything but look askance upon a country schoolmistress, raised in Ireland, without so much as a single titled blood relative, and a gaming house proprietor for an uncle? And if they knew she herself had been an inmate of the worst of his establishments . . .

She closed her eyes. His sisters—he himself—*anyone,* for that matter—must never know about that. She was ineligible enough on so many other counts. She hadn't even a penny to her name which she did not earn herself. No, she had no place in the life of the Reverend Mr. Adrian Carstairs, or the bishopric he undoubtedly one day would occupy.

She remained with her class, though only part of her mind wrestled with their artistic inabilities. The rest, contrary to her strict orders, dwelt on Adrian, upstairs in the attics, dragging about furniture with his injured wrist. She should go to help him. She *couldn't* go, for to be in the same room with him, knowing she must keep a barrier between them, proved a torture beyond endurance.

The arrival of her Uncle Thaddeus in the early afternoon severely undermined her willpower. He greeted her with a warm hug and kiss on the cheek, then set her aside to study her. "You look perturbed, my dear. Has aught occurred?"

"Nothing new." She moved away, not wanting her perceptive relative to note how deep her unhappiness lay. "Ad—Mr. Carstairs's wrist is healing, though how it can when he persists in hauling about that heavy furniture—"

"Is he doing that now?" Mr. Danvers interrupted.

He set forth at once to assist his friend and Daphne, abandoning her charges to Cousin Beatrice, followed in his wake. Surely she could spend an hour or two with Adrian without betraying how much she reveled in his company—especially since they would not be alone. With Uncle Thaddeus present, she could not help but behave in a circumspect manner, and Adrian's attention would be diverted from her.

When they entered the lumber room, Adrian straightened up from where he bent over a trunk. He looked tired, she thought. Lines of strain that might well be pain showed on his face. These eased, as if with a conscious effort. Only the tight set of his mouth betrayed the damage done to his wrist by his day's labors.

"Mr. Danvers." Adrian crossed the wide expanse of now-empty floor to greet her uncle.

Mr. Danvers clasped Adrian's outstretched hand. "You have made a great deal of progress. I have come to offer what aid I can."

"And so have I." Daphne joined them. Adrian's frowning gaze touched her, compelling her to look into his eyes. She resisted, though it wasn't easy. This would be a difficult afternoon for her, more so than she'd realized.

Only activity would help. She turned at once to the open trunk with its stacks of mildewed leather-bound volumes and began unloading them, leaving Adrian and her uncle to pick up a broken bed frame and drag it across the hall. She sank to her knees and continued her methodical work, but could not prevent her mind from wandering.

She held one of the pieces—a very important piece—of this terrible puzzle. She knew of the existence of the paintings—or at least that several people *believed* in their existence. If they were hidden here, and she could find them, the paintings could be sold to finance the Seminary until this ghost scandal faded from memory and new pupils sought admission. Finding the paintings would also rid them of the ghosts—for what else could be behind the hauntings *except* cover for the marauder's entry into the Dower House to search for the hidden Selwood legacy? She should tell Adrian. . . .

The prospect of his coming face to face with Uncle Percival, which of course Adrian would wish to do once he learned of his presence, destroyed her determination.

What a dreadful state of affairs. She was so very fond of the old rogue; yet he could destroy her entire life with one incautious word. And Percival, she knew all too well, never guarded his tongue. He would tell Adrian at once of the close ties of affection that bound her to her disreputable relative, of their hand-to-mouth days in Covent Garden. Percival would be proud of that time, of the success he had made. And in his enthusiasm, he would ruin her.

Uncle Thaddeus and Adrian appeared at her shoulder, and she realized they waited for her to finish the trunk. She drew out the last of the books, then followed them across the hall to begin the tedious job of replacing the contents. Already, the two men had gone on to a heavy wingback chair.

It took her eleven trips back and forth to carry the heavy pile of books. When she finished, she paused to watch Adrian attempt to move a very large trunk. It didn't budge an inch, almost as if it had been nailed to the floor. With a sigh, she dusted her hands and prepared to remove the contents of this, as well.

Adrian dropped on one knee beside it, feeling for the catch. "It's locked," he said after a moment. "I don't suppose there are keys?"

"Perhaps we could move it if we all three pulled?" Daphne suggested. She joined her uncle at one handle, while Adrian took the other.

Even with the three of them tugging at it, it remained where it stood. Daphne dropped her hold in disgust, then realized Adrian regarded the ancient repository with a speculative frown. "Are you searching for the magic words to open it?" she asked.

"Not words." He knelt before it once more, examining the carving on the edge of the lid. "Daphne, have you ever seen anything like this before?"

She went to his side, all too aware of him. With an effort, she focused her attention on the intricate decorations in the wood. "It's similar to those old casks in—" She broke off, her eyes widening. "In the cellar," she breathed.

Adrian cast her a swift smile in which no trace of tiredness or pain remained. "As you say. Now," he peered at the line where the lid joined the body. "If I cannot find the triggering mechanism—and I'm willing to bet I cannot, or I would have done so on the casks by now—I believe we can force this."

"And once it is open, we can find how the mechanism is hidden!" she exclaimed. "And then we can go to the cellar—"

"Let us find it, first." Laughter sounded in his voice, his whole manner that of a hound having found its scent. His hands slid along the wooden fruit and flowers, pressing and probing, yet finding nothing.

Daphne watched for a few minutes, her own fingers aching to search, too. Uncle Thaddeus stood quietly at her side, his intent gaze never leaving Adrian and the trunk. They'd have to force it, she supposed. She drew back, her gaze sweeping the room. Nothing. But surely there would be tools somewhere—like the nearest fireplace. She fetched the poker from her chamber.

As she re-entered, Adrian looked up, grinned, and thanked her. He took the instrument, eyed the jointure of the trunk's lid and body for a moment, then placed the pointed end of the tool just to the right of the lock, wriggled it firmly into place, then applied pressure.

For several moments nothing happened. Then, with a protesting screech and groan, the trunk shuddered. A splintering crack and tearing sound followed, and the poker lowered, raising the lid. Adrian dropped his weapon and swung the trunk fully open. All three of them stared down into the empty space.

"But—" Words to express her disbelief failed Daphne. She shook her head, feeling betrayed, lost—cheated.

She had hoped, she had been so very certain, they had found their answer. . . .

Adrian dropped to his knees once more and felt within, his expression intent. "Ahh . . ." The exclamation escaped him as his hand closed upon something Daphne could not see. The next moment, the bottom of the trunk lifted away. Chill air rushed about them as they stared down into a gaping crawlspace beneath.

"We've found it," he said, triumph ringing in his deep voice.

Chapter Seventeen

"No wonder our ghost seemed to just drop out of sight," Daphne exclaimed. "But why is the passage *here?*" She looked from the open trunk to the room's outer walls; the nearest, along the side with the windows, stood a good twelve feet away. "Why not just place it over there? That would have made more sense."

"But we might have found it with little trouble, then." Adrian's gray eyes danced with inner lights, and enjoyment shone on his chiseled features. "Whoever designed this did it for secrecy. Where better to hide such a passage than in the middle of a storage trunk in the middle of a storage room?"

"Where, indeed?" Mr. Danvers shook his head. "That you found it at all is amazing."

Daphne sank back on her heels. "I think I had stopped believing in it," she said at last. "It still doesn't seem possible. And the opening mechanism—?"

Adrian ran a finger along the rim of the trunk's lid, and his mouth tightened. "Destroyed, I'm afraid." His gaze strayed to the gaping hole before them. "Which leaves only one way to discover how it worked." He looked up at Mr. Danvers, laughter in his eyes. "Do you care to join me?"

A narrow, enclosed place ... Daphne *hated* anything like that. And if it led to the tunnel, underground ... she shuddered. The awkwardness of her narrow skirts would be the least of her problems, but she wouldn't back down now. "You're not leaving me behind," she informed them.

"I think," Adrian said slowly, "that for this first trip it might be best. We have no idea in what state of repair—or disrepair—we might find the passage. The dust and mildew alone may be suffocating. Nor do we know where it will let out. It might be very long."

"I—" She hesitated, wanting to explore, yet not wanting to enter that dark, confining passage.

"Let me just fetch a lantern," he said. "I'll want someone here, guarding our exit, in case we run into trouble. If the stairs are rotted and we fall through, I would rather we not all be on them. Someone must be able to fetch help."

It was *not* a weakness in her to acquiesce to this plan. Someone did need to stay here. It would accomplish nothing for her to demand to be the one to brave the dark, restricting area with its dust and spiders and who knew what else. She nodded her agreement, and he strode from the room, his step springing.

Mr. Danvers settled with care on the top of a teetering Queen Anne escritoire that had one elegantly curved foot missing. "I am more glad than ever he is here," he said.

Daphne deemed it prudent to return no answer to this. "Do you suppose it will let out in the cellars or in the underground passage beyond?" she asked instead.

To that, her uncle could make no certain guess. "Though it seems we may shortly find out," he added, as the approaching tread of booted feet sounded along the corridor.

Adrian re-entered, bearing a lighted lantern in his hand and followed closely by Elspeth. Becoming color touched the woman's cheeks as she greeted Mr. Danvers, then she quickly turned her attention to the trunk.

"I never would have believed it," she exclaimed. "To think we have lived in this house all our lives and never so much as suspected! It quite depresses me. What fun we might have had with it."

Mr. Danvers smiled. "And only think what your young ladies might do with it."

Her appalled gaze flew to his. "Merciful heavens," she said, and a soft laugh escaped her. "We must take every care they do not find out about this, or one of the little wretches will be hurt for certain."

"I think we should find out what state it is in." Adrian clambered over the side of the huge trunk, dropped to hands and knees, ducked his head and, holding the light before him, vanished into the tunnel. After a moment, Mr. Danvers followed suit, though with noticeably less enthusiasm. A minute later, Adrian's muffled voice drifted back to them. "I've reached the wall and the stairs."

"There's a surprising amount of room here," Mr. Danvers's voice added.

Daphne exchanged an uneasy look with Elspeth. "Be careful," she called.

No answer came back. Had they already passed out of hearing distance? No light could she see, either. Daphne found herself staring into a dark passage, still and stuffy. Adrian had been right about the dust and the mildew. She stifled a sneeze and leaned farther into the now bottomless trunk to try to detect any movement or sound. Nothing reached her.

"We can only wait." Elspeth sounded frustrated as she leaned forward, gripping the edge of the great trunk. "I do hope the stairs are not rotted out. If he—if one of them falls through, he might be seriously injured."

"I doubt either will." Daphne forced a more positive note into her voice than she herself felt. It seemed all too likely an eventuality to her, but she saw no reason to distress Elspeth further.

The minutes crept past, and nothing happened. No shouts for help reached them; neither man returned. Daphne remained where she knelt, hands clenched together until her nails bit into her palms.

"What can be happening?" Elspeth cried at last.

That settled it. Daphne rose. "I'm going to find out." She ran down the hall to fetch her chamberstick, lit it, then carried it carefully back, shielding the fragile flame from any chance breezes caused by her movement.

Elspeth stood by the trunk, gazing into the dark depths. "It doesn't feel *too* cold," she said as Daphne entered. She looked up, a determined expression on her sweet face. "I'm going with you."

Daphne hesitated. "Do you not think one of us should remain here—in case something happens?"

"I could not bear the waiting. Perhaps you would care to stay?"

Daphne's lips twitched. "Not for anything." She hesitated at the edge, gave Elspeth an encouraging if somewhat shaky grin, and climbed inside.

The mustiness of the ages stifled her as soon as she crawled within the wooden tunnel. It *was* narrow . . . and close. Dust tickled her nose, and she stifled an impulse to scramble back out into open air. But Adrian—and her Uncle Thaddeus—were somewhere below.

From behind her, she heard the creak of boards as Elspeth followed. Too late; she couldn't turn back now, not without sending her cousin scrambling backwards as well. She might as well get on with it at once, the sooner to come out on the other side.

And if it led nowhere but a dead end?

She *would* think of something like that. Clutching her candlestick, she inched forward on her knees, hampered by her narrow skirt. How many feet had she estimated from the wall? Twelve? It felt like miles.

She pushed forward, then suddenly found herself with space about her. She faced a wall, but the floor dropped away to her left into a flight of stairs, and the ceiling lifted well above her head. She rose to her feet, gripping at the wall with her free hand.

"Go down so I can stand up." Elspeth's head bumped into her knee.

Daphne descended the first few steps with care. They seemed solid enough, though very steep—and they didn't squeak or protest. That surprised her.

Within the narrow stairwell, the walls seemed to close about her once more. She clenched her jaw, thought about open meadows, and forced herself down three more stairs. At least she could stand erect and feel space in front of her. Behind, Elspeth crowded close, one hand on her shoulder for guidance. The single candle shed only enough light for Daphne to see the next step or two; Elspeth must be moving blind.

Then abruptly she faced another wall: the side of the Dower House. Here the passage widened a few inches, enough to ease the eerie sensation that the walls sought to crush her. Still, the stairs fell away at a sharp angle, making the descent perilous.

Elspeth's grip tightened on her shoulder. "How far do you think we have come?" she whispered. It sounded unnaturally loud in the still confines.

"Not far enough," Daphne muttered, and forged onward and downward before her courage deserted her.

Ages crept by, and suddenly Daphne found her candle reflecting off another wall before her. A stirring in the air sent the flame dancing, then it settled. The stairs reached a tiny landing, turned to the left once more and continued their steep descent.

Daphne drew a shaky breath. "It cannot be much farther," she declared, more to encourage herself than Elspeth.

"N–no." Elspeth sounded doubtful.

Daphne pressed on, and after only twenty more stairs she encountered another wall before her. It took her a moment to realize she stood within an open space, the floor about six foot square, the sides curving inward to meet overhead in a rounded arch. She held the candle aloft, and its light glinted off a metal handle set in the straight wall before her. She turned it, and the panel before her swung silently outward.

Light flooded inside, and Daphne stumbled out as a ark shape loomed from the side, grasping her arm. A artled gasp escaped her, then she relaxed as she recog- ized Adrian's smiling gaze.

"Hold that door," he called to Mr. Danvers, who as- sted Elspeth free. "I didn't realize you intended to follow s." He still supported her, one hand beneath her elbow.

With reluctance she moved away. "You took so readfully long, our curiosity got the better of us."

"Just as well. This closes far too easily, and we ouldn't find the opening mechanism on this side. We ere about to return upstairs and try again." He moved the cask behind them.

Daphne studied it with interest. "So that's where we ame out. Yes, the carving really is like that on the unk, isn't it?"

Adrian bent over the handle, tracing his fingers along e edge, then searching the carving about the outside f the great oaken container. "This was crafted with nsiderable skill," he said at last, sounding disgusted. 'll have to dismantle it to find the means to open it on is side."

"But that will alert our ghosts we've discovered the air," Daphne protested.

Adrian rubbed his chin, his gaze straying to the back all of the cellar where more massive casks and the wine cks stood in a row. "The opening device is bound to be e same, and in a similar location. If I could find it ere—" He broke off, his expression intent. "What if it kes *two* people to operate? If that's the case, then the echanism need not be on the cask at all, but—"

He looked about, alert, his gaze seeking. "Somewhere ong this wall . . ." His voice trailed off as he began his stematic search, testing every carving and timber he uld find. At last, against the stone wall at the base of e last cask in the row, a support beam gave very ightly under the pressure.

"There." Satisfaction sounded in his voice. "How

very simple, when one realizes the principle of needing more than one person. Mr. Danvers, if you will stand by the cask and test it? And Daphne, would you mind going back inside? Then if this fails, you may open the door for us once more."

"To be sure," she said, and hoped her voice didn't sound as hollow to them as it did to her. "I can think of nothing I should like more."

She'd brought it on herself, she supposed. Bracing her nerve, she allowed her uncle to help her into the great cask. The massive front swung shut upon her, enclosing her in darkness once more, but she barely had time to grit her teeth before the latch clicked and the front eased open, freeing her.

Uncle Thaddeus stood before her, smiling in triumph, and held out his hand. "We have found the key."

Relieved, she jumped down.

Adrian strode up to them, nodded in satisfaction at the open cask, then turned to study the ones that lined the back wall. "One of these," he said slowly, "should be the entrance for the tunnel to the Manor House."

Daphne swallowed and tried to keep her countenance. "How delightful. Another enclosed place. Now all you must do is find *that* opening mechanism."

He checked the line of casks as thoroughly as he had those on the other wall, but this time the base timber remained immovable. Frowning, he stepped back, his gaze resting on first one, then another. "The wine rack," he said at last, and strode over to this last possibility.

It looked solid, Daphne thought, and the carved pattern decorated the solid wood here, as well. A flicker of anticipation raced through her. Yet how did this really help them, after all? The ghosts mostly had been seen *outside* the Academy. They still did not know—

Adrian's "Ah!" interrupted her thoughts. He stood with one hand on a board that protruded from the rack just below the level of his elbow. "Will each of you test a cask?"

Mr. Danvers took the one nearest the far corner, Elspeth took the next, and Daphne stood before the third. Each grasped the edge of the barrel, but nothing happened. Disappointed, Daphne moved to the fourth, where Elspeth joined her. Mr. Danvers went to stand beside Adrian. Daphne tensed, and the wood shifted ever so slightly beneath her fingers.

Or had she imagined it? "Try it again," she called, and this time gripped with both hands. "I think it's giving a little, but it's not opening."

Mr. Danvers took Adrian's place, and Adrian came to her side, feeling for himself that almost imperceptible change as Mr. Danvers activated the mechanism. "This is it," he said, "but I'd wager it's been locked from the other side."

"Or possibly blocked off," Elspeth suggested. "It would be just the sort of thing my grandfather would have done."

"Then our ghosts aren't using it?" In spite of herself, disappointment dragged at Daphne. "All this effort for nothing!"

"Not necessarily." Adrian still studied the cask front. "There have been voices back there. Even if no one has entered the Dower House through here, that passage beyond is certainly being used. And," he added, "we have no reason to think this doorway is not, as well. Our ghosts may have secured it on their side to keep us from stumbling across it. There is a reason the Seminary is being haunted, and whatever lies beyond this wall must be part of it."

Daphne hugged herself. The reason. The missing paintings? But if they lay on the other side of this wall, they would already have been found. And if they were hidden elsewhere? She shook her head, but that did nothing to clear her thinking.

Try again, she ordered herself. Who even knew of the existence of the paintings? Her Uncle Percival, of course. He'd known Elspeth's father. That meant he

265

knew Cousin George's father, as well. Then did George know of the paintings? And what of those two rough-looking men? Did they try to enter the Dower House through the old passage to search for the paintings?

"Perhaps," Adrian said slowly, breaking the silence that had engulfed them, "Miss Susannah Ingels and her brother know of the tunnel. Their estate lies near here, does it not? They might be using it to frighten students away from the Seminary. It is not that difficult—" he cast a conspiratorial grin at Daphne, "—to break into the Manor House cellars."

Elspeth sighed. "That sounds like something Miss Davenport might encourage, if Susannah ever mentioned it to her."

The paintings might not be involved at all, Daphne realized—except in the case of Uncle Percival. Perhaps their frustrated guess of days before held true after all, and each of the various ghosts haunted the place for his or her own reasons.

"Should we force it?" Elspeth looked from Mr. Danvers to Adrian, then back again.

"We would not be able to disguise the damage, once it had been done." Mr. Danvers looked to Adrian. "What do you think?"

"I would rather not ruin it," he said. "I think I will try to find the entrance from the other end. Selwood's cellar is much the same as this one. We should be able to find the mechanism."

"But I cannot remain here this night," Mr. Danvers protested. "I must return to my parish. I will make arrangements for tomorrow—or send a message if I cannot."

Adrian ran a hand over his wrist, frowning. It must be paining him, Daphne realized. All that heavy work, and despite how casually he treated it, she knew the swelling could not have left it entirely. If he encountered one of their ghosts, he would be at a disadvantage. By tomorrow night, though, he would have had a chance to rest—without spending a day moving heavy furniture.

"That would be perfect," Daphne said. "That will give us time to plan a strategy in case we encounter any stray specters. And tonight we can keep watch down here in case anyone tries to gain entrance."

With that, the others agreed, and they headed out of the cellar—not by the secret passage, but into the hallway by the kitchens. Elspeth led the way, accompanied by Mr. Danvers. Daphne, directly behind the couple, could not help but notice the surreptitious glances Elspeth directed at Uncle Thaddeus. They held considerable warmth, too, she realized.

Was her uncle aware of Elspeth's growing regard? Somehow, she doubted it. He was the sweetest man, so very perceptive—where others were concerned. But not, she knew full well, where it involved himself. He might have realized that Elspeth's affections had become engaged, but he would remain oblivious to the fact that he was their object.

Poor Elspeth. Uncle Thaddeus tended to be such a solitary person. Though a wife—the right wife—was exactly what he needed. She would have to make certain he realized that. She glanced at Adrian, then away at once. Elspeth and Uncle Thaddeus, at least, should be happy.

Forcibly, she returned her attention to their immediate problems. Tomorrow night, Adrian and her uncle would enter the Manor House and seek the entrance to the underground passage. Part of her wanted to go with them—but the more imaginative part contemplated a passage buried under the earth, and quailed. Yet she couldn't let them go alone, with her not knowing what occurred. . . .

They saw Mr. Danvers to the door, then Adrian headed up the stairs to spend a few quiet hours with Herodotus. The girls would not be finished with their last lessons of the day for some time yet, Daphne realized. Leaving Elspeth to join her sisters, she slipped into the library for a bit of solitude of her own.

She had no more settled herself before the hearth than a light tapping sounded on the French doors. She looked up to see Cousin George standing there, his brows knit, his hands clasping the greatcoat he had draped over his shoulders. The rest of his costume was as immaculate—and startling—as ever.

As she rose, she eyed the pistachio-colored coat—another new one—and found no fault in it beyond the nipped-in waist and the elaborately wide lapels. She could not quite like the violet and green tones of his waistcoat, which to her seemed somewhat garish, but she had to admit he had gone to considerable pains over the intricate folds of his neckcloth. She let him in and recoiled at the scent of Russian oil too liberally applied.

"How do you go on, dear Coz?" he asked. He searched her face. "You look tired, m'dear, really too tired." He advanced to the fireplace and peered into the mirror, his fingers—covered in green kid leather—checking the points of his shirt collar. Apparently satisfied, he turned back to her. "Have there been any more hauntings?"

Daphne hesitated only a moment. "All has been quiet," she assured him.

George tugged at the green riband that held his quizzing glass. "Has your resident clergyman not yet managed to exorcise your ghosts? He must—he really must—" he broke off and clenched his hands together.

"Why are you so concerned about it?" she asked. "Have they started to haunt you?"

His fingers clenched, then smoothed the strips of silk. "My dear, I am glad it is you and not our cousins I found. Just between us—you won't tell them, will you?" He darted an anxious glance at her.

"What?" Daphne temporized.

He turned to face the flames and spoke over his shoulder without looking at her. "I find myself in the teensiest bit of a bind, you see. In fact," he added with a rush of candor, "my pockets are wholly—but wholly!—to let. I cannot risk the rent being even the least bit late this quarter, or I shall positively find myself dunned at my door. And what makes it worse," he added, turning a haggard face to her, "I'm devilishly fond of my cousins, you know I am. I hate the thought of pressuring them. I hate this whole deplorable situation, for that matter. It's so very unpleasant."

"I'd noticed," Daphne murmured.

"And it is not right for the poor old girls to be put to such bother and worry." He ran an agitated hand through his hair, disarranging the perfect order of his locks. "There's no need to tell them I was here, you know. I just wanted to see if you'd made any progress." He gave her a weak smile that faded at once, and headed out into the snow.

Daphne watched his departure, frowning. She could not doubt his distress; but did it mean he was innocent—or afraid of their discovering his guilt? She could only hope he was not behind this terrible affair, for that would only increase any ensuing scandal which she dreaded would descend upon them once the haunting was solved. The Seminary could be destroyed just as easily by any following gossip or shocking revelations.

Sobered, she went to assist her cousins with their pupils.

Herodotus, Adrian decided, had not progressed this well since first he'd arrived here. He stretched his stiff back, then looked over the several pages of translation he had just completed, and the running commentary he had kept that would make up the major portion of his dissertation. Amazing how making progress on one problem aided his work on another.

Nor had he yet needed to light his branch of working candles. He glanced out the window, surprised to see the light only just fading. From the uncanny sounds drifting up from below, he guessed the girls had gathered in the drawing room for an hour of musical torture. He would take a walk, he decided prudently, then return refreshed to tackle the next segment—when the girls had dispersed to pursue other occupations.

He donned his outdoor clothes and slipped quietly down the stairs, giving the drawing room a wide berth. Surely there must be many aspects of this life Daphne would not miss in the least, if he could ever induce her to leave her post. He still had that problem to solve.

Frowning, he let himself out the back way without encountering anyone and strode toward the stable to check on Achilles. As he leaned against the stall door rubbing the big brute's nose, a clatter of hooves sounded on the cobbled stones and he turned to see Squire Romney ride in on his showy black.

The man raised his riding crop in salute. "Just coming to have a word with you. Something I want you to see."

Adrian strolled up to the man's horse and laid a hand on its neck. "What is that?"

"Saddle a horse," came the response.

Adrian looked over his shoulder to where Hobson, the sole groom, curried a chestnut mare. "Is there a saddle mount here?"

"Aye, sir. Use 'im for takin' messages."

A few minutes later, Adrian found himself facing a flea-bitten roan, Roman-nosed and well up in flesh. It turned a placid eye on him, then resumed its somnolent state. He heaved the saddle over the broad back, cinched the girth, then set his jaw. He swung up, refusing to acknowledge the protest from his healing wrist. "Where are we going?" he asked Romney as he joined him.

"Across my lands. Should be there before it's too dark to see."

Curious, Adrian prodded his hulking beast forward, and it lumbered from the yard at Romney's side. Much to Adrian's surprise, when Romney broke into a trot, his own animal picked up a shambling version of the gait, and in a very few minutes they reached the path cutting across the Selwood land onto Romney's estate.

Here the heavy underbrush and thick surrounding trees made seeing more difficult, and they reined in once more, resuming the strolling pace Adrian's mount seemed to prefer. After traversing somewhat more than a mile, Adrian became aware of a dull thudding noise. His curiosity growing by the minute, he urged his mount forward, and emerged at last from the trees into a fallow field. Perhaps two hundred yards away stood a barn. Romney motioned for silence and led the way along the line of trees. Apparently, that barn was their destination.

At a distance of about seventy-five yards from it, Romney dismounted and tied his reins to a tree branch. Adrian did the same, then followed as the man crept along a hedge. At last the Squire stopped and pointed.

Adrian peered through the gathering darkness. Two men wielded hammers on the building, which listed heavily to one side. Several new posts lay on the ground beside them. The men turned to pick up one of these, and Adrian recognized them with a start of surprise. He had seen them before, late one night, paying a very threatening call on George Selwood.

Romney, at his side, nodded. "Selwood's friends. And look."

From inside the barn a gentleman emerged, tall but slight of build. Even in the fading light, Adrian recognized the sneering features of young Mr. Reginald Ingels.

"This is the Ingels's estate?" Adrian asked.

Romney nodded, his expression grim. "Never trusted that young man. All flash and no bottom. Couldn't shoot a brace of pheasants if they were bagged for him. Well, what do you think of his laborers' harrying poor Selwood? I tell you, this whole business means trouble."

Chapter Eighteen

Daphne curled into the chair by her window and gazed down at the wintry landscape below. Adrian had already taken up his position—but not quite the one she had expected. After contemplating the dank, dark cellar, he had thought a few moments, then rigged up an ingenious device. And only a real ghost would get by him.

Much to her admiration, he had set up an arrangement of string across the fronts of the oak casks. If either door budged during the night, it would pull at the strings, which in turn would tug at the pots on the kitchen table to which he had tied the other end. Even if he drifted off to sleep—which was not impossible, given the warmth of the oven fires—the noise would awaken him. He had settled quite comfortably for the night with a fresh pot of steaming coffee, a plate of rolls provided by Cook, and his dissertation to bear him company. Daphne almost envied him.

She sighed and rested her chin on the heel of one hand. Below, the hall clock chimed midnight, each soulful bong fading into the otherwise silent darkness. She yawned and blinked eyes that tended to drift closed.

A single, distant chime brought her awake. She must have dozed off. She stretched and peered into the night. Nothing . . .

A figure moved along the line of trees, and she tensed. One of the ghosts. She watched, eyes narrowed, as it stood, arms crossed before it, tapping a foot, gazing up at the windows. It opened one hand, weighing something it held, as if it contemplated throwing whatever it was. Rocks, she supposed. And if her guess were correct, this particular ghost would undoubtedly select the wrong window, and probably break it into the bargain.

She collected the oil lamp that burned low beside her bed, turned it up, and waved it in front of the window. The figure outside waved back. No need to disturb Adrian for this one—in fact, far better not. She donned her pelisse, exchanged her slippers for half-boots, and let herself out into the dark corridor.

A few minutes later, she slipped out of the library into the freezing night. She didn't have to wait. Her ghost detached himself from the terrace shrubbery and clumped up to her, a beaming smile on his cherubic countenance. She faced him squarely. "What on earth are you doing here, Uncle Percival?"

He harrumphed. "A fine greeting, me darlin'. I wanted to see you, and this was the only thing I could think of, since you had the infernal impertinence to order me not to show myself. I'm hurt, I tell you, hurt that you are ashamed of your old uncle."

"I'm not in the least ashamed of you, but our poor cousins have already had more scandal than is good for their school. Now, do spare me the theatrics. What brought you?"

He eyed her sideways. "I've seen some nasty looking men hanging about the place. Didn't like the look of 'em at all. After my paintings, I make no doubt. Wanted to warn you, that's all."

Daphne squeezed his hand. "Are there two of them? Then they're probably the ones we've seen. It's very sweet of you to be concerned, Uncle Percival."

He huffed. "What else can I do but keep a watchful avuncular eye on you? And you can't stop me, either. I know my duty to my family, whatever you may think. Now, you go back inside, girl, before you catch your death. I'll just stick around here for a bit and make sure no one tries to get in."

"There's no need—" she began.

He held up his hand. "I'll have no arguments from you, m'dear. In with you, and have a good night's sleep for once, secure in the knowledge your old uncle is not far away."

It would be useless to protest; once Uncle Percival had set his mind to something, there would be no budging him. Touched by his unexpectedly sincere concern, she stood on tiptoe and kissed his cheek. He beamed at her and shooed her toward the house. She re-entered the library, turned about to say goodnight, but he had already vanished into the shadows.

Smiling, she threw the bolt and turned about, only to find Adrian standing before her, his arms folded, his expression grim. She opened her mouth, groped for words, but they escaped her. She stared helplessly at his clouded countenance.

"I thought it was only Miss Trevellian who kept liaisons with ghosts in the early hours of the morning." He kept his tone level; the accusation lay solely in his eyes.

"I—it's not what you think," she managed, and was annoyed by the guilty heat that flamed her cheeks.

"It isn't? What, bye the bye, *do* I think?"

Her face burned. "That is most ungentlemanly of you. Oh!" she exclaimed as she caught the glint in his eyes. "You are teasing me. That is most unkind."

He smiled, though he did not relax his attitude. "Who was that?"

She was undone. Nothing would keep him from ferreting out the truth now that he scented a mystery about her. It would be better he heard it from her than from someone else. She crossed to a chair and sank into it as the shattered fragments of her existence crashed about her feet.

"My Uncle Percival." Amazingly, only the slightest tremor sounded in her voice. Now that disaster lay upon her, she felt surprisingly calm. Adrian would know the worst, and being a man of infinite good sense, he would withdraw from her, remaining friendly—but nothing more.

"You did not invite him in?"

Daphne swallowed, then forged ahead. "He is quite delightful, but—" She broke off, finding the words even harder than she had expected. Her gaze remained fixed on her folded hands.

"Somewhat of an embarrassment at times?" Adrian suggested. He sat on the arm of the sofa. "Every family has a black sheep or two," he pointed out. "I have a couple myself. My sister Nell spends most of her time trying to keep them out of Halliford's orbit."

"Does she?" Daphne didn't meet his gaze, but welcomed this side issue. "I'll have you know I have met most of your family, and while I admit they are not quite in the common way, they are far from black sheep."

Adrian shook his head. "You've never met my uncle and aunt. Sir Henry and Lady Carstairs—and she will never let you forget the title. No, my dear, I have hidden them away to spring upon you as a nasty surprise one day. Now, tell me about Uncle Percival."

She drew a quavering breath, and plunged ahead. "He runs a gaming establishment. He left the one he had in London rather hurriedly just under four years ago, and now resides on the Continent—an arrangement, I believe, necessitated by Bow Street. His most recent venture was in Italy, though it appears he had to close it rather suddenly as well." Why hadn't she admitted the rest, about Covent Garden and her own role? Was she truly so lacking in courage? Or did she dread seeing him turn from her?

"And he came here hoping to borrow money?" Adrian suggested.

At least she could purge part of her conscience. She grasped at this topic. "If only that were all. He has come, he says, to locate the Selwood family treasure." Briefly, she told him of the paintings. "And if he believes they exist, there might be others who do, also."

Adrian studied the toe of one gleaming topboot. "Paintings. I believe one of your cousins mentioned them before, but as having been stolen."

She nodded. "Now it appears their grandfather may have hidden them, instead. But Adrian, my uncle is quite determined to find them and make off with them, and I cannot allow that. If they do indeed exist, my cousins have need of them—and they would be rightfully theirs!"

"And if he is looking for them, then it is likely others are, as well." He paced to the fire. "This puts a very different light on the matter, does it not? A fortune in valuable paintings. That might well be worth driving the Seminary out of business."

"You mean my Cousin George? But—he seems so worried for us."

He reached for the poker and gave the embers a contemplative stir. "It wouldn't necessarily have to be him—though who, outside of the family, would know of this treasure?"

"Someone their grandfather trusted?" It didn't sound very plausible to her own ears.

"What matters," Adrian said, resuming his pacing, "is that we be the first ones to find these paintings, if they exist, to secure them for your cousins. We can then make their discovery known, which should put a stop to the hauntings."

She nodded, but raised her frowning gaze to his face. "Where," she asked, "are we likely to locate them? We have searched this house thoroughly for secret passages and hiding places. What does that leave?"

Adrian stopped his perambulations before her, and a slow smile lit his eyes. "Our end of the underground tunnel?" he suggested.

* * *

The next morning passed for Daphne with incredible slowness. She fidgeted about the art room, barely keeping her patience under control as Marianne Snowdon arranged colors on her paper with determined imprecision. A vague figure, which Daphne recognized as a ghost, appeared to one side of the page, dabbed in with tones of gray. Prudently, she ignored it. It would be a long term—if the Seminary survived to complete it.

Toward afternoon, unable to remain longer indoors, she took her charges, armed with sketching pads, for a ramble through the frozen countryside. A brisk tramp along the snowy paths to the stream that still ran in spite of the icy patches went a long way toward renewing her energies. Jane walked with Marianne, their friendship apparently restored. They seemed to enjoy themselves, and the other young ladies, after exclaiming for the first few minutes over the dreadful cold, soon forgot to complain and began seeking out picturesque scenes to add to their collection of drawings.

At the first opportunity, Daphne drew Jane aside. "You are no longer angry with Marianne?"

Jane shook her head, beaming. "It was only because she would flirt so with Mr. Carstairs. But Miss Breame says he has eyes for no one but you, and is oblivious to Marianne, so that makes everything all right, does it not?"

"Jane—" Daphne broke off, shaking her head.

"I won't breathe a word of it," Jane promised, solemn-faced. "All the others say we must not, for fear Mr. Carstairs might overhear."

"You may tell everyone, Jane, that I—I have no interest in Mr. Carstairs. He is excellent company, but that is all. Is that understood?"

Jane looked crestfallen. She nodded, glum, and strode off to rejoin her friends. A minute later, the girls surrounding her turned to stare at Daphne and shake their heads.

That should put a stop to the gossip. Daphne turned away. She wished it were as easy to convince her heart.

They returned in the gathering dusk, thoroughly chilled but laughing. Daphne, trying to emulate their cheery mood, ushered them into the drawing room where Cook had prepared steaming cocoa and biscuits for them, a high treat. The only thing missing, Daphne reflected as she looked about at the happy girls, was Adrian.

Her heart wrenched. She hadn't made a complete confession to him. And now, to make it worse, he would be on the lookout for Uncle Percival, and would undoubtedly encourage her disreputable relative to relate his adventurous history—which would reveal her own shocking past. She'd been a fool last night, a coward. And every minute she now delayed made it all the harder to reveal the truth.

Where was Adrian at the moment? Resting, she hoped. He certainly had not done so during the night. He had conducted morning prayers without betraying any exhaustion, though she had seen the lines about his eyes. How long, she wondered, could a man go on like that without sleep? But his energy seemed boundless, his enjoyment of the unsettling events uncurtailed.

The session in the drawing room after dinner that evening wracked her nerves. She had seen nothing of Adrian, let alone had a chance for private speech with him. And now she would be busied with seeing her charges into their beds, while he undoubtedly kicked his heels in the library, anxious to begin his housebreaking. She wished she might accompany him, but knew it to be a forlorn hope.

As soon as she made her final check on the young ladies, she returned below stairs, then hesitated at the library door. Should she tell him now? But there might be so little time. Her Uncle Thaddeus would be arriving

278

soon, and Elspeth. She might begin only to be cut off, and that would be intolerable.

Elspeth hurried down the stairs and joined her in the hall, and that settled the matter. Half-relieved and half-regretful, she followed her cousin into the library, where Adrian stood by the French doors. He looked so calm, so capable—not at all like one about to embark on a potentially dangerous venture.

The warmth in his eyes as they rested on her nearly proved her undoing. She looked away, not able to meet the caress of his gaze. She needed something to do, something to occupy her. . . . She hurried to the fire to add an unnecessary log to the already comfortable blaze.

"Sophronia and Beatrice have retired for the night," Elspeth informed them. "I feel rather guilty, not telling them what we are about, but they would worry so." She sighed. "I believe I shall read. Why do you two not play piquet?"

Piquet. He would be a worthy opponent, but how could she sit *tête-à-tête* with him without revealing how very wrong everything had become? She couldn't tell him the truth, not in front of Elspeth. And he was not a man to be put off for long. He would have the full story from her, and then he would understand, and agree there could be nothing between them but friendship, a pale shadow of what she longed for.

She searched for cards, taking her time, delaying as long as she could, until Adrian unearthed a deck from a desk drawer. She managed to waste several more minutes positioning a table before the fire, but then he came up behind her, bearing a chair, and a minute later she faced him across the short space as he shuffled. His gaze, though, rested on her face, his eyes piercing and perceptive.

"When I get back," he said softly—so softly Elspeth could not hear, "you may tell me as much or as little as you wish. But do not be so distressed. It always seems true that nothing is ever as bad as one dreads."

She nodded, not meeting his gaze, blinking back the tears that stung her eyes. He would make the telling easy. But what came after—no, he could do nothing to change the inevitable outcome for her. He would leave without her. At least he would hold his tongue, she had no doubt of that. If Uncle Percival could be packed safely off to the Continent once more, her secret would remain inviolate, she at least could retain her position here at the Seminary.

But it would be a very empty, lonely position without Adrian nearby, his gray eyes brimming with enjoyment, his energy infecting her, his strength protecting her, his arms holding her for brief but soul-stirring moments. . . .

He dealt. She gathered her cards and ordered her mind under the pretense of sorting her hand. Play came naturally to her—it would, after Uncle Percival's tutelage—allowing her to recover her composure; and Adrian proved every bit as good a player as she'd anticipated, forcing her to concentrate on her choices. She lost the first hand ignobly, and immediately demanded a rematch.

They were well into their fifth hand when Adrian straightened. "Someone's coming up the drive." He strode out to the hall.

A moment later Daphne heard the front door open. The deep cadences of men's voices followed, too low for her to hear, then Uncle Thaddeus, wrapped in a great-coat and scarf, entered the room.

"Adrian is taking my horse to the stable," he said. "Good evening." He took Elspeth's hand.

She rose. "Pray sit by the fire, you must be quite frozen from your ride. Let me get you some wine." She crossed to a small pier table where a decanter rested, kept there for the refreshment of visiting parents, and filled a glass with deep ruby liquid. This she handed to Mr. Danvers, then moved quickly away.

Mr. Danvers's gaze rested upon her for a long moment, his expression somber, then he turned to Daphne. "Has anything new occurred, my dear?"

"I believe we now know what our ghosts are after." Quickly, she told him of the unexpected appearance of Uncle Percival and his revelations about the paintings. Elspeth she had told earlier in the day.

Mr. Danvers listened in silence. Once his gaze drifted to Elspeth, who sat in a chair and stared into the hearth, and his mouth set in a tired line. When Daphne finished, he nodded. "If we can find these paintings, then we can save the Seminary. For your sake, Miss Elspeth, I hope we can."

"We must!" Elspeth exclaimed. "But the more I think of it, the worse the situation seems. Cousin George must be involved—I can see no other way."

"Then surely it becomes only a family matter," Mr. Danvers suggested.

"If it were only the family involved, we might be able to hush it up. But the students!" Elspeth shook her head, and tears glinted on her long lashes. "The scandal will be dreadful, and every one of our remaining pupils will be taken from us by their outraged parents. And I cannot blame them!"

Mr. Danvers drew a chair to her side. "If we find the paintings, you will not lose your home, at least."

"Our home." A shaky laugh escaped Elspeth. "It is our lives I worry about. Could you envision my sisters without the Seminary? They would be lost, they would have no purpose. It would be too dreadful."

Mr. Danvers offered her his handkerchief, and she accepted it with a sniff. "And you?" he asked gently. "Can you envision no life for yourself away from the Seminary?"

"I could not bear a life of inactivity." She spoke from the depths of the muslin square.

Daphne sank to her knees at her cousin's side. "We may yet be able to escape scandal. No matter who is responsible, we should suffer no more than a brief notoriety, which the funds from the paintings will help us weather. We will come about, never fear."

Adrian rejoined them, and Elspeth straightened, dabbed at her eyes, and solemnly returned Mr. Danvers's handkerchief. They settled down to a game of whist and passed the next two hours in relative peace, their only conversation having to do with the play. They all, Daphne noted, kept glancing at the clock, but not one of them mentioned what lay ahead.

At last, when the hands stood at twenty minutes past one, Adrian gathered the discarded cards from the last hand, shuffled once, then placed the deck on the center of the table. "I believe it is time we left you ladies to a game of piquet. Mr. Danvers, are you ready?"

Daphne followed them to the back door, keeping her growing unease under control. Still, as the two men let themselves out into the quiet night, armed with a lantern, she could not prevent herself from catching Adrian's sleeve. "Be careful," she whispered.

The smile he flashed held both confidence and enjoyment. "You may be very sure we shall." With one finger, he just touched her cheek. "Will you keep watch over the front of the house?"

She fought the desire to clasp his hand. "I would rather come with you." In spite of the suffocating tunnel they might well enter.

"We'll be back before you know it—and very possibly through the cellar." With that, he slipped away into the darkness with her uncle.

Daphne hugged herself against the cold. She didn't like this at all, but what could she do? She would not be easy again until they returned, safe and unharmed. With dragging steps, she returned to the library where the fire burned bright.

Elspeth looked up from the chair before the hearth where she sat with an unopened book clutched in her hands. "They are off?" she asked in a woebegone tone. "I do hope they will be all right."

"Of course they will." With effort, Daphne inserted a rallying note into her voice. "Why do you not go to my room and watch over the front of the house?"

Elspeth eyed her with suspicion. "And you?"

"I'll take the cellar," Daphne decided. "And I shall come up here to make sure no one tries to enter from the terrace."

With that, they parted to take up their stations. Daphne donned her shawl, but she had a shrewd suspicion it would not be sufficient against the cold of the basements. At least Elspeth would pass the night in comparative comfort.

Sitting on the table in the dank, freezing dark proved every bit as unpleasant as Daphne had expected. If only she could light a fire for warmth. Then she could read or play patience by the glow. Instead, she sat here with nothing to occupy her mind except worry for her uncle and Adrian.

She could imagine, all too vividly, a terrifying number of things that could go wrong with their expedition. What if those two men lay in wait for them, armed and ready to attack? What if they found the tunnel, only to have it collapse on them? What if—

She could not go on this way, not without driving herself into a screaming fit. Nothing happened here; she felt like she wasted her time. When she stood near the far wall, only silence greeted her. She might as well check the library.

There, too, all lay in stillness. At least it was warmer than in the cellar. While she was at it, she might as well go up to her room and collect her pelisse.

She mounted the steps, taking care not to make any noise that might rouse the girls, and crept along the hall to her room. The door stood slightly ajar, to allow Elspeth a view of the corridor, as well—in case anyone tried to emerge from the lumber room. As Daphne pushed her door wider, the deep sound of even breathing reached her.

Elspeth sat in the comfortable chair before the window, a comforter drawn up to her chin, her head turned against the cushioned back. Fast asleep. Nor did Daphne have the heart to awaken her. She would just add this room to her tour. She extracted her pelisse from the wardrobe without rousing her cousin, looked out the window to find nothing amiss, then returned to the library for a perfunctory check before going on to the cellar.

How far had the men gotten by now? she wondered as she repeated her self-appointed rounds. She should have gone with them, despite the numerous objections. Anything would have been better than waiting, not knowing, worrying like this. She arrived at her chamber on that thought and found Elspeth still peacefully slumbering. A slight smile just touching her lips, Daphne peeped out her window.

And froze.

A ghost slipped across the drive, making for the terrace outside the library doors. Uncle Percival again, she realized. Would he make a nightly habit out of dropping by this way? She had best see him and find out what he wanted, then convince him to go home. The last thing she wanted would be Percival marching through underground tunnels, searching for those paintings.

She hurried down the stairs to the library once more, then crossed to the French doors. To her surprise, no one waited without. Had he backed off to find her window and hurl rocks at it? She reached for the bolt, only to find it already open.

Open? Surely it had been secure last time she checked! She stepped back, eyeing it with distrust, as if it were a coiled serpent that might strike at her.

Open. Uncle Percival might have done it. He might well number lock-picking among his various questionable skills. And if he had let himself into the Dower

House, and without notifying her of his arrival, that could only mean he intended to search for the paintings.

She hurried from room to room on the ground floor, peeking into each, but nowhere did she see his flamboyant figure sounding the walls or pulling back the rugs. So where was he? The cellars, of course, she realized in dismay. If he had known of this treasure's existence, he might well know of the secret passage, perhaps even the underground tunnel, perhaps even other hiding places they had not yet discovered. She had better get after him.

Indignant at this high-handed behavior, she stormed down to the cellar. As she turned in at the door, she saw the dim glow of a candle or shuttered lantern at the far end. She marched forward, and had advanced perhaps ten feet into the room before she realized the front of the fourth oak cask against the back wall stood open. The light came from within—or rather, from beyond.

From the secret tunnel.

Her heart seemed to fill her chest and beat in her ears. The tunnel. She could hardly believe it, after all the searching. Adrian and Uncle Thaddeus had actually found it. She started forward, then slowed.

Where were they? Why had they not come at once upstairs to tell her? Probably because they wanted to continue their explorations, perhaps locate the paintings.

Her indignation swelled. The least they could do would be to allow her—and Elspeth—to take part in that. And so she would tell them. Still, she found herself advancing on the great cask on tiptoe.

It seemed eerily silent down here. Too silent. The chance remained, she reminded herself, that someone other than Adrian and her uncle might have opened it. She reached the cask's edge, took tentative hold on it, and peered within.

Light shone from a single lantern hung on a timbered wall, from which beams and supports stuck out in various directions. The pale glow bathed this end of the tunnel, sending shadows dancing backward perhaps ten feet. It must be almost seven feet high, and at least that wide, broadening to more than ten feet at the tunnel mouth.

And just to the left of where she stood, piled high on the stone floor, lay an array of items that robbed her of breath. For a moment she stared, astonished, at an assortment of art objects, gold plate and jewels. No paintings, but this—this veritable treasure trove. Could this be the Selwood legacy? She took a hesitant step inside, staring about in wonder.

Had this lain here for sixty-odd years, securing the future of the Selwood ladies? In awe, she picked up a chased silver candelabrum, running her finger along the beautiful lines. The beautiful *clean* lines. Very little dust clung to the surface, and only minimal tarnish. She replaced it on the floor and bent to examine a hideous epergne. No, it must have been placed here only days before, not years.

She glanced about, and noticed the absence of cobwebs. And that iron hook from which the lantern hung, not a speck of rust marred it. It had been replaced sometime recently—but not within the last hour, she would bet on that. And Adrian had heard voices coming from here.

Not the Selwood legacy, but a thieves' den.

That, finally, made sense. Stolen goods, hidden at the end of the tunnel by—whom? Cousin George and his disreputable visitors?

She stepped backward, dismayed, her mind still whirling. This explained the hauntings, to frighten people away when the culprits wished to bring more treasures to this hiding place. They now had something tangible to hand over to the authorities. Bow Street might even become involved. The hauntings would come to an end—but at what cost to the Seminary? How could it survive the ensuing scandal? How *dare* George leave his ill-gotten goods here, practically beneath the school, involving his cousins in his filthy schemes?

Somehow, that infuriated her more than the rest. If only her cousins could be spared—but there seemed no way. At least they could sell the paintings to tide them over the worst.... Daphne looked around, and with a sinking heart she realized she could see no paintings. She'd been so certain they lay behind all these troubles, yet they had nothing to do with it. For all she knew, they didn't even exist!

Where was Adrian? She peered down the tunnel, beyond the shadows and into darkness. Why didn't he come back?

Or had he not opened the passageway in the first place?

Tensing, she glanced over her shoulder, but nothing moved. What did she do now? Wait?

Someone had opened this passage. Presumably, that someone would shortly return to close it. Where, in the meantime, could that someone have gone? Her gaze flew toward the oak cask with the stair leading to the attic. The attic, with Elspeth asleep in a room with the door open, only yards away. She didn't want to leave the cellar, but if Elspeth heard noises and awoke.... She had to check on her, make sure no one had used the secret stair.

Seemingly, no one had. The attic floor remained quiet. Daphne crept to her room and peeked in, and in relief saw Elspeth still slumbered in peace. Nothing—or no one—had disturbed her.

She looked along the hallway toward the lumber room, and swallowed—which did nothing to relieve the dryness of her throat and mouth. She had to check, to see if it showed signs of anyone having been there. She had to take a step down the corridor, then another, and another, until she reached that room....

She did it, to the accompaniment of her pulse pounding in her ears. Now, she had only to open that door. . . . She stood for a full minute with her fingers grasping the handle, her ear pressed against the panel. No sounds issued forth. Bracing her nerve, she eased it open a crack.

Only pale moon and starlight illuminated the chamber, bathing the few remaining pieces of furniture in a soft glow. No shadows wavered, no sharp intake of breath hissed from the corners. Nothing. She gathered her courage and went in.

The great trunk, now restored to a pretence of being undamaged, remained exactly as they'd left it. Daphne crept around to the back, checking for the piece of paper which they had suspended there from beneath the closed lid. That had been Adrian's idea, so they would know if it had been disturbed. Apparently, it had not. Which left her nowhere nearer knowing to where the person who opened the tunnel entry had vanished. Unless . . .

Uncle Percival! She had forgotten him. It *had* been him she'd seen—hadn't it? Where had he gotten lost? Or, if he knew about the paintings, did he perhaps know how to open the secret doors in the cellar? What if the passage had not been blocked on the other side, but merely required a further opening device—such as a key? Uncle Percival might have let himself in, then gone exploring for his paintings. If he failed to find them, he undoubtedly would return to pick over the thieves' loot and console himself with that. By now he might even have encountered Adrian and Uncle Thaddeus.

She retraced her steps, hurrying, wondering what might await her. A scraping from the cellar reached her as she neared, and she slowed, finishing the last few steps in caution—though it was probably only Uncle Percival, returning to the treasure. She should have guessed his involvement at once. She crept through the darkness to where the light barely showed through the opening in the cask. Sure enough, a white-robed figure bent over the stolen goods within.

Indignant, she marched forward. "Don't you dare touch anything," she ordered.

The man spun about, rising, revealing not the good-natured countenance of her scapegrace uncle, but the threatening scowl of one of Cousin George's late night visitors. She shrank back, too startled to do more than shake her head as she collided with the end of the cask.

The man sprang after her, grasping her arm, and she saw no more than his swinging fist before it connected with her temple.

Chapter Nineteen

All that followed remained a stunned blur for Daphne. Tearing sounds penetrated through her daze, and somehow that seemed incongruous. She felt herself shoved about, but lacked the energy to protest or struggle. The ground felt hard beneath her; she must have fallen to the stone floor.

As her head began to clear, she tried to crawl away— only to discover her ankles had been bound and her hands were confined behind her. She squinted at the ties at her feet, which resembled strips of bed linen. Or a ghost's white robe.

She leaned back against the timbered wall, her head throbbing. A foul taste lingered in her mouth, and she bit into another of the begrimed rags. Another strip wrapped about her head, preventing her from spitting it out.

A boot scraped on the paving, and the next moment her captor stood over her, a malevolent glint in his eye, his fingers toying with the blade of a rather nasty-looking knife. "You shouldn't 'ave come down 'ere," he said, and grinned.

The shadowiness of the figure looming over her turned it all into a nightmare. It couldn't be as bad as it seemed, Daphne tried to tell herself. Yet in this dark recess where she now lay, she could barely make out his features, and somehow that made it worse.

A tuneless whistle that might have been an Irish air, shaky at first then growing in volume, approached, accompanied by the steady tread of footsteps. Daphne couldn't figure out from which end of the tunnel. The man above her tensed, crouching beside her, all but invisible here where the light from that single lantern didn't quite reach.

Both whistling and footsteps stopped abruptly. "And what have we here?" came Uncle Percival's familiar voice.

Daphne tensed, struggling, but the man pressed the point of his knife against her neck. She could make a sound to warn Percival, but at what cost to herself? And knowing Percival, he would only poke around to investigate the cry rather than taking prudent flight. That would get them nowhere. Perhaps she'd have a better chance once the man moved away from her side to tackle her uncle.

The next moment the scrabbling sounds of someone climbing through the open cask reached her. They stopped, and a loud intake of breath announced Percival's discovery of the treasure horde.

"And where are the leprechauns?" he said softly, almost reverently. "I don't even remember the rainbow, but sure enough, it's me pot of gold." He stepped down into the tunnel, and, a broad grin on his face, swooped to scoop up a small chased silver box.

Daphne's captor lunged toward him. Daphne tried to scream, a muted, voiceless cry, and Percival spun to face her. The man seized a candlestick and brought it down on her uncle's head. For one moment Percival remained standing, staring toward Daphne with a blank expression, then dropped with a thud to the stone floor.

Daphne fought against her bonds, but in vain. Percival lay still. Too still? If only she could reach him. She raged inwardly—the only way open to her.

Their captor looked from one to the other of them, nodded as if satisfied, then climbed into the cask and

291

disappeared toward the cellar beneath the Dower House. The scraping of his boots ended with a thud as he jumped to the floor on the other side. After a moment, the faintest sound of rapping reached her, followed by an eerie screech that set her teeth on end. A hinge, she told herself. It was only a hinge.

A minute later, the man reappeared in the tunnel, eyed them both, then grasped the bulky form of Percival just below the shoulders, heaved him over, and dragged him toward the cask. Daphne chewed at the filthy rag in her mouth, but to no avail. Nor did any amount of struggling do other than tighten the bonds that confined her wrists and ankles.

All too soon the man returned once more. He picked her up with an ease she found infuriating, tossed her over his shoulder as if she were no more than a sack of meal, and carried her, in her turn, through the cask.

The glow from the tunnel barely illuminated the immense cellar. She could make out little in the dimness, but her captor seemed to know what he was about. He bore her a short distance along the side wall to a cask that stood open, its large, round front no more than a shadowy shape against the darkness that surrounded them. He dumped her unceremoniously inside.

She braced herself for hitting the wooden bottom, but instead landed on something soft. Uncle Percival, she guessed. She rolled off him and dragged herself to her knees in time to see the front swing close in her face.

Darkness enveloped her, and she fought back an urge to scream. Throwing herself against the front did no good, only leaving her with an aching shoulder to show for the effort. She sank back on her heels, closing her eyes, forcing herself to think rationally. The musky odor of oak soaked long in brandy surrounded her. This wasn't the cask with the stairway leading to the attic. She maneuvered around, but the most cursory examination of her prison proved it to possess no other exit.

She turned her attention to reviving Uncle Percival,

no easy task with her wrists confined behind her. It might be kinder to let him lie in oblivion, but he might be able to untie her, and she wanted to be ready when their captor came to let them out.

If he came to let them out . . .

Adrian stood in the dark hall at the Manor, his lantern mostly covered, contemplating the great walnut stair that wound its way into the darkness of the floor above.

Mr. Danvers clasped his hands before him, and a deep frown creased his brow. "I cannot believe George Selwood is aware of the use to which that tunnel has been put—so many items of such considerable value!— yet how could he not know? I tell you, Adrian, I do not like this in the least."

Adrian rubbed his free hand across the stubble of beard that roughened his jaw. "Selwood has insisted from the beginning the hauntings are genuine, but that's been a pretence, no doubt of that. Which means he's tried to keep us from investigating. He's also been afraid, and I don't think that's been an act. No, he must know about that treasury down there, and it has him badly frightened."

Mr. Danvers nodded. "It is time we send someone for the constable. I cannot believe that treasure is aught but ill-gotten."

"No, it is undoubtedly stolen. But before we call in the authorities, I should like to give Selwood a chance to extricate himself. He might even be of assistance in capturing the culprits if we promise to help him get free of this tangle."

Mr. Danvers did not look happy. "For Daphne and Miss Elspeth's sakes, I should like to see their cousin well out of this," he admitted. "And the scandal for the school, if Mr. Selwood should be arrested—" He shook his head.

"Then let us see to it he is not." Adrian started for the steps.

Mr. Danvers followed, and together they mounted with care to the next floor. Some prior knowledge of the floor plan, Adrian decided, might have been helpful. Aside from the oil lamps that burned low on the stairs, no other lights illuminated the darkness.

He considered a moment, frowning at the possibilities that jumbled in his mind. If Selwood expected his unwelcome visitors, he probably would be in one of the downstairs rooms, awaiting their arrival. Instead, the house lay in stillness and Selwood had retired for the night.

Thus assured he was unlikely to raise any alarm by displaying his lantern, he drew back the cover and let the full arc of brightness sweep the broad corridor. The doors all stood shut. He started to his right, opening each in turn, and found nothing but Holland covers and the musty air of disuse. He returned to the stairs, then started in the other direction.

The second door he tried opened into an anteroom, and at once he felt the difference in temperature. Somewhere in the near vicinity, a fire performed its welcome work. Through a crack in the doorway directly before him, he glimpsed the flickering light of the flames.

Adrian shuttered his light and set it on a table. He would not need it within the bedchamber beyond. He eased his way into the room to see the hearth burning low, almost down to embers. Selwood, it seemed, had retired early.

Cold, pale moonlight filtered through a crack in the draperies, and a small lamp burned softly on the bedside table. More than sufficient illumination, Adrian decided. He crossed to the great bedstead and yanked back the curtains.

The figure within started, sitting upright, jerking the covers up to its chin. The wide, frightened eyes of George Selwood peered out from beneath his skewed nightcap and blinked in the darkness. His gaze came to rest on Adrian, and he shrank back with a gasp.

"You have a few things to explain, Selwood." Adrian kept his voice purely conversational and inviting, without any hint of accusation.

"I—I have?" Selwood peered at his visitor. "Carstairs, is that you? What the devil do you mean by this—this outrage?"

"That's what we're here to discover. You are acquainted with Mr. Danvers, are you not? Your cousin Daphne's uncle?"

Selwood shifted in the bed and pulled a pillow behind himself. "We have met. I was not, however, aware I had issued invitations to a party in my chamber this night."

"I'm more interested in the party at the end of the tunnel."

"The—" Selwood swallowed, setting his Adam's apple bobbing. "What—what tunnel?"

"Cut line, Selwood. We found the mechanism that opens the cask in your cellar, and we have been to the end of the tunnel that must butt up against the Dower House. We were not, however, able to find the opening that connects the cellar at that end. And I must admit, we quickly became far more interested in what we found down there."

"You—you found something?" he asked weakly. He looked from one to the other of them with a sickly smile. "How—how interesting. What?"

"That's what I expect you to tell me—as well as what's been going on. If you tell us enough, we might be able to get you out of this mess."

"Out of—" For a moment, a glimmer of hope shone in his drawn face, but it faded at once. "I don't know what you're talking about, really, I don't. I haven't the faintest idea. What do you mean, barging in here, disturbing my sleep, talking a pack of nonsense, making veiled threats—"

295

"Threats?" Adrian's brow rose. "We haven't once mentioned the constables, have we?"

"You—you've summoned them?" The last remnants of color drained from Selwood's face, and the hands that still clasped the edge of the comforter trembled. "I'll be ruined. We all will." He sank back against the pillows, horror patent on his countenance.

Adrian glanced at Mr. Danvers, then back at Selwood. "There might still be a way out," he suggested.

Selwood merely groaned and shook his head. "What hope have we?" he moaned.

"You might begin by telling us the whole story," Adrian invited. "Who are those two men who visit you at night?"

"Devils." Vehemence sounded in Selwood's voice. "Devils."

"From the beginning, I think." Adrian's steady gaze rested on Selwood, compelling.

Selwood shook his head. "You can't protect me. No one can. They'll kill me if the constables come."

Adrian raised politely skeptical brows. "And how could they manage that feat if they are under arrest?" Selwood remained silent for a long moment, his posture tense in the bed, but Adrian could tell he listened. "How involved are you in their thieving ring?" he added.

At that, a shuddering sigh escaped Selwood. "I'm not, really I'm not. But I hoped—oh, how I hoped!—no one would ever find out about it."

"It was only a matter of time," Adrian pointed out. "How long have you known about the tunnel?"

"Always," Selwood said. "My father told me."

"And about the paintings?" Adrian prodded gently as the man fell silent.

Selwood glared at him. "I thought they might be in the passage. Then technically they wouldn't be part of the contents of the Dower House."

Adrian nodded, encouraging, keeping his temper

under firm check. "So you hired those men to search the tunnel."

Selwood nodded, miserable. "We had first to find the opening."

"You didn't know the mechanism?"

Again, Selwood shook his head. "They found it. So quickly, in fact, my search seemed destined for success. They explored every inch of that passage, then said locating the paintings might take considerable time. Then the hauntings started."

"How did you find those men?" Adrian kept his tone level, inviting confidences.

Selwood stared at him, his expression one of surprise. "They came to me looking for odd jobs. Expert carpenters, you know. They sounded like just the fellows to locate the hidden mechanism for the tunnel, so I took them on." His face clouded once more. "I should have known, I really should. It was all too good to be true."

Adrian refrained from agreeing out loud. Had coming to Selwood been a stroke of luck on their part? Or had the men known of the existence of the tunnel in advance? If Selwood had visited an inn, been in his cups, he might have mentioned his search and never remembered afterwards. The men might have come in the hope of finding the paintings, then when that search proved a failure, turned the tunnel to another, more profitable, use. "Go on," he said through gritted teeth. "When did you discover what they were about?"

Selwood hesitated. "Only recently. Very recently. I—I didn't go into the tunnel."

"Why not?"

"They said it was dirty and full of spiders and rats."

Adrian drew a steadying breath. "You weren't the least bit curious about how their search progressed?"

"Of course." Selwood pleated the covers with nervous fingers. "Only they said I'd be in their way. They wouldn't show me the mechanism, either, so I could go in on my own."

"And you allowed them to get away with that?"

Selwood cast a sideways glance at him. "I don't see where I had much choice," he muttered. "Not at first, at least. They were careful, very careful, always making sure I wasn't around. But I didn't trust them. It occurred to me they might be planning to find the paintings and keep them for themselves." He sounded outraged at the thought of such duplicity, as if his own motives and behavior were above reproach. "So one night I sneaked down and caught the cask door as it closed behind them. I still don't know how the mechanism works," he added, annoyed.

"So you followed them?" Adrian pursued.

Selwood nodded. "And I saw what they had down there. The most amazing things. I couldn't believe it at first. For one minute . . ." His voice trailed off, but a touch of longing lingered in his expression. "Well, I soon realized it couldn't be any horde belonging to my family, that all of it must be stolen. I told them I wouldn't stand for my tunnel being used for that sort of thing, but they just laughed at me."

"Why didn't you go to the authorities?" Mr. Danvers, who had kept silent until now, demanded.

Selwood stared at him, shocked. "I couldn't. They said I was as involved as they were, and if they were arrested, they'd tell the Runners the whole scheme was mine, but I'd gotten scared and was trying to lay all the blame on them. The scandal!" He broke off, shaking his head, apparently beyond speech for a few moments. With a visible effort, he went on. "Ruined," he gasped. "Me, my cousins, their school. All of us. There was nothing, not a single thing, I could do but keep silent and hope no one discovered what they were about."

"Well, we have," Adrian announced. He turned to Mr. Danvers, who stood on the opposite side of the bed, his expression concerned. "I think we can keep him out of this, but we'd best bring in the law tonight."

An incautious footstep outside in the anteroom

proved Adrian's only warning. He gathered himself for a flying lunge, but when the door burst open, two men stepped in, both armed with horse pistols. With a wave of a barrel, one of them gestured Adrian away from the bed. Mr. Danvers circled around to join him on the far side.

"Well, Your Highness." The other man slouched against the jamb, grinning. "Rather late to be entertaining visitors."

"What are you doing here?" Selwood barely got the words out of his throat.

The man's grin broadened. "Listening. That weren't a very good idea of yours, not good at all," he said to Adrian. "We don't want to go calling in no Runners, now, do we?"

"What're we going to do with 'em, Freddy?" the other asked. He never took his gaze from his captives.

"Same thing I done with the others." Freddy straightened and jerked his head. "Come on. No time to lose."

The others. Adrian moved slowly where the man directed him, giving himself a chance to think and plan. By "the others" did he mean Daphne and Miss Elspeth? He could only hope Mr. Danvers did not come to that same conclusion, though no other seemed possible. What had this Freddy done with them? At this moment, Adrian only wanted to get his hands about the man's throat and choke the answer out of him.

But getting himself shot would accomplish little—unless Selwood's servants heard the pistol fire and came to investigate. More likely they'd cower in their beds. For the moment, Adrian abandoned the idea of heroics. A better chance might present itself—and he wanted to know where Daphne was before these men could use her as a hostage, bargaining their knowledge of what they had done with her for their own release. Nor could he do anything that might place Mr. Danvers in jeopardy. Chafing at these restrictions, Adrian permitted himself to be hustled out of the chamber, along the corridor, down the stairs.

Selwood, shivering in his nightshirt, his cap still cocked over one eye, had not even had the chance to bundle himself into his brocade dressing gown or thrust his feet into his Turkish slippers. The man addressed as Freddy ordered him to lead the way to the cellars, and George did, all the while casting frantic glances over his shoulder at the two weapons. Little heart and no courage, Adrian guessed. He could not count on Selwood's support in any escape from this situation.

That situation might be turning very ugly, he was well aware. All three of them could identify these two men. It was possible they would simply be left in the tunnel. Bound and gagged, they might well be unable to escape.

More likely, though, the men would not want to take any chances. The odds were very slim that anyone who did not know of the existence of the tunnel would ever think to look for bodies left so deep under the earth. Miss Beatrice and Miss Sophronia Selwood would certainly raise a hue and cry at their disappearance, but it seemed likely the opening mechanism for the tunnel would elude them and any other searchers. And even if they did manage to open it, it would be far too late as far as he, Mr. Danvers, Selwood—and very possibly Daphne and Miss Elspeth—were concerned.

They reached the cellar, and the nameless man took up a position by the cask where he could still keep his pistol pointed at Adrian. Freddy strolled along the wine rack, his aim never wavering from Mr. Danvers, until he reached the polished board Adrian himself had found earlier. A moment later a dull click sounded, and their other captor dragged open the front of the cask on well-oiled hinges. He stepped back and waved Adrian inside.

"And don't try nothing, or the reverend 'ere will get shot," the man added.

Adrian felt like a complete fool. Still, there was little

he could do but comply—at least for the moment. An opportunity to do more would come—he would make that opportunity at whatever cost before he simply gave up and let these two get away with whatever they now planned.

Only a faint light from the low-burning oil lamps illuminated their way. Adrian increased his pace, only to be ordered at once to slow down. This he did, tensed, listening for any sound to indicate one or the other of the men might be about to shoot him in the back. But nothing occurred; they continued through the semi-darkness, their shadows dancing erratically about the timbered walls.

If only one had burned out, Adrian might have seized his chance. His best hope would be for Mr. Danvers and himself to separate as far as possible. He didn't bother including Selwood in his hazy plan. The man trudged along in his nightrail, despondent, shoulders stooped and feet dragging, as if he went to his death.

He might well be doing just that. They all might. Which made it imperative to escape.

Ahead, Adrian could just make out the dull gleam of the treasure horde. Would Daphne and Miss Elspeth be there, bound . . . or dead? He quickened his pace once more, his agonized gaze searching into the dark recesses, both hoping for and dreading a glimpse of her. Yet even by the wavering light, and through shadows that advanced and retreated, he could see that no human figures awaited them.

Did that mean they didn't have Daphne captive, after all? Hope surged within him, along with a determination to make sure she never fell into their clutches. He turned back to the others, to find himself facing Freddy and his horse pistol.

"Let's just shoot 'em right here," the man said. "Be a lot easier in the long run."

Chapter Twenty

Adrian kept very still. Mr. Danvers's sharp intake of breath broke the sudden silence, followed the next moment by a moaning whimper from George Selwood. The dandy's knees trembled, and for a moment Adrian expected him to topple forward.

"Wouldn't that make things rather awkward?" Adrian kept his voice calm, with just a hint of boredom coloring the words. He examined the nails of his left hand in an attitude of indifference, while actually checking his wrist for strength. He wouldn't be able to put the full force of a punch behind it, but he still had his right, and that he could use to advantage. He had to delay whatever these two planned for him until he could be certain Daphne was safe.

Freddy and his companion exchanged uneasy glances. "Why should it be awkward?" Freddy demanded. "Don't see why it should. What's awkward is having to hold these here pistols on you."

"You could always put them down," Adrian suggested.

"No we couldn't." Freddy's companion puckered his brow in concentration. "Wouldn't work. Wouldn't 'ave no control over you lot, we wouldn't."

Freddy guffawed. "Put 'em down. That's a right good one, that is."

Apparently not good enough, though. The guns

didn't waver. Adrian braced himself for a lunge as Freddy steadied his pistol and squinted down the barrel at Adrian's chest.

A sound—more a shuffle—that had been playing about the corners of his consciousness for a few moments, finally penetrated. Footsteps, and they approached. He cleared his throat. "It seems," he announced in that same carefully unconcerned drawl, "we are about to have company."

"Back," Freddy ordered, and waved them toward the shadows.

Selwood ducked away into the darkness where he was ordered. Mr. Danvers took one step, then hesitated as Adrian made no move to comply.

"Why?" Adrian asked. "You surely don't suppose you could hide so many of us, do you?"

The booted footsteps came closer, striking in an even pace across the stone floor of the passage. Adrian peered through the dim light and could make out a shadowy shape approaching. A man, greatcoat swinging about his booted lower legs, very broad in the shoulder. The figure passed beneath one of the infrequently placed oil lamps.

"Romney," Selwood breathed in relief. "We're saved."

Their two captors shifted slightly but made no other acknowledgment of the newcomer's arrival.

Romney slowed as he reached the last light, and his eyes widened, as if for the first time he saw how many figures stood there in the shadows. He came to an abrupt halt and stared from one to the other of them. "What the devil has been going on here?" he demanded.

Adrian's eyes narrowed; the question, he realized, had not been directed at either himself or Selwood, but at the two thieves.

"We're 'olding pistols on 'em," Freddy's literal companion announced, regarding Romney like a hound awaiting praise.

Freddy snorted. "Looks like we're going to have to move the stash," he said, his tone regretful.

"You mean you've been careless." Romney's eyes glittered in the lamp light. "I thought we agreed to maintain the utmost secrecy. Sam?"

"Did keep it secret," Freddy's companion asserted. "They didn't follow us, they went and found it all on their own. And you told us no one could." He quailed under Romney's kindling eye. "This weren't no fault of ours. We done our best."

"Now, there ain't no call to get all nattered about it." Freddy appeared immune to Romney's rising wrath. "What's done is done. This lot won't cause us no more problems. Any number of bodies can stay hidden down here. Who's to find the way in again? Once we seal off the entrances, no one won't ever think to look, nor find 'em if'n they do."

"Bodies." Romney sounded disgusted. "You've wasted my hiding place. All these years I've waited to put it to good use, and now you just throw it away as a graveyard. And you have the—"

A loud pounding sounded from beyond the cask leading to the cellar beneath the Dower House. Romney stiffened, alert.

"More of 'em," Freddy said. "But don't you worry, none, sir. They're all taken care of."

Romney directed a fulminating look at his henchman which caused the fellow to look abashed. He grasped the lantern from its wall hook, climbed into the cask, then strode through the short wooden passage. Freddy and Sam exchanged troubled glances, and Adrian grasped his opportunity. He set off after Romney.

" 'Ere, now," Sam protested.

Adrian pretended to ignore him. If this was Freddy's other captive . . . Daphne . . .

"All of you," he heard Freddy say behind him, and a

304

few moments later Mr. Danvers assisted the hapless, trembling Selwood into the cask and after them.

On the other side, Romney followed the sounds of pounding until he reached the fourth cask from the end on the long wall. He didn't hesitate, but with a series of quick pulls on various locations, he released the mechanism. Four, Adrian counted, and probably in a specific order, one releasing the next. No wonder he hadn't found it; he'd sought no more than a single- or at most a double-controlled device.

Selwood stiffened. "How the devil did you know the secret?" he demanded as the front of the cask snapped open a few inches.

Romney gave a short laugh. "You had even more chances than I did to learn about this place. Played in these cellars more often than I did when we were children. But I listened when our elders talked. You never cared for aught but winning our games. So I learned things, and you did not." A sneer crept into his voice. "Things I saw no need to share with you." He pulled the cask door wide.

Adrian pushed forward to look within, relief flooding him as he saw by the glowing lantern Daphne's blazing eyes. Then fury surged through him to see her so, bound and confined. She knelt on the wood, arms behind her, a gag fastened about her mouth. She must have been kicking the side, he realized. Next to her, a middle-aged gentleman of slight build and a developing paunch lay slumped against the wall. A distinguished brow, flamboyant dress—Adrian didn't recognize him and spared him no more than a glance. He returned his attention to Daphne. He had found her. Somehow, he must get her free of this.

A wordless cry of pent-up rage escaped her. Romney peered inside, and Daphne sank to a half-sitting position, moving forward in the process, and lashed out with her daintily slippered feet.

Romney jumped backward in time to avoid a telling

305

kick aimed at his stomach, and chuckled. "My dear——" he began.

"You will all stand still," came the quavering voice of Miss Elspeth. "You will not move a muscle—and do not turn about!" The order came from directly behind them, shaky but determined.

Rather than obey, every one of them spun around to see Elspeth standing about ten feet away with an unlit lantern in her hand and no weapon.

"I told you not to turn," she declared, indignant.

Adrian grasped his opportunity, the only one he was likely to have. Freddy stood closest to him. Adrian launched himself against the man, striking with his good hand at the wrist that held the pistol. It took Mr. Danvers only a moment to follow suit, turning on the man called Sam. Adrian, rolling on the floor with his opponent, saw Selwood dart back through the cask. Making his escape, Adrian realized with disgust, leaving Daphne bound and helpless.

He wrenched his right arm free from Freddy's grip and swung, connecting with the man's jaw. Freddy rolled away, scrambling for the pistol that lay a few feet from them. Adrian followed. Where was Romney? Elspeth, he realized as he kicked the pistol from Freddy's grasp, swung her lantern like a weapon, keeping Romney cornered, away from them.

"Stand back," came a shaky cry from out of the darkness.

Adrian, by instinct, ducked low, ramming his head into Freddy's chest. Just over his left shoulder something flew by, and Romney gave a sharp exclamation and dropped to his knees. A large silver epergne clattered at his side. Selwood, Adrian realized; he hadn't deserted them.

Elspeth swung her lantern once more, hitting Romney in the shoulder, and his lantern crashed to the floor. Glass shattered, then flames burst high into the air as the oil spilled out, spreading across the ground. Romney yelled, diving backward, beating at the edges of his greatcoat that had been splattered, and now burst into flame. The conflagration roared for no more than a few moments, then flickered, dying down as rapidly as it had exploded.

An instant later the fire extinguished, plunging them into blackness.

It took considerable effort for Daphne, with both her ankles and wrists bound, to struggle once more to her knees. All the while, she remained vividly aware of the struggle taking place without. She hadn't hurt Squire Romney in the least, she reflected, infuriated with her failure. Nor had she done anything to help herself or the others.

Erect again, she inched forward to the edge of her cask. At least the door to her makeshift prison had been left open. The flames that had illuminated the scene with ferocious brightness wavered, then died, plunging everything into darkness. What occurred? Where was Adrian? She could still hear the grunts and clamor of struggle, of men rolling on the stone flagging, of fist connecting with solid body. What went on?

"Daphne?" Elspeth's trembling voice reached her. Amid the other sounds she discerned the shuffling of slippered feet crossing the floor. "Daphne?" Elspeth's tone wavered in uncertainty.

Daphne gave another of her wordless cries. The next moment hands touched her face and shoulder, then sought the cloth that bound about her head. Daphne winced as her hair tangled in the knot, but then the tie fell away. Daphne made urgent noises again, and the fingers found her mouth, then pulled the stifling cloth free.

Daphne gasped, drawing in dank, musty air. "Thank you," she managed. "My hands—" She turned as best she could, offering her bound wrists to her cousin.

307

Elspeth groped in the dark down Daphne's arms and quickly pulled at the ends of the cloth that fastened them. With surprising rapidity, these, too, fell away. Apparently Daphne reflected ruefully, her captor had not held a high opinion of her ability to escape or he would have secured her with more efficient knots. She sat back and went to work on her feet.

She yanked loose the last tie, crawled free of the cask, then stood in the cellar. She could see nothing, only hear the sounds of fighting. How did they know what they did? If she tried to help, she might inadvertently make things worse.

She needed light, she knew. Somewhere on that floor would be Elspeth's unbroken lantern. Yet she hesitated to get in the way of the men and their struggle.

She cast an anxious glance about, and caught the faint glow from within the cask leading back to the tunnel. Her stomach clenched; she would have to go through there. They needed light. Gripping Elspeth's arm, she led the way toward the glimmer and entered the passage once more.

The nearest lantern hung a good twenty-five yards away. Far too conscious of the solid earth above her head, pressing relentlessly down upon the top of the curved tunnel, she ran toward the light. If only she might find a pistol while she was at it; it probably wouldn't matter that she didn't know how to use one. She could wave it to good effect. Any weapon, for that matter, would be better than none. And Adrian . . .

The thought of Adrian, hampered by his injured wrist, drove her on. If all else failed, she would use the lantern as had Elspeth.

She reached the lamp, dragged it from its hook, and raced back to the cellar as fast as her cramped limbs would carry her, Elspeth at her heels. They pushed their way through the cask that formed the passage, and their light flooded the scene before them.

For one moment, Daphne stood at the edge of the

308

cask, while Elspeth stepped down to the cellar floor. Daphne followed, raised the lantern, and saw a sudden blur of movement to her right. An arm shot out, hooking her about the neck. Another poised at her side, and the light flickered along the blade of a knife held against her ribs.

"Stand away," a deep voice shouted, "unless you want Miss Selwood killed."

Romney. She recognized the voice and stiffened, furious with herself for providing him with such an opportunity.

The men fell apart. Elspeth, partway into the room, froze, staring at her in horror. Close beside her, Adrian sat back, disheveled, his hands in a chokehold about—Daphne blinked. About Uncle Percival's neck? Farther behind, she saw Uncle Thaddeus struggling with one of the thieves. The other lay on the floor unconscious.

Adrian wasted no time. He shifted his grip on the hapless Percival and hurled him against Daphne's legs, knocking her backwards into Romney and throwing them both to the stone floor. Daphne rolled away from the knife, to freedom, as Adrian, grasping Selwood's hurled epergne, swung it, bringing it down on the Squire's head.

Adrian stumbled forward, grasped her as she dragged herself to her feet, and enveloped her in a brief but crushing embrace. In the next instant, he had scooped up the fallen knife and spun to face the thief who now stood over the crumpled form of Uncle Thaddeus. The thief backed away, his wary gaze on Adrian's determined approach.

Daphne recovered the lantern and saw a glint of metal from the stone floor near the base of the oak cask. She stooped and grabbed a pistol which shook abominably in her hand. She presented it to Adrian, who threw her a grin that made her almost forget all she had gone through that night.

Elspeth took an unsteady step forward, then sank to

her knees beside the inert from of Mr. Danvers. Daphne reached her side and knelt, groping for her uncle's pulse, while Adrian held the pistol on their one uninjured enemy.

"He's only unconscious," Daphne announced, relieved. She rose slowly, leaving Uncle Thaddeus to Elspeth's tender care.

The thief took another step backward, as if afraid. His furtive gaze scanned the ground, then he took another step, this time a little to the right, toward the line of casks. Daphne's gaze narrowed, then only a couple of yards away she spotted the other pistol.

"Adrian," she said as calmly as she could, "please tell him to move in the other direction."

"Do it," came Adrian's sharp command.

The man hesitated, giving Daphne her chance. She swooped forward, keeping clear of the thief's reach, and kicked the pistol farther away. She scrambled after it and picked it up.

From out of the darkness—from under one of the long tables—Cousin George emerged. "Is it over?" he asked, voice trembling. "Have we won?" He went to Daphne's side, his hand just touching her arm as if he sought her protection.

Adrian drew a deep breath. His hand remained steady as it held the pistol. "Explain," he ordered the remaining thief.

" 'Im." The man jerked his head to where Romney lay unconscious against the wine racks. "It were 'is idea. The jobs. Knowing where things could be 'iddenlike 'til it would be safe to sell 'em. Playing at ghosts to scare them silly chits away."

"How long have you been stealing things?" Daphne demanded. "Why haven't we heard of any robberies? So much—"

The man snorted. "Not from 'round 'ere," he said in disgust. "We've brought that lot from all over England." Pride sounded in his voice.

Uncle Percival, who had been sitting quietly against the line of casks, strolled forward, brushing himself off. He straightened his coat with care and turned his considering eye on Adrian. "Being used as a weapon is not quite the way I would have chosen to be of assistance, perhaps, but there, one can't always choose one's course, can one? Delighted to have played my part." He held the epergne under one arm. He patted it, and both tone and look took on a reproving aspect. "I am appalled, sir, that such an excellent bit of silver work has been damaged."

Adrian's lips twitched. "You have my profound apologies. Though under the circumstances I would rather it had been that epergne than Miss Selwood."

Percival gave vent to a lusty sigh. "She is a treasure, is she not? My dearest niece. Never have I beheld her equal with a deck——"

"Uncle Percival!" Daphne exclaimed, aghast.

He beamed on her. "Ah, me darlin'." His gaze, though, strayed back toward the cask, the tunnel beyond, and undoubtedly the more readily spendable treasure within.

"I think," Adrian said, "we had best get this lot secured before they regain consciousness."

"An excellent plan," Percival agreed. "You, my good man," he gestured to Cousin George, then blinked. "George, is it not? Well, well." His face became a mask of disapproval. "In your nightrail, of all things. What has this world come to?" He clicked his tongue. "Make yourself of use. I believe my ghost sheet must be about here somewhere. Be quick and tear it into strips, there's a good fellow."

Adrian stood back, holding the pistol, while the others bound wrists and ankles. Uncle Percival, Daphne noted, knew what he was about; he worked with an efficiency that made her wonder about his life for the past few years. All the while, he whistled between his teeth, a lilting, off-key melody.

When they'd finished with the last of their captives, Adrian handed Percival the pistol, then checked the knots and nodded approval. "Well done."

Adrian's voice sounded strained, Daphne noted with concern. He leaned back against the cask leading to the tunnel, catching the open door with his good hand as if to steady himself. The door gave an eerie creak, a splintering shudder, then it swung. Adrian caught his balance, stepping back into the cellar, and the front of the cask separated in half on protesting hinges—into two separate doors.

Daphne stepped forward, catching the two pieces, pulling them apart. There, before them, a figure loomed out of the darkness. It took Daphne a moment to realize she stared at a painting of a man in Elizabethan garb. No, not Elizabethan, she realized.

"That—that's King Henry the Eighth," she stammered.

"Holbrook's work." Uncle Percival breathed out an exultant sigh. "Me darlin', you've found our treasure."

"Holbrook," Daphne repeated. "Do you mean—? It must be worth a fortune."

"Ah, me darlin', it's what I've been trying to tell you." Uncle Percival regarded it with a beatific smile.

Cousin George sighed, a sound of pure disgust. "On the Dower House side," he muttered. The next moment, his expression shifted, and he cast a considering glance at Elspeth.

"You will not be thinking of raising the rent," Daphne said sharply. "Besides, you cannot."

George's shoulders sagged. "No," he said dully. "No, of course not."

"The doors." Adrian, who had been examining the edge that had separated, shook his head. "What better hiding place? Once we found them, we'd only think of them as the way into the tunnel or the stairs. Who would thing twice about them again? To conceal something *within* the doors themselves, that was a stroke of genius."

He looked over his shoulder, a sudden glinting smile dancing in his eyes, enchanced by the glow of the oil lamp Daphne clutched. "How many paintings," he asked, "were missing when the evaluation was made?"

"Four," pronounced Percival, the family expert.

"And all within the Dower House," Daphne said pointedly. "Adrian, will you help me open the cask for the stair to the attic?"

"An excellent guess, I should think."

Together, they worked the mechanism, and the front of the cask swung wide. After only a few minutes of searching, with Adrian at her side, she triggered the next device. Here, too, the door swung in half and she found herself facing the portrait of a woman garbed for the same era as King Henry.

Percival gave vent to a deeply satisfied sigh and went to the cask that had held him prisoner. A few minutes later, he revealed a third painting. The fourth they found within the cask next to it.

"We can save the school," Daphne breathed, not quite believing their fortune. "We can really save it."

Percival rubbed his knuckles along his jaw line, his expression pensive. "Each one worth a fortune," he declared. "Surely, me darlin', the school can get by on just three."

"Four," Daphne informed him.

He fixed a reproving glare on her and opened his mouth.

"Daphne, my love, is it true?" Elspeth called from the floor. Mr. Danvers now sat at her side, watching them.

"Uncle—?" Daphne hurried to them.

"I am quite recovered." Mr. Danvers hauled himself to his feet, but made no protest when both Elspeth and Daphne took his elbows for support.

In fact, it seemed to Daphne he leaned most gratefully against Elspeth. Prudently she stepped away. Neither of the other two seemed to notice.

Elspeth dragged her gaze from Uncle Thaddeus. "The paintings—is it true? Will they really be enough to save the Seminary? Oh, Daphne, Mr. Carstairs—" She broke off, tears filling her eyes. "Oh, how—how happy my sisters will be. And—Cousin Percival, is it not?" She gave a shaky laugh. "How very long it has been, to be sure."

"Dear lady." He swept her an elegant bow, hampered somewhat by the epergne he still held, and carried her fingers to his lips. "How it pains me that it must be so short a reunion, but I fear with my finances in such desperate straits, I must flee these shores once more."

"You're going?" Daphne asked, both hopeful and sorry to see the last of her delightfully outrageous relative.

"You shall not go with your pockets wholly to let," Elspeth vowed. "Surely you deserve some reward for your part in this night."

"Dear Cousin." He beamed on her, and once more kissed the hand he still retained. "Spoken like the true lady you are."

Daphne shook her head in mock sorrow. "I am quite eclipsed," she murmured. "But you will still leave?" she added, louder. Elspeth might be willing to share the largesse, but she could not possibly welcome the scandals that inevitably followed in Percival's wake.

"Ah, me darlin'." A wistful glint shone in his eyes. "Italy . . . no, perhaps Paris. I have always had a fancy for an establishment in that great city. Just off the Rue St. Honore, I believe. Yes." He became lost in a rapturous dream.

"Does the Seminary," Mr. Danvers asked, reclaiming Elspeth's attention, "mean as much to you as it does to your sisters?" An odd note sounded in his voice.

Elspeth hesitated. "I care for it for their sake," she
314

said at last. "I could not imagine them without it, it has for so long been the mainstay of their lives."

"And yours?" A touch of urgency edged his words.

Again she hesitated, as if weighing her answer with care. "I have no other focus for my energies," came the reply, slightly muffled. She kept her gaze lowered, refusing to meet his.

"And if you had one?" Mr. Danvers raised her hands, drawing her reluctant gaze to his face. "Would they be capable of running the school without your assistance?"

"I—I would need much to occupy me." A shy smile wavered upon her lips.

"I believe," Mr. Danvers responded, "the wife of a country vicar could not complain of boredom."

"Nor of anything else," breathed Elspeth, gazing at him as if mesmerized.

Mr. Danvers wasted no more time with words. With commendable presence of mind, he gathered his unprotesting lady into his arms and kissed her.

Daphne turned away, both glad and depressed. She would miss Elspeth; the seminary would not be the same without her gentle humor. It would seem empty. Her whole life would seem empty.

She could always, she supposed, join Uncle Percival in Paris. There seemed little left for her here in England. Only Jane to need her still, and all too soon Jane would make her debut and Daphne would be left alone to dwindle into an ape leader, a spinster schoolmistress. . . .

"Daphne," Uncle Thaddeus called, a surprisingly serious note in his voice. Elspeth still nestled in the curve of his arm, her expression glowing. "You *do* know what is best for yourself. Don't let stubbornness keep you from choosing it."

Stubbornness. If that only were all that stood in her way . . .

Adrian caught up to her as she reached the foot of the stairs, his hand closing on her shoulder. She didn't meet his gaze. Instead, she took the offensive. "I suppose you will be leaving, now. I—I must thank you for all your help."

"I know how much you hate accepting favors. So perhaps you would be willing to do me one in return." For once, a note of seriousness underlined that deep, compelling voice.

Daphne glanced up, met the burning intensity of his gaze and looked quickly away. "There is nothing I could do to sufficiently discharge the debt I owe you." She inserted a note of finality into her words and started away from him.

"Isn't there? As your uncle so memorably pointed out, the wife of a country vicar would never be bored. Could you not come to enjoy such a life?"

More than anything in the world! her heart cried. Tears stung her eyes and she shook her head, not trusting herself to look up. He was a gentleman, one considerate of the feelings of others. He wouldn't press her. . . .

He caught her hand, his hold determined yet gentle. "You know we can work together—how much you have contributed to our effort here. I cursed my clumsiness in hurting my wrist at first, but it has certainly proved to me—and to you, as well, I should hope—how much of a partnership we might have." That injured hand strayed to her cheek, his touch a caress. He brushed an errant tendril from her eyes, then trailed his fingers down to her lips.

Resolutely, she studied the top button of his waistcoat. Her tears threatened to escape, but with great effort she held them back, shaking her head, unable to command her voice. "I—I am quite ineligible," she managed. "I am—am sensible of the—" she sniffed and fought to keep her shoulders from shaking with the sob she repressed "—the honor you do me, but—"

"I've done you no honor at all," came his smiling reply. His arm slid about her waist, drawing her closer. "I have enough illustrious relations to know myself no matrimonial prize. All I offer you is a life of hard, but very satisfying, work. Come, can you not bring yourself to share it with me?"

She blinked rapidly, but it did little to clear the unshed tears from her eyes. They clung to her lashes, and more took their place. "It—it is I who am no matrimonial prize," she managed.

"I think that's for me to decide." His head bent toward hers, and his mouth found a very sensitive spot near her ear.

For a moment, she let herself rest against him, then she thrust herself away, her hands on his upper arms. "You do not know!" she cried. "Adrian, I—it would ruin you to wed such a one as I."

"I admit," he said maddeningly, gathering her to him once more, "I would find myself frequently distracted from my parishioners, but I fail to see how that would ruin me."

"Oh, must you make this so difficult?" Her agony sounded in her voice. "I must choose what is best for you, as well. And that is for you *not* to be saddled with me."

The teasing light faded from his eyes. "Come, love, confess the worst to me. What skeletons lurk in your cupboards?" He held her firmly, tenderly, allowing her no chance for escape.

"I should have told you before." She hadn't the heart to free herself, yet she knew she should. She would not be able to bear it when, after hearing the truth, he would be the one to set her aside. "I—my past—"

His hand caressed the nape of her neck where her hair hung loose. "What is past, is past," he murmured. "It's a future I'm talking about. Our future."

She wrenched herself free, leaving part of her heart behind. "A girl from a gaming hell has no place in a vicarage!" There, she'd said it at last. Now he'd know, he'd hesitate, realize the truth of her words. . . .

Strong hands caressed her shoulders. "One of Uncle

Percival's, I presume?" Amusement, mingled with warmth, sounded in that deep voice. "My poor darling, is that what has haunted you these last few days? Fear the old rogue would reveal your disreputable secret?"

Somehow, he didn't seem to be taking all this as seriously as he should. "You—you ought to be appalled," she informed him, and sniffed. Where was a handkerchief when she needed one?

He placed the much-needed linen in her hands. With a murmured "thank you," she dabbed at her brimming eyes. He turned her firmly to face him, cupping her chin in his hand and forcing her face up so he could look fully into her eyes. Determinedly, she refused, keeping her gaze lowered, unable to meet that searching look.

"Have I never told you of my sister Nell's shameful past?" Laughter sounded in his voice.

She peeked up at him, guarded. "The duchess—"

"Very nearly *not* the duchess, my love," he informed her. "She first met Halliford while she modeled a gown for his mistress."

Daphne stared at him. "The duchess?" The lovely, self-assured, elegant duchess of Halliford? A shop assistant?

"He didn't recognize her later, of course," Adrian went on. "But she was so convinced a duke would never marry a mere seamstress's helper—when he learned the truth—she tried to run away from him."

Just as Daphne must run from the duchess's brother, now. She shook her head, trying to draw back. "Halliford is a duke," she reminded him. "Nothing your sister ever might have done could ruin his future. Not like yours."

"Ah, yes, mine. That bishop's palace, do you mean?"

Mutely, she nodded her head. At last, he began to see reason. So why didn't she feel relieved?

"And what, my beloved, makes you think I would want to be a bishop? It sounds deadly dull, to me. I could not see either of us happy involved in the intrigues and political maneuverings of such an office. No, if you have hopes of such a husband, you must look elsewhere. I hope you do not, though," he added with determination, "for I intend to have you for my wife."

Somehow, she found herself held tightly against his chest once more. "It—it would be wrong in me to marry you," she murmured, somewhere in the vicinity of his collar.

He tipped her chin up, his mouth finding hers with a force that robbed her of breath. She closed her eyes, clinging to him, knowing she should not. How could she tear herself away, how . . . ? Conscious thought faded as she melted against him, returning his kiss with the passion she had held so firmly in check. Until now.

He released her slowly, and his lips brushed her eyes. "It would be much more wrong," he informed her, "not to say grossly improper, for you to refuse me, after behaving in such a shocking fashion with a clergyman."

A shaky giggled escaped her. "You—you are quite abominable," she managed.

"That sounds more like you, love."

"Ah, me darlin'." Percival stood at their elbows, a benign smile on his genial countenance. "He is quite right. A hasty marriage, I should recommend. And I shall bestow my avuncular blessings upon the match."

Daphne, her cheeks heated at the embarrassment of being caught in Adrian's arms, tried to pull free, but found Adrian unwilling to comply. She relaxed against him once more. "I believe we can do quite well without your blessings, Uncle."

"No, my love, how can you say it?" That familiar note of enjoyment once more colored Adrian's tone. "One never knows when the meagerness of my stipend will force us to seek your uncle's professional services."

Percival beamed. "A gentleman of profound wisdom. Daphne, I congratulate you on your excellent judgment. But—" he waved a finger at Adrian, "I'll have you know I trained her properly. Not much she can't tell you about fuzzing the cards. But if she's forgotten, you may count upon my assistance." He enveloped them in the warmth of his complacent smile.

Daphne eyed him in amused exasperation. "I suppose you now feel you have done all in your power to ensure his future happiness?"

"But have I not?" He shook his head in reproof. "Have I not bestowed upon him the two greatest gifts I possess? You—and my invaluable knowledge? No," he held up his hand, then reversed the gesture to smother a yawn. "You need not thank me, sir. It is a delight. I shall now depart for my hostelry to seek my bed. But not," he added, "before I call in the watch to deal with our captives." Yawning once more, he started up the dark steps to the hall above.

Adrian brushed his chin along the top of Daphne's tumbled hair. "Despite the blessings of both your uncles, you have returned me no answer, yet."

She looked up earnestly to meet the burning intensity of his gaze. "My past—"

"Your past," he informed her, "shall undoubtedly one day stand us in excellent stead. I have always felt that a vicar with no worldly experience must be of little use to his parishioners. Well, my love?"

He kissed her once more, gently at first, then with an increasing need that left her in no doubts about the sincerity of his wishes. It also dissolved the last of her good intentions. When she could speak again, a shaky sigh escaped her. "I suppose I have now compromised you hopelessly, and there is nothing for it but to marry you and right you in the eyes of the church."

"Nothing whatsoever," he informed her with perfect gravity. He fitted her more snugly against himself. "Now kindly compromise me again."